ALTERNATE TALES OF ALTERNATE WORLDS—

From a distant future in which Earth is a backwater planet in a Galactic Empire, and only a man from the planet's own past can offer both Earth and Empire a possible means of peaceful coexistence. . . .

To a time outside of time, when the humans called Eternals have set themselves up as the keepers of Reality, ready to alter entire timelines to preserve their chosen History. . . .

To an age when man explores a power that seems to deny the very laws of gravitation. . . .

Welcome to never before revealed universes of the imagination—

THE ALTERNATE ASIMOVS

"FASCINATING AND ENTERTAINING!"
—*Knoxville News-Sentinel*

"A WONDERFUL ADDITION FOR THE ASIMOV FAN'S LIBRARY."—*Charleston Evening Post*

THE ALTERNATE ASIMOVS
BY
ISAAC ASIMOV

A SIGNET BOOK

NEW AMERICAN LIBRARY

ACKNOWLEDGMENTS

"Belief" copyright 1953 by Street & Smith Publications, Inc.; copyright renewed 1980 by Isaac Asimov.

 SIGNET TRADEMARK REG. U.S. PAT. OFF. AND FOREIGN COUNTRIES
REGISTERED TRADEMARK—MARCA REGISTRADA
HECHO EN CHICAGO, U.S.A.

SIGNET, SIGNET CLASSIC, MENTOR, ONYX, PLUME, MERIDIAN and NAL BOOKS are published by NAL PENGUIN INC., 1633 Broadway, New York, New York 10019

First Signet Printing, April, 1988

1 2 3 4 5 6 7 8 9

PRINTED IN THE UNITED STATES OF AMERICA

To Kate Medina and Jennifer Brehl,
the latest of a long line of editors who have
painstakingly guided me (and sometimes bullied me)
through the intricacies of the writer's craft.

CONTENTS

INTRODUCTION

Every once in a while I do a book that is *not* my own idea. This is one of them. I particularly want you all to know that it is not my own idea, so let me explain to you how it all came about.

Back in 1964, Dr. Howard Gotlieb of the Boston University Library got the notion of collecting my papers. The B.U. Library specialized in twentieth-century American authors, under which heading I fall. What's more, I was (and still am) a member of the Boston University faculty, so it seemed particularly appropriate to include me.

This struck me, at the time, as a grotesque idea. I considered my "papers" to be junk (and I still believe that today, in my heart of hearts). Whenever they accumulated to an uncomfortable degree, I burned them in the barbecue pit in the backyard of my house in Newton, Massachusetts. (I used that barbecue pit for nothing else.)

When I said as much to Dr. Gotlieb, he was horrified. He explained to me the importance of contemporary records of important literary figures (and apparently when he used that phrase he meant me). He also described the vast number of students of literature who would gain their much-desired Ph.D.'s as a result of their meticulous studies of my first drafts, and how useful this would be to aspiring authors of centuries and millennia hence.

I believe none of this, but Dr. Gotlieb was (and is) one of the sweetest and nicest men ever invented by a creative

Deity (assuming the existence of one), and I hadn't the heart to disappoint him. So I gave him all the material I could find that had escaped the barbecue pit, and then began sending him additional material as it accumulated.

He received copies of all the books I published in every edition I could get hold of (book club, paperback, foreign, etc.). I sent him manuscripts, both first drafts and final copies. I sent him all my correspondence and fan mail. I sent him an intact copy of every magazine that had an essay or story of mine in it, so that, for instance, he now has about twenty years' worth of *The Magazine of Fantasy and Science Fiction*, ten years of *American Way*, and every copy of *Isaac Asimov's Science Fiction Magazine*. It's all stored in a special vault.

The accumulated material over these last twenty years and more is mountainous and is growing steadily. Every couple of weeks I lug a mass of assorted papers, magazines, and books to Doubleday and Company, which very kindly mails it to "Isaac's vault."

I try not to think of it. Some poor soul in Dr. Gotlieb's office must be forced to go through it all, and arrange it, and classify it, and file it in some rational way so that any particular piece of paper can be found quickly on demand. (I know. There have been a few times when I have wanted something, and they located it for me at once.)

I also fear the ultimate results. That vault can only hold so much. Some day it will explode, and I can imagine the headline in *The Boston Globe:* "Asimov Vault Explodes. Commonwealth Avenue Devastated. Twenty Killed. Hundreds Hurt."

And it will be all my vault.

That gives you the first portion of the story behind this book. Carry on.

In the last five years or so I have taken to editing anthologies of various kinds, and in great numbers. I have, as of now, over eighty such anthologies to my credit.

Naturally, this sort of nefarious activity is well beyond my abilities. You will not be surprised, then, to hear that in almost all cases, I have co-conspirators at my side. The two most loyal and accommodating of these are Martin Harry Greenberg and Charles G. Waugh. Marty lives in Wisconsin, Charles lives in Maine, and I live in Manhattan, so we are well spread out. We maintain contact by means of letters, phone calls, and occasional visits. (*They* make the visits. I don't travel.)

It's an ideal anthological conspiracy. Charles has an enormous collection of publications and an infallible memory for everything he has read, and is deeply in love with a photocopying machine. He can therefore supply us with any kind of stories we want. As for Martin, he has an uncontrollable passion for writing for permissions, for taking care of all records, and for the receiving and sending out of all checks. He also visits editors for the purpose of hypnotizing them into agreeing to additional anthologies by the dozen.

That leaves me only the task of reading the stuff they send me, making decisions as to what goes where, writing introductions and occasional headnotes, and delivering the manuscripts to the various publishers (since almost all of them are virtually within walking distance of my home, if it is a nice day).

Naturally, Marty and Charles have developed a proprietary interest in me.

You will therefore understand that once, a couple of years ago, when Charles was visiting Boston, one of the "sights" he intended to see was "Dr. Asimov's vault." (Charles is a quintessential Wasp, and will *not* address me by my first name, though I repeatedly urge him to. Marty, who is no more a Wasp than I am, is more relaxed.)

I don't know how long Charles spent in the vault, breathing in the invigorating odor of old paper and poring over dead items of Asimoviana, but it seems he came across some material I had long forgotten. I'm not sure that the material deserves the name of "curiosa," but it was certainly curious. What particularly interested Charles was that he came across some old versions of a few well-known stories of mine that were, for one reason or another, markedly different from those same items as later published. It seemed to him that there might be some reader interest in these old versions. He even made a list of the relevant items.

He mentioned this the next time he spoke to Marty, and Marty mentioned it to me the next time he spoke to me. Marty even had a name for the book: *The Alternate Asimovs.*

My reaction was immediate and enthusiastic. "Marty," I said, "you're crazy."

He said, "May I mention it to Doubleday?"

"Go ahead," I said, laughing heartily. I was sure they would chase him out of the office to the accompaniment of streams of opprobrious language. Serve him right, I thought.

Either I had underestimated Marty's persuasiveness, however, or the good nature of Kate Medina, my then editor at Doubleday, or both, because the next thing I knew I found myself staring at a contract.

Muttering imprecations under my breath, I wrote to good old Howard at the B.U. Library, and the *next* thing I knew I had piles of old paper on my desk representing some of the items Charles had mentioned.

You understand, then, why I disclaim this book. Some of you may think, "Well, there goes Asimov and his inordinate vanity, thinking anyone would be interested in his old junk." But it's not so. The fault is entirely that of Howard Gotlieb, Charles Waugh, Martin Greenberg, and Kate Medina.

—Still, having read this far while standing in the bookstore and browsing, you might as well pay your money and take the book home with you. I wouldn't want Howard, Charles, Martin, and Kate to be disappointed in their notion that you would be interested.

1

GROW OLD
ALONG WITH ME

FOREWORD

Now that you've brought the book home with you, let me present the first item—my novella, "Grow Old Along with Me."

On May 26, 1947, the editor of *Startling Stories* asked me to write a 40,000-word novella for the magazine. At the time I had been selling to science fiction magazines for nearly nine years, and had already handled the length. Two years before, I had written "The Mule" for *Astounding Science Fiction,* and that had been 50,000 words long.

Startling was asking, specifically, for an "*Astounding*-type story," so it seemed to me that it would be a piece of cake.

It took me all summer to write it, however, because I was also working on my Ph.D. research at the time. I finished it on September 22, 1947. It ended substantially longer than had been requested (49,000 words), but that didn't bother me. Since the magazines pay by the word, that just meant additional money.

The title of the novella I took from the first line of

Robert Browning's "Rabbi Ben Ezra," which is a paean
to old age. That gave the title an ironic significance, in
view of the plot of the story. I was only twenty-seven at
the time, and I was still able to view the matter of old
age with detachment.

But then, to my astonishment (and rage), *Startling*,
having held on to the story for three weeks, rejected it.
I was humiliated, for I hadn't had a rejection in five
years. To get one now from a second-rate magazine,
after I had spent a whole summer on it and after receiving their approval when I had (at their request) let them
see sections of it as I wrote, seemed more than I could
bear. I am routinely disappointed when I get rejections
(and I get some even now), but I can bear them philo-
sophically. This was the one and only time I was
enraged.

I tried the story at *Astounding*, and it was rejected
again. There was some hope that a small, semi-profes-
sional publishing house, which was being established
for the publication of science fiction novels, might do it
for next to no money, but even that fell through.

It was the worst literary fiasco of my life till then, and
the wonder is that I didn't throw the damned manuscript away. Fortunately, this was a decade before I had
bought the house with the barbecue pit in the backyard, or I would surely have burned it. As it was, the
apartment I then lived in didn't have a barbecue pit in
the living room, so I just put the manuscript in a drawer
and tried to forget about it.

In 1949, however, Doubleday and Company was
planning to start a hard-cover science fiction line, the
first by any general publisher. My friend, the science
fiction writer Frederik Pohl, had learned of this, so he
came to me and suggested I show Doubleday "Grow
Old Along with Me." I strongly demurred, because I
was in no mind to suffer new humiliation over this
turkey I had written, but Fred was most persuasive and
I said I would think about it.

On March 11, 1949, I decided that it would be
unprofessional of me to decide on behalf of an editor

that a story was unsuitable. I therefore walked over to Fred Pohl's apartment. (In those days, I was too impecunious to take a taxi, and too naive to think of making a phone call to check if he were home.) Naturally, he wasn't home and his eight-year-old stepdaughter, who was alone in the house, answered the bell. (In those days, eight-year-old children were not yet firmly indoctrinated never to open the door to casual callers.)

You must understand that ordinarily I treat my manuscripts as though they were diamond-studded. I always bring them in to a publishing house and place them directly into editorial hands, when I can. When the publishers are out of town, I am forced to mail the manuscripts, but I always call up in a reasonable time to make sure they have arrived. This time, though, so little did I care for "Grow Old Along with Me" that I indifferently handed the manuscript to the child at the door with instructions to give it to her father.

And then, a little to my astonishment, Walter L. Bradbury, the editor at Doubleday, liked the novella and said that if I would expand it to 70,000 words or so, Doubleday would publish it. What's more, he paid me $150 just for agreeing to do it, and promised me another $350 once the task was finished. Thereafter, of course, the book might earn royalties in addition. I was staggered by this munificence and by the vision of oriental splendor for the future.

It took me six and a half weeks to do the revision and extension of the book, and I was through on May 20, 1949. Doubleday accepted it, but asked for a new title. I was only too ready to drop the old one, which I associated only with misery and embarrassment, and I suggested *Pebble in the Sky*.

Pebble in the Sky was published on January 19, 1950. It was the very first book of what has amounted now to over 330 altogether, of which fully 100 have been published by Doubleday.

Even after this, I retained a carbon of the original "Grow Old Along with Me" long enough to be able to hand it, along with other stuff, to Howard Gotlieb at the Boston University Library. Of course, I had a whole mass of old manuscripts in a box in the attic of my Newton home and I didn't look through it in detail, so I didn't know that this particular item was included until Charles Waugh told me he had seen it in the vault.

Now here it is, exactly as originally written for *Startling* except for the correction of typos and minor infelicities.

Grow Old Along with Me

PROLOGUE

As everyone knows who has ever tried, a story can be told in two ways. You can either start at the beginning and work towards the end, or start at the end and work towards the beginning. In this particular case, the beginning is Joseph Schwartz, retired tailor of Chicago, U.S.A., anno Domini 1947, while the end is Bel Arvardan, non-retired archaeologist of Baronn, Sirius Sector, 827 Galactic Era.

Actually, there's a third way of spinning a yarn, and that's to start at both ends and work towards the middle. And since, O gentle reader (incidentally, the phrase when actually used some centuries back referred not to the kindliness of the reader but to his assumed "gentle"—i.e., "noble"—birth, as distinguished from the common herd, who, the author presumably felt, had not the wit nor the selective taste to read his works)—

—But to backtrack—

And since, O gentle reader, the two ends toward the middle method sounds a little confusing, we will try that, and demonstrate that it isn't so at all.

It is only that we shall have to take one end at a time, since our first name is not Gertrude nor our last name Stein. At the toss of a coin, we begin with Joseph Schwartz—

PART I: JOSEPH SCHWARTZ

CHAPTER 1 *Between One Footstep and the Next*

Joseph Schwartz, retired tailor, etc., although lacking what the sophisticates of today call a "formal education," had expended much of an inquisitive nature upon random reading. By the sheer force of indiscriminate voracity, he had gleaned a smattering of practically everything, and by means of a trick memory had managed to keep it all straight.

That is to explain why, on this very sunny and very bright early summer day of 1947, Schwartz could stroll his way along the pleasant streets of suburban Chicago and quote Browning to himself. Specifically, he was quoting the poem "Rabbi ben Ezra," which he knew by heart, having read it twice when he was younger, and which we shall not bore you by repeating in full. Actually, it was the first two lines that appealed to him—and to us—and those went:

> *Grow old along with me!*
> *The best is yet to be . . .*

Schwartz felt that to its fullest. After the struggles of youth in Europe and those of his early manhood in the United States, the serenity of a successful maturity was pleasant. With a house of his own and money of his own, he could, and did, retire. With a wife in good health, a daughter safely married, a grandson to soothe these last, best years—what had he to worry about?

There was the atom bomb, of course, and this somewhat lascivious talk about World War III, but Schwartz was a believer in the goodness of human nature. He didn't think there would be another war, so he smiled tolerantly at the children he passed and silently wished them a speedy and not too difficult ride through youth to the peace of the best that was to be—

* * *

And in another part of Chicago stood the Institute for Nuclear Studies, in which men had no theories about the essential worth of human nature, since no quantitative instrument had yet been designed to measure it. When they thought about it at all, it was merely to wish that some stroke from heaven would prevent the damned ingenuity of humanity from turning every innocent and interesting discovery into a deadly weapon.

Yet in a pinch, the same man who could not find it in his conscience to curb his curiosity into nuclear studies that might someday kill half of Earth, would risk his life to save his comrade's.

It was the blue glow behind the chemist's back that first attracted the attention of Dr. Smith.

He peered at it as he passed the half-open door. The chemist—a cheerful youngster—was whistling and splicing two wires. For a moment there was no action, and then some instinct stirred.

Dr. Smith dashed inside, and with a frenzied motion of a yardstick he snatched up, swept the contents of the desk top to the floor. There was the deadly hiss of molten metal, and Dr. Smith felt a drop of perspiration slip to the end of his nose and poise there.

The youngster took time to collect his wits, which had been scattered in the other's rush. He stared blankly at the concrete floor along which the silvery metal had already frozen in thin splash marks, still radiating heat strongly.

Dr. Smith said breathlessly, "What's been going on here?"

"There wasn't *anything* going on here," the chemist yammered. "That was just a sample of crude uranium. I'm making an electrolytic copper determination— What *could* have happened?"

"I don't know. There was the blue corona— Uranium, you say?"

"*Crude* uranium, and that isn't dangerous. Purity is one of the most important qualifications for fission.

Besides which, it isn't plutonium and it wasn't being bombarded."

"And," said Dr. Smith thoughtfully, "it was below the critical mass." He stared at the soapstone desk, at the burned and blistered paint of the cabinets. "Yet uranium melts at about 1800 degrees centigrade, and this place must be saturated with all varieties of stray radiations and emanations. When the metal cools, young man, it had better be chipped up and collected, and thoroughly analyzed."

He stepped to the opposite wall and felt thoughtfully at a spot about shoulder height.

"What's this?" he said to the chemist. "Has this always been here?"

"What, sir?" The young man stepped up nervously and glanced owlishly at the spot the older man indicated. It was a tiny hole, as if made by a thin nail driven into the wall and withdrawn—but driven through plaster and brick for the full thickness of the building's wall, since through it daylight could be seen.

The chemist shook his head. "I never noticed that before, but I never looked for it, either."

"Well—let's get out of here. We'll send in our radiation men to check the place, and you and I will spend a siege in the infirmary."

"Radiation burns, you mean?" The chemist paled.

"We'll find out."

There were no signs of radiation burns in either. Blood counts were normal and a study of the hair roots revealed nothing. Nor did any symptoms develop. Nor, in all the Institute, was anyone found, either then or in the near future, to explain why a crucible of crude uranium, well below critical size and under no direct neutronic bombardment, should suddenly grow red-hot and melt.

The only conclusion was that nuclear physics had queer and dangerous crannies left in it.

No connection was drawn between all this and the fact that, during the next few days, there were some items in the newspapers reporting disappearances. No one important was concerned, no one semi-important, no one of the slightest interest—to anyone but ourselves.

For one of the disappearances was recorded as follows:

"Joseph Schwartz, height, five feet six inches, weight, one hundred sixty-five pounds, partly bald, with graying hair, has been missing from his home for three days. When last seen, he was wearing—" and so on and so on.

There was no further report on the matter.

To Joseph Schwartz it had happened between one step and the next. He had lifted his right foot, when for a moment he felt dizzy—as though for the merest trifle of time a whirlwind had lifted him and turned him inside out—and when he placed his right foot down again, all the breath went out of him in a gasp, and he felt himself slowly crumple and slide down to the grass.

He waited a long time with his eyes closed—and then he opened them.

It was true! He was sitting on grass, where previously he had been walking on concrete. *The houses were gone!* The white houses, each with its lawn, squatting there, row on row—all gone!

And it was not a lawn he was sitting on, for the grass was growing rank, untended, and there were trees about, many of them, with more on the horizon.

That was when the worst shock of all came, because the leaves on those trees were ruddy, some of them, and in the curve of his hand he felt the dry brittleness of a dead leaf. He was a city man—but he knew autumn when he saw it.

Autumn! Yet when he had lifted his right foot, it had been a June day, with everything a glistening green.

He spoke to himself out loud—for even the sound of his own voice was a soothing element in a world otherwise completely strange. And that voice was low and tense and panting.

He said, "In the first place, I'm not crazy. I feel inside like I always felt. There must be something else possible.

"A dream?" He considered. "How can I tell if it's a dream or not?" He pinched himself and felt the nip, but shook his head. "I can always dream I feel a pinch. That's no proof."

He looked about him confusedly. Could dreams be so clear, so detailed, so lasting? He had read once that most dreams last not more than five seconds, that they are induced by trifling disturbances to the sleeper— and that the apparent length of the dreams was an illusion.

Despairingly, he shifted the cuff of his shirt upward and stared at his wristwatch. The second hand turned and turned and turned. If it was a dream, the five seconds were going to stretch madly.

He looked away and wiped futilely at the cold dampness of his forehead. "What about amnesia?"

He did not answer himself, but slowly buried his head in both hands. If between the rising of a foot and the replacement thereof, the mind skips three months or a year and three months or ten years and three months— If it picks you up in June 1947 and drops you in September or October heaven-knows-when—how can you tell?

But that couldn't be. Schwartz looked at his shirt. It was the one he had put on that morning, or what should have been that morning, and it was a fresh shirt. He bethought himself, plunged a fist into his trouser pocket, and brought out an apple.

He bit into it wildly. It was fresh and still had a lingering coolness from the Frigidaire that had held it two hours earlier—or what should have been two hours.

That left him with the dream—maybe—

It struck him that the time of day had changed. It was late afternoon—or at least the shadows were lengthening. The quiet desolation of the place was borne in upon him suddenly.

He lurched to his feet. Obviously, he would have to

find people—any people. And, as obviously, he would have to find a house, and the best way to do that would be to find a road.

Automatically, he turned in the direction in which the trees seemed thinnest, and walked.

The slight chill of evening was creeping inside his shirt and the tops of the trees were becoming dim and forbidding, when he came upon that straight and impersonal streak of macadam. He lunged toward it and felt the hardness under his feet.

Along either direction was absolute emptiness, and for a moment he felt the cold clutch again. He had hoped for cars. It would have been the easiest thing to wave them down and say—he said it aloud in his eagerness—"Going toward Chicago, maybe?"

What if he were nowhere near Chicago? Well, any large city. He had only four dollars and twenty-seven cents in his pocket, but there were always the police—

He was walking along the highway—walking along the middle—watching in both directions. The setting of the sun made no impression upon him, or the fact that the first stars were coming out.

No cars. Nothing. And it was getting to be really dark.

He thought that first dizziness might be coming back, because the horizon at his left glimmered. Through the gaps in the trees there was a cold blue shine. It was not the leaping red he imagined a forest fire would be like, but a faint and creeping glow. And the macadam beneath his feet seemed to sparkle ever so faintly. He bent down to touch it, and it felt normal. But there was that tiny glimmer that caught the edges of his eyes.

He was getting hungry and really, really frightened when he saw that spark to the right.

It was a house. He shouted wildly and no one answered, but it was a house. The sharp instinct of fright and hunger and loneliness told him that, so he turned off the road and went plunging cross-country, across ditches, around trees, through the underbrush and over a creek, till he was there—with his hands reaching out to touch the hard white structure.

It was neither brick, nor stone, nor wood, but he never paid that the least mind. It looked something like porcelain, but he didn't give a hoot. He was just looking for the door, and when he came to it and saw no bell, he kicked at it and yelled like a madman.

He heard the stirring inside, and the sound of a human voice. He yelled again.

"Hey, in there!"

There was a faint, oiled whir, and the door opened. A woman emerged, a spark of alarm in her eyes. She was tall and wiry, and behind her was the gaunt figure of a hard-faced man in work clothes.

To Schwartz they were beautiful as only the sight of friends to a man alone could be beautiful.

The woman spoke, and her voice was liquid but peremptory, and Schwartz reached for the door to keep himself upright. His lips moved—uselessly—and in a rush, all the clammiest fears returned to choke his windpipe and stifle his heart.

For the woman spoke in no language Schwartz had ever heard.

CHAPTER 2 The Disposal of a Stranger

Loa Maren and her stolid husband were playing cards in the cool of the evening, while the shrouded figure in the motor-driven wheelchair in the corner drowsed over his book-film. It was a usual scene—the short interval between work and sleep.

Arbin Maren fingered the thin, smooth rectangles carefully as he considered the next play. And as he slowly made his decision, the pounding at the door sounded and the hoarse yells that didn't quite coalesce into words.

His hand lurched and stopped just above the card it was going to pluck from the group he held. Loa's eyes grew fearful, and then she stared at her husband with a trembling lower lip.

Arbin said, "Get Grew out of here. Quickly."

Loa said nothing. She was at the wheelchair, making soothing sounds with her tongue.

The sleeping figure gasped and stumbled awake. He straightened his lolling head and groped for the bookfilm, which he had dropped into the blanket that covered his legs.

"What's the matter?" he demanded irritably.

"Shh. It's *all* right," muttered Loa vaguely, and wheeled the chair into the next room. She closed the door and placed her back against it, thin chest heaving as her eyes sought those of her husband. There was that pounding again.

They stood close to each other as the door opened, almost defensively, and the hostility peeped from them as they faced the short, plump man who smiled faintly at them.

Loa said, "Is there anything we can do for you?", then jumped back as the man gasped and put a hand out to stop himself from falling.

"Is he sick?" asked Arbin stupidly. "Here, help me take him inside."

The hours after that passed, and in the quiet of their bedroom Loa and Arbin prepared slowly for bed.

"Arbin," said the woman.

"What do you want?"

"Is it safe?"

"Safe?" He seemed to avoid her meaning deliberately.

"The man— The man we took into the house. Who is he?"

"How should I know?" was the irritated response. "Can we refuse shelter? Tomorrow, if he lacks identification, we'll inform the Regional Security Board and that will be the end of it." He composed himself.

But his wife broke the returning silence, her thin voice more urgent. "You don't think he might be an

agent of the Society of Ancients? There is Grew, you
know."

"He is not a police agent, Loa. Forget that. Do you
suppose that they would go through an elaborate trick-
ery for the sake of a poor old man in a wheelchair?
Could they not enter by daylight and with legal search
warrants? Please— Don't romanticize. Besides, why
should they suspect anything? Our produce this season
will be the full quantity demanded of us according to
the set quota for our land, assuming a working force
of three people—"

"Yes, yes. But then, Arbin, I have been thinking. If
he is not a policeman, he can't be from Earth."

"What? You mean a man from the outer worlds?
That's more ridiculous still. Why should a man of the
Empire come to this dead world—"

"Exactly. Because no one would look for him here.
He doesn't speak the language, does he? He babbles.
Can *you* understand him? A single word? Don't you
see that we can make use of him? If he is a stranger on
Earth, he will have no registration with the Census
Board, and he will be only too glad to avoid reporting
to them. We can use him on the farm, in the place of
my father, and it will be three people again, not two,
that will have to meet the quota for three this next
season."

She looked anxiously at the uncertain face of her
husband, who considered long, then said, "Sleep, Loa.
We shall speak further in the common sense of
daylight."

The whispering ended, the light was put out, and
eventually sleep filled the room, and the house.

The next morning it was the turn of Grew to consider the matter. He was a man who had been strong
and active. His shoulders were broad, his upper arms
well fleshed. Nothing anywhere tattled of fifty-five.
Yet his legs, two cylindrical masses of nerveless matter, were slowly shriveling and wasting away, so that
by all the customs of Earth, he should have been

reported for painless disposal that his place might be
taken by a younger and fitter man.

It was with a pained glance at those legs, dead these
two years, that he said, "Your troubles, Arbin, apparently arise from the fact that I am registered as a
worker, so that the produce quota is set at three. This
is the second year I have lived past my time. It is
enough."

"We will not discuss that." Arbin was troubled.
"We have produced enough."

"In two years there will be the Census, and I will go
anyway."

"You will have two more years of your books and
your rest. Why should you be deprived of that?"

"Because others are. And what of Loa? Will she
last another season? Do you think I have not seen her
when she was so tired that she couldn't walk—couldn't
gather the strength to weep? Of what use to me is my
life at the cost of my daughter's death?"

"There is this man," suggested Arbin eagerly. "What
do you think?"

"A stranger," mused Grew. "He comes knocking at
the door, from nowhere, speaks unintelligibly. —Who
is he?"

The farmer shrugged. "He is mild-mannered, and
frightened to death. He babbles and babbles, and then
huddles there, without moving, lost somewhere in his
own mind."

"What if he is insane?— And like myself, avoiding
the authorities."

"That doesn't sound likely." But Arbin stirred
uneasily.

"You tell yourself that because you want to use
him. —Well, then, the problem is how to dispose of
this stranger to our best advantage. Do you know
what I would do? I'd take him to town."

"To Chica?" Arbin was horrified. "That would be
ruin."

"Not at all," said Grew calmly. "Do you remember
the visicast last week? —The Institute for Nuclear Re-

search has an instrument that is supposed to make it easier for people to learn. They want volunteers. Take him."

Arbin shook his head helplessly. "I know nothing of it. —But Grew, they'll ask for his registration number, and you know it's only inviting investigation to have things in improper order. Then they'll find out about you."

"You're wrong, Arbin. The Institute wants men because the machine is still experimental. I'm sure they won't ask questions. If the stranger dies, he'll probably be no worse off than he is now —Here, Arbin, hand me the book-projector and set the mark at reel six."

When Schwartz opened his eyes that morning, it was to feel that dull, heart-choking pain that feeds on itself, the pain of a familiar world lost.

Once before he had felt it, and there was that momentary flash that lit up a forgotten scene into sharp brilliance. He, a youngster, in the snow of the wintry village—with the sleigh waiting—at the end of whose journey would be the train—and after that, the great ship.

The longing, frustrating fear for the world of the familiar united him for the moment with that twenty-year-old who had emigrated to America. Somehow he had decided all this could not be a dream—

He jumped up as the light above the door blinked on and off and the meaningless baritone of his host sounded. Then the door opened and there was breakfast—a mealy porridge that he did not recognize but that tasted faintly like corn mush (with a savory difference) and milk.

He said, "Thanks," and nodded his head vigorously.

The farmer said something in return and picked up Schwartz's shirt from where it hung on the back of the chair. He inspected it carefully from all sides, paying particular attention to the buttons. Then, replacing it, he flung open the sliding door of a closet, and for the first time Schwartz became visually aware of the warm milkiness of the walls.

"Plastic," he muttered to himself, using that all-inclusive word with the finality laymen usually do. He noted further that there were no corners or angles in the room—all planes fading into each other at a gentle curve.

But the other was holding objects out toward him and making gestures that could not be mistaken. Schwartz obviously was to wash and dress.

With help and directions, he obeyed. —Except that he found nothing with which to shave, nor could gestures to his chin elicit anything but an incomprehensible sound accompanied by a look of distinct revulsion on the part of the other. He scratched at his gray stubble and sighed windily.

And then he was led to a small, elongated, bi-wheeled car, into which he was ordered by gestures. The ground sped beneath them and the empty road moved backward on either side, until low sparkling-white buildings rose before him, and there, far ahead, was the blue of water.

He pointed eagerly. "Chicago?" It was the last gasp of hope within him, for certainly nothing he ever saw looked less like that city.

The farmer made no answer at all—

CHAPTER 3 *The Ruler and the Ruled*

Ennius was in his fourth year as Procurator of the tiny province of Terra. As the direct representative of the Emperor, his social standing was, in a way, on a par with Viceroys of huge Galactic Sectors that sprawled their gleaming volumes across hundreds of cubic parsecs of space. That was, perhaps, an academic comfort to his wife and daughter.

Actually, however, the post of Procurator of Terra was little better than exile. No riches or splendor here. No court functions at which to sparkle, nor the bustle of trade and life. There were instead the empty palaces on the slopes of the continental mountains, where alone the atmospheric radioactivity was low enough for continual inhabitation—That, and a quarrelsome population who hated him and the Empire and whose eternal wretched internecine feuds had to be judged and balanced.

His escapes were rare and short. They had to be short, for here in Chica, at ease for the moment, it was necessary to wear lead-impregnated clothes at all times, even while sleeping, and to dose oneself continually with metaboline.

He was discoursing upon that very fact in the ancient Institute for Nuclear Research where he was visiting the one Earthman in all the planet whom he could treat as an equal.

"Metaboline," he said, holding up the vermilion pill for inspection, "is perhaps a true symbol of all that your planet means to me, my friend. Its function is to heighten all metabolic processes, while I sit here immersed in the radioactive cloud that surrounds me and that you are not even aware of." He swallowed it. "There! Now my heart will beat more quickly; my breath will pump a race of its own accord; my liver will boil away in those chemical syntheses that, medical men tell me, make it the most important factory in the body— And for that I pay with a siege of headaches and lassitude afterwards."

Dr. Shekt listened with some amusement. He was usually referred to as "near-sighted Shekt," not because he wore glasses or was in any way afflicted, but merely because long habit had given him the unconscious trick of peering closely at things, of weighing all facts anxiously before saying anything. He was tall and elderly, and his withered figure stooped in a question mark.

But he was well read in much of Galactic culture, and he was relatively free of the trick of universal hostility and suspicion that made the average Earthman so repulsive to that man of the Empire, Ennius.

Shekt said, "I'm sure you don't need it. Metaboline

is just one of your superstitions, confess it. If I were to substitute sugar pills without your knowledge, you'd be none the worse."

"You say that in the comfort of your own environment. —Do you deny that your basal metabolism is higher than mine?"

"I know that it is a superstition of the Empire, Ennius, that we men of Earth are different from other human beings, but that's not really so. Are you coming here as a missionary of the anti-Terrestrians?"

Ennius groaned. "By the life of the Emperor, your comrades of Earth are themselves the best such missionaries. Living here, cooped up on their deadly planet, festering in their own anger, they're nothing but a standing ulcer in the Galaxy.

"I mean it. What other planet's inhabitants have so much ritual in their daily lives that they adhere to with such masochistic fury? Not a day passes but I receive delegations from one or another of your ruling bodies asking the death penalty for some poor devil whose only crime has been to invade a forbidden area, to evade the Sixty, or perhaps merely to eat more than his share of food."

"Ah, but you always grant the death penalty. Your idealistic distaste seems to stop short at resisting."

"The Stars are my witness that I struggle to deny the death. But what can one do? The Emperor will have it that all the subdivisions of the Empire are to remain undisturbed in their local customs—and that is right and wise, since it removes popular support from the fools who would otherwise kick up rebellion on alternate Tuesdays and Thursdays. Besides, were I to remain obdurate when your Councils and Senates and Chambers insist on the death, such a shrieking would arise, and such a wild howling and denunciation of the Empire and all its works, that I would sooner sleep in the midst of a legion of devils for twenty years than face such an Earth for ten minutes."

Shekt sighed and rubbed the thin hair back upon his skull. "I wish I could deny your statement, Procurator, but I cannot. Yet we are no different from you of the outer worlds, merely more unfortunate. We are crowded here on a world all but dead, immersed in a sea of radiation that imprisons us, surrounded by a huge Galaxy that rejects us. What can we do against the feeling of frustration that burns us? Would you, Procurator, be willing that we send our surplus population abroad?"

Ennius shrugged. "Would I care? It is the populations themselves that would. They don't care to fall victim to Terrestrial diseases."

"Terrestrial diseases!" Shekt scowled. "It is a nonsense that should be eradicated. We are not carriers of death. Are you dead for having been among us?"

"To be sure," smiled Ennius, "I do everything to prevent undue contact."

"It is because you yourself fear the propaganda created, after all, only by the stupidity of your own bigots."

"What, Shekt, no scientific basis at all to the theory that Earthmen are themselves radioactive?"

"Why, certainly they are. How could they avoid it? So are you. So is everyone on every one of the hundred million planets of the Empire. We are more so, I grant you, but scarcely enough to harm anyone."

"But the average man of the Galaxy believes the opposite, I am afraid, and is not desirous of finding out by experiment. Besides—"

"Besides, you're going to say, we're different. We're not human beings, because we mutate more rapidly due to atomic radiation, and have therefore changed in many ways. —Also not proven."

"But believed."

"And as long as it is so believed, Procurator, and as long as we of Earth are treated as pariahs, you are going to find in us the characteristics to which you object. If you push us intolerably, is it to be wondered at that we push back? Hating us as you do, can you complain that we hate in our turn— No, no, we are far more the offended than the offending."

Ennius was chagrined at the anger he had aroused. Even the best of these Earthmen had the same blind spot, the same feeling of Earth against all the universe.

He said tactfully, "Shekt, forgive my boorishness, will you? Take my youth and boredom as excuse. You see before you a poor man, a young fellow of forty—and forty is the age of a babe in the professional civil service—who is grinding out his apprenticeship here on Earth. It may be years before the fools in the Bureau of the Outer Provinces remember me long enough to promote me to something less deadly. So we are both prisoners of Earth and both citizens of the great world of the mind in which there is distinction of neither planet nor physical characteristics. Give me your hand, then, and let us be friends."

The lines on Shekt's face smoothed out, or more exactly, were replaced by others more indicative of good humor. He laughed outright. "The words are the words of a suppliant, but the tone is still that of the Imperial career diplomat. You are a poor actor, Procurator."

"Then counter me by being a good teacher, and tell me of this Synapsifier of yours."

"What, you have heard of the instrument? You are a physicist among your other hobbies?"

"All knowledge is my province. Seriously, Shekt, I would really like to know."

The physicist peered closely at the other and seemed doubtful. He rose, and his gnarled hand rose to his lip, which it pinched thoughtfully. "I scarcely know where to begin."

"Well, Stars above, if you're considering at which point in the mathematical theory you are to begin, abandon them all. I know nothing of your Probability Factors in Electronic Neuro-Chemistry."

Shekt's eyes twinkled. "Yet you have the name of the branch of mathematics correct."

"A mistake. It came first to my mind, and had I not thought it gibberish, I would not have said it. What is your Synapsifier?"

"Well, essentially it is a device intended to increase the learning capacity of a human being."

"Really? Does it work?"

"I wish we knew. The essentials are these. The nervous system in man—and in animals—is composed of neuroproteins, which are nothing but huge molecules in very precarious electrical balance. The slightest stimulus will upset one, which will right itself by upsetting the next, which will repeat the process, until the brain is reached. The brain itself is an immense grouping of similar molecules that are connected among themselves in all possible ways. Since there are something like ten to the twentieth power (that is, a one with twenty zeroes after it) such neuroproteins in the brain, the number of possible combinations is of the order of factorial ten to the twentieth power, which is a number so large that if all the electrons and protons in the universe were universes themselves, and all the electrons and protons in those universes again became universes—then all the electrons and protons in all the universes so created would still be nothing in comparison. —Do you follow me?"

"Not a word, thank the Stars. If I even attempted to, I should bark like a dog for sheer pain of the intellect."

"Hmp. Well, in any case, what we call nerve impulses are merely the progressive electronic unbalance that proceeds along the nerves to the brain and then from the brain back along the nerves. Do you get that?"

"Yes."

"Well, blessings on you for a genius, then. As long as this impulse continues along a nerve cell, it proceeds at a rapid rate, since the neuroproteins are practically in contact. However, nerve cells are limited in extent, and between each nerve cell and the next is a very small partition of non-nervous tissue. In other words, two adjoining nerve cells do not actually connect with each other."

"Ah," said Ennius, "and the nervous impulse must jump the barrier?"

"Exactly! The partition drops the strength of the impulse and slows the speed of its transmission according to the square of its width. And this holds for the brain as well. Imagine, now, if some means could be found to lower the dialectric constant of this partition between the cells.

"The dia-what constant?"

"The insulating strength of the partition. The impulse would jump the gap more easily. You would think faster and learn faster."

"Well, does it work?"

"I have tried the instrument on animals."

"And with what result?"

"Why, that most died of denaturation of brain protein—coagulation, in other words, like hard-boiling an egg."

Ennius winced. "There is something ineffably cruel about the cold-bloodedness of science. What about those that didn't die?"

"Not conclusive, since they're not human beings. The burden of the evidence seems to be favorable. —But I need humans. You see, it is a matter of the natural electronic properties of the individual brain. Each brain gives rise to micro-currents of certain type. None exactly duplicate—like fingerprints, or the blood-vessel patterns of the retina—if anything, even more individual. The treatment, I believe, must take that into account, and if I am right, there will be no more denaturation. —But I have no human beings on whom to experiment. I ask for volunteers but—" He spread his hands.

"I certainly don't blame them, old man," and Ennius grimaced. "But seriously, should the instrument be perfected, what do you intend doing with it?"

The physicist shrugged. "It's not for me to say. It would be up to the Grand Council."

"You would not consider making it available to the Empire?"

"The Grand Council. See them."

Ennius shook his head. "They would allow nothing to leave the Earth. Would you talk with them?"

"I? What could *I* say?"

"Why, that if Earth could produce a Synapsifier that could do what you say, and would make it available to the Galaxy, some of the restrictions on emigration to other planets might be broken down."

"What," said Shekt sarcastically, "and risk epidemics and our differentness and our non-humanity?"

"You might," said Ennius quietly, "even be removed en masse to another planet. Consider it."

The signal light flashed hysterically, and Shekt clicked the communicator. "What is it?"

"Doctor Shekt. We have a volunteer."

"A what?"

"A volunteer, sir. There is someone here who is willing to offer himself as a subject."

The physicist's face grew gaunt. "I'll be right there." He wheeled in his chair. "You will excuse me, Procurator."

"Certainly. How long does the operation take?"

"It's a matter of hours. Do you wish to watch?"

"I can imagine nothing more gruesome, my dear Shekt. I'll be in the State House till tomorrow. Will you tell me the result?"

Shekt seemed relieved. "Yes, certainly."

"Good. —And think over what I said."

When Ennius left, Dr. Shekt, quietly and cautiously, touched the communicator and a young technician entered hurriedly, white robe sparkling clean, long brown hair carefully bound back.

Shekt said, "There is *really* a volunteer? A *volunteer*—and not another subject sent in the usual manner?"

"Yes," was the emphatic response. Then a note of caution entered. "You think we had better get rid of him?"

"No. I'll see him." But Shekt's mind was a cold whirl. So far, secrecy had been absolute. The mere fact of a volunteer was disturbing. —And immediately after Ennius's visit. Shekt himself had but the vaguest knowledge of the giant misty forces that were now beginning to wrestle back and forth across the blasted face of Earth, but he knew enough to feel himself at the mercy of them.

CHAPTER 4 *The Volunteer in Spite of Himself*

Arbin was uneasy in Chica. He felt surrounded. Somewhere in Chica, one of the largest cities on Earth— they said it had 50,000 human beings in it—somewhere there were officials of the outer Empire. He had never seen a man of the Galaxy, but in Chica his neck was continually twisting in fear that he might. If pinned down, he could not have explained how he would identify a non-Earthman even if he saw one, but it was in his very marrow to feel that they were somehow different.

He looked back over his shoulder as he entered the Institute. His bi-wheel was parked in an open area, with a six-hour coupon holding a spot open for it—was the extravagance itself suspicious? —Everything frightened him now. The air was full of eyes and ears.

If only the strange man would remember to remain hidden in the bottom of the rear compartment. He had nodded violently—but had he understood?

And then somehow the door was open in front of him, and a voice had broken in on his thoughts. "What do you want?"

It sounded impatient; perhaps it had already asked him that same thing several times.

He answered hoarsely, words choking out of his throat like dry powder, "Is this where a man can apply for the Synapsifier?"

The receptionist looked up sharply and said, "Sign here."

Arbin put his hands behind his back and repeated huskily, "Where do I see about the Synapsifier?" Grew had told him the name, but the word came out queerly—like so much gibberish.

But he was understood, for the young woman be-

hind the desk pressed her lips together and kicked the
signal bar at the side of her chair violently.

Arbin was fighting desperately for a lack of notori-
ety and failing miserably in his own mind. This girl
was looking hard at him. She'd remember him a thousand years later. And then he turned, with a wild
desire to end the entire bad business and leave.

—But someone was coming rapidly out of another
room, and the receptionist was pointing to him. "Volunteer for the Synapsifier," she was saying. "Won't
give his name."

Arbin turned to face him. "Are you the man in
charge?"

"I'll take you to him." Then, eagerly, "You want to
volunteer for the Synapsifier?"

"I want to see the man in charge," Arbin said
woodenly.

The new fellow frowned, then left. There was a
wait. Then—finally—there was the beckon of a finger—

Dr. Shekt peered helplessly at the gnarled farmer
across the desk. His age, thought Shekt, was probably
under forty, but he looked ten years older. His cheeks
were reddened beneath the leathery brown, and there
were distinct traces of perspiration at the hairline and
the temples, though the room was cool. The hands
were fumbling at each other.

Shekt said uneasily, "Now, my dear sir, I don't see
why you should insist on these conditions, but you
may have your way. You may keep your name to yourself *and* your residence and everything about yourself.
Tell me as much as you feel necessary, and no more.
Go ahead."

The farmer ducked his head, as a sort of rudimen-
tary gesture of respect. "Thank you. It's like this, sir.
We have a man about the farm, a distant—uh—relative
—he helps, you understand—"

Arbin swallowed with difficulty, and Shekt nodded
gravely.

Arbin continued, "He's a very willing worker and a

very *good* worker—we had a son, you see, but he died—and my good woman and myself, you see, need the help—she's not well—we could not get along scarcely without him." He felt that somehow the story was a complete mess.

But the gaunt scientist nodded. "Is it this relative of yours you wish treated?"

"Why yes, I thought I had said that—but you'll pardon me if this takes me some time. You see, this poor fellow is not—exactly—right in his head." He hurried on furiously, "He is not sick, you understand. He is not wrong so that he has to be put away. He's just *slow*. He doesn't talk, you see."

"He can't talk?" Shekt seemed startled.

"Oh—he can. It's just that he doesn't like to. He doesn't talk *well*."

The physicist looked dubious. "And you want the Synapsifier to improve his mentality, eh?"

Slowly Arbin nodded. "If he knew a bit more, sir, why, he could do some of the work my wife can't, you see."

"He might die, do you understand that?"

Arbin looked at him helplessly, and his fingers writhed furiously.

Shekt said, "I'd need his consent."

The farmer shook his head slowly, stubbornly. "He won't understand you." Then, urgently, almost beneath his breath, "Why, look, sir, I'm sure you'll understand me. You don't look like a man who doesn't know what a hard life is. This man is getting old. It's not a question of the Sixty, you see, but what if in the next census they think he's a half-wit and—and take him away. We don't like to lose him. But—" and Arbin's eyes swiveled involuntarily at the walls as if to penetrate them by sheer will and detect the listeners that might be behind. "—But what if the Ancients don't like that? Maybe trying to save an afflicted man is against the Customs—but life is hard, sir, and it would be useful to you. You've asked for volunteers?"

"Yes, yes. —You needn't worry; we'll take care of

you. Suppose you drive your car around to the back,
and I'll help you bring in your relative."

His arm dropped in friendly fashion to Arbin's shoulder, who grinned spasmodically. To Arbin, it was like
a rope loosening from about his neck.

Shekt looked down at the plump, balding figure
upon the couch. The patient was unconscious, breathing deeply and regularly. He had spoken unintelligibly; had understood nothing. Yet there had been none
of the physical stigmata of feeble-mindedness. Re-
flexes had been in order, for an old man.

Old! Hmm.

He looked across at Arbin, who watched everything
with a glance like a vise.

"Would you like us to take a bone analysis?"

"No," cried Arbin. Then, more softly, "I don't want
anything that might be identification."

"It might help us if we knew his age," said Shekt.

"He's fifty," said Arbin, shortly.

The physicist shrugged. It didn't matter. Again he
looked at the sleeper. When brought in, the subject
had been, or seemed, dejected, withdrawn, uncaring.
Even the Hypno-pills had apparently aroused no suspicion. They had been offered him; there had been a
quick, spasmodic smile, and he had swallowed them—

The technician was already rolling in the last of the
rather clumsy units that together made up the Synapsifier. At the touch of a push button, the polarized
glass in the windows of the operating room underwent
molecular rearrangement and became opaque. The
only light was the white one that blazed its cold brilliance upon the patient suspended in the multi-hundred-
kilowatt diamagnetic field some two inches above the
operating table to which he was transferred.

Arbin still sat in the dark there, understanding nothing but determined in deadly fashion to prevent somehow, by his presence, the harmful tricks he knew he
had not the knowledge to prevent.

The physicists paid no attention to him. The elec-

trodes were adjusted to the patient's skull. It was a
long job. First, there was the careful study of the skull
formation by the Ullster technique that revealed the
winding, tight-knit fissures. Shekt smiled to himself
grimly. Skull fissures weren't an unalterable quantitative measure of age, but they were good enough. The
man was older than the claimed fifty.

And then after a while he did not smile. He frowned.
There was something else wrong with the fissures.
They seemed odd—not quite— For a moment, he was
ready to swear that the skull formation was a primitive
one, a throwback, but then— The man was subnormal
mentally. Why not?—

He said wearily to the assisting technician, "The
wires here and here, and here." Tiny pricks and the
insertion of the platinum hairs. "—Here, and here."

A dozen connections, probing through skin to the
fissures, through the tightnesses of which could be felt
the delicate shadow-echoes of the micro-currents that
surged from cell to cell in the brain.

Carefully they watched the delicate ammeters stir
and leap as the connections were made and broken.
The tiny needle-point recorders traced their delicate
spiderwebs across the graphed paper, in irregular peaks
and troughs.

Then the graphs were removed and placed on the
illuminated opal glass. They bent low over it, whispering.

Arbin caught disjointed flashes: "—remarkably
regular—look at the height of this quinternary peak—
think it ought to be analyzed—clear enough to the
eye——"

And then for what seemed a long time there was a
tedious adjustment of the Synapsifier. Knobs were
turned to vernier adjustments, then clamped, and their
readings recorded. Over and over again, the various
electrometers were checked and new adjustments were
necessary.

Then Shekt smiled at Arbin and said, "It will all be
over very soon."

The large machinery was advanced upon the sleeper

like a slow-moving and hungry monster. Four long wires were dangled to the extremities of his limbs, and a dull black pad of something that looked like hard rubber was carefully adjusted at the back of his neck and held firmly in place by clamps that fitted over the shoulders. Finally, like two giant mandibles, the opposing electrodes were parted and brought downward over the pale, pudgy head, so that each pointed at a temple.

Shekt kept his eyes firmly on the chronometer; in his other hand was the switch. His thumb moved; nothing visible happened—not even to the fear-sharpened senses of the watching Arbin. After what might have been hours but was actually less than three minutes, Shekt's thumb moved again.

His assistant bent hurriedly over the still-sleeping Schwartz, then looked up triumphantly. "He's alive."

There remained yet several hours, during which a library of recordings were taken, to an undertone of almost wild excitement. It was well past midnight when the hypodermic was pressed home and the sleeper's eyes fluttered.

Shekt stepped back, bloodless and weary. He dabbed at his forehead with the back of a hand. "It's *all* right." He turned to Arbin wistfully. "Would you want to leave him with us for a few days for further tests? No harm would come to him."

But the look of alarm in the other's eyes, the instantaneous leap of suspicion into the lines of his face, were answer enough.

Shekt shrugged and held out his hand. Arbin seized it in a silent but fervent shake.

Dr. Shekt did not sleep that night. The rising sun found him—or would have found him if the windows had been readjusted to transparency—still seated in the operating room, in slowly agonizing reflection.

The excitement and thrill of the operation was over, and there was again room for the horrors and uncertainties of thought.

Had he wanted volunteers? The orders given him had been to avoid volunteers.

His thoughts raced sardonically. To be sure, he knew nothing—officially—of the strategic aims of the Society of Ancients and of the High Minister of Earth. But from their attitude toward the Synapsifier, much could be deduced.

For two years the Synapsifier had been under test, and for two years he had been watched and hampered at every step with a sharpness of official caution that had spoken in a shout. —And the secrecy was against the Galactic Empire.

He had some seven or eight papers that might have been published in the *Sirian Journal of Neurophysiology*. These papers moldered in his desk. Nothing like complete secrecy existed, of course. That might have been penetrated and become intolerably suspicious, as an action. Instead, information was given out in an atmosphere of simple frankness—yet subtly distorted. The Synapsifier became a sort of impractical and obscure scientific device, of huge dream value, but little actual use.

Yet Ennius was inquiring. Was he suspecting something about it?—or about something bigger? Was the Empire suspecting what he himself fearfully suspected; that Earth was planning another of its futile rebellions?

Three times in two hundred years, Earth had risen. Three times, under the banner of a claimed ancient greatness (Shekt's shoulders shook in a bitter and silent merriment at the thought), Earth had rebelled against the Imperial garrisons. Three times they had failed—of course—and had not the Empire been enlightened, and the Galactic Councils, by and large, statesmanlike, Earth would have been bloodily erased from the roll of inhabited worlds.

But now, a fourth time? Impossible.

Then why this attitude toward the Synapsifier? Why certain other things? The sect of the Zealots was out in the open again—once again pounding the drums of the mythical Imperial past of Earth, once again spreading their hate of the men of outer space. And the Council of Ancients suffered it.

Were they mad? Or horribly sane? Was the Synapsifier eventually to be used to breed a race of superintellects? It was a dramatic thought: a world of artificial geniuses avenging the wrongs of a hundred thousand years.

But no, that would take time. Who should know that better than he? Then, perhaps to treat a few key men—those who would count—

His thoughts descended to Earth. What of this man he had just treated? This volunteer who had come despite the feeble publicity campaign for subjects designed simultaneously to turn away suspicion *and* volunteers, so that only the "trusted" volunteers sent him by the High Minister should be tested.

Perhaps—perhaps he had better inform the High Minister of this. Perhaps he should have consulted him first. A spasm of fear shook him. He was fifty-eight years old. The next census would get him, unless the High Minister ordered otherwise—and even on this miserable, burning mud ball of Earth, he wanted to live—

His hand reached for the communicator and he punched the combination that would lead directly to the High Minister's private rooms.

CHAPTER 5 *Of Lava and of Rock*

The High Minister was a man of lava, and his Secretary was a man of rock. There you had the two men in a nutshell—even if the kernels consisted of metaphor. The contrast was perhaps not too uncommon, for look here—

The High Minister was the most important Earthman on Earth, the recognized ruler of the planet by direct and definite decree of the Emperor of all the Galaxy—subject, of course, to the orders of the Emperor's Procurator. The Secretary was no one at all, really—merely a member of the Society of Ancients, appointed by the High Minister to take care of certain details, and—theoretically—dismissable at will.

The High Minister was known to all the Earth, and looked up to as the supreme arbiter on matters of custom. It was he who announced the exemptions to the Sixty, and it was he who judged the breakers of ritual, the defiers of rationing and of production schedules, the invaders of restricted territory, and so on. The Secretary was known to nobody, not even by name, except the Society of Ancients, and, of course, the High Minister himself.

The High Minister had a command of language and made frequent speeches to the people, speeches of high emotional content and copious flow of sentiment. The Secretary preferred a short word to a long one, a grunt to a word, and silence to a grunt.

So it might seem strange that in a case such as the present—that is, when Dr. Shekt faced both—it was at the Secretary that his dodging glance caught and held.

Approximately a month had passed since the experiment upon the "volunteer" (in Shekt's mind, that was how the incident was always thought of, including quotation marks), and in that time, he had felt the soft stranglehold about him tighten.

And now the High Minister sat in his richly woven armchair and patted lightly at the upholstered arm rest with a soft hand. The Secretary stood behind him with veiled eyes and was quite motionless.

The High Minister said, "We regret, Dr. Shekt, more than ever that the incident occurred."

The physicist felt his breath catch. He could not quite force a smile, or even a look of blank equanimity. He said faintly, "There is then proof of your Wisdom's former suspicions?"

"Why, such proof as we consider ample for disturbed sleep. We have found your man. —He is close to your city. —A farmer—he—his wife—this relative. On the records, they are three. A dead son, as he

said. The third man is in his fifties, as he said." He
looked up at his Secretary. "Is it not so?"

And the Secretary nodded once.

Shekt lifted a palm and said, "But then—"

"Ah, yes. But probe a bit deeper. Is it likely that
the Empire in their designs upon us would employ
falsities crudely false? Rather expect them to resemble
the truth greatly. We have searched the records more
closely—and the farmer is as he says and his wife as
she says. But the third man, *the* man, is *not*. The man
on our records is the father of the woman. He is tall,
dark, not bald, and we have his trimensional photo,
his retina pattern, and his blood form. *Your* man, as
you know, is short, stout, bald, and his face and attri-
butes are not on our records." He looked up again.
"Is it not so?"

The Secretary nodded once.

"But—then who is he?" asked Shekt.

"You are curious too, then? Why, it is something to
be curious about, is it not? Consider, that in all our
records of living men, we lack him."

Shekt stirred in the uncomfortably hard chair that
was reserved for such as were given the honor of
audience and were yet of sufficient worth to be shown
a little consideration. "Why, Your Wisdom, an explanation suggests itself to me that involves nothing very
unusual."

"I would like to hear it."

"It may be that this man's father-in-law, the farmer's that is, died recently and his death was not reported. This other, the man experimented upon, a
stranger, a distant relative, a friend, anybody, might
have been subject himself to the Sixty. To escape at
least to the next census he might be taking the place of
the father-in-law."

The High Minister's round face cracked in the bland,
cynical smile of one who surveys human virtue and
finds it a null. "So that the farmer and his wife risked
their own lives by breaking the Customs."

"That may be where the Synapsifier fits in. By volunteering this man, they might hope to win him exemption from the Sixty and themselves immunity from their crime."

The Secretary opened his mouth and made a sound like a frog croaking. The High Minister looked up quickly. "What is it?"

The Secretary spoke—a cold, clipped voice. "Except that the father-in-law has been located, alive, paralyzed, himself evading the Sixty."

"Then they might be hoping for an exemption for him as well," said Shekt quickly.

"In the month since the experiment," said the High Minister sweetly, leaning forward, "nothing has been heard from these people regarding exemptions, immunities, or anything else."

"Then they may simply want another worker about the farm, and lack the courage to apply for anything." Dr. Shekt was suddenly desperate. "Your Wisdom, I thoroughly believe these people to be honest Earthmen. If they cheat, it is for their lives' sake. I have pledged them my word they would be protected—"

"*Your* word is not binding upon me," snapped the High Minister. "Who gave *you* the right to extend protections? Is it *their* lives you are fighting for, or your own?"

Shekt's eyes involuntarily dropped before the other's blaze.

He said, "Yet the experiment increased my knowledge of the Synapsifier, and so should help all Earth. That is worth a return."

"It is worth a return also from the Empire."

Shekt rebelled. "Are you implying that I have had any dealings at all with the Empire on the matter?"

"Ennius has seen you. That is an admitted fact."

"I have told you of that," said Shekt patiently. "The invention naturally would interest the Empire. He was frank enough. He asked me point-blank if I would make it available to the central Government. I told you his offer—freedom for Earth—transfer of all of us to another planet."

Once again the Secretary croaked, and Shekt started
at the sound. It dawned upon him that the Secretary,
by that croak, intended a laugh.

The High Minister curled a lip. "Yes, the Empire is
lavish with its promises, but where is the freedom that
is given to a slave freely by his master? Do you dream?
Give them the Synapsifier, and how strangely and
mistily they will forget once again that there is an
Earth. Where are the promises of food to us during
the famine five years ago? Shipments were refused
because we lacked Imperial credits, and Earth manu-
facturers would not be accepted, as being radioactively
contaminated. Where were the Imperial credits? A
hundred thousand died of starvaion."

Shekt breathed with difficulty. He said in a choking
voice, "If we ourselves had not been too stubborn to
come to a reasonable agreement over the—"

The High Minister smashed his fist against the desk
between them and rose, gleaming in his red cloak.
"Silence. Are you trying to remove the blood-guilt of
Earthman lives from the Galactic Empire? Have a
care, Dr. Shekt. That blood-guilt will soon be repaid
now, and it will be repaid equally upon the heads of
those renegade Earthmen—"

The Secretary might have coughed ever so lightly,
or nudged his superior. In any case, there was a pause
and then a change in tone.

"Consider," said the High Minister coldly, "that
this Ennius comes to you and pokes his patrician outer-
world nose into your Synapsifier. And consider that as
he does so, a farmer comes in with every evidence of
agitation and proposes, as the subject of a test, a man
from outside Earth. —Yes, why do you play the open-
mouthed fish? A man not on our records is a man not
of Earth. You see no connection there?"

Shekt said nothing.

The High Minister said with a firm authority, "You
are going to publish a paper now. The Synapsifier is a
moderate success. It has given faintly positive results
with one man, inconclusive results with others, killed a

few. Give as much inconsequential detail as will carry conviction without information. Remember, no great interest must be aroused. —And if Ennius visits you again, or any man of the Galaxy—*hold your tongue.* Remember that your own Sixty is on the way, and that we are not at all satisfied with you."

Shekt, pale and drawn, dropped his head and said nothing. It was the end of the interview.

And then the High Minister and the Secretary were alone, and the latter sat down in negligent fashion in the chair that Dr. Shekt had previously occupied. The light and fire had momentarily died in the High-Ministerial countenance. He looked merely perturbed.

"Do you think he is safe, Brother? Eh?"

The Secretary shrugged, and grunted with neither the respect nor the awe necessarily due a High Minister. His title of "Brother" was sufficient evidence of membership in the powerful Society of Ancients.

"A word to Ennius, Brother," the High Minister went on, "and we may be destroyed. This Shekt is an Assimilationist. You heard his remarks on the famine. These cowards who believe in conciliation are dangerous."

The cold stolidity of the Secretary's face stopped the expression of further doubts. He said, "Shekt knows nothing of our plans. Shekt is, as you say, a coward, and consequently may burn within, but will remain silent—and we need him as yet." The Secretary went on deliberately, "Furthermore he is not half the danger that fools in high places are who gush forth torrents containing but the driblets of sense."

The High Minister burned at the cheekbones. "What do you mean?"

"I mean your talk of blood-guilt and repayment. Our greatest weapon is that no one could conceive of a victory of Earth over the Galaxy. Our obvious and immense weakness is our strength, for they do not watch us. Leave it that way, Your So-called Wisdom.

Don't threaten. And don't worry about the Synapsifier. Even that is a side issue."

The High Minister swallowed, and if the gleam of hatred in his eyes could have been turned into action, it might have been the worse for the Secretary. But it could not, and all concerned knew it could not.

The High Minister said, "Now then, what of this spy? This Agent T, as you refer to him?"

"Nothing. We watch, and wait. He was too easily located. He makes no effort at concealment or at reaching Ennius."

For a while, the High Minister pondered. His long, carefully tended fingers went to his lower lip and pinched. "You mean we are intended to catch the spy."

"Ah," and the Secretary croaked drily. "You are absorbing wisdom. Certainly. And therefore we don't. We watch—and wait."

"How long?"

"Till Ennius makes the next move—or until we are ready, in which case ours will be the *last* move."

And he smiled an extraordinary smile—for it was as devoid of humor as a lemon of sweetness.

And then the Secretary was alone. He slumped lazily in the soft, rich armchair that the High Minister had previously occupied. His eyes were fixed distantly upon the ceiling, his hands were clasped gently in his lap, and his thoughts roved sharply.

The exact nature of these thoughts would not quite fit in with the orderly narration of the tale, but they concerned themselves little with Dr. Shekt, with the High Minister, or even with Ennius.

Instead, there was the picture of a planet, Trantor—from whose huge, planet-wide metropolis all the Galaxy was ruled. And there was the picture of a palace whose spires and sweeping arches he had never seen in reality; that no other Earthman had ever seen. He thought of the invisible lines of power and glory that swept from sun to sun in gathering strings, ropes, and cables to that central palace and that abstraction, the Emperor, who was, after all, merely a man.

His mind held that thought fixedly—the thought of that power which alone could bestow a divinity during life—concentrated in one who was merely human.

Merely human! Like himself!

CHAPTER 6 *The Mind That Changed*

The coming of the change was dim in Joseph Schwartz's mind. There had been that first shattering fear, already as strange and old in his mind as the picture of Chicago itself. There was the trip to Chica, and its strange, raveled ending. He thought of that often.

For one thing, it was the only time in the half year since this had all happened that he had left the farm. For another, the memory seemed to stop short—

Many times he had tried to follow that memory along—step by step, slow inch by slow inch—as though to trap by sheer careful persistence the key to the change that had come since then.

Many times in his mind the thin man in charge had offered that pill—white, ellipsoidal. He had taken it and swallowed it quickly. A drug, of course. Cure, or kill, or nothing. At the time he didn't care.

And then—

Well, and then—

That's where the clearness ended and the ragged shreds of recollection came to taunt him. He could remember nothing but the farm thereafter—and headaches. No, not quite headaches. Throbbings, rather, as though some hidden dynamo in his brain had started working and with its unaccustomed action was vibrating every bone of his skull.

There had been Grew in his wheelchair at his bedside, repeating words and pointing, or making motions. And one day he stopped speaking nonsense and began talking English. —Or no, he himself—he, Joseph Schwartz—had stopped speaking English and begun talking nonsense. —Except that it wasn't nonsense anymore.

Then, when the autumn was become really golden, things were clear again and he was out in the fields working. It was amazing the way he picked it up. He *never* made a mistake. There were complicated machines that he could run without trouble after a single explanation.

He waited for the cold weather, and it never quite came. The winter was spent in clearing ground, in fertilizing, in preparing for the spring planting in a dozen ways.

He questioned Grew, tried to explain what snow was, but the latter only stared and said, "Frozen water falling like rain, eh? Oh, snow! On other planets, they say—not here."

Schwartz watched the temperature thereafter, and found that it scarcely varied from day to day—and yet the days first shortened and then lengthened quite as would be expected in a northerly location—say, as northerly as Chicago. And he wondered if he was on Earth.

He tried· reading some of Grew's book-films, but gave up. People were people still, but the minutiae of daily life the knowledge of which was taken for granted, the historical and sociological allusions that meant nothing to him—these forced him back.

The puzzles continued: the uniformly warm rains, the wild instructions he received to remain away from certain regions. For instance, there had been the evening that he had finally become too intrigued by the shining horizon—the blue glow to the south—

He had slipped off after supper, and when not a mile had passed the almost noiseless whirr of the bi-wheel engine had come up behind him, and Arbin's wild shout. He had stopped and been taken back.

Arbin had paced back and forth before him and said, "You stay away from anywhere that it shines at night."

He had asked mildly, "Why?"

And the answer came with biting incisiveness, "Because it is forbidden."

But that night had a great importance for Schwartz, for it was during that short mile towards the Shiningness that he first became aware of the Mind Touch. He was never able to describe it to anybody else. He hadn't seen anybody, or heard anybody, or exactly touched anything.

Not exactly— It had been *something* like a touch, but not anywhere on his body. It was in his mind. —Not exactly a touch, but a presence—a somethingness there.

And it occurred again and again with increasing frequency.

It was only a month previously that it began to dawn upon him that he always knew when either Arbin or Loa was in the house—even when he had no reason for knowing. It was a hard thing not to take for granted, since it seemed so natural.

He experimented, and found that he knew exactly where any of them were—at any time. He could distinguish between them, for the Mind Touch differed from person to person.

He said nothing about it.

It was in the early spring that he felt the Touch during the planting—the original Touch, the one he had felt in that short trip towards the Shiningness. He came to Arbin that evening and said, "What about that patch of woods past the South Hills, Arbin?"

"Nothing about it," was the gruff answer. "It's Ministerial Ground."

"What's that?"

Arbin seemed annoyed. "Belongs to the High Minister."

"But it's not cultivated."

"It's not intended for that." Arbin's voice was shocked. "It was a great Center. —In ancient days."

"How ancient? What was its name?" The questions came quickly, as did Schwartz's breath.

But Arbin shrugged it off impatiently. "I don't know

how ancient. —And only the learned men—the Society of Ancients—know the names of the ancient Centers. What business is it of yours, anyway? Look, Joseph, if you want to remain here safely, curb your curiosity. Tend to your job."

"Does anybody live there?"

"No!" Arbin walked away.

But it was from there that the strange Mind Touch came, and there was to it a threatening overtone that made him uneasy.

—He was younger these days too. Not so much in the physical sense, to be sure. He was thinner in his stomach and broader in his shoulders. His muscles were harder and springier, and his digestion was better. That was the result of work in the open, but there was something else. It was his way of thinking.

Old men tend to forget what thought was like in their youth—they forget the quickness of the mental jump, the daring of the youthful intuition, the agility of their insight. They become accustomed to the more plodding varieties of reason, but because this is more than made up for by the accumulation of experience, old men think themselves wiser than the young.

But to Schwartz experience remained, and it was with a sharp delight that he found he could understand things at a bound—that he gradually progressed from following Arbin's explanations, to anticipating them, to leaping on ahead. And as a result, he felt young in a far more subtle way than any amount of physical excellence could account for.

And now the planting was over, and Schwartz felt he had to know—a number of things. It came out finally on a spring evening over a game of chess with Grew in the arbor.

Chess, somehow, hadn't changed—except for the names of the pieces. Grew told him of variations thereof—such as four-handed chess, in which each player had a board, touching each other at the corners, with a fifth board filling the hollow in the center as a common no-man's-land. There were three-dimensional chess games in which eight transparent boards were placed one over the other and each piece moved in three dimensions as it had formerly moved in two, and in which the number of pieces and pawns was doubled and the win came when a simultaneous check of both enemy kings occurred. There were even the popular varieties, in which the original positions of the chessmen were decided by throws of the dice, or where certain squares conferred advantages or disadvantages to pieces upon them, or where new pieces with strange properties were introduced.

But chess itself, the original and unchangeable, was the same—and the tournament between Schwartz and Grew had completed its first hundred games.

When he began, Schwartz had a bare knowledge of the moves, and he lost constantly in the first games. But that had changed, and the games were becoming different now—after Schwartz had begun winning. Gradually Grew had grown slow and cautious, had taken to smoking his pipe into glowing embers in the intervals between moves, and had finally subsided into rebellious and querulous losses.

Grew was White and his pawn was already on King 4. Schwartz took his seat in the gathering twilight and sighed. The games were really becoming uninteresting, as more and more he became aware of the nature of Grew's moves before they could be made. It was as if Grew had a window in his skull.

They used a "Night-board" that glowed in the darkness in a checkered blue-and-orange glimmer. The men, in the sunlight ordinary lumpish figures of a reddish clay, were metamorphosed at night. Half were bathed in a creamy whiteness that lent them the look of a cold and shining porcelain, and the others sparked in tiny glitters of red.

The first moves were rapid. Schwartz's own King's Pawn met the enemy advance head-on. Grew brought out his King's Knight to Bishop 3; Schwartz countered with Queen's Knight to Bishop 3. Then the White Bishop leaped to Queen's Knight 5, and Schwartz's

Queen's Rook's Pawn slid ahead a square to drive it back to Rook 4. He then advanced his other Knight to Bishop 3.

The shining pieces slid across the board with an eery volition of their own as the grasping fingers lost themselves in the night.

Then Schwartz said tensely and abruptly, "Where am I?"

Grew looked up in the midst of a deliberate move of his Queen's Knight to Bishop 3 and said, "What?"

"What planet is this?" Schwartz moved his Bishop to King 2.

"Earth," was the short reply, and Grew castled with great emphasis, first the tall figurine that was the King moving, and then the lumpish Rook topping it and resting on the other side.

That was a thoroughly unsatisfactory answer. The word Grew had used Schwartz translated in his mind as "Earth." But what was "Earth"? Any planet is "Earth" to those who live on it. He advanced his Queen's Knight's Pawn two spaces, and again Grew's Bishop had to retreat, to Knight 3 this time. Then Schwartz and Grew, each in turn, advanced the Queen's Pawn one space, each freeing his Bishop for the battle in the center that would soon begin.

Schwartz asked, as calmly and casually as he could, "What year is this?"

Grew paused. He might have been startled. "What *is* it you're harping on today? Don't you want to play? This is 827 G.E. Does that satisfy you?" He stared frowningly at the board, then slammed his Queen's Knight to Queen 5, where it made its first assault. Schwartz dodged quickly, moving his own Queen's Knight to Rook 4 in counterattack. Then the skirmish was on in earnest. Grew's Knight seized the Bishop, which leaped upwards in a bath of red fire to be dropped with a sharp click into the box where it might lie, a buried warrior, until the next game. —And then the conquering Knight fell instantly to Schwartz's Queen. In a moment of over-caution Grew's attack faltered and he moved his remaining Knight back to the haven of King 1, where it was relatively useless. Schwartz's Queen's Knight now repeated the first exchange, taking the Bishop and falling prey in its turn to the Rook's Pawn.

And now another pause, and Schwartz asked mildly, "What's G.E?"

"What?" demanded Grew bad-humoredly. "You're still wondering what year this is? Well, it's 827 of the Galactic Era; 827 years since the foundation of the Galactic Empire; 827 years since the coronation of Frankenn the First. —It's your move." And he concluded in a thunder.

But the Knight that Schwartz held was swallowed up in the grip of his hand. He was in a fury of frustration. He said, "Please—" and put the Knight down on Queen 2. "Do you recognize any of these names: Asia, America, the United States, Russia, Europe—" He groped for identification.

In the darkness Grew's pipe was a sullen red glow and his dim shadow hunched over the shining chessboard as if of the two it had the less life.

Schwartz tried again. "Do you know where I can get a map?"

"No maps," growled Grew, "unless you want to risk your neck in Chica. I'm no geographer. I never heard of the names you mention."

—Again the vague threat that seemed to be hanging over him always: "—risk your neck—"

He asked doubtfully, "The sun has nine planets, hasn't it?"

"Ten," was the uncompromising answer.

Schwartz hesitated— Well, they *might* have discovered another. He counted on his fingers, then, "How abou the sixth planet? Has it got rings?"

Grew was slowly moving the King's Bishop's Pawn forward two squares and Schwartz instantly did the same. Grew said, "Saturn, you mean? Of course it has rings." He was calculating now. He had the choice of

taking either the Bishop's Pawn or the Knight's Pawn,
and the consequences of the choice were not too clear.

But to Schwartz, sure now of Earth's identity, the
chess game was less than a trifle. Questions quivered
along the inner surface of his skull, and one slipped
out. "And your book-films are real? There are other
worlds? With people?"

And now Grew looked up from the board, eyes
probing uselessly in the darkness. "Are you serious?"

"Are there?"

"By the Galaxy! *I believe you really don't know.*"

Schwartz felt humiliated in his ignorance. "Please—"

"Of course there are worlds. Millions! Every star
you see has worlds, and most that you don't see. It's
all part of the Empire."

Delicately—inside—Schwartz felt the faint echo of
each of Grew's intense words as they sparked directly
from mind to mind. He felt the mental contacts growing stronger with the days. Maybe soon he could hear
those tiny words in his mind even when the person
thinking them *wasn't* talking.

He said huskily, "How long since it's all happened,
Grew? How long since the time there was only one
planet?"

"What do you mean?" Grew was suddenly cautious.
"Are you a member of the Ancients?"

"Of the what? I'm not a member of anything—but
wasn't Earth once the only planet? —Well, wasn't it?"

"The Ancients say so," said Grew grimly, "but who
knows? Who really knows? The worlds up there have
been up there all history long, as far as I know."

"But how long is that?"

"Thousands of years, I suppose. Fifty, a hundred— I
can't say."

Thousands of years! Schwartz felt a gurgle in his
throat and pressed it down in panic. All that between
two steps? A breath, a moment, a flicker of time—and
he had jumped thousands of years?

But now Grew was making his next move—he was
taking the other's Bishop's pawn, and it was almost

mechanically that Schwartz noted mentally the fact
that it was the wrong choice. Move fitted to move in
his mind with no conscious effort. His King's Rook
swooped forward to take the foremost of the now-
doubled White Pawns. White's Knight advanced again
to Bishop 3. Schwartz's Bishop moved to Knight 2,
freeing itself for action. Grew followed suit by moving
his own Bishop to Queen 2.

Schwartz paused, before launching the final attack.
He said, "Is Earth still boss?"

"Boss of what?"

"The Emp—"

But Grew looked up with a roar at which the chessmen quivered. "Listen, you, what are you getting at,
anyway? The Ancients say it was once, but does it
look it?" There was a smooth whir as Grew's wheelchair circled the table. Schwartz felt grasping fingers
on his arm.

"Look! Look there!" Grew's voice was a whispered
rasp. "You see the horizon? You see it shine?"

"Yes."

"*That* is Earth—all Earth. Except here and there,
where a few patches like this one here exist."

"I don't understand."

"Earth's crust is radioactive. The soil glows, always
glowed, will glow forever. Nothing can grow. No one
can live— You really don't know that? Why do you
suppose we have the Sixty?"

The paralytic subsided. He circled his chair about
the table again. "It's your move."

The Sixty! —Again that phrase, and always with the
indefinable Mind Touch of menace. Schwartz's chess
pieces played themselves, while he wondered with a
tight-pressed heart. His King's Pawn took the opposing Bishop's Pawn. Grew moved his Knight to Queen
4 and Schwartz's Rook sidestepped the attack to Knight
4. Again Grew's Knight attacked, moving to Bishop 3,
and Schwartz's Rook avoided the issue again to Knight
5. But now Grew's King's Rook's pawn advanced one
timorous square and Schwartz's Rook slashed forward.

It took the Knight's Pawn, checking the enemy King. Grew's King promptly took the Rook, but Schwartz's Queen plugged the hole instantly, moving to Knight 4 and checking. Grew's King scurried to Rook 1, and Schwartz brought up his Knight, placing it on King 4. Grew moved his Queen to King 2 in a strong attempt to mobilize his defenses, and Schwartz countered by marching his Queen forward two squares to Knight 6, so that the fight was now in close quarters. Grew had no choice; he moved his Queen to Knight 2, and the two female majesties were now face to face. Schwartz's Knight pressed home, taking the opposing Knight on Bishop 6, and when the now-attacked White Bishop moved quickly to Bishop 3, the Knight followed to Queen 5. Grew hesitated for slow minutes now, then advanced his Queen up the long diagonal to take Schwartz's Bishop.

And now he paused, and drew a relieved breath. His sly opponent had a Rook in danger with a check in the offing, with his own Queen ready to wreak havoc. And he was ahead a Rook to a Pawn.

"Your move," he said with satisfaction.

But Schwartz said finally, "What—what is the Sixty?"

There was a sharp unfriendliness to Grew's voice. "Why do you ask that? What are you after?"

"Please," humbly. "I am a man with no harm in me. I don't know who I am, or what happened to me. Maybe I'm an amnesia case."

"Very likely," was the contemptuous reply. "Are you escaping from the Sixty? Answer truthfully."

"But I tell you I don't know what the Sixty is!"

It carried conviction. There was a long silence. To Schwartz, Grew's Mind Touch was ominous, but he could not—quite—make out words.

Grew said slowly, "The Sixty is your sixtieth year. Earth supports twenty million people, no more. To live, you must produce. If you cannot produce, you cannot live. Past Sixty—you cannot produce."

"And so—" Schwartz's mouth remained open.

"You're put away. It doesn't hurt."

"You're killed?"

"It's not murder." Stiffly, "It *must* be that way. Other worlds won't take us, and we must make room for the children some way. The older generation must make room for the younger."

"Suppose you don't tell them you're sixty."

"Why shouldn't you? Life after sixty is no joke— And there's a census every ten years to catch anyone that is foolish enough to try to live. Besides, they have your age on record."

"Not mine." The words slipped out. Schwartz couldn't stop them. "Besides—I'm only fifty—next birthday."

"It doesn't matter. They can check by your bone structure. Don't you know that? There's no way of masking it. They'll get me next time. —Say, it's your move."

Schwartz disregarded the urging. "You mean they'll—"

"Sure. I'm only fifty-five, but look at my legs. I can't work, can I? There are three of us registered in our family and our quota is adjusted on a basis of three workers. When I had the stroke and was crippled past cure, I should have been reported, and then the quota would have been reduced. But Arbin and Loa wouldn't do it, because they're fools, and it has meant hard work for them—till you came along. But they'll get me next year. —Your move."

"Is next year the census?"

"That's right. —Your move."

"Wait!" urgently. "Is *everyone* put away after sixty? No exceptions at all?"

"Not for you and me. The High Minister lives a full life, and members of the Society of Ancients; certain scientists; or those performing some great service. Not many qualify. Maybe a dozen a year. —*It's your move!*"

"Who decides who qualifies?"

"The High Minister, of course. Are you moving?"

But Schwartz stood up. "Never mind. It's check-mate in five moves. My Queen is going to take your Pawn to check you, you've got to move to Knight 1, I bring up the Knight to check you, you move to Bishop

2, my Queen checks you at King 6, you move to
Knight 2, my Queen goes to Knight 6, and when
you're then forced to Rook 1, my Queen mates you at
Rook 6.

"Good game," he added automatically.

Grew stared long at the board, then, with a cry,
dashed it from the table. The gleaming pieces rolled
dejectedly about on the floor.

But Schwartz was conscious of nothing—nothing,
except the overwhelming necessity of escaping. For
though Browning said:

> Grow old along with me!
> The best is yet to be . . .

that was in an Earth of teeming billions and of unlimited food. The best that was to come now was the
Sixty—and death.

—Schwartz, you see, was sixty-two.

It was then that Schwartz knew two things. The first
was simple and inevitable. He had to live, somehow,
anyhow. Death might come easily and naturally to
those who were used to the thought all their lives, but
not to him.

The second thing of which he was aware, however,
was more subtle. It came in a moment of insight that
followed from no logic other than the heightened per-
ceptions of fear. It was that the strange Mind Touch of
the Ministerial Ground—the one with the undercur-
rent of hostility, the one he had first detected on his
abortive trek to the shining horizon—was watching
him. Watching him with the specific purpose of keeping him where he was; of not letting him escape.

Undoubtedly, he was trapped.

—Trapped in the strangeness of the dim future and
already condemned to absolute death.

INTERMISSION

We leave Joseph Schwartz in the afore-described predicament—temporarily—in accordance with the promise in the first five paragraphs of this story. What follows afterward can best be understood by scooting to another end of the tale now, and working backward to the proper point. —Or not exactly backward, either, but more at an angle of 120 degrees.

It will all be clear eventually, I promise you.

And, as indicated at the very beginning, we must proceed to a consideration of Bel Arvardan, archaeologist of Baronn, Sirius Sector, citizen of the Galactic Empire.

PART II: BEL ARVARDAN

CHAPTER 7 One World—or Many

In the year 827 G.E., now under consideration, Arvardan was thirty-five, ruggedly handsome to an extent that might be considered queer in a scientist— but then archaeology is an outdoor science in its field aspects, and Arvardan had traveled through more regions of the Empire than many a professional traveler at his age.

In view of his physical appearance, it might be strange—or not, depending upon the cynicism of the observer—that he remained a bachelor. He himself denied it, claiming he was married to his work, but truth compels us to state that few women, if any, were impressed with the legality of such a marriage contract. At least, they tried hard enough to make a bigamist out of him.

But come to think of it, all that is incidental. In fact, it has nothing to do with the story—except in a way.

The following, while perhaps less interesting, is more pertinent. Bel Arvardan graduated as Senior Archaeologist at the quite unprecedented age of twenty-three from the School of Archaeology of Arcturus University. His Senior Dissertation was entitled: "On the Antiquity of Artifacts in the Sirius Sector with Considerations of the Application Thereof to the Radiation Hypothesis of Human Origin."

That dissertation marked the beginning of a career of iconoclasm. From the first, Arvardan adopted as his own the hypothesis advanced earlier by certain groups of mystics who were more concerned with metaphysics than with archaeology—i.e., that Humanity had originated upon some single planet, and had radiated by degrees throughout the Galaxy. This was a favorite theory of the fantasy writers of the day, and a favorite sneer of almost every respectable archaeologist of the Empire.

But Arvardan was a force to be considered by even the most respectable, for within the decade he became the recognized authority on the relics of the pre-Empire cultures still left in the eddies and quiet backwaters of the Galaxy.

For instance, he had written a monograph on the mechanistic civilization of the Rigel Sector, where the development of automation created a separate culture that persisted for centuries, till the very perfection of the machines reduced human initiative to the point where the vigorous fleets of the Warlord Moray took easy control. Where orthodox archaeology attributed such atypical cultures to differences in race not yet ironed out by intermarriage, Arvardan proved the automated culture to be a natural outgrowth of the economic and social forces of the times and of the region.

Then there were the barbarous worlds of Ophiuchus, which the orthodox had long upheld as samples of primitive Humanity not yet advanced to the stage of interstellar travel. Every textbook used those worlds as evidence of the Merger Theory—i.e., that Humanity had originated independently on many worlds based upon a water-oxygen chemistry with proper intensities of temperature and gravitation, due to the inevitable working of biological law, and that as interstellar travel was discovered, the various races met and merged.

Arvardan, however, uncovered traces of the early civilization that had preceded the then-thousand-year-old barbarism of Ophiuchus and proved that the earliest records of the planet showed traces of interstellar trade and that Man had emigrated to the region in an already civilized state.

And now the pursuit of his pet theory had led him to probably the least significant planet of the Empire—the planet called Earth. It is there we join him.

We meet Arvardan in that one spot of Empire on all Earth—the desolate heights of the plateaus north of the Himalayas. There, where radioactivity was not, and never had been, there gleamed a place that was not of Terrestrial architecture. In essence, it was a copy of the Viceregal Palaces that existed on more fortunate worlds. The soft lushness of the grounds was made for comfort. The forbidding rocks had been covered with topsoil, watered, immersed in an artificial climate—and converted into five square miles of lawns and flower gardens.

The cost in energy involved in this performance was terrific by Earthly calculations, but it had behind it the completely incredible resources of two hundred million worlds, continually growing in number. (It has been estimated that in the Year of the Galactic Era 827, an average of fifty new planets each day were achieving the dignity of provincial status, this condition requiring the attainment of a population of 500,000,000.)

In this patch of non-Earth lived the Procurator, and sometimes, in this artificial luxury, he could forget that he was a Procurator and remember only that he was an aristocrat of great honor and ancient family.

His wife was perhaps less often deluded, particularly at such times as, topping a grassy knoll, she could see in the distance the sharp, decisive line separating the grounds from the fierce wilderness of Earth. It was then that not all the colored fountains (luminescent at night, with an effect of cold liquid fire), flowered walks, or idyllic groves could compensate for the knowledge of their exile.

So perhaps Arvardan was welcomed even more than protocol might call for. To Ennius, for instance, Arvardan was a breath of Empire, of spaciousness, of boundlessness.

Arvardan for his part found much to admire.

He said, "This is done well—and with taste. It is amazing how a touch of the central culture permeates the most outlying districts of our Empire."

Ennius smiled. "It is not as I would wish it. It seems to me to be a shell which rings hollowly when I touch it. When you have considered the Procuratorial staff, the Imperial garrison—both here and in the important planetary centers—and an occasional visitor such as yourself, you have exhausted all the touch of the central culture that you speak of. It seems scarcely enough."

They sat in the colonnade in the dying afternoon, when the sun was glinting downward toward the mist-purpled jags of the horizon, and the air seemed so heavy with the scent of growing things that its motions were merely sighs of exertion.

It was, of course, not quite suitable even for a Procurator to show too great a curiosity about the doings of a guest, but that does not take into account the inhumanity of day-to-day isolation from all the Empire.

Ennius said, "Do you plan to stay for some time, Dr. Arvardan?"

"Oh, as to that I can scarcely say. As long as I feel necessary—which is an indefinite answer, I'm afraid. You see, when one searches for something of whose nature he is unaware, and which he is unsure of recognizing when he finds it, or of interpreting after recognizing it, or of convincing others of the correctness of his thoughts, or—But how did I get into this, Procurator?"

"I seem to gather a sense of confusion," smiled Ennius.

"And so there is. Much confusion. Perhaps some will be cleared up, once I poke my nose into the prehistoric past of this planet."

Ennius raised his eyebrows. "Why this planet? If any spot in the Galaxy lacks history, this is it."

"That may *seem* to be so, but I think you have it exactly twisted. This is a very unique world."

"Not at all," said the Procurator stiffly, "it is a very ordinary world. It is more or less a pigpen of a world, or a horrible hole of a world, or a cesspool of a world, or almost any other particularly derogatory adjective you care to use. And yet with all its refinement of nausea, it cannot even achieve uniqueness in villainy, but remains an ordinary, brutish peasant world."

"But," said Arvardan, somewhat taken aback by

the energy of the inconsistent statements thus thrown at him, "the world is radioactive."

"Well, what of that? Some thousands of planets in the Galaxy are radioactive, and some considerably more so than Earth."

It was at this moment that the soft-gliding motion of the motile cabinet attracted them. It came to a halt within easy hand-reach.

Ennius gestured toward it and said to the other, "What would you prefer?"

"I am not particular. —A lime twist, perhaps."

"That can be handled. The cabinet will have the ingredients. With or without Chensey?"

"Just about a tang of it," said Arvardan, and held up his forefinger and thumb nearly touching.

"You'll have it in a minute."

Somewhere in the bowels of the cabinet perhaps the most universally popular mechanical offspring of human ingenuity went into action—a non-human bartender whose electronic soul mixed things not by jiggers, but by atom counts; whose ratios were perfect every time; and which not all the inspired artistry of anyone merely human could match.

The tall glasses appeared from nowhere, it seemed, as they waited for them in the appropriate recesses.

Arvardan took the green one and for a moment felt the chill of it against his cheek. Then he placed the rim to his lips and tasted.

"Just right," he said. He placed the glass in the well-fitting holder in the arm of his chair and said, "Thousands of radioactive planets, Procurator, just as you say, but only one of them is inhabited. This one, Procurator."

"Well—" Ennius smacked his lips over his own drink and seemed to lose some of his sharpness against its velvet. "Perhaps it *is* unique in that way. It's an unenviable distinction."

"The uniqueness is not just in that." Arvardan spoke deliberately between occasional sips. "It goes further. Biologists have shown—or claim to have shown—that on planets in which the intensity of radioactivity in the atmosphere and in the seas is above a certain point, life will not develop. Earth's radioactivity is above that point by a considerable margin."

"Interesting. I didn't know that. I should say that was definite proof that Earth life is fundamentally different from that of the rest of the Galaxy."

"Not at all," was the vehement response. "That's the old view; completely blasted, Procurator. All life is fundamentally one, in that it is based upon protein complexes in colloidal dispersion. We call it protoplasm. And the effect of radioactivity that I just talked of is based upon the quantum mechanics of the protein molecule. It applies to you, to me, to Earthmen, to spiders, and to germs.

"You see, proteins, as I probably needn't tell you, are immensely complicated groupings of amino acids and certain other specialized compounds, arranged in intricate three-dimensional patterns that are as unstable as sunbeams on a cloudy day. It is this instability that is life, since it is forever changing its position in an effort to maintain its identity—in the manner of a long rod balanced on an acrobat's nose.

"But this marvelous protein must first be built up out of inorganic matter, before life can exist. So at the very beginning, by the influence of the sun's radiant energy and in those huge solutions we call oceans, organic molecules gradually increase in complexity from methane to formaldehyde, to sugars and starches in one direction and from urea to amino acids and proteins in another. It's a matter of chance, of course, and the process on one world may take millions of years, and on another, a hundred. It has been shown that 'millions' is by far the more probable figure.

"Now, physical organic chemists have worked out with great exactness the whole reaction chain involved, and particularly the energetics thereof, and it is known beyond the shadow of a doubt that several of the crucial steps require the absence of radiant energy. If this strikes you as queer, Procurator, I can only say

that photo-chemistry (the chemistry of reactions induced by radiant energy) is a well-developed branch of
the science, and there are innumerable cases of very
simple reactions that will go in one of two different
directions, depending upon whether they take place in
the presence or absence of quanta of light energy.

"In ordinary worlds, the sun is the only source of
radiant energy. In the shelter of clouds, or at night,
the carbon and nitrogen compounds combine and re-
combine, in the fashions made possible by the absence
of those little bits of energy hurled into the midst of
them by the sun—like bowling balls into the midst of
an infinite number of infinitesimal tenpins.

"But on radioactive worlds, sun or no sun, every
drop of water—even in deepest night—even five miles
under—sparkles and bursts with darting gamma rays,
kicking up the carbon atoms—activating them, the
chemists say—and forcing the reactions to proceed
only in certain ways, ways that never result in life.
And believe it or not, there is rigid mathematical
evidence—and experimental, as well—for every bit of
this."

Arvardan's drink was gone. He placed the empty
glass on the waiting cabinet. It disappeared instantly.

"Another one?" asked Ennius.

"Ask me after dinner," said Arvardan. "I've had
quite enough for now."

And Ennius tapped a shining fingernail upon the
arm of his chair and said, "You make the process
sound quite fascinating, but if all is as you say, then
what about the life on Earth? How did *it* develop?"

"Well, there— You see, even you are beginning to
wonder. That's what makes it fascinating."

"Unless," said Ennius with a casual shrug, "the
rigid mathematics you speak of is slightly wrong. It is
amazing, the rigidity of some of the science that has
failed in the past."

"Quite so! But rigid mathematics has far more often
endured than failed—and there is an explanation in
the case of Earth that fits very nicely."

"Ah, I might have scented it. You have a pet hypothesis of your own."

"Quite," agreed Arvardan, "and it is simple. Radioactivity in excess of the minimum required to prevent life is not sufficient to destroy life already formed. It might modify it, but, except in huge excess, it will not destroy it. —You see, the chemistry involved is different. In the first case, simple molecules must be prevented from building up, and in the second, already formed complex molecules must be broken down. Not at all the same thing."

"I don't get the application of that at all," said Ennius.

"Isn't it obvious? Life on Earth originated *before* the planet became radioactive. My dear Procurator, it is the only possible explanation that does not involve denying either the fact of life on Earth or enough chemical theory to upset half the science."

Ennius gazed at the other quite in horror. "But you can't mean that."

"Why not?"

"Because how can a world *become* radioactive? The life of the radioactive chemicals in the planet's crust is in the millions of years. They must have existed indefinitely in the past."

"But there is such a thing as artificial radioactivity, Procurator—even on a huge scale. There are thousands of nuclear reactions of sufficient energy to create all sorts of radioactive isotopes. If we were to suppose that human beings might use some applied nuclear reaction in industry, without proper controls, or even in war, if you can imagine anything like a war proceeding on a single planet, most of the topsoil might be converted into artificially radioactive materials. What do you say to that?"

The sun had expired in blood on the mountains, and Ennius's thin face was ruddy in the reflection. The gentle evening wind stirred and the drowsy murmur of the carefully selected varieties of insect life upon the Palace grounds was more soothing than ever.

Ennius said, "It sounds very artificial to me—an ad hoc hypothesis made up to cover facts, but very improbable. For one thing, I can't conceive using nuclear reactions in war, or letting them get out of control to this extent in any manner. Now, if you had said subetheric radiations—"

"But you underestimate nuclear reactions because you're living in the present. To you, nuclear reactions are like—well, fire. Destructive, but controllable. In the case of fire, you can use fireproof materials for construction. You can use water, sand, carbon dioxide, carbon tetrachloride, nitrogen, and so on. But what if someone—or some army—used fire without knowing how to control it? —Well, apply that to nuclear reactions."

"Hmm," said Ennius, "you sound like Shekt."

"Who's Shekt?" Arvardan looked up quickly.

"An Earthman. A biologist. He told me once that Earth might not always have been radioactive."

"Ah. Well, that's not unusual, since the theory is certainly not original with me. It's part of the *Book of the Ancients*, which is the traditional, or mythical, history of prehistoric Earth. I'm saying what it says, except that I'm putting its rather elliptical phraseology into equivalent scientific statements."

"The Book of the Ancients?" Ennius seemed surprised —and a little upset. "Where did you get that?"

"It wasn't easy, but I did. Parts of it, anyway. Why do you ask?"

"It is a revered book of a radical sect of the Earthmen, and it is forbidden for outsiders to read it. I wouldn't broadcast the fact that you did, while you're here. Non-Earthmen have been lynched for less."

"You make it sound as if the Imperial police power here is defective."

"It is in cases of sacrilege. A word to the wise, Professor Arvardan."

A melodious chime sounded a vibrant note that seemed to harmonize with the rustling whisper of the trees. It faded out slowly, lingering as though in love with its surroundings.

Ennius rose. "I believe it is time for dinner. Will you join me, sir, and enjoy such hospitality as this husk of Empire on Earth can afford."

An occasion for an elaborate dinner came infrequently enough. An excuse, even a slim one, was not missed. So the courses were many, the surroundings lavish, and the women bewitching. And, it must be added, Professor B. Arvardan of Baronn was lionized to quite an intoxicating extent.

He took advantage of his audience to repeat much of what he had said to Ennius. It was met with grateful throbbings of excitement and much whispering and exclamations, with profound, if turgid, questioning on the part of the men, and squeals and shocks on the part of the women.

It was quite successful, except that Ennius sat throughout with a mechanical smile on his lips that seemed even more uneasy than the light crease on his forehead.

And then one emeraldized dame, with a billowing pink-and-white heaving of the bosom asked, "But Professor Arvardan, do you really expect to *prove* your theory here?"

"I may," replied Arvardan cheerfully. "I'm going to investigate the radioactive areas. If I find human relics and artifacts *there*, what deduction can be drawn but the existence of life before the radioactivity?"

It was during this rather short speech that all excitement and babble died away, so that at the end the archaeologist stared about in the sudden cold silence.

A man in military uniform said shortly, "You imagine that to be safe, sir?"

Arvardan lifted his eyebrows. "Why, the radioactivity is not as bad as all that. We'll be amply protected, and we'll make liberal use of long-range mechanical devices for archaeological research. There should be little danger."

Ennius leaned toward him and said significantly,

"I'm sure the Colonel was not referring to the radioactivity. He means that the High Minister will not allow any violation of Forbidden Areas, which include all that are radioactive and some that aren't."

Arvardan frowned. "Well, I don't see that that should concern us, Procurator. I have a Writ of Permission from the Emperor, and my research is of great value to science."

But the Procurator shook his head. "A Writ of Permission won't help. The Emperor himself couldn't enter the radioactive areas without the High Minister's permission—or a war against these fanatics of Earth." There was a general murmur of agreement to that.

"In fact," continued Ennius, "if you would listen to my very urgent advice, you'd drop it all and leave."

And so the dinner ended on a very flat note.

CHAPTER 8 Darkening—at the Right

The Procurator's Palace was scarcely less a fairyland at night. The evening flowers (none native to Earth) opened their fat white blossoms in festoons that extended their delicate fragrance to the very walls of the Palace. Under the polarized light of the moon the artificial silicate strands, woven cleverly into the stainless alabaster alloy of the Palace structure, sparked a faint violet against the milkiness of their surroundings.

Ennius looked at the stars. To him they were the real beauty, since they were the Empire.

Earth's sky was of an intermediate type. It had not the unbearable glory of the skies of the Central Worlds, where star elbowed star in such blinding competition that the black of night was nearly lost in a coruscant explosion of light. Nor did it possess the lonely grandeur of the skies of the Periphery, where the unrelieved blackness was broken at great intervals by the dimness of an orphaned star—with the milky lens shape of the Galaxy spreading across the sky, the individual stars thereof lost in diamond dust.

On Earth, two thousand stars were visible at one

time. Ennius recognized Sirius, round which circled one of the ten largest planets of the Empire. And Arcturus, of course, capital of the sector of his birth. The sun of Trantor, the Empire's capital world, was lost somewhere in the Milky Way. Even under a telescope it was just part of a general blaze.

He felt a soft hand on his shoulder, and his own went up to meet it.

"Flora?" he whispered.

"Shall I have breakfast brought out here, Ennius?" came his wife's half-amused voice. "Do you know that it's almost dawn?"

"Is it?" He smiled fondly up at her and felt in the darkness for the brown ringlet that hovered next her cheek. He tugged at it. "And must you wait up for me and shadow the most beautiful eyes in the Galaxy?"

She freed her hair and replied gently, "You are trying to shadow them yourself with your sugar syrup, but I've seen you this way before. What worries you tonight, dear?"

Ennius shook his head in the shadows and said, "I don't know. I think maybe an accumulation of little things has finally sickened me. First the matter of Shekt and his Synapsifier, and now the complete obtuseness and stupidity on the part of the Government. —And other things, other things. Oh, what's the use, Flora— I'm doing no good here at all."

"Surely, this time of the morning isn't quite the moment for putting your morale to the test."

But Ennius was speaking through clenched teeth. "These Earthmen! Why should so few be such a burden to the Empire? They are quarrelsome and difficult, and at the same time, so shrewdly accurate in their annoyances—as if they knew by instinct where our weaknesses lay. Do you remember, Flora, when I first was appointed to the Procuracy—the warnings I received from old Faroul, the last Procurator, as to the difficulty of the position? —He was right. Absolutely." He paused, lost in himself, then continued, apparently at a disconnected point. "Yet if anything seems clear,

it is that the resentment of these Earthmen has led
them into dreams of rebellion—"

He looked up at her. "Do you know that it is the
doctrine of the Society of Ancients that Earth was at
one time the sole home of Humanity, that it is the
center of the race, and that it shall once again become
the center of the race?"

"Yes," she said soothingly, "I know." It was always
best at these times to let him talk himself out. She
knew that also.

"And there are actually extreme groups," he went
on, "that claim this mythical Second Kingdom of Earth
to be at hand, that warn that the Empire will be
destroyed in a general catastrophe which will leave
Earth triumphant in all the pristine glory—" and his
voice shook, "of a backward, barbarous, soil-sick
world. —Except that in the last year or two, we hear
them no longer."

"Why, that is good."

"No, that is bad. That is the first of the little things I
mention. As long as the fanatics are allowed freely to
spew their sewage, why, no one takes them seriously;
neither we nor the general population of Earth. But
when they are hushed suddenly, then it occurs to me
that the High Minister wishes no attention attracted to
their doctrines, and that can be so only when the
doctrines become official."

"Oh, isn't that long-roundabout reasoning, Ennius?
Besides, what can these poor people here *do?* Should
we take them so seriously? It's their only source of
amusement, this great dream of world dominion of
theirs. Why deprive them of it?"

"Well, that's not all. For instance, what's going on
with the Synapsifier?" Ennius frowned thoughtfully at
the dullness that was overcoming the polished darkness of the Eastern sky. "Shekt tells me its purpose
was to increase the mental capacity of human beings.
Is he telling me everything? And even if that were all,
is it already operating on Earthmen, in order to cut

down the vast odds of one world to two hundred million?"

"By making all Earthmen clever? I thought you said it didn't work."

"That is what Shekt says, not I. —And he takes care to avoid me now. My letters to him are answered impersonally and, I believe, are censored. They're very strange letters. I tried to visit him a month ago in Chica, but he could never be located—somehow. It's all very puzzling—and disturbing."

And then he turned to her and groped for her hands in the dim starlight. His voice was urgent. "Now listen to me, Flora. There's no use hashing this over. There's a good deal you don't know. There's a good deal you *can't* know. But this I will say. There is going to be rebellion on Earth—something like the Uprising of 750, except that it will probably be worse. That is why I am sitting here and waiting for the sunrise."

"But—if you're so certain— Are we prepared for it?"

"Prepared!" Ennius's laugh was a bark. "*I* am. The garrison is in readiness, and fully supplied. What can possibly be done with the material at hand, I have done. But Flora, I don't want to have a rebellion. I don't want my Procuracy to go down in history, as the Procuracy of the Rebellion. I don't want my name linked with death and slaughter. I'll be decorated for it, but a century from now the history books will call me a bloody tyrant. What about the Viceroy of Santanni in the Sixth Century? Could he have done other than he did? He was honored then, but who has a good word for him now? I would rather be known as the man who prevented a rebellion and saved the worthless lives of these fools." He sounded quite hopeless about it.

"Are you so sure you can't, Ennius—even yet?" She sat down beside him and brushed her fingertips along the line of his jaw.

He caught at them and held them tightly. "How can I? The Imperial Government is deliberately heading

for the worst. Why do they send this madman, this
Arvardan, here? I can do nothing now."

"But dear, I don't see that this archaeologist will do
anything so awful. I'll admit he sounds like a faddist,
but what harm can he do?"

"Why, isn't it plain? He wants to be allowed entry
in the Forbidden Areas. He'll be stopped."

"Well—"

"But *I* won't stop him. I *can't* stop him. I know it's a
foolish theory of most people that Viceroys can do
anything, but it just isn't so. That man has a writ of
permission from the Bureau of Outer Provinces, and
approved by the Emperor. That supersedes me. I can
do nothing without appealing to the Central Council,
and that would take months—and what reasons could
I give? And if I tried to stop him by force, it would be
an act of rebellion—and you know how ready the
Central Council is to remove any executive they think
is overstepping the line, ever since the Civil War of
the Eighties. What good would that do, then? I'd be
replaced by someone who wasn't aware of the situation at all, and Arvardan would eventually go ahead
anyway."

"You *said* he'd be stopped."

"By the High Minister! And then how will we ever
convince him that it is not a Government-sponsored
project, that the Empire is not conniving at deliberate
sacrilege?"

"Oh, he can't be that touchy."

"He can't?" Ennius reared back and stared at his
wife. The night had lightened to a slatiness in which
she was just visible. "You have the most touching
naiveté. He certainly *can* be that touchy. Do you
know that Earth, for instance, will allow no outward
sign of Imperial domination on their world because of
their insistence that Earth is the rightful ruler of the
Galaxy? Do you know what happened once when the
Emperor's insignia was raised in their Council Chamber at Washenn—just as it is present in every planetary Council Chamber in the Galaxy as a symbol of

the Imperial Unity? I'll tell you what happened. The lunatics tore it down, and by evening the entire miserable town was in arms against our soldiery. Eventually we had to give in to them."

"You mean," she said incredulously, "that the Imperial insignia was not replaced?"

"It was never replaced. By the Stars, it was not. Earth is the only one of hundreds of millions that has no insignia in its Council Chamber— And now Arvardan is going to try to penetrate the Forbidden Areas. What can they be thinking of in Trantor? —And worse yet, he is preaching their own radical doctrine at them. This professor-idiot honestly believes that Earth *is* the home planet—*the* home planet—of the human race. Imagine throwing fuel on the fire like that! I grant you he's sincere—but even if he were completely correct, Flora, what can those bungholes at the Bureau of Outer Provinces be thinking of?"

"Will you tell me one thing honestly, Ennius?"

"If I can."

"What are you really expecting? You're not just worried, love, you're nearly in a panic. Are you expecting a test-tube explosion? —Or something worse?"

Ennius avoided her eyes. "I have no reason to expect anything worse."

"But you do." She gazed earnestly at him in the growing dawn. "You shouldn't hide anything from me. It's worse than wrong—it's unsuccessful. You *do* expect something worse."

"Flora, I've told no one." There was something tortured in his eyes. "It isn't even a hunch. —Maybe four years on this world is too long for any sane man. It's just that it seems to me that no sane planet would rebel against an Empire of two hundred million worlds."

"They've done it before."

"Yes, but they seem so confident this time." He looked up with a keen surprise, as though he had just put his finger on something that had eluded him.

He repeated with energy, "That's it, they seem confident. By the Stars, they really believe they can have their own way. More than that. They believe they can *compel* us— You know, Flora, these people have their mysticisms. They have to, in order to bear their realities. Can they really be so firm in their Faith in some Destiny or some Force—something that has meaning only to them—that can give the victory to them?

"That can't be. You see—even granting that the ordinary Earthman thinks that Fate will someday restore Earth's supposed overlordship of the Galaxy—surely the rulers of Earth cannot think so. They at least know the need of the prosaic weapons of war that even Fate finds handy in its decisions. Maybe— Maybe— Maybe—"

"Maybe what, Ennius?"

"Maybe they have their weapons?"

"That will allow one world to defeat two hundred millions? You *are* panicky."

"But they are so confident."

"Oh, how do you know? They have revolted before. Maybe they were just as confident then. And maybe they're not confident now—maybe your own sick imagination wishes the attribute upon them. —Now look, the sun will be up shortly. Shall we just sit quietly for a while? Then you'll feel better and you'll be able to think it all over and make sense out of it."

And then for half an hour—in that spot of the Galaxy at least—there was peace, and when the Sun rose it gleamed ruddily upon an arbor in which the Imperial Representative on Earth and his wife were asleep on each other's shoulders.

They never did see the sunrise.

CHAPTER 9 *Darkening—at the Center*

Bel Arvardan took passage in the Terrestrial Air Transport Company's largest jet Stratospheric, traveling between Everest and the Terrestrial capital, Washenn. He traveled alone, leaving his ship and the members of his expedition to engage themselves in last-minute preparations.

This he did deliberately, out of the reasonable curiosity of a stranger and an archaeologist toward the ordinary life of men inhabiting such a planet as Earth.

—And for another reason too. It was to look at the Earthmen for himself in the light of the strange hints of the Procurator.

Arvardan was from the Sirian sector, the sector above all in the Galaxy where anti-Terrestrian prejudice was strongest. Yet he did not believe he had succumbed to it. Of course, he had grown into the habit of thinking of Earthmen in certain set, caricature-types, and even now the word "Earthman" seemed an ugly one to him—but he wasn't really prejudiced—

At least, he didn't think so. For instance, if an Earthman had ever wished to join an expedition of his, or work for him in any capacity—and had the training and the ability—he would be accepted. If there were an opening for him, that was. He pondered the matter and decided that he would certainly eat with an Earthman, or bunk with one, or in all ways treat them as he would treat anyone else. Yet he would always be conscious of the fact that an Earthman was an Earthman—he couldn't help that. That was the result of a childhood immersed in an atmosphere of bigotry so complete that it was almost invisible, till you left it and looked back.

Yet here he was in a plane with only Earthmen about him, and he felt perfectly natural.

What was it that Ennius had against them, though? He had made every effort to argue away the research into the radioactive areas. And he had been driving at something—something sinister and threatening about Earthmen—without ever being clear or definite.

Again Arvardan looked about at the undistinguished and normal faces of his fellow passengers. They were supposed to be different. But could he tell them from others in a crowd? He didn't think so.

The plane itself was, in his eyes, a small affair of imperfect construction. It was, of course, atomic powered, but the application of the principle was far from

efficient. For one thing, the power unit was not well
shielded, and it occurred to Arvardan that the presence of stray gamma rays and a high neutron density
in the atmosphere might well strike Earthmen as less
important than it would strike others.

And then the view caught his eyes. From the dark
wine purple of the extreme stratosphere, Earth presented a fabulous appearance. Beneath him the vast
and misted land areas in sight (obscured here and
there by the patches of sun-bright clouds) showed a
desert orange. Behind, rapidly overtaking the fleeing
stratoliner, was the soft and fuzzy nightline within
whose dark shadow was the sparking of the radioactive areas.

His attention was drawn from the window by laughter among the others, centering about an elderly couple, comfortably stout and all smiles.

Arvardan nudged his neighbor. "What's going on?"

His neighbor paused to say, "They've been married
forty years, and they're making the Grand Tour."

"The Grand Tour?"

"You know. All around the Earth."

The elderly man, flushed with pleasure, was re-
counting volubly his experiences and impressions, while
his wife joined in periodically in the best of humors.
To it all the friendly audience listened with the greatest pleasure, so that to Arvardan it seemed that
Earthmen were as warm and human as any people in
the Galaxy.

And then someone asked, "And when is it that
you're scheduled for the Sixty?"

"In about a month," came the ready, cheerful answer. "Sixteenth April."

"Well," said the questioner, "I hope you have a
nice day for it."

"She's coming with me," said the elderly man, jerking a thumb at his genial wife. "She's not due for
about three months after that, but there's no point in
her waiting, she thinks, and we might as well go together. Isn't that it, Chubby?"

"Oh yes," she said, and giggled rosily. "Our children are all married and have homes of their own, and I'd just be a bother to them. Besides, I couldn't enjoy the time anyway without the old fellow—so we'll just leave off together."

Arvardan interrupted the general babble to clear up a point on which he had a distinct suspicion.

He said to his neighbor, "What does he mean by the Sixty? He isn't referring to euthanasia, is he?" Arvardan knew of the custom, but only academically. It was now borne in on him that it actually applied to living human beings.

The man addressed favored Arvardan with a long and suspicious stare. He said, "Well, what do you think he meant?"

It was answer enough. Arvardan, rather appalled, looked on at the general merriment that such a subject could give rise to.

Apparently the entire list of passengers was engaged in a simultaneous arithmetical calculation of the time remaining to each, a process involving conversion factors from months to days that occasioned several disputes.

One small fellow with tight clothes and a determined expression said fiercely, "I've got exactly twelve years, three months, and four days left. Twelve years, three months, and four days. Not a day more; not a day less."

Which someone qualified by saying reasonably, "Unless you die first, of course."

"Nonsense," was the immediate reply. "I have no intention of dying first. Do I look like the sort of man who would die first? I'm living twelve years, three months, and four days, and there's not a man here with the hardihood to deny it." And he looked very fierce indeed.

A youngish man took a long, dandyish cigarette from between his lips to say darkly, "It's well for them that can calculate it out to a day. There's many a man living past his time."

"Ah, surely," said another, and there was a general nod, and a rather inchoate air of indignation arose.

"Not," continued the young man, interspersing his cigarette puffs with a complicated flourish intended to remove the ash, "that I see any objection to a man—or woman—wishing to continue on past their birthday to the next General Assembly day, particularly if they have some business to clean up. It's these sneaks and parasites that try to go past to the next census, eating the food of the next generation—" He seemed to have a personal grievance there.

Arvardan interposed gently, "But aren't the ages of everyone registered? They can't very well pass their birthday too far, can they?"

There was a general silence admixtured with contempt at the foolish idealism expressed. Someone said at last, diplomatically, "There isn't much point living past the Sixty, I suppose."

"Not if you're a working man, or a farmer," shot back another vigorously. "How about the administrators, though, and the city men—"

Finally the elderly man, whose fortieth wedding anniversary had begun the conversation, ventured his own opinion, emboldened perhaps by the fact that, as a current victim of the Sixty, he had nothing to lose. "As to that," he said, "it depends on who you know." And he winked with a sly innuendo. "I knew a man once who was sixty the year after the 810 census and lived till the 820 census caught him. He was sixty-nine before he left off. Sixty-nine!"

"But how could he do that?"

"He had a little money, and his brother was an Ancient. There's nothing you can't do if you've got that combination."

And there was general approval of that sentiment, which was reinforced by the youngish man with the cigarette. "If you don't have any of the ready green, though, you might as well march off on your birthday morning, or twenty Ancients will be at your door the next day to get you—"

"And fine your children, most likely," added someone else.

To all of this Arvardan listened with the greatest astonishment. And perhaps some of this showed in his face, for his neighbor, who had been scowling at him since his question concerning the Sixty, said abruptly, "You have a queer way of speaking. Are you from the western continents?"

Arvardan found the eyes of all upon him, each with its own sudden spark of suspicion in it. Did they think him a member of this Society of Ancients of theirs? Had his questioning seemed the cajolery of an *agent provocateur?*

He met that by saying, in a burst of frankness, "I'm not from anywhere on Earth. I'm Bel Arvardan from Baronn, Sirius Sector."

He might as well have dropped an atomic explosive capsule into the middle of the plane.

The first silent horror on every face turned rapidly into angry, bitter hostility that flamed at him. The man who had shared his seat rose stiffly and crowded into another, where the pair of occupants squeezed closely together to make room for him.

Faces turned away. Shoulders surrounded him, hemmed him in. For a moment, Arvardan burned with indignation. Earthmen to treat *him* so. And then he relaxed. It was obvious that bigotry was never a one-way operation; that hatred bred hatred.

He completed the journey silent and alone.

CHAPTER 10 *Darkening—at the Left*

The grounds of the college of Ancients in Washenn are nothing if not sedate. Austerity is the key word, and there is something authentically grave about the clustered knots of novices taking their evening stroll among the trees of the Quadrangle—where none but Ancients might trespass. Occasionally the green-robed figure of a Senior Ancient might make its way across the lawn, receiving reverences graciously.

And once in a long while the High Minister himself might appear—

—But not as now, at a half run, almost in a perspiration, disregarding the respectful raising of hands, oblivious to the cautious stares that followed him, the blank look at one another, the slightly raised eyebrows—

He burst into the Legislative Hall by the private entrance and broke into an open run down the empty, step-ringing ramp. The door that he thundered at opened at the foot-pressure of the one within and the High Minister entered.

His Secretary scarcely looked up from behind his small, plain desk, where he hunched over a midget Field-shielded Televisor, listening intently and allowing his eyes to rove over a quire or so of official-looking communications that piled high before him.

The High Minister rapped sharply on the desk. "What is this? What is going on?"

The Secretary's eyes flicked coldly at him, and the Televisor was clicked off. "Greetings, Your Wisdom."

"Greet me no greetings!" retorted the High Minister impatiently. "I want to know what is going on."

"In a sentence, our man has escaped."

"You mean the man who was treated by Shekt with the Synapsifier—the one who babbled a strange language —the one on the farm outside Chica—"

It is uncertain how many qualifications the High Minister in his anxiety might have rattled out, had not the Secretary interrupted with an indifferent, "Exactly."

"Why was I not informed? Why am I never informed?"

"Immediate action was necessary, and you were engaged. I substituted therefore, to the best of my ability."

"Yes, you are careful about my engagements when you wish to do without me. Now, I'll not have it. I will not permit myself to be bypassed and sidetracked. I will not—"

"We delay," was the reply at ordinary speaking volume, and the High Minister's half-shout faded. He

coughed, hovered uncertainly on further speech, then
said,

"What are the details?"

"Scarcely any. After six months of patient waiting,
with nothing to show for it, this man—Agent T, as our
reports refer to him—left."

"Wasn't he followed?"

"Quite. Four hours along the Highway, eastward.
Then he was lost."

"How lost?"

"That is the puzzling part, since there is no reasonable explanation."

"What do you mean, no reasonable explanation?
How can there be no reasonable explanation? How
are we to achieve our purposes, if at crucial moments
there is suddenly no reasonable explanation?"

"Our own man has been questioned. He speaks of a
headache; blinding pain, bright lights whirling before
his eyes, dizziness; is uncertain as to length of seizure.
Half an hour, perhaps."

"Impossible. He has been bribed."

"Or attacked," said the Secretary with composure.
"We are not the only ones who may have more methods of attack than is generally known."

The High Minister paled perceptibly. "But what are
we to do now?"

"Find Agent T. Obviously the Empire has an organization on Earth we know nothing of. Agent T, when
found, will provide the clue to it, unless he is top man
himself. Which would be even better."

The High Minister turned away and bit his lip in a fit
of brain-racing. Then he said over his shoulder, "What
about the farmer with whom Agent T has been living?"

"Nothing. He was questioned and discarded—a mere
tool, of no value to them or us."

Then, for the first time, the Secretary volunteered a
statement. "You have an appointment four hours from
now with a Professor Bel Arvardan."

The other waved a hand with angry negligence.
"Cancel it."

"Not at all. You had better see him."

"Why?" He whirled. "Who is this What's-his-name? What does he want?"

"You should have asked that first. He's an archaeologist of the Empire."

"And what in all the Galaxy have I to do with archaeology? Or with archaeologists?"

"Nothing. But a man of the Empire wants to see you on the very day Agent T eludes us."

"Oh—" and the High Minister, as if suddenly tired, half-collapsed into the straight-backed, armless chair in the corner. "This is all past my understanding. I am lost."

"Yes," murmured the Secretary, allowing a faint smile to appear on his lips. "Ennius, our worthy Procurator, has sent us a note forewarning us of the archaeologist."

"I have not received that either. I tell you, I am told nothing of what occurs. It is disgraceful—"

"Why, I tell you now, Your Wisdom. Ennius affirms expressly that this Arvardan has no official connection with himself or the Empire, and has no understanding of our customs; and hopes that we treat him with tolerance and understanding, in view of his ignorance. —Oh, yes, he greets us fraternally."

The High Minister said, "He sounds a little too earnest. I don't believe a word of it."

"It will be your business to judge that. Who or what Arvardan is, we don't know—but we mean to find out and to lose no sight of him till that is done."

Then, as the High Minister was about to leave, the Secretary lifted a finger—

"Your Wisdom!"

The High Minister turned.

The Secretary said, "About Arvardan again. It would be best if you attempt no deep strategy. Be yourself, and as eloquent as you please, provided you say nothing. Restrict yourself to a mission of confusion and delay. —And smile. Your present expression will give you away."

*   *   *

Bel Arvardan arrived in good time, and was able to look about him. To a man well acquainted with the architectural triumphs of all the Galaxy, the College of Ancients can scarcely seem more than a brooding block of steel-ribbed granite, fashioned in an archaic style. To one who was an archaeologist as well, it might signify in its gloomy, nearly savage austerity the proper home of a gloomy, nearly savage way of life. Its very primitiveness marked the turning back of eyes to the far past—

As for the High Minister, his robe was new and glistening in its freshness. His forehead showed no trace of haste or doubt; perspiration might have been a stranger to it.

And the conversation was friendly indeed. Arvardan was at pains to mention the well-wishings of some of the great men of the Empire to the people of Earth. The High Minister was as careful to express the thorough gratification that must be felt by all Earth at the generosity and enlightenment of the Imperial Government.

Arvardan expounded on the importance of archaeology to Imperial philosophy; on its contribution to the great conclusion that all humans of whatever world of the Galaxy were brothers—and the High Minister agreed blandly and pointed out that Earth had long held such to be the case, and could only hope that the time would shortly come when the rest of the Galaxy might turn theory into practice.

Arvardan smiled very shortly at that and said, "It is for that very purpose, Your Wisdom, that I have approached you. The differences between Earth and some of the Imperial Dominions neighboring it rest largely, perhaps, on differing ways of thinking. Still, a good deal of friction can be removed if it can be shown that Earthmen are not different, racially, from other Galactic citizens."

"And how do you propose to do that, sir?"

"Well, that is not easy to explain in a word. As

Your Wisdom may know, the two main currents of archaeological thinking are commonly called the 'Merger Theory' and the 'Radiation Theory.' "

"I am acquainted with a layman's view of both."

"Good. Now the Merger Theory, of course, involves the notion that the various types of humanity, evolving independently, interbred in the very early, scarcely documented days of primitive space travel. A conception like that is necessary to account for the fact that Humans are so alike one to the other now."

"Yes," commented the High Minister dryly, "and such a conception also involves the necessity of having several hundred separately evolved beings of a more or less human type so closely related chemically and biologically that interbreeding is possible."

"True," exclaimed Arvardan with enthusiasm, "an impossibly weak point. Yet most archaeologists ignore it and adhere firmly to the Merger Theory, which would imply that in isolate portions of the Galaxy there might be sub-species of humanity who remained different, who didn't interbreed—"

"You mean Earth," commented the High Minister.

"Earth *is* considered an example. The Radiation Theory, on the other hand—"

"Considers us all descendants of one planetary group of humans."

"Exactly."

"My people," said the High Minister, "because of the evidence of our own history, and of certain writings that are sacred to us and cannot be exposed to the view of outsiders, are of the belief that Earth itself is the original home of humanity."

"And so I believe as well, and I ask your help to prove this point to all the Galaxy."

"You are optimistic. Just what is involved?"

"It is my conviction, Your Wisdom, that many primitive artifacts and architectural remains may be located in those areas of your world that are now, unfortunately, masked by radioactivity. The age of the remains could be accurately calculated from the radio-active decay present and compared—"

But the High Minister was shaking his head. "Please! You must speak no more on the subject."

"But why not?" Arvardan frowned in thorough amazement.

"For one thing," said the High Minister reasonably, "what do you expect to accomplish? If you prove your point, even to the satisfaction of all the worlds, what does it matter that a million years ago all of you were Earthmen? After all, a billion years ago we were all apes, yet we do not admit present-day apes into the relationship."

"Oh come, Your Wisdom, we are not so unreason-able."

"There's nothing unreasonable about it, sir. Isn't it reasonable to assume that Earthmen in their long iso-lation have so changed from their emigrating cousins, especially by influence of radioactivity, as to now form a different race?"

Arvardan bit at his lower lip and answered reluc-tantly, "You argue well on the side of your enemies."

"Because I ask myself what my enemies will say. So you will accomplish nothing, sir, except perhaps to further exacerbate the hatred against us by proving our past greatness."

"But," said Arvardan, "there is still the matter of the interests of pure science, the advance of knowledge—"

The High Minister lifted his eyebrows in a half-humorous regret. "I would hate to stand in the way of that. I speak now, sir, as one gentleman of the Empire to another. I myself would cheerfully help you, but my people are a proud and obstinate race who over centu-ries have withdrawn into themselves because of the—uh—lamentable attitude towards them of parts of the Galaxy. They have certain taboos, certain fixed customs —which even I could not offer to violate."

"And the radioactive areas—"

"—are one of the most important taboos. Even if I

were to grant you permission, and certainly my every impulse is to do so, it would merely provoke rioting and disturbances, which would not only endanger your life and those of the members of your expedition, but would in the long run bring down upon Earth the disciplinary action of the Empire. I would betray my position and the trust of my people if I were to allow that."

"But I am willing to take all reasonable precautions. If you wish to send observers with me— And, of course, it is taken for granted that I will consult you before publishing any results obtained—"

The High Minister shrugged. "You tempt me, sir. It is an interesting project. But you overestimate my power, even if we leave the people themselves out of consideration. I am not an absolute ruler. In fact, my power is sharply limited—and all matters must be submitted to the consideration of the Society of Ancients before final decisions are possible."

Arvardan shook his head. "This is most unfortunate. The Procurator warned me of the difficulties— yet I was hoping that— When can you consult your legislature, Your Wisdom?"

"The Presidium of the Society of Ancients will meet three days hence. It is beyond my power to alter the agenda, so it may be a few days more before the matter can be discussed. —Say a week."

Arvardan nodded abstractedly. "Well, it will have to do. —By the way, Your Wisdom—"

"Yes."

"The Procurator mentioned one of your scientists—a Dr. Shekt—in passing. I have heard since of a Synapsifier he has developed, a machine concerned with the neurochemistry of the brain. Do you know where I might locate him?"

The High Minister had stiffened visibly, and for several moments said nothing. Then, "I believe I know the man you mean. What is your business with him?"

"Well, I have been working a little on a project

involving the classification of humanity into encephalographic groups—brain-current types, you understand."

"Umm— The device, I understand, was not a success."

"Well, maybe not, but there may be some information I could find useful. He wouldn't be in Washenn, would he?"

"I believe you will find him at the Institute for Nuclear Studies in Chica. Of course, there must be no mention of your intentions with regard to the Forbidden Areas."

"That is understood, Your Wisdom." He rose. "I thank you for your courtesy and your kind attitude, and can only hope that the Council of Ancients will be liberal in this case."

Once again, after Arvardan had left, the High Minister showed his capacity for change. He remained for a long time afterward in a frozen state of thought.

Two months—

Two months had been scheduled to elapse before the Day. The "space bullets" would not be ready till then. —And now the forces of the Galaxy seemed to be converging: Agent T, this archaeologist, the traitor Shekt—

Earth—against all the Galaxy.

The High Minister's hands were trembling gently.

CHAPTER 11 "—Its Ugly Head"

In the half year that had elapsed from the day that Dr. Shekt's Synapsifier had been used on Joseph Schwartz (or Agent T, depending on your viewpoint), the physicist had changed completely. Physically not so much, though perhaps he was a thought more stooped, a shade thinner. It was his manner—abstracted, fearful. He lived in an inner communion, withdrawn from even his closest colleagues, and from which he emerged with a reluctance that was plain to the blindest.

Arvardan, of course, had not the opportunity of

comparing this state with that of an earlier Shekt, and therefore accepted the other's attitude for what it seemed—an abrupt and odd rudeness.

He felt embarrassed, there in the anteroom of the carefully darkened apartment, quite obviously an unwelcome intruder.

He chose his words. "I would never have dreamed of imposing upon you to the extent of visiting your home, Doctor, were it not that the Procurator assured me of your friendliness to men of the Galaxy."

It was apparently an unfortunate phrase, for Dr. Shekt jumped at it. "Now, he does wrong to impute any especial friendliness to strangers as such. I have no likes and dislikes. I am an Earthman. If you care to make a formal appointment with my secretary at the Institute—"

Arvardan's lips compressed, and he half turned—

"You understand, Dr. Arvardan," the words were hurried and whispered, "I am sorry if I seem rude, but I really cannot—"

"I quite understand," the archaeologist said coldly, though he did not understand at all. "Good day, sir."

Dr. Shekt smiled feebly. "If you will make an appointment—"

"I am very busy, Dr. Shekt."

He turned to the door, raging inwardly at all the tribe of Earthmen, feeling within him, involuntarily, some of the catchwords that were bandied so freely on his home world. For instance, the proverbs "Politeness on Earth is like dryness on the ocean" or "An Earthman will give you anything as long as it costs nothing and is worth less."

His arm had already broken the photoelectric beam that opened the front door when he heard the flurry of quick steps behind him and a hist of warning in his ear. A piece of paper was thrust in his hand, and when he turned there was only a flash of red as a figure disappeared.

He was in his rented ground-car before he unraveled the paper in his hand. Words were scrawled upon it:

"Ask your way to the Great Playhouse at eight this evening. Make sure you are not followed."

He frowned ferociously at it and read it over five times, then stared all over it, as though expecting invisible ink to bound into visibility. Involuntarily, he looked behind him. The street was empty. He half raised his hand to throw the silly scrap out the window, hesitated, then stuffed it into his vest pocket.

Undoubtedly, if he had had one single thing to do that evening other than what the scrawl had suggested, that would have been the end of it—and perhaps of several thousands of billions of people. But as it turned out, he had nothing to do—

At eight o'clock he was making his slow way as part of a long line of ground-cars along the serpentine way that apparently led to the Great Playhouse. He had asked only once, and the passerby questioned had stared suspiciously at him (apparently no Earthman was ever free of that all-pervasive suspicion) and said curtly, "You just follow all the rest of the cars."

Apparently all the rest of the cars were going to the Playhouse, for when he got there he found all being swallowed one by one by the huge maw of the underground parking lot. He swung out of line and crawled past the Playhouse, waiting for he knew not what.

A slim figure dashed down from the pedestrian ramp and hung outside his window. He stared at it, startled, but it had the door open and was inside in a single gesture.

"Pardon me," he said.

"Oh, hush." The figure hunched down low in the seat. "Were you followed?"

"Should I have been?"

"Don't be funny. Go straight ahead. Turn when I tell you. —My goodness, what are you waiting for?"

The voice was soprano. A hood had shifted down to the shoulders and light brown hair was showing. Blue eyes stared up at him.

"Move on," she ordered peremptorily.

He did, and for fifteen minutes, except for an occasional muffled but curt direction, she said nothing. He stole glances at her, and thought with a sudden pleasure that at least she was pretty—but she had no eyes for anything but the road.

Mostly she looked behind.

They stopped, or Arvardan did, at the girl's direction —at the corner of an unpeopled residential district. After a careful pause the girl motioned him ahead once more, and they inched down a drive that ended in the gentle ramp of a private garage.

The door closed behind them, and the light in the car was the only source of illumination.

She said earnestly, "Now look here, I don't think anyone followed us, but if you hear any noise at all, you throw your arms tight around me, and—and—you know."

He nodded gravely. "I believe I can improvise without any trouble. Is it necessary to wait for noise?"

The girl reddened. "You don't have to joke about it. That's just a move to avoid suspicion of our real intentions. *You* ought to see that."

Arvardan dropped his hands helplessly into his lap and quirked a corner of his lip upward. "My dear girl, I swear to you I see nothing. I am not at all acquainted with your Earth customs, and if it is taken here as normal for a young female to be quite so aggressive in her amorous attentions (if that is what these are), I hope you'll forgive my ignorance and explain exactly what you want."

The girl breathed in sharply, and her eyes were dark with pride. "You're being quite hateful about this, and just as soon as we're through here, I'm going to cut you dead. —Meanwhile, you quit pretending. I know you're an Imperial agent."

"I?" with sudden energy.

"Certainly. That's why I brought you here. They

don't know about *this* place, and they don't know about *me*."

"Who are 'they'?"

"The Ancients, of course. I don't blame you for not trusting me, but you think it over. You've got to trust somebody, and I'm the logical person, aren't I? I'm risking my life to have this talk with you."

He looked at her curiously. She seemed suddenly young—he wondered if she were twenty-one yet—but then she was more than merely pretty— He felt himself drifting into side issues and returned to the point.

He said gently, "May I think about it? It's a horribly important decision, this matter of trusting people, isn't it?"

She nodded at that. "Well then, I'll give you fifteen minutes. Time is very important, though, and you must make up your mind to trust me by then. —I won't say a word."

She clasped her hands in her lap and looked firmly ahead through the windshield that afforded a view only of the blank wall of the garage ahead.

He watched her whimsically. The smooth, soft line of her chin belied the attempt at firmness into which she forced it, and her nose was straight and thinly drawn. Her complexion had that peculiar rich overtone so characteristic of Earth—yet her features had none of the grotesqueries so well known in the Sirian caricatures of Earthmen.

He caught the corner of her eye upon him. It was hastily withdrawn and turned forward again—then slid round a second time in shy curiosity.

"What's the matter?" he said.

She turned to him and caught her underlip in two teeth. "I was watching you."

"Yes, I could see that. Smudge on my nose?"

"Uh-uh." Her hair seemed to float gently and hover each time she shook her head. "You're the first Galaxy man I've ever seen except the Procurator—and he's always bundled up in so much lead clothing, he just looks like a sack of potatoes."

"I'm different?"

"Oh yes. —Aren't you afraid of the radioactivity in the air? You're just wearing ordinary clothes."

"Well, so are you—except that they look very extraordinary indeed when you wear them."

She dimpled. "I was born here. But I thought Galaxy men were different."

"Well then, they're not as different as you suppose. I don't think the radioactivity is as bad as all that. —I don't feel sick yet. My hair isn't falling out." He pulled at it. "My stomach isn't in knots, and I'll probably still have children some day, if I ever go about it in the proper fashion."

He said that gravely, and her eyes narrowed at him. Then she laughed and said, "You're crazy."

"Hmm. You'd be surprised how many very intelligent and famous archaeologists have said that—and in long speeches, too."

"Well, you are. You're not like Earthmen."

"So you keep saying. Why am I different?"

"You're friendly. Earthmen are always so suspicious."

"Ah now, that's just soft soap. You can't fool an old hand like myself with that. I haven't said I'll trust you yet."

"Oh, you will," and she nodded confidently, "because if you weren't going to, you wouldn't still be sitting here."

"Are you under the impression that I have to force myself very hard to sit here next to you? If you are, you're wrong, you know. Besides, it might be a pretty deep scheme of my own to worm out all your secrets without giving myself away at all."

"How can you? I'm not an enemy of yours, or the Empire's."

"But how could I know that? Maybe you're an enemy agent, getting all set to entwine me in her evil allure. How about that?"

She looked haughty again. "I'm not that type of girl at all."

"You look as if you could be. Glamorous female

enemy agents always act innocent, though. That's their evil way."

Her haughtiness gave way, and she giggled. "You're crazy all the *way*." Then she was a bundle of business. "Anyway, the fifteen minutes are up. Are you ready to trust me?"

"Well," he lifted his eyebrows, leaned one tanned arm on the steering mechanism, and watched her thoughtfully. "I don't see how I can answer when I don't even know who you are. What's your name?"

She gasped, and her mouth stayed open. "Oh golly, I haven't told you."

"No, you haven't. And naturally, it makes me think you don't trust me. The thing has to be mutual."

"But you saw me at Dr. Shekt's house."

"I saw a flash of red dress, I think, but that's all. Was that you?"

She nodded. "Uh-huh. I'm Dr. Shekt's daughter. I'm Pola Shekt."

"Well. I'm Bel Arvardan. How do you do, Pola?" He held out a hand into which hers disappeared for a moment, and they shook seriously. He said, "I don't have to call you Miss Shekt, do I?"

Pola wrinkled her forehead. "Would you rather?"

He grimaced. "I think that would be awful, don't you?"

"Then you can call me Pola. Shall I call you Bel?"

"I don't answer to anything else, you know."

"Are we ready for business now?"

"Any kind," he said fervently.

She smiled at him, and in the brilliance of her smile Arvardan was suddenly conscious of a queer type of electric shock playing about internal organs he didn't know he possessed.

He said, "Now you tell me everything."

"Well, I don't know how much you know, being an Imperial agent, but I can tell you one thing anyway. The fate of the whole Galaxy is at stake. I'm sure of it."

Arvardan's first impulse was to laugh. She seemed

so serious, and the melodrama fell so sweetly from her lips. And then, between the impulse and the act, he remembered a few things. There were the vague and threatening hints of Ennius; there was the hatred and deadly animosity of the men in the plane when they learned of his Galactic origin; there was the High Minister and his suspicions; Dr. Shekt and his queerness. He decided not to laugh, at least for a while.

Instead he said solemnly, "Go on. Please tell me the details."

Her voice dropped to a tight whisper. "Earth is going to revolt."

He couldn't resist a moment of amusement. "No!" he said, opening his eyes wide. "All of it?"

But Pola flared into instant fury. "Now don't you be so smart. It's very serious, because it might destroy all the Empire."

"Earth will do all that?" Arvardan struggled against a burst of laughter. He said gently, "Pola, how well do you know your Galactography?"

"As well as anybody, teacher, and what has that to do with it, anyway?"

"It has this to do with it. The Galaxy has a cubic volume of several million cubic light years. It contains two hundred million inhabited planets, and an approximate population of five hundred quadrillion people. Right?"

"I suppose."

"Now, Earth is one planet, with a population of twenty millions, and no resources besides. In other words, there are twenty-five billion Galactic citizens to every Earthman—so what harm can Earth do?"

"There are?" For a moment the girl seemed to sink into doubt, then she emerged. "But it's so. My father is sure of it, and he knows."

"Earth has revolted before," Arvardan reminded her. "Three times—and no particular damage was done."

"This time it's different."

"My dear girl," said Arvardan (almost by itself, his

hand had moved forward to pat her cheek in a not-too-brotherly fashion, but he diverted its course and pulled at his ear instead), "My dear girl, I admit this is a fascinating interview. It has elements of mystery, intrigue, and above all, a lovely conversationalist. But I can't understand what it is you're trying to tell me."

"Oh," she cried, "I think this isn't at all the way I planned it. I thought that if you were an Imperial agent you'd know all about most of it, and then we could work together. —With my father."

"Your father?" asked Arvardan dryly. "You mean Dr. Shekt, who was so anxious to see me that he never let me pass the threshold of his house."

"But he couldn't," Pola said earnestly. "Couldn't you see that? The High Minister has been having him watched and followed for months now, and he didn't *dare* speak to you. But why do you suppose I got you out here? It's for him; *he's* arranged it."

"Oh— Well, where is he, then? Here?"

"Is it after ten?"

"Yes."

"Then he should be upstairs now—if they haven't caught him." She looked about with an involuntary shudder. "We can get into the house directly from the garage now, and if you'll come with me—"

She had her hand on the knob that controlled the car door, when she froze. Her voice was a husky whisper. "There's someone coming. —Oh, quick—"

The rest was smothered. It was anything but difficult for Arvardan to remember her original injunction. His arms swept about her with an easy motion, and in an instant she was warm and soft against him. Her lips trembled upon his. For about ten seconds he swiveled his eyes to their extremes in an effort to see that first crack of light or hear that first footstep, but then he was drowned and swept under by the sweetness of it all. It was quite a while before she broke away from him, and for a moment they rested, cheek against cheek.

He said, with a dreamy pleasure, "It must have been only a traffic noise."

"I suppose," she whispered, and was suddenly away from him, arranging her hair and adjusting the collar of her dress with prim and precise gestures. "I think we had better go into the house now. Put out the car light. I've got a pencil-flash."

He stepped out of the car after her, and in the new darkness she was the vaguest shadow in the little pock-mark of light that came from her pencil-flash.

She said, "You'd better hold my hand. There's a flight of stairs we have to go up."

His voice was a whisper behind her. "You don't hear anything now, do you, Pola? I'll make a noise myself if it will help."

She stopped and turned. He could not see her, but there was a delightful haughtiness in her voice. "Oh, don't think you got away with anything, *Doctor* Arvardan. It so happens that I never did hear any noise in the first place."

And she would have gone on, but his hand on hers tightened as he said grimly, "Well, in *that* case—"

And after a minute or two Pola said, in a queer, strangled voice, "You've made me drop my flash."

It lay there in a tiny pool of light. He picked it up for her, and for a moment turned it upon her flushed face.

She said, "I suppose you think that was very smart."

He replied calmly, "Very. And very nice too."

"Oh come along, do."

But all the way up the stairs, in the safety of the gloom, Pola smiled.

CHAPTER 12 *The Odds That Vanished*

They met in a back room on the second story of the house, with the windows carefully polarized to complete opaqueness. Pola was downstairs, alert and sharp-eyed in the armchair from which she watched the dark and empty street.

Shekt's stooped figure wore an air somehow different from that which Arvardan had observed some ten hours previously. The physicist's face was still haggard, and infinitely weary, but where previously it had seemed uncertain and timorous, it now bore an almost desperate defiance.

"Dr. Arvardan," he said, and his voice was firm, "I must apologize for my treatment of you in the morning. I had hoped you would understand—"

"I must admit I didn't, sir, but I believe I do now."

Shekt seated himself at the table and gestured toward the bottle of wine. Arvardan waved his hand in a deprecating gesture. "If you don't mind, I'll have some of the fruit instead. —What is this? I don't think I've ever seen anything like it."

"It's a kind of orange," said Shekt. "I don't believe it grows outside Earth. The rind comes off easily." He demonstrated, and Arvardan, after sniffing at it curiously, sank his teeth into the winy pulp. He came up with an exclamation. "Why, this is delightful, Dr. Shekt. Has Earth ever tried to export these objects?"

"The Ancients," said the physicist grimly, "are not fond of trading with the outside. Nor are our neighbors fond of trading with us. It is but an aspect of our difficulties here."

And Arvardan felt a sudden spasm of fury overcome him. "That is the most stupid thing yet. I tell you, I could despair of human intelligence when I see what can exist in men's minds."

Shekt shrugged with a lifelong tolerance. "It is part of the nearly insoluble problem of anti-Terrestrialism, I fear."

"What makes it so nearly insoluble," exclaimed the archaeologist, "is that no one seems to really want a solution. How many Earthmen respond to the situation by hating all Galactic citizens indiscriminately? Do they want equality, mutual tolerance—no. They want only their own turn as top dog."

"Perhaps," said Shekt sadly. "But that is only a surface effect. Give us the chance, and a new generation of humans would grow up like all others. The Assimilationists, with their tolerance and belief in the universality of humanity, have more than once been a power on Earth. I am one. But it is the Zealots—that is, the extreme nationalists—with their dreams of past rule and future rule that have the organization. It is against them that the Empire must be protected."

Arvardan frowned wearily. "The revolt Pola spoke of?"

"Dr. Arvardan," Shekt said grimly, "it's not too easy a job to convince anyone of such an apparently ridiculous possibility as Earth conquering the Galaxy, but it's true. I am not physically brave, and I am most anxious to live. You can imagine, then, the immense crisis that must now exist to force me to run the risk of committing treason with the eye of the local administration already upon me."

"Well," said Arvardan, "if it is that serious, I had better tell you one thing immediately. I am not an Imperial agent. I have no connection at all with the Imperial government. I am exactly what I seem to be—an archaeologist on a scientific expedition that involves only my own interests. I'm sure you had better see the Procurator with this."

"That is exactly what I cannot do, Dr. Arvardan. It is that very contingency against which the Ancients guard me. When you came to my house, I thought you might be a go-between. That he suspected."

"He may suspect—I cannot answer for that. But I am not a go-between. I'm sorry."

"But you are here, and you are a citizen of the Empire. You can see him afterward." There was a look of infinite pleading on his face.

Arvardan was uneasy. At the moment he was convinced that he was dealing with an elderly and eccentric paranoid, perhaps harmless, but thoroughly cracked. Yet he remained. He did not analyze his reasons, though a shrewd observer might have suspected that a small matter of light brown hair and blue eyes, currently in another room, might have had something to do with it.

In any case, he leaned back in his chair. "Well, it's your risk. I'll help if I can, but I promise nothing."

"Hear me out. I ask no more. —Dr. Arvardan, you have heard of my Synapsifier?"

"The Procurator made mention of it. Otherwise I haven't."

"And what has the Procurator said?"

"That it was an interesting failure. Designed to improve learning capacity, I believe?"

Shekt was chagrined. "Yes, Ennius undoubtedly thinks it is a failure. It was so publicized, and the eminently successful results have been suppressed—deliberately."

"Hmm. A rather unusual display of scientific ethics, Dr. Shekt."

"I admit it. But I am fifty-six, sir, and if you know anything of the customs of Earth, you know that I haven't long to live."

"Exceptions are made for noted scientists, among others, I have read."

"Certainly. But it is the High Minister and the Council of Ancients that decide on that, and there is no appeal from their decisions, even to the Emperor. I was told that the price of life was secrecy concerning the Synapsifier and hard work for its improvement." The older man spread his hands helplessly. "Could I know then of the outcome, of the use to which the machine would be put?"

"And the use?" Arvardan extracted a cigarette from his shirt-pocket case and offered one to the other, who refused it.

"If you'll wait a moment— One by one, after my experiments had reached the point where I felt the instrument might be safely applied to human beings, certain of Earth's biologists were treated. In each case they were men I knew to be in sympathy with the Zealots—the extremists, that is. They all survived, though secondary effects appeared after a time. One was eventually brought back for treatment. I could not save him— But in his dying delirium—I found out."

It was close upon midnight. The day had been long, and much had happened. But now something was stirring within Arvardan. He said tightly, "I wish you'd get to the point."

Shekt said, "I beg your patience. I must explain thoroughly if you're to believe me. You know, of course, of Earth's peculiar environment—its radioactivity—"

"Yes, I have a fair knowledge of the matter."

"And of the effect of this radioactivity upon Earthmen."

"Yes."

"Then I won't belabor the point. I need only say that the incidence of mutation on Earth is greater than in the rest of the Galaxy. The idea of our enemies that Earthmen are different thus has a certain basis of physical truth. To be sure, the mutations are minor, and most possess no survival value. If any permanent change has occurred in Earthmen, it is only in some aspects of their internal chemistry which enable them to display greater resistance to their own particular environment—greater resistance to radiation, more rapid healing of burned tissues—"

"Dr. Shekt, I am acquainted with all you say."

"Then has it ever occurred to you that these mutational processes occur in living species on Earth other than human?"

There was a short silence, and then Arvardan said, "Why no, I hadn't, though, of course, it is quite inevitable, now that you mention it."

"That is so. It happens. Our domestic animals exist in greater variety than on any other inhabited world. The orange you ate is a mutated variety, which exists nowhere else. It is this, among other things, that makes the orange so unacceptable for export. Outsiders suspect it as they suspect us—and we ourselves guard it as a valuable property peculiar to ourselves. And of course, what applies to animals and plants applies also to microscopic life."

And now indeed Arvardan felt the thin pang of fear enter.

He said, "You mean—bacteria."

"I mean the whole domain of primitive life. Protozoa, bacteria, and the self-reproducing proteins that some people call viruses."

"And what are you getting at?"

"I think you have a notion of that, Dr. Arvardan. You seem suddenly interested. You see, there is a belief among your people that Earthmen are bringers of death, that to associate with an Earthman is to die, that Earthmen are the bearers of misfortune, possess a sort of evil eye—"

"I know all that. It is merely superstition."

"Not entirely. That is the dreadful part. Like all common beliefs, however superstitious, distorted, and perverted, it has a speck of truth at bottom. Sometimes, you see, an Earthman carries within his body some mutated form of microscopic parasite which is not quite like any known elsewhere, and to which, sometimes, outsiders are not particularly resistant. What follows is simple biology, Dr. Arvardan."

Arvardan was silent.

Shekt went on, "We are caught sometimes too, of course. A new species of germ will make its way out of the radioactive mists and an epidemic will sweep the planet, but by and large, Earthmen have kept pace. For each variety of germ and virus, we build our defense over the generations, and we survive. Outsiders don't have the opportunity."

"Do you mean," said Arvardan, with a strangely faint sensation, "that contact with you now—" He pushed his chair back.

Shekt shook his head. "Of course not. We don't *create* the disease; we merely carry it, under very unfavorable conditions. If I lived on your world, I would no more carry the germ than you would. And even here, it is only one of every quadrillion germs, or one out of every quadrillion of quadrillions, that is dangerous. The chances of your infection right now

are less than that of a meteorite penetrating the roof
of this house and hitting you. —*Unless* the germs in
question are deliberately searched for, isolated, and
concentrated."

Again a silence, longer this time. Arvardan said, in
a queer strangled voice, "Have they been doing that?"

"Yes. For innocent reasons—at first. Our biologists
are, of course, particularly interested in the peculiari-
ties of Earth life, and recently isolated the virus of
Common Fever."

"What is Common Fever?"

"A mild endemic disease on Earth. That is, it is
always with us. Most Earthmen have it in their childhood, and its symptoms are not very severe. A mild
fever, a transitory rash, and swelling of the joints, combined with an annoying thirst. It runs its course in four
to six days, and we are thereafter immune. I've had it.
Pola has had it. However, on occasion, a member of
the Imperial garrison is exposed to it, and usually he
dies within twelve hours. He is then buried—by
Earthmen—since any other soldier approaching also
dies.

"The virus, as I say, was isolated ten years ago. It is
a nucleoprotein—as are most filtrable viruses—which,
however, possesses the remarkable property of containing an unusually high concentration of radioactive
carbon and nitrogen. When I say unusually high, I
mean fifty percent. It is supposed that the effects of
the organism on its host is largely that of its radiations,
rather than its toxins. Naturally, it would seem logical
that Earthmen, who are adapted to gamma radiation,
are only slightly affected. Original interest in the virus
centered about the method whereby it concentrated
the radioactive isotopes. As you know, no chemical
means can separate isotopes, nor can any other known
organism—but the direction of research changed.

"I'll be brief, Dr. Arvardan. I think you see the
rest. Experiments might be conducted on animals from
outside Earth, but not on foreign men. The numbers
of outsiders on Earth were too few to allow several to

disappear without notice. Nor could premature discovery, of course, be allowed. So it was a group of bacteriologists that were sent to the Synapsifier to return with insights enormously developed. It was they who developed a new mathematical attack on protein chemistry and on immunology, which enabled them finally to form an artificial strain of virus that was designed to affect Galactic human beings only. Tons of the crystallized virus now exist."

Arvardan was haggard. He felt the drop of perspiration glide sluggishly down his temple and cheek.

"Then you are telling me," he gasped, "that Earth intends to set loose this virus on the Galaxy; that they will initiate a gigantic bacteriological warfare—"

"—which we cannot lose and you cannot win. Exactly. Once the epidemic starts, millions will die each day, and nothing will stop it. Frightened refugees fleeing across space will carry the virus with them, and if you attempt to blow up entire planets, the disease can be started again in new centers. There will be no reason to connect the matter with Earth. By the time our own survival becomes suspicious the ravages will have progressed so far, the despair of the outsiders will be so deep, that nothing will matter to them."

"And all will die?" The appalling horror did not penetrate—could not.

"Perhaps not. Our new science of bacteriology works both ways. We have the antitoxin as well, and the means of production thereof. It might be used in case of early surrender."

In the horrible blankness that followed—during which Arvardan never thought of doubting the truth of what he had heard, the horrible truth that at a stroke wiped out the odds of twenty-five billion to one—Shekt's voice was small and tired.

"It is not Earth that is doing this. A handful of leaders, perverted by the gigantic pressure that excluded them from the Galaxy, hating those who keep them outside, insanely wanting to strike back at any cost—

"Once they have begun, Earth must follow. What else can it do? In its tremendous guilt, it will have to finish what it started. Would it allow enough of the Galaxy to survive and risk punishment? And yet can it prevent it? Surely some far corners will escape, some few may be immune—enough to remember the eternal hatred that will result, and to avenge.

"And before I am an Earthman, I am a man. Must trillions die for the sake of millions? Must a civilization spreading over a Galaxy crumble for the sake of the resentment, however justified, of a single planet? And will we be better off for all that? The power in the Galaxy will reside still on those worlds with the necessary resources—and we have none. Earthmen may even rule at Trantor for a generation, but their children will become Trantorians, and in their turn will look down upon the remnant on Earth.

"And besides, is there an advantage to Humanity to exchange the tyranny of a Galaxy for the tyranny of Earth? No—no, there must be a way out for *all* men, a way to justice and freedom."

His hands stole to his face and behind their gnarled fingers he rocked gently to and fro.

Arvardan had heard all this in a numbed haze. He mumbled, "There is no treason in what you have done, Dr. Shekt. I see in you, rather, the oneness of Humanity. How must we stop this? How?"

There was the sound of running footsteps, the flash of a frightened face into the room, the door left swinging open.

"Father— Men are coming up the walk."

Dr. Shekt went gray. "Quickly, Dr. Arvardan, through the garage." He was pushing violently. "Go to Ennius. Tell him what I've told you. Take Pola, and don't worry about me. I'll hold them back."

But a man in a green robe waited for them as they turned. He wore a thin smile and carried, with a casual ease, a Neuronic Whip, the weapon that stunned with the maximum of pain. There was a thunder of fists at the main door, a crash, and the sound of pounding feet.

Dr. Shekt muttered helplessly to Arvardan, "It's the High Minister's secretary."

"True," the man in green advanced, "and you almost got away. But not quite. —Hmm, a girl too. Injudicious. —And our Imperial friend, the innocent archaeologist."

Arvardan said evenly, "I am a Galactic citizen, and I dispute your right to detain me—or, for that matter, to enter this house—without legal authority."

"I," and the Secretary tapped his chest gently with his free hand, "am all the right and authority on this planet—within the month, perhaps in the Galaxy. —We have all of you, even Agent T, now."

"Agent T?" said Arvardan blankly.

"The man who calls himself Joseph Schwartz. He too is captured, and he is waiting for you."

The last thing Arvardan was conscious of was that smile, expanding—and the flash of the Whip. He toppled through a crimson sear of pain into unconsciousness.

INTERMISSION

And so, as previously explained, both ends meet in the middle. We followed Joseph Schwartz first and Bel Arvardan second, and both now end together. To be sure, the mutual situation is not comfortable, since the meeting takes place under rather helpless conditions for both.

Nevertheless, a third part remains, in which we can take up the meeting and follow the remaining events in which both are equally and simultaneously concerned.

The diagram of this narration can therefore be represented as follows:

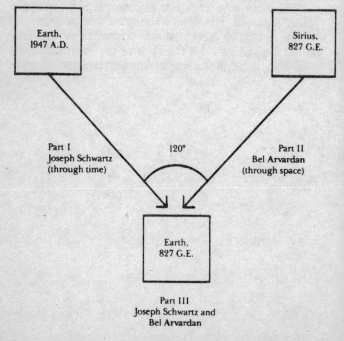

Earth,
1947 A.D.

Sirius,
827 G.E.

Part I
Joseph Schwartz
(through time)

120°

Part II
Bel Arvardan
(through space)

Earth,
827 G.E.

Part III
Joseph Schwartz and
Bel Arvardan

As you can see, therefore, the story has been told from both ends towards the middle, as promised.

The reason for going into the matter in such detail, I suppose, is that most authors have the urge to explain the actual physical structure of their stories, as distinct from such minor details as plots and climaxes. I've finally obeyed that urge. Fascinating, isn't it?

PART III:
JOSEPH SCHWARTZ AND BEL ARVARDAN

CHAPTER 13 *Coalescence*

For the moment, Schwartz was resting uneasily on a hard bench in one of the small sub-basement rooms of the Chica Hall of Correction.

The "Hall," as it was commonly termed, was the great token of the local power of the High Minister and those surrounding him. It lifted its gloomy shadow in a rocky, angular height that overshadowed the Imperial barracks beyond it, just as its shadow clutched at the Terrestrial malefactor far more than did the unexerted authority of the Empire.

Within its walls, many an Earthman in past centuries had waited for the judgment that came to one who falsified or evaded the quotas of production, who lived past his time or connived at another's such crime, or who was guilty of attempting subversion of the local government. Occasionally, when the local prejudices of Terrestrial justice made particularly little sense to the sophisticated and usually blasé Imperial government of the time, a conviction might be set aside by the Procurator, but this meant insurrection, or at the very least, wild riots.

Ordinarily, where the Council demanded death, the Procurator yielded.

Of all this, Joseph Schwartz, very naturally, knew nothing. To him, awareness consisted of a small room, its walls transfused with but a dim light, its furniture two hard benches and a table, plus a small recess in the wall that served as washroom and sanitary convenience combined. There was no window for a glimpse of sky, and the drift of air into the room through the ventilating shaft was feeble.

He rubbed the hair that circled his bald spot and sat up ruefully. His attempt at escape to nowhere (for

where on Earth was he safe?) had been short, not
sweet, and had ended here.

It had undoubtedly been a foolish and useless
attempt—

But he knew so little of this horrible world. To leave
by night or cross-country would have entangled him in
mysteries, would have plunged him into radioactive
danger pockets of which he knew nothing—so with the
boldness of one with no choice, he had struck out
upon the Highway at broad noon.

He was thoroughly aware of that enemy Mind Touch
at all times. For six months, it had been watching
him—and now it followed. At no time did he see
anyone. Actually, he dared not look, dared not turn
around, dared not show that he was other than at
ease. For at the beginning, when he *had* watched and
tried to flush out the man behind him, the Mind Touch
had changed subtly. From merely menace, it had become caution, from caution, doubt—and Schwartz became aware that his nemesis was armed, that should
he, Schwartz, seem to be aware of danger, he would
be brought down rather than allowed to escape—

So he walked on, knowing that he remained within
range of a weapon that held death. His back was stiff
in the anticipation of he knew not what. How does
death feel? —How does death feel? The thought jos-
tled him in time to his steps, jounced in his mind,
jiggled in his subconscious, until it went past endurance.

He turned toward the grassy shoulder of the Highway. He had been passing down a gentle decline, and
half a mile of it stretched upward to end sharply against
the sky in green and gray. Was there a scurry in the
fields up there? Was that something new and deadly in
the Mind Touch? Was a gun being leveled? Was aim
being taken?

He yelled at the nothingness he stared at, waving his
arms in a wild fury.

"Leave me alone, why don't you? What have I done
to you? —Go away! —*Go away!*"

He ended in a cracked shriek, his forehead ridged

with hate and fear of the creature who stalked him, and his mind alive with enmity. His thoughts heaved and thrust at the Mind Touch, attempting to evade the clingingness of it, rid itself of the breath of it—

—And it was gone. Suddenly and completely gone. There had been the momentary consciousness of overwhelming pain—not in himself, but in the other—then nothing. —No Mind Touch. It had dropped away like the grip of a fist growing lax and dead.

For many minutes, he waited—

Nothing— No Mind Touch—

He turned and walked again; the Mind Touch did not return.

Occasionally a vehicle sped by. None stopped for him, and he was glad of it. He slept in an open field during that following night, and the next morning was within the outskirts of Chica.

It was a mistake.

He excused it to himself in any number of ways as he sat there on the hardness of the bench in that cell. —He was a big-city man. He had been in Chica once, whereas all the rest of Earth was completely strange to him. He might be lost in the anonymity of crowds. He might even get a job—

But it was a mistake, despite all that.

It was early morning, and the motion of the populace was still thin and sporadic, but even so, the Mind Touches were for the first time numerous. They amazed and confused him.

So many! Some drifting and diffuse; some pointed and intense. There were men who passed with their minds popping in tiny explosions; others with nothing inside their skulls but perhaps a gentle rumination on the breakfast just completed.

At first Schwartz turned and jumped with everyone that passed, taking each as a personal contact; but within the hour he learned to ignore them—

He was hearing words now that he had never experienced back on the farm; thin, eery phrases, disconnected and wind-whipped; far off, far off— And with them, living, crawling emotion and other subtle things that cannot be described—so that all the world was a panorama of boiling life visible to himself only.

He found he could penetrate buildings as he walked, sending his mind in as though it were something he held on a leash, something that could suck its way into crannies invisible to the eye and bring out the bones of men's inner thoughts.

It was before a hugely stone-fronted building that he halted, for there was that distant Mind Touch that to him might mean a job. They were looking for workers in there. —He became conscious, for the first time, that he was hungry.

He stepped inside, where he was promptly ignored by everyone. He had never learned to read this language of new Earth, only to speak and understand it, so the directing signs meant nothing to him. He touched someone's shoulder.

"Where do I see about a job, please?"

"Through that door!" The Mind Touch that reached him was full of annoyance and suspicion.

—Through the door, and then the thin, point-chin fellow who fired questions at him and fingered the classifying machine onto which he punched the answers.

Schwartz stammered his lies and truths with equal uncertainty.

But the personnel man began, at least, with a definite unconcern. The questions were fired rapidly, "Age —Fifty-two? Hmm. State of health —Married— How many children— Experience— Worked with textiles? —Well, what kind? —Thermoplastic? —Elastomeric? —What do you mean, you think all kinds— Who did you work with last? —Spell his name— You're not from Chica, are you— Where are your papers? —You'll have to bring them here if you want action taken— What's your registration number?—"

Schwartz was backing away. He hadn't foreseen this end when he had begun. And the Mind Touch of the man before him was changing. It had become suspicious to the point of single-trackedness, and cautious too. There was a surface layer of sweetness and good-fellowship that was so shallow and overlay animosity so thinly as to be more dangerous than anything else.

"I think," said Schwartz nervously, "that I'm not suited for this job."

"No, no, come back," and the man beckoned at him. "We have something for you. Just let me look through the files a bit." He was smiling, but his Mind Touch was clearer now, and even more unfriendly.

He had punched a buzzer on his desk—

Schwartz, in a sudden panic, rushed for the door.

"Hold him!" cried the other instantly, dashing from behind his desk.

Schwartz struck at the Mind Touch, striking violently with his own mind, and he heard a groan behind him. He looked quickly over his shoulder. The personnel man was seated on the floor, face contorted and temples buried in his palms. Another man bent over him, then, at an urgent gesture, headed for Schwartz. Schwartz waited no more.

He was out on the street, fully aware now that there must be an alarm out for him with a complete description made public, and that the personnel man, at least, had recognized him.

He ran and doubled along the streets blindly. He attracted attention, more of it now, for the streets were filling up—suspicion, suspicion everywhere—suspicion because he ran—suspicion, because his clothes were wrinkled and ill-fitting—suspicion, because his face seemed to have hair on it, tiny gray hairs—

Schwartz groaned when he noticed that last in more than one fleeting Mind Touch. Apparently none of these new people had hair on their face. Arbin hadn't had any shaving equipment, and he'd had to improvise his own, using a steel cutter of some sort. —But where could he shave now, and unless he shaved, his beard would betray him.

In the multiplicity of Mind Touches and the confusion of his own fear and despair, he could not identify the true enemies, the ones in whom there was not only suspicion but certainty—and so he hadn't the slightest warning of the Neuronic Whip.

There was only that awful pain, which descended like the whistle of a lash and remained like the crush of a rock. For seconds he coasted down the slope of that descent into agony, before drifting into the black.

—And now he sat on the bench in the cell with his Mind reaching out, and contacting only danger and death.

The door opened, and he was on his feet, in tense fear. His knees and hips panged with stiff pain as they straightened, so that he almost fell.

It was a man in green uniform with a metal object held ready in his hand, which Schwartz knew to be dangerous.

"Come with me."

Schwartz followed him, speculating— He had stopped the first follower on the road to Chica. He had nearly knocked out the personnel man that morning. How many could he handle? —He'd better wait, before one last great effort.

It was a large room that he was brought into. The guard closed the door behind him, remaining outside himself.

Schwartz looked about him.

"Approach, Joseph Schwartz." There was a raised platform at the front of the room, like the judge's bench in a courtroom. Upon a high armchair of complicated design sat the man in the long green robe who had spoken.

He walked up slowly, and was conscious first of the two men and a girl who were seated in simple wooden chairs with arms and legs queerly stiff.

"Do you recognize these people, Joseph Schwartz?" asked the robed man.

Schwartz looked at them, then pointed. "I saw him once."

It was Shekt he pointed at. The physicist responded wearily, "I treated him with the Synapsifier, and it is

the only contact I ever had with him. You know that. I
protest this—"

"Silence! How about you, Dr. Arvardan?"

"I never saw him," was the curt, hostile response.

"We'll see about that after a while," came the grim
reply.

Chapter 14 *Descent into Despair*

The Secretary watched the four before him with a
savage sense of satisfaction. The girl he tended to
ignore, but otherwise it was a clean sweep. There was
the Earthman traitor, the Imperial agent, and the mysterious creature they had been watching for half a
year. It was doubtful that in a case so urgent and
crucial any of the enemy of smaller moment would
know enough to be dangerous.

To be sure, there was still Ennius, and the Empire.
Their arms, in the person of spies and traitors, were
pinioned, but there remained an active brain somewhere—perhaps to send out other arms.

The Secretary leaned forward, hands clasped, and
spoke quietly and gently. "Now it is necessary to make
things absolutely clear. There is war between Earth
and the Galaxy—undeclared as yet, but war nevertheless. You are our prisoners and will be treated as
necessary under the circumstances. Naturally, the recognized punishment is death—"

"Only in the case of legal and declared war," broke
in Arvardan fiercely.

"Legal war?" sneered the Secretary. "What is *legal*
war? Earth has *always* been at war with the Galaxy,
whether we made polite mention of the fact or not."

"Don't bother," said Shekt to Arvardan huskily.
"Let him have his say. We're in no position to argue."

Arvardan could feel life beginning to tingle in his
fingertips. He moved his arm with a gigantic effort
that brought the perspiration to his forehead—but managed to touch Pola's elbow. She did not feel it; that
was obvious. But she saw it after a while and looked

up at him with a feeble little smile, no spark of anything but apprehension in it. Arvardan tried to throw encouragement into his own expression, and failed—

The Secretary was speaking. "As I say, all lives here are forfeit, but nevertheless can be bought. Are you interested in the price?"

Shekt looked at him briefly. "What are you proposing?"

"This. Obviously, word of our plans has leaked out. How it got to Dr. Shekt is not difficult to see, but how it got to the Empire is puzzling. We would like to know, therefore, just what the Empire does know. How about it, Arvardan?"

"I am an archaeologist," said Arvardan bluntly. "I don't know anything at all about what the Empire knows—but I hope they know a damned lot."

"So I imagine. Well, you may change your mind. Think, all of you."

Throughout Schwartz contributed nothing, nor did he raise his eyes.

The Secretary waited, then said, perhaps a trifle savagely, "Then I'll outline the price to you of your non-cooperation. Dr. Shekt and the girl, his daughter, who, unfortunately for herself, is implicated to a deadly extent, are Earth citizens. Under the circumstances, it will be most appropriate to have both subjected to the Synapsifier. You understand, Dr. Shekt?"

The physicist's eyes were pools of pure horror.

"Yes, I see you do," said the Secretary. "It is, of course, possible to allow the Synapsifier to damage brain tissue just sufficiently to allow the production of an acerebral imbecile. It is a most disgusting state, one in which you will have to be fed or starve, be cleaned or live in filth, be shut up or remain a study in horror to all who see. It may be a lesson to others in the great day that is coming.

"As for you," and the Secretary turned to Arvardan, who was tugging at his wooden arms with wild vehemence and succeeding only in lifting them halfway, "and your friend Schwartz, you are Imperial citizens,

and therefore suitable for an interesting experiment.
We have never tried our concentrated Fever virus on
you Galactic dogs. It would be interesting to show our
calculations correct. —A small dose, you see, so that
death is not instant. The disease might work its way to
the inevitable over a period of a week, if we dilute the
injection sufficiently. It will be very painful."

And now he paused and watched them through
slitted eyes. "That," he said, "is the alternative to a
few well-chosen words at the present time. —And
Arvardan, don't think that your release from paralysis
will help you. I am armed and have half an army
outside which will be signaled into action the moment
you move out of your seat."

Arvardan sank back, face brick red with effort and
frustration.

Dr. Shekt muttered, "How do we know that you
won't have us killed anyway, once you have what you
want of us?"

"You have my assurance that you will die horribly if
you refuse. You will have to gamble on the alternative. What do you say?"

"Can't we have some time?"

"Time? Certainly. You may have two hours." The
Secretary, in the plenitude of power, tossed the words
to them with the same gesture that he would throw a
bone to a dog.

"May we be left together?"

"Why not?" and the Secretary smiled grimly. "With
an appropriate guard outside the door, and a fresh
supply of paralysis, I think none of you will attempt
anything foolish. —And," as an afterthought, "I will
take the girl with me, as an earnest of your good
intentions."

The hall in which they were left was evidently one
used for assemblies of several hundred. The prisoners
were lost and lonely in its size. Nor was there anything
to say. Arvardan's throat burnt dryly and he turned
his head from side to side with a futile restlessness.

Shekt's eyes were closed and his lips were colorless and pinched.

Schwartz remained apart. His state of apathy was complete. He had made no gesture of resistance, even when the little brown rods had pressed close to each arm and leg, so that first they tingled and then passed out of his control. The Mind Touches of the other two rested lightly upon him, and he sifted them cautiously.

Arvardan whispered fiercely. "Shekt. —Shekt, I say."

"What? —What?"

"What are you doing? Going to sleep? Think, man, think!"

"Why? What is there to think of?"

"Who is this Joseph Schwartz?"

"Don't *you* believe me? He was brought to me for treatment under the Synapsifier, and he was treated. I know nothing more."

"But then, why? Why was he treated?" Arvardan felt the faintest stirrings within him. "Maybe he *is* an Imperial agent."

"And if he is? Look at him. He's as helpless as we. —Maybe if we tell some sort of concerted story, they might wait, and eventually we might—"

The archaeologist's lip curled. "Live, you mean. With the Galaxy dead and civilization in ruins? Live? I might as well die."

"I'm thinking of Pola," muttered Shekt.

"I am too," said the other, "but what's there to do? Don't let your hopes deceive you. We won't live under any circumstances." Then, as though to escape from the thought, escape anywhere, he shouted, "You. Whatchername! Schwartz!"

Schwartz raised his head and allowed a glance to ooze out toward the other. He said nothing.

"Who are you?" demanded Arvardan. "How did you get mixed up in this? What's your part in it?"

And at the question, all the injustice of everything descended on Schwartz. All the harmlessness of his past, all the infinite horror of the present burst in upon him, so that he said in a fury, "Me? How did I get mixed up in it? Listen, I'm a nobody. I'm an honest man and a hard-working tailor, till I retired, that never bothered anybody. I hurt nobody, I worked hard, I took care of my family. —And then, for no reason, for *no reason*—I came here."

"To Chica?" asked Arvardan.

"No, not to Chica," shouted Schwartz in wild derision. "I came to this whole blasted world. —Oh, what do I care if you believe me or not. My world is in the past. My world had land and food and two billion people, and it was the *only* world."

Arvardan fell silent before the verbal assault. He turned to Shekt. "Can you understand him?"

"Do you realize," said Shekt in feeble wonder, "that he has hair on his face?"

"Right," said Schwartz defiantly, "and I have wisdom teeth and an appendix. —And I wish I had a tail to show you. *I'm from the past. I traveled through time.* —Now leave me alone." He ended with a sob.

The two scientists looked at each other briefly. Arvardan lowered his voice. "Mad, I suppose. I can't blame him."

"I wonder. —I remember his skull sutures now. They were primitive, very primitive."

Arvardan was amazed. "You mean— Oh come, it's impossible."

"I've always supposed so." For the moment Shekt's voice was a feeble imitation of normality, as though the presence of a scientific problem had switched his mind to that detached and objective groove in which personal matters disappeared. "They've calcuated the energy required to displace matter along the time axis, and a value greater than infinity was arrived at, so the project has always been looked upon as impossible. But others *have* talked of the possibility of 'time-faults,' analogous to geological faults, you know— Spaceships *have* disappeared, for one thing, in almost full view. There's the famous case of Hor Devallow in ancient times, who stepped into his house one day and never came out, and wasn't inside either. —And then there's the planet you'll find in the Galactography books of the last century which was visited by three expeditions that brought back full descriptions—and then was never seen again.

"Then there are certain developments in nuclear chemistry that seem to deny the law of conservation of mass-energy. They've tried to explain that by postulating the escape of some mass along the time axis. Uranium nuclei, for instance, when mixed with copper and barium in minute but definite proportion, under the influence of light gamma irradiation, set up a resonating system—"

"Wait," and Arvardan frowned intensely. "Never mind all that. There isn't time. Let me ask him a few questions— Look, Schwartz."

Schwartz looked up again.

"Yours was the only world in the Galaxy?"

Schwartz nodded.

"But you only thought that. I mean, you didn't have space travel so that you could check up."

"No."

"Or atomic power?"

"We had an atomic bomb— Uranium— I guess that's what made this world radioactive. There must have been a war after I left—with atomic bombs."

"It all fits so far," muttered Arvardan tensely. Then, "All right, then. You had a language then, of course."

"Lots of them."

"Which did you use?"

"English."

"Well, say something in it."

For six months or more, Schwartz had said nothing in English. But now, with lovingness, he said slowly, "I want to go home and be with my own people."

Arvardan turned to Shekt. "Is that the language he used when he was Synapsified?"

"I can't tell," said Shekt, in mystification. "Queer sounds then and queer sounds now. How can I relate them?"

"Well, never mind— What's your word for 'mother' in your language, Schwartz?"

Schwartz told him.

"Uh-huh. How about 'father'—'brother'—'one'—the numeral, that is—'two'—'three'—'fire'—'hand'—"

This went on and on, and when Arvardan paused for breath, his expression was one of awed bewilderment.

"Shekt," he said, "either this man is genuine, or I'm the victim of as wild a nightmare as can be conceived. He's speaking a language practically equivalent to the inscriptions found in the fifty-thousand-year-old strata on Sirius, Arcturus, Alpha Centauri, and twenty others."

"Are you sure?"

"Am I *sure?* Of course I'm sure. I'm an archaeologist. It's my business to know. I've been translating the ancient tongue for years, and here is a man who speaks it."

For an instant, Schwartz felt his armor of aloofness cracking. For the first time he felt himself regaining the individuality he had lost. The secret was out; he was a man from the past—*and they accepted it.* It proved him sane, stilled forever that haunting doubt, and he was grateful. —And yet he held aloof.

It was Shekt's turn now. He asked his questions hungrily: "Have you felt any bad effects as a result of the Synapsifier?"

Schwartz didn't know the word, but caught the thought.

"No," he said.

"I see you learned our language rapidly afterwards. Wasn't that unusual for you?"

"I always had a very good memory," was the cold response.

"And so you feel no different now from before you were treated?"

"That's right."

Dr. Shekt's eyes were hard now, and he said quickly, "What am I thinking?"

And with complete amazement Schwartz began,

"That I can read—" Then he stopped abruptly. "How did you find out?"

But Shekt had dropped him. He had turned his white, helpless face to Arvardan. "He can sense minds, Arvardan. —How much I could do with him. And to be here. —To be helpless."

"What—what—what—" Arvardan popped wildly.

"He can sense minds! I've been wondering about it ever since they brought him in— Arvardan, you remember the bacteriologist I told you about, the one who died as a result of the effects of the Synapsifier? One of the first symptoms of mental breakdown was his claim that he could read minds. —And he *could*. I found that out before he died. It's been my secret. I've told no one—but it's possible, Arvardan; it's possible. You see, with the lowering of brain-cell resistance, the brain may be able to pick up the magnetic fields induced by the microcurrents of others' thoughts, and reconvert it into similar vibrations in itself. —It's the same principle as that of any ordinary recorder. It would be telepathy in every sense of the word—"

Schwartz maintained a stubborn and hostile silence as Arvardan turned slowly in his direction. "Are you sure, Shekt? But we might be able to use that. Is this true, Schwartz?" The archaeologist's mind was spinning wildly, working out impossibilities. "There may be a way out now. There *must* be a way out."

But Schwartz was cold to the tumult in the Mind Touch he sensed so clearly. He said, "For me, maybe. I'll be valuable to them."

"To them!" exclaimed Arvardan, with a strong revulsion. "What do you mean?"

"I mean I'm an Earthman, and you're an outsider. That's plain, isn't it?" It was out now, and Schwartz was glad of it.

It took time for Arvardan to understand, and when he did he heaved, again futilely, at the paralysis that held him. Schwartz felt the dark menace of the Mind Touch, which lay like a blanket over his own. He "pushed" at it with an almost savage humor, and was rewarded by the sudden wince of pain on Arvardan's face.

"I did that," he said. "Want more?" ·

Arvardan subsided. —Then, "But the Earthmen want to kill you too."

Slowly, Schwartz had gathered fury. For an hour he had lain there, thinking. For an hour memories of his own youth had returned, memories he hadn't revived for years. It was a queer amalgamation of past and present that finally brought forth his indignation now.

But he spoke calmly, restrainedly. "They want to kill me because they think I'm one of you, that's all. I suppose you blame them. I suppose you think it's criminal for an oppressed and small people to try to overturn their tyrants. Don't you have a Galaxy of your own, with all the stars in the sky to play with? Do you need Earth also? Earthmen are not welcome anywhere in all your worlds. Can't you spare them their own remnant of Earth at least?"

"He talks like a Zealot," said Arvardan with contempt.

Schwartz burned the more at it. "Oh yes, you're a fine sample of the product the Galaxy sends us. You are tolerant and wonderfully big-hearted, and admire yourself because you treat Dr. Shekt as an equal. But underneath—yet not so far underneath that I can't see it plain in your mind—you are uncomfortable with him. You don't like the way he talks or the way he looks. In fact, you don't like *him,* even though he would like to betray Earth. —And you kissed a girl of Earth recently, and look back upon it as a weakness. You're ashamed of it—"

Arvardan had struggled against the torrent of words unavailingly, and now stopped, red-faced and open-mouthed.

Schwartz turned to Shekt with an unmitigated blaze. "And what are you after? Your fear of death sticks to you, you reek of it, your Mind Touch is full of it. —Do you think you'll escape the Sixty by betraying your planet, and living on over the corpses of your own people?"

But Shekt faced him now, with the dignity that came of a last desperation. He said simply, "If you can sense minds, investigate mine. Look! Look deeply! Find anything dishonorable in it if you can. See if it is not true that I could have avoided the Sixty easily enough if I had cooperated with the madmen who will ruin the Galaxy. See if it is not by opposing them that I am losing my life. —And see if I have any wish to harm Earth or Earthmen."

It stopped Schwartz, since in these matters it was impossible to fool him. Shekt's mind was open to him, and to Schwartz the mind was incontrovertible evidence. There could be no lie in it that did not leave its unavoidable mark in jumble and confusion.

And Shekt was not lying.

The physicist went on. With his tired eyes closed he continued wearily, "You can sense minds. Have you inspected the High Minister's? Or that of his Secretary? What do you know of what they're planning to do?"

"Revolt," said Schwartz reluctantly. "Fight for their rights. There are germs involved."

"Germs!" Shekt ground out bitterly. "Do you know how many will die?" Schwartz was silent. "I think you do now. Don't believe me, if you wish, but inspect the Secretary's mind when he returns. You may be too late then. If you live on, you live in a ruined Galaxy, with a ruined humanity. Perhaps you wish it."

"No, no." To Schwartz it was all obvious. Even the Mind Touch of the Secretary seemed suddenly to be clear now. Earlier it had been mostly a paean of woe to the Galaxy; the details had been dim; he had not been watching; but—but now—

Arvardan was speaking. "All right, Schwartz, look at me now. Read my mind. I was born on Baronn in the Sirius sector. I lived my life in an atmosphere of anti-Terrestrialism, so I can't help what flaws and follies lie at the roots of my subconscious. But look on the surface, and tell me if ever since I was thirteen I have been a bigot in any way.

"Schwartz, you don't know our history! You don't know of the thousands and tens of thousands of years in which Man spread through the Galaxy—the wars and misery. You don't know of the first centuries of the Empire, when still there was merely a confusion of alternating despotism and chaos. It is only in the last two hundred years now that our Galactic government has been a representative one. Under it, the various worlds are allowed their cultural autonomy—have been allowed to govern themselves—have been allowed voices in the common rule of all.

"At no time in history has Humanity been as free from war and poverty as now; at no time has their economy been so wisely adjusted; at no time have their prospects for the future been as bright. —And would you want a few megalomaniacs to destroy it all?

"Earth's grievance is legitimate and will be solved someday, if the Galaxy lives. But what these few will do now is no solution, it is merely the descent into despair."

Schwartz was moved. All those worlds to die—to fester and dissolve in horrible disease. —Was he an Earthman after all? Simply an Earthman? In his youth he had left Europe and gone to America; was he not the same man despite that? And if after him, men had left a torn and wounded Earth for the worlds beyond the sky, were they less Earthmen? Was not all the Galaxy his—all—all—descended from himself and his brothers—

He said, "I am with you. Is there any way I can help?"

"How far out can you reach for minds?" asked Arvardan eagerly, with a hastening quickness as though afraid still of a last change of mind.

"I don't know— There are minds outside. Guards, I suppose."

"Can you reach Pola? —The girl who was here?"

"I don't know what her Touch is like," Schwartz explained, almost timidly. He hated revealing limitations.

"Well, look for her," pleaded Arvardan. "See if you can find anything that's familiar."

There was a long silence, in which both the others devoured Schwartz with their eyes. Arvardan was trying to move—he felt the tingle in his legs that might signify returning life.

And then out of the soft stillness Schwartz's voice came low and tense. "I think it may be her— Fear and anger— It's a girl's mind, I'm sure of it. It—it seems to have a sort of girlishness about it." He looked up. "I can't explain."

"Is she alive?" asked Shekt in anguish. "Is she hurt?"

"I can't sense any pain. Oh— It's she. She's thinking of you, Dr. Shekt, and—" For a moment he seemed puzzled.

He said to Arvardan, "You're not a relation of hers, are you?"

Arvardan shook his head.

"Or a close friend?"

Arvardan hesitated. "I met her last night."

Schwartz seemed to listen, then shrugged his shoulders. He said nothing further, but Arvardan felt his heart bound queerly at the implications of the silence. Ashamed of kissing her, was he. If they could only get out of this. If only they could live. He would show that pudgy hair-face—

But aloud he said, "How about the Secretary—the man who left us here?"

A longer pause—the minutes stretched by unendurably.

Schwartz said, "Your minds are in the way. Don't watch me. —Think of something else."

They tried to. Another pause. Then, "No—I can't—I can't."

Arvardan struggled with his feet. He could move them a bit now, although every such motion resulted in an almost unbearable twinge. He said, "How hard can you hurt someone? The way you hurt me a while back, I mean?"

"I can knock a man down."

"How do you do it?"

"I don't know. It just gets done. It's—it's—" Schwartz looked almost comically helplessly in his effort to put the wordless into words.

"Can you handle more than one at a time?"

"I've never tried. —Maybe not."

Shekt interrupted. "Are you thinking of trying it on the Secretary when he comes back, Arvardan?"

"Why not?"

"How will we get out? Even if we caught the Secretary alone and killed him, and I don't think Schwartz is capable of that, there are hundreds waiting for us outside." Then, with an almost savage outcry, "It's hopeless, I tell you!"

But Schwartz interrupted huskily, "I've got him."

"Whom?" It came from both at once.

"The Secretary. It's his Mind Touch. —I know."

"Don't let him go." Arvardan almost rolled over in his attempts at exhortation—and tumbled out of the chair, so that he lay on the floor with one half-paralyzed leg working futilely to wedge underneath his body and lift. "Suck him dry. Get all the information you can."

Schwartz reached out until his head ached. Until now, Mind Touches had come to him rather than vice versa. He hadn't been able to avoid them. But now he clutched; he clawed out with the tendrils of his own mind, blindly, clumsily, like an infant thrusting out fingers it can't quite handle for an object it can't quite reach.

Painfully, he caught wisps. "Triumph! He's sure of the results. —Something about space bullets. —He's started them. —No. Not started. —Something else. —It's the space bullets that please him."

"What are space bullets?" demanded Arvardan.

"I don't know," wailed Schwartz. "It's just space bullets in his mind— I can't get the picture— Wait,

wait— little ships— little ships with no men— I can't get any more."

Shekt groaned. "Don't you get it, Arvardan? They're automatically guided missiles to carry the virus— Aimed at various worlds—"

"But where are they kept, Schwartz?" insisted Arvardan. "Look, man, look—"

"There's a building. I—can't—quite—see. —Five points—a star—and Sloo—"

Shekt broke in again. "That's it. By all the stars in the Galaxy, that's it. The Temple of Senloo. It's surrounded by radioactive pockets on all sides. No one would *ever* go there but the Ancients. Is it on a river, Schwartz?"

"Yes—yes—yes."

"When, Schwartz, when?"

"I can't see the day, but soon—soon— His mind is bursting with that— It will be very soon." His own head seemed bursting with the effort.

Arvardan was dry and feverish as he raised himself finally to his hands and knees, though they wobbled and gave under him.

"Schwartz, listen to me," he cried urgently. "I want you to do something."

But Schwartz was babbling now. "He's coming— He's coming here. —And he's going to have us killed. —It's deep and firm in his mind—" His voice sank and stopped as the door opened.

—It was then that Arvardan quite, quite despaired.

CHAPTER 15 *Duel! —With and Without Weapons*

The Secretary's voice was one of cold derision. "Dr. Arvardan! Had you not better return to your seat?"

Arvardan looked up at him, conscious of the cruel indignity of his own position, but there was no answer to make, and he made none. Slowly he allowed his aching limbs to lower him to the ground. He waited there, breathing heavily, hoping wildly for delay. If his limbs could return a bit more; if he could make a last lunge; if he could frighten that cold maniac into using his weapon—

That was no Neuronic Whip that dangled so gently from the smoothly gleaming Flexiplast belt that held the Secretary's robe in place. It was a full-size blaster that would shred him to atoms in an instantaneous point of time. —A quick death that he would never feel.

Strange that at that moment the thought of Pola pressed itself upon him; strange that he should so desire to live—

The Secretary said, "You all seem the worse for my absence. —Have you anything to say to me?"

It was quite obvious that no one had, and as obvious that to the Secretary this was not unwelcome.

He went on. "It doesn't matter. Your information is no longer important. We have advanced the hour of striking. I had thought the supply of virus to be smaller than it was. —Amazing what pressure will do, even on those who swear more speed is impossible."

At this point Schwartz interrupted thickly. "Two days— Less— Let's see— Tuesday—six in the morning— Chica time."

The blaster was in the Secretary's hand. He advanced in abrupt strides and towered over Schwartz's drooping figure.

"How did you know that?"

Schwartz stiffened; somewhere mental tendrils bunched and grasped. Physically, his jaw muscles clamped rigorously shut and his eyebrows curled low, but these were purely irrelevant. Within his brain there was that which reached out and seized hard upon the Mind Touch of the other.

To Arvardan, for precious, wasting seconds, the scene was meaningless; the Secretary's sudden motionless silence was not significant.

Schwartz muttered gaspingly, "I've got him. —Take away his gun— I can't hold on—" It died away in a gurgle.

And Arvardan understood. With a lurch he was on

all fours again; then slowly, grindingly, he lifted himself by main force to an unsteady erectness.

The Secretary might have been struck by the Medusasight. On his smooth and unfurrowed forehead perspiration gathered slowly, and his expressionless face hinted of no emotion. —Only that right hand, holding the blaster, showed any signs of life. Watch closely, and you might see it jerk ever so gently; note the curious flexing pressure of it upon the contact button; a gentle pressure, not enough to do harm, but returning—and returning—

"Hold him tight," gasped Arvardan with a ferocious joy. He steadied himself on the back of a chair and tried to gain his breath. "Let me get to him."

His feet dragged. He was in a nightmare, wading through molasses, swimming through tar, pulling with torn muscles at the back of a row of seats till he was drawn level, then reaching out so slowly—so slowly—to another row, and dragging again.

He was not conscious of the terrific duel that proceeded before him.

The Secretary had only one aim, and that was to put just the tiniest force into his thumb—three ounces, to be exact, since that was the contact pressure required for the blaster's operation. To do so, his mind had only to instruct a quiveringly balanced tendon, already half-contracted.

Schwartz had only one aim, and that was to restrain that pressure—but in all the inchoate mass of sensation presented to him by the other's Mind Touch, he could not know which particular area was alone concerned with that thumb. So it was that he bent his efforts to produce a stasis, a complete stasis—

The Secretary's Mind Touch heaved and billowed against restraint. It was a quick and fearfully intelligent mind that confronted Schwartz's untried control. For seconds it remained quiescent, waiting—then, in a terrific, tearing attempt, it would tug wildly at this muscle or that—

To Schwartz, it was as if he had seized a wrestling

hold which he must maintain at all costs, though his opponent threw him about in frenzies.

—But none of this showed. Only the nervous clenching and unclenching of Schwartz's jaw, the quivering lips, bloodied by the biting teeth—and that occasional soft movement on the part of the Secretary's thumb, straining—straining—

Arvardan paused to rest. His outstretched finger just touched the fabric of the Secretary's tunic, and he felt he could move no more. His agonized lungs could not pump the breath his dead limbs required. His eyes were blurred with the tears of effort, his mind with the haze of pain.

He gasped, "Just a few more minutes, Schwartz— Hold him, hold him—"

Slowly, slowly Schwartz shook his head. "I can't— I can't—"

And indeed, to Schwartz all the world was slipping away into dull, unfocused chaos. The tendrils of his mind were becoming stiff and non-resilient.

The Secretary's thumb pressed once again upon the contact. It did not relax— The pressure grew by tiny stages.

Schwartz could feel the bulging of his own eyeballs, the writhing expansion of the veins in his forehead. He could sense the awful triumph that gathered in the mind of the other—

—Then Arvardan lunged. His stiff and rebellious body toppled forward, hands outstretched and clawing.

The yielding, mind-held Secretary toppled with him— The blaster flew sideways, clanging along the hard floor.

Schwartz felt the captive mind wrench free almost simultaneously, and fell back, his own skull a tangled jungle of confusion.

The Secretary struggled wildly beneath the clinging dead weight of Arvardan's body. He jerked a knee into the other's groin with a vicious strength, while his clenched fist came down sideways on Arvardan's cheekbone. He lifted and thrust—and Arvardan rolled off in huddled agony.

The Secretary staggered to his feet, panting and disheveled—and stopped again.

Facing him was Shekt, half reclining. His right hand, shakingly supported by the left, was holding the blaster, and although it quivered, the barrel pointed at the Secretary.

"You pack of fools," shrilled the Secretary, passion-choked, "what do you expect to gain? I have only to raise my voice—"

"And you, at least," responded Shekt weakly, "will die."

"You will accomplish nothing by killing me," said the Secretary bitterly, "and you know it. You will not save the Empire you would betray us to—and you would not save even yourselves. —Give me that gun and you will go free."

He extended a hand, but Shekt laughed wistfully. "I am not mad enough to believe that."

"Perhaps not, but you are half-paralyzed," and the Secretary broke sharply to the right, far faster than the physicist's feeble wrist could veer the blaster.

But now his mind, as he tensed for the final jump, was utterly and entirely on the blaster he was avoiding. Schwartz extended his mind once again in a final jab, and the Secretary tripped and slammed downward as if he had been clubbed.

Arvardan had risen painfully to his feet. His cheek was red and swollen and he hobbled when he walked. He said, "Can you move, Schwartz?"

"A little," came the tired response. Schwartz slid out of his seat.

Arvardan bent over the prone Ancient and pulled his head back, none too gently. "Is he alive?" He felt futilely for a pulse with his still-numb fingertips, and then placed a palm beneath the green robe. He said, "His heart's beating, anyway. —You've a dangerous power there, Schwartz. —What do we do next?"

Shekt said, "There's the Imperial garrison in Fort

Dibburn not half a mile away. Once there, we're safe and can get word to Ennius."

"Once there! There must be a hundred guards outside, with hundreds more between here and there—"

"There's still Schwartz."

The plump Earthman looked up at the sound of his name and shook his head. "I'm not very good at it. I can't hold him very long."

Shekt said earnestly, "Because you're not used to it. Listen, I've got a notion as to what it is you do with your mind. It's a receiving station for the electromagnetics of the brain. I think you can transmit also. Do you understand?"

Schwartz seemed painfully uncertain.

"You must understand," insisted Shekt. "You'll have to concentrate on what you want him to do—and first we're going to give him his blaster back."

"What!" The outraged exclamation was neatly double.

Shekt raised his voice. "He's got to lead us out of here. We can't get out otherwise, can we? —And how can it look less suspicious than to allow him to be obviously armed?"

"But what if I can't hold him?" demanded Schwartz. He was flexing his arms, slapping them, trying to get back into the feel of normality.

"It's the chance we take. Try it now, Schwartz. Have him move his arm." His voice was pleading.

The Secretary moaned as he lay there, and Schwartz felt the reviving Mind Touch. Silently, almost fearfully, he let it gather strength—then spoke to it. It was a speech that included no words; it was the silent speech you send to your arm when you want it to move, a speech so silent you are not yourself aware of it.

And Schwartz's arm did not move; it was the Secretary's that did. The Earthman looked up with a wild smile, but both Shekt and Arvardan had eyes only for the Secretary: that recumbent figure with a lifting head, eyes from which the glaze of unconsciousness was vanishing, and an arm that peculiarly and incongruously jerked outwards at a ninety-degree angle.

Schwartz bent to his task.

The Secretary lifted himself up in angular fashion, nearly, but not quite, overbalancing himself. And then, in a queer and involuntary way, he danced.

It lacked rhythm; it lacked beauty; but to the three who watched—to Schwartz most of all—it was a thing of indescribable awe. For in that moment the Secretary's body was under the control of a mind not materially connected with it.

Slowly, cautiously, Shekt approached the robot-like Secretary and, not without a qualm, extended his hand. In the open palm thereof lay the blaster, butt first.

"Let him take it, Schwartz," said Shekt.

The Secretary's hand reached out and grasped the weapon clumsily. For a moment it shifted rapidly, and was grasped for action. For a moment there was a sharp, devouring glitter in his eyes. And then it all faded. Slowly, slowly the blaster was put into its place in the belt and the hand fell away.

Schwartz's laugh was high-pitched. "He almost got away there." But his face was white as he spoke.

"Well? Can you hold him?"

"He's fighting like the devil. —But it's not as bad as before."

"That's because you know what you're doing," said Shekt, with an encouragement he did not entirely feel. "Transmit, now. Don't try to hold him; just pretend you're doing it yourself."

Arvardan broke in. "Can you make him talk?"

There was a pause—then a low, rasping growl from the Secretary. —Another pause; another rasp.

"That's all," panted Schwartz.

"Never mind, then. We may get by without."

The memory of the next two hours was something no two of those that took part in the queer odyssey could duplicate. Dr. Shekt, for instance, had acquired a queer rigidity in which all his fears were drowned in

one breathless and helpless sympathy with the inwardly
struggling Schwartz. Throughout he had eyes only for
that round face as it slowly furrowed and twisted with
effort. Even when they joined Pola he had hardly time
for more than a moment's glance, a quick pressure of
the hand.

It was Arvardan who strode to her, Arvardan who
explained the situation in queer, jumbled phrases. She
had not been far, nor was the movement from the
assembly room to the small office in which she had
been detained an eventful one. The guards outside the
door had saluted sharply at the appearance of the
Secretary, who returned the salute in a fumbling, flat
way. They passed unmolested.

It was only when they left the Hall of Correction
that Arvardan became conscious of the madness of it
all. —Yet even then, Arvardan felt himself drowning
in Pola's eyes. Whether it was the life that was being
snatched from him, the future that was being destroyed
about him, the eternal unavailability of the sweetness
he had tasted—whatever it was, no one had ever seemed
so completely and devastatingly desirable.

In after-time, she was the sum of his memories.
Only the girl—

Pola did not understand at all. The queer, abstracted
attitude of Schwartz; the dead angularity of the Secretary's walk; the impossible things Arvardan had said,
which she had but half grasped— The sunny brightness
of the morning burned down upon her unaccustomed
eyes, so that Arvardan's down-turned face blurred
before her. She smiled up at him and was conscious of
that strong, hard arm on which her own rested so
lightly. That was the memory that lingered afterward.
—Flat, firm muscle lightly covered by glossy-textured
plastic cloth, smooth and cool under her wrist—

Schwartz was in a sweating agony. The curving drive
that led away from the side entrance from which they
had emerged was largely empty. For that, he was
hugely thankful.

Schwartz alone knew the full cost of failure. In the

enemy Mind that he controlled, he could sense the unbearable humiliation, the surpassing hatred, the utterly horrible resolves. He had to search that Mind for the information that guided him—the position of the official ground-car, the proper route to take— And in searching, he also experienced the galling bitterness of the determined revenge that would lash out, should his control waver for but the tenth part of the second.

The secret fastnesses of the Mind in which he was forced to rummage remained his personal possession forever. In after-times, there came the pale gray hours of many an innocent dawn during which once again he had guided the steps of a madman down the dangerous walks of an enemy stronghold.

Schwartz gasped at the words when they reached the ground-car. He dared not relax sufficiently to utter connected sentences. He choked out quick phrases, "Can't—drive car—can't—make him—make drive—complicated—can't—"

Shekt soothed at him with a soft clucking sound. He dared not touch him; dared not speak in an ordinary way; dared not distract Schwartz's mind for a second.

He whispered, "Just get him into the back seat, Schwartz. I'll drive. I know how. From now on, just keep him still."

About the Secretary's part in all this it is impossible even to speculate. —Captive of his own prisoners; armed, but helpless against unarmed men; it is perhaps not even desirable to investigate the matter.

The Secretary's ground-car was a special model. Because it was special, it was different. It attracted attention. Its green headlight turned to the right and left in rhythmic swings as the light dimmed and brightened in emerald flashes. Men paused to watch. Ground-cars advancing in the opposite direction moved to the side in a respectful hurry.

Had the car been less noticed, had it been less obtrusive, the occasional passerby might have had time

to note the pale unmoving Ancient in the back seat—
might have wondered—might have scented danger—

But they noticed only the car, so that time passed—

A soldier blocked the way at the gleaming chromium gates that rose sheerly in the expansive, overwhelming way that marked all Imperial structures, in sharp contrast to the squat and brooding architecture of Earth. His huge force gun shot out horizontally in a barring gesture, and the car halted.

Arvardan leaned out. "I'm a citizen of the Empire, soldier. I'd like to see your Commanding Officer."

"I'll have to see your identification, sir."

"That's been taken from me. I am Bel Arvardan of Baronn. I'm on the Procurator's business, and I'm in a hurry."

The soldier lifted a wrist to his mouth and spoke softly into the transmitter. There was a pause while he waited for an answer—and then he lowered his rifle and stepped aside. Slowly the gate swung open.

CHAPTER 16 *The Deadline That Approached*

It was at noon, perhaps, that the High Minister at Washenn inquired via televisor after his Secretary and a search for the latter failed. The High Minister was displeased; the minor officials at the Hall of Correction were perturbed.

Questioning followed, and the guards outside the assembly room were definite that the Secretary had left with the prisoners at 10:30 in the morning. —No, he had left no instructions. —They could not say where he was going; it was, of course, not their place to ask.

The girl was also gone. A new set of guards was equally uninformative— A general air of anxiety mounted and swirled.

At 2 P.M., the first report arrived that the Secretary's ground-car had been seen that morning—no one had seen if the Secretary was within—some thought he had been driving, but had only assumed so, it turned out—

By 2:30, it had been ascertained that the car had entered Fort Dibburn.

At not quite 3, it was finally decided to put in a call to the Commandant. A lieutenant had answered.

It was impossible at that time, they learned, for information on the subject to be given. However, His Imperial Majesty's officers requested that order be maintained for the present. It was further requested that news of the absence of a member of the Society of Ancients not be generally distributed until further notice.

That was enough. Men engaged in treason cannot take chances, and when one of the prime members of a conspiracy is in the hands of the enemy, it can only mean discovery or betrayal. These were reverse sides of a single coin. Either would mean death.

Word went out—

The population of Chica stirred. The professional demagogues were on the street corners. The secret arsenals were broken open and the hands that reached in withdrew with weapons. There was a twisting drift towards the fort, and at 6 P.M. a new message was sent to the Commandant, this time by personal envoy.

This activity was not matched by events within the Fort. It had begun dramatically, when the young officer meeting the entering ground-car reached out a hand for the Secretary's blaster.

"I'll take that," he said curtly.

Shekt said, "Let him take it, Schwartz."

The Secretary's hand lifted the blaster and stretched out; the blaster left it—and Schwartz, with a heaving sob of breaking tension, let go.

Arvardan was ready. When the Secretary lashed out like an insane steel coil released from compression, the archaeologist pounced upon him, fists pumping down hard.

The officer snapped out orders. Soldiers were running up. When rough hands laid hold of Arvardan's shirt collar and dragged him up, the Secretary was

limp upon the seat. Dark blood was flowing feebly
from the corner of his mouth. Arvardan's own already
bruised cheek was open and bleeding.

He straightened his hair shakily. Then, pointing a
rigid finger, he cried firmly, "I accuse that man of
conspiring to overthrow the Imperial Government. I
must have an immediate interview with the Commanding Officer."

"We'll have to see about that, sir," said the officer
civilly. "If you don't mind, you will have to follow
me—all of you."

And there, for hours, it rested. Their quarters were
private and reasonably clean. For the first time in
twelve hours they had a chance to eat, which they did,
despite considerations, with dispatch and efficiency.
They even had the opportunity of that further necessity of civilization—a bath.

Yet the room was guarded, and as the sun descended toward the horizon Arvardan finally lost his
temper and cried, "But we've simply exchanged
prisons."

The dull, meaningless routine of an army camp drifted
about them, ignoring them. Schwartz was sleeping and
Arvardan's eyes went to him. Shekt shook his head.
"Not yet. —That's for desperation."

"But there are only thirty-nine hours left."

"I know—but wait."

A cool voice sounded. "Which of you claims to be a
citizen of the Empire?"

Arvardan sprang forward.

"Follow me," said the soldier.

The Commanding Officer of Fort Dibburn was a
colonel grown stiff in the service of the Empire. In the
profound peace of the last generations there was little
in the way of "glory" that any army officer could earn
and the Colonel, in common with others, had earned
none. But in the long, slow rise from military cadet,
he had seen service in every part of the Galaxy—so
that even a garrison on the neurotic world of Earth

was to him but an additional chore. He wanted only the peaceful routine of normal occupation. He asked nothing but the usual—and now this was denied him.

He seemed tired when Arvardan entered. His shirt collar was open and his tunic with its blazing yellow Spaceship and Sun of Empire hung loosely over the back of his chair. He cracked the knuckles of his right hand with an abstracted air, as he stared solemnly at Arvardan.

"A very confusing story, all this," he said. "Very. May I ask your name?"

"Bel Arvardan, sir, of Baronn—archaeologist on an approved research expedition to Earth."

"I see. I am told you have no papers of identification."

"They were taken from me, but the rest of my expedition is at Everest. The Procurator himself will identify me."

"Very well." The Colonel crossed his arms and teetered backward on his chair. "Suppose you give me your side of the story."

"I have been made aware of a dangerous conspiracy on the part of a small group of Earthmen to overthrow the Imperial Government by force, which, if not made known at once to the proper authorities, may well succeed in destroying both the Government and much of the Empire itself."

"I find that a very rash and farfetched statement. May I have the details?"

"Unfortunately, I feel it vital that the details be told to the Procurator himself in person. I request therefore to be put into communication with him now, if you don't mind."

"Umm. —Let us not act too hurriedly. Are you aware that the man you have brought in is Secretary to the High Minister of Earth?"

"Perfectly!"

"And he is a prime mover in this conspiracy you mention."

"He is."

"Your evidence."

"I cannot discuss the evidence with anyone but the Procurator."

The Colonel frowned and regarded his fingernails. "Do you doubt my competency in the case?"

"Not at all, sir. But only the Procurator has the authority to take the decisive action required in this case."

"What decisive action do you refer to?"

"A certain building on Earth must be bombed and totally destroyed within thirty hours, or the lives of most of the inhabitants of the Empire will be lost."

"What building?" asked the Colonel wearily.

Arvardan snapped back. "May I be connected with the Procurator, please?"

There was a pause of deadlock. The Colonel said stiffly, "You realize that in forcibly kidnapping an Earthman, you have rendered yourself liable to trial and punishment by the Terrestrial authorities? Ordinarily, the Imperium will protect its citizens as a matter of principle, and insist upon a Galactic trial. However, affairs on Earth are delicate—I have strict instructions to risk no avoidable clash—so that unless you answer my questions fully, I will be forced to turn you and your companions over to the local authorities."

"But that would be a death sentence! For yourself too!—Colonel, I am a citizen of the Empire, and I demand an audience with the Pro——"

A buzzer on the Colonel's desk interrupted him. The Colonel turned to it, closing a contact. "Yes?"

"Sir!" came the clear voice. "A body of natives have encircled the Fort. It is believed they are armed."

"Has there been any violence?"

"No, sir."

There was no sign of emotion on the Colonel's face. "Artillery and aircraft are to be made ready—all men to battle stations. Withhold all fire except in self-defense. Understood?"

"Yes, sir. An Earthman under flag of truce wishes audience."

"Send him in. —Also send the High Minister's Secretary here again."

And now the Colonel glared coldly at the archaeologist. "I trust you are aware of the appalling nature of what you have caused."

"I demand to be present at the interview," cried Arvardan, nearly incoherent with fury, "and I further demand the reason for your allowing me to rot under guard here for six hours while you closet yourself with a native traitor."

"Are you making any accusations, sir?" demanded the Colonel, his own voice ascending the scale.

"No, sir. —But I will remind you that you will be accountable for your actions hereafter, and that you may well be known in the future, if you have a future, as the destroyer of your people."

"*Silence!* I am not accountable to you, at any rate. —We will conduct affairs henceforward as I choose. Do you understand?"

The Secretary passed through the door held open by a soldier. On his purpling, swollen lips there was a brief, cold smile. He bowed to the Colonel and remained completely unaware, to all appearances, of the presence of Arvardan.

"Sir," said the Colonel to the Earthman, "I have communicated to the High Minister the details of your presence here and the manner in which it came about. Your detention here is, of course, entirely—uh—unorthodox, and it is my purpose to set you free as soon as I can. However, I have here a gentleman who, as you probably know, has lodged against you a very serious accusation, one which, under the circumstances, we must investigate—"

"I understand, Colonel," said the Secretary calmly. "However, as I have already explained to you, this man has been on Earth, I believe, only three or four days, and his knowledge of our internal politics is non-existent. This is a flimsy basis indeed for any accusation."

Arvardan retorted in anger, "I am not the only one who makes the accusation."

The Secretary did not look at the archaeologist either then or later. He spoke exclusively to the Colonel. He said, "One of our local scientists is involved in this, one who, approaching the end of his normal sixty years, is suffering from delusions of persecution—and another man of unknown antecedents and a history of idiocy. —Scarcely better."

Arvardan jumped to his feet. "I demand to be heard—"

"Sit down," said the Colonel coldly and unsympathetically. "You have refused to discuss the matter with me. Let the refusal stand. —Bring in the man with the flag of truce."

It was another member of the Society of Ancients. Scarcely a flicker of the eyelid betrayed any emotion on his part at the sight of the Secretary. The Colonel rose from his chair and said, "Do you speak for the men outside?"

"I do, sir."

"I assume, then, that this riotous and illegal assembly is based upon a demand for the return of your fellow countryman here."

"Yes, sir. He must be immediately freed."

"Indeed! Nevertheless, the interest of law and order and the respect due His Imperial Majesty's representatives on this world require that the matter cannot possibly be discussed while men are gathered in armed rebellion against us. You must have your men disperse."

The Secretary spoke up pleasantly. "The Colonel is perfectly correct, Brother Cori. Please calm the situation. I am perfectly safe here, and there is no danger—for anybody. Do you understand? —For anybody. It is my word as an Ancient."

"Very well, Brother. I am thankful you are safe."

He was ushered out.

The Colonel said curtly, "We will see that you leave here safely as soon as matters in the city have returned to normal."

Arvardan was again on his feet. "I forbid it. You will let loose the would-be murderer of the human race. I demand an interview with the Procurator by my constitutional rights as a Galactic citizen." Then, in a paroxysm of frustration, "Will you show more consideration to an Earthman dog than you will to me?"

The Secretary's voice sounded over that last near-incoherent rage. "Colonel, I will gladly remain until such time as my case is heard by the Procurator, if that is what this man wants. An accusation of treason is serious, and the suspicion of it—however farfetched—may be sufficient to ruin my usefulness to my people. I would really appreciate the opportunity to prove to the Procurator that none is more loyal to the Empire than myself."

The Colonel said stiffly, "I admire your feelings, sir, and freely admit that were I in your place, my attitude would be quite different. —I will attempt contact with the Procurator."

Arvardan said nothing more until led back to his cell.

He avoided the glance of the others. For a long time he sat motionless, with a knuckle pinched between gnawing teeth.

Until Shekt said, "Well?"

Arvardan shook his head. "I just about ruined everything."

"What did you do?"

"Lost my temper; offended the Colonel; got no-where— I'm no diplomat, Shekt."

The physicist was on his feet, withered hands clasped behind his back. "What about Ennius? Is he coming?"

"I suppose so. —But at the Secretary's own request, which I can't understand."

"The Secretary's own request— Then I'm afraid Schwartz is right."

"Huh? What has Schwartz been saying?"

The plump Earthman was sitting on his cot. He

shrugged his shoulders when the eyes turned to him and spread out his hands in a helpless gesture. "I caught the Secretary's Mind Touch when they took him past our room just now. —He's already had a long talk with this officer you spoke to."

"I know— What about it?"

"There's no worry or fear in his mind; only hate. —And now it's mostly hate for us, for capturing him, for dragging him here. We've wounded his vanity; he's lost face. He intends to get even with us. I saw little daydream pictures in his mind. —Of himself, single-handed, preventing the Galaxy from doing anything to stop him, even while we, with our knowledge, work against him. He's giving us the odds, and then will smash us anyway and triumph over us."

"You mean he will risk his plans, his dreams of Empire, to vent a little spite at us? That's mad."

"I know," said Schwartz with finality. "He *is* mad."

"And he thinks he'll succeed?"

"That's right."

"Then we must have you, Schwartz. We'll need your mind. Listen to me—"

But Shekt was shaking his head. "No, Arvardan, we couldn't work that. I woke Schwartz when you left and we discussed the matter. His mental powers, which he can describe only dimly, are obviously not under perfect control. He can stun a man, or paralyze him, or control the larger voluntary muscles even against the subject's will, but that's about all. In the case of the Secretary, he couldn't make the man talk, the small muscles about the vocal cords being beyond him; he couldn't coordinate motion well enough to have him drive a car; he even balanced him while walking only with difficulty. Obviously, then, we couldn't control Ennius, for instance, to the point of having him issue an order, or write one. I've thought of that, you see—" Shekt shook his head as his voice trailed away.

Arvardan felt the desolation of futility descend upon him. "Where's Pola?"

"Sleeping in the other room."

He would have longed to wake her— Longed—oh, longed for a lot of things.

Arvardan looked at his watch. There were only thirty hours left.

CHAPTER 17 *The Deadline That Passed*

Arvardan looked at his watch. There were only six hours left.

He looked about him now in a dazed and hopeless way. They were all here now—even the Procurator, at last. Pola was next to him, her warm little fingers on his wrist and that look of fear and exhaustion on her face that more than anything else infuriated him against all the Galaxy.

Maybe they all deserved to die, the stupid, stupid— stupid—

He scarcely saw Shekt and Schwartz. They sat on his left. And there was the Secretary, his lips still swollen, one cheek bruised green, so that it must hurt like the devil to talk—and Arvardan's own lips stretched into a furious smile at the thought and his fists clenched and writhed—

Facing all of them was Ennius, frowning, uncertain, dressed in those heavy, shapeless, lead-impregnated clothes.

He was stupid, too— Arvardan felt a thrill of hatred shoot through him at the thought of these Galactic rulers, who wanted only peace and ease. Where were the conquerors of three centuries back? Where?—

Six hours left—

Ennius had received the call from the Chica garrison some eighteen hours before, and had streaked half around the planet at the summons. The motives that led him to that were obscure. Essentially, he had thought, there was nothing to the matter but a regrettable kidnapping of one of these green-robed curiosities of superstitious, hag-ridden Earth. —That and the

obscure and undocumented accusations. Nothing the
Colonel on the spot could not have handled.

And yet there were his own forebodings of Terrestrial rebellion, and there was Shekt— Shekt was in
this—

He sat now facing them, thinking, quite conscious
that his decision in this case might hasten a rebellion,
perhaps weaken his own position at court, ruin his
chance at advancement— As for Arvardan's long speech
just now about virus strains and unbridled epidemics,
how seriously could he take it? After all, if he took
action on the basis of it, how credible would the matter sound to his superiors?

So he postponed the matter in his mind by saying to
the Secretary, "Surely you have something to say in
this matter?"

"Surprisingly little," said the Secretary, with easy
confidence. "Merely to ask what his evidence is in all
this."

"Your Excellence," said Arvardan, outraged, "I have
already told you that the man admitted it in every
detail, at the time of our imprisonment day before
yesterday."

"Perhaps," said the Secretary, "you choose to credit
that, Your Excellence, but it is simply an additional
unsupported statement. Actually, the only facts to which
outsiders can bear witness are that *I* was the one
violently taken prisoner, not they; that it was *my* life
that was in peril, not theirs. Now I would like my
accuser to explain how he could find all this out in the
half week that he has been on the planet, when you,
the Procurator, in years of service have found nothing
to my disadvantage."

"There is reason in what the Brother says," admitted Ennius heavily. "How *do* you know?"

Arvardan replied stiffly, "Prior to the accused's confession, I was informed of the conspiracy by Dr. Shekt."

"Is that so, Dr. Shekt? And how did you find out?"
The Procurator's glance shifted to the physicist.

Shekt said, "Dr. Arvardan was admirably thorough

and accurate in his description of the use to which the Synapsifier was put and concerning the dying statements of the bacteriologist, F. Smitko."

"But Dr. Shekt, the dying statements of a man known to be in delirium are not of very great weight. You have nothing else?"

Arvardan interrupted by striking his fist on the arm of his chair and roaring, "Is this a law court? Has someone been guilty of violating a traffic ordinance? We have no time to weigh evidence. I tell you, we have till six in the morning, five and a half hours, to wipe out this enormous threat. —You knew Dr. Shekt well at one time. Have you known him to be a liar?"

The Secretary interposed instantly, "No one accuses Dr. Shekt of deliberately lying, Your Excellence. It is only that the good doctor has, of late, been greatly concerned over his approaching sixtieth birthday. I am afraid that a combination of age and fear have induced slight paranoiac tendencies, common enough here on Earth. —Have you noticed no change in him in the past months?"

Ennius had, of course. By the Stars, what was he to do?

But Shekt's voice was calm, quite normal. He said, "I might say that for the last half year I have been under the continual watch of the Ancients, that letters from you to me have been opened, that my answers to you have been censored, but it is obvious that all such complaints would be attributed to the paranoia spoken of. However, I have here Joseph Schwartz, the man who volunteered as a subject for the Synapsifier one day last autumn when you were visiting me at the Institute."

"I remember." There was a feeble gratitude in Ennius's mind that the subject had, for the moment, veered. "Is that the man?"

"Yes," said Shekt. "The exposure to the Synapsifier was uncommonly successful, since he had a photographic memory to begin with, as I found out recently.

At any rate, he now has a mind that is sensitive to the thoughts of others."

And Ennius leaned far forward in his chair and cried in a shocked amazement, "What? Are you telling me he reads minds?"

"That can be demonstrated, Your Excellence. —But I think the Brother will confirm the statement."

The Secretary darted a quick look of hatred at Schwartz, boiling in its intensity and lightning-like in its passage across his face. He said, with but the most imperceptible quiver in his voice, "It is quite true, Your Excellence. This man they have here has certain hypnotic faculties, though whether that is due to the Synapsifier or not, I don't know. I might add that this man's subjection to the Synapsifier was not recorded, a matter which you'll agree is highly suspicious."

"It was not recorded," said Shekt quietly, "in accordance with my standing orders from the High Minister," but the Secretary merely shrugged his shoulders at that.

Ennius said peremptorily, "What about this Schwartz? What do his mind-reading powers, or hypnotic talents, or whatever they are, have to do with the case?"

"Shekt intends to say," put in the Secretary, "that Schwartz can read my mind."

"Is that it? —Well, and what is he thinking?" asked the Procurator, speaking to Schwartz for the first time.

"He's thinking," said Schwartz, "that we have no way of convincing you of our side of the case."

"Quite true," scoffed the Secretary, "though that deduction scarcely calls for much mental power."

"And also," Schwartz went on, "that you are a poor fool, afraid to act, desiring only peace, hoping by your justice and impartiality to win over the men of Earth, and all the more a fool for so hoping."

The Secretary reddened. "I deny all that."

But Ennius shrugged it off. He said to Schwartz, "And what am *I* thinking?"

Schwartz replied, "That even if I could see clearly

within a man's skull, I need not necessarily tell the truth about what I see."

The Procurator's eyebrows lifted in surprise. "You are correct, quite correct. —Do you maintain the truth of the claims put forward by Drs. Arvardan and Shekt?"

"Every word of them."

"Hmp. Yet unless a second such as you can be found, one who is not involved in the matter, your evidence would not be valid in law, even if we could obtain general belief in you as a telepath."

"But it is not a question of the law," cried Arvardan, "but of the safety of the Galaxy."

"Your Excellence," the Secretary rose in his seat, "I have a request to make. —I would like to have this Joseph Schwartz removed from the room."

"Why so?"

"This man, in addition to reading minds, has certain powers of mental force. I was captured by means of a paralysis induced by this Schwartz. It is my fear that he may attempt something of the sort now against me, or even against you, Your Excellence."

Arvardan rose to his feet, but the Secretary overshouted him to say, "No hearing can be fair if a man is present who might subtly influence the mind of the judge by means of admitted mental gifts."

Ennius made his decision quickly. An orderly entered and Joseph Schwartz, offering no resistance, nor showing the slightest sign of perturbation on his moonlike face, was led away.

To Arvardan, it was the final blow—

As for the Secretary, he rose now, and for the moment stood there—a tall, grim figure in green, strong in his confidence.

He began in serious, formal style. "Your Excellence, all of Dr. Arvardan's beliefs and statements rest upon the testimony of Dr. Shekt. In turn, Dr. Shekt's beliefs rest upon the dying delirium of one man— And all this, Your Excellence, *all this* occurred after Joseph Schwartz was submitted to the Synapsifier.

"Who, then, is Joseph Schwartz? Until Joseph

Schwartz appeared on the scene, Dr. Shekt was a
normal, untroubled man. You yourself, Your Excellency, spent an afternoon with him the day Schwartz
was brought in for treatment. Was he abnormal then?
Did he inform you of treason against the Empire? Did
he seem troubled? Suspicious? He says now that he
was instructed by the High Minister to falsify the results of the Synapsifier tests. Did he tell you that then?
Or only now, *after* that day on which Schwartz appeared?

"Again, who is Joseph Schwartz? He spoke no known
language at the time he was brought in. So much we
found out for ourselves later, when we first began to
suspect the stability of Dr. Shekt's reason. He was
brought in by a farmer who knew nothing of his identity nor any facts about him. None have since been
discovered.

"Yet this man has strange mental powers. He can
stun at a hundred yards by thought alone. I myself
have been paralyzed by him; my arms and legs were
manipulated by him; my mind might have been manipulated if he had wished.

"I believe, however, that Schwartz did manipulate
the minds of these others. They say I captured them;
that I threatened them with death; that I confessed to
treason and to aspiring to Empire— Yet ask of them
one question, Your Excellence. Have they not been
thoroughly exposed to the influence of Schwartz, that
is, of a man capable of controlling their minds?

"Is not perhaps Schwartz the traitor? If not, who *is*
Schwartz?"

The Secretary seated himself, calm, almost genial.

Arvardan felt as though his brain had mounted a
cyclotron and was spinning outward now in faster and
faster revolutions— What answer could one make? That
Schwartz was from the past? What evidence? That he
himself recognized a genuinely primitive speech? —But
with a manipulated mind? After all, how could he tell
his mind had not been manipulated? Who *was* Schwartz?
—What had convinced him so quickly and so surely of

this great plan of Galactic conquest?—One man's word? —One girl's kiss? —Or Joseph Schwartz?

He couldn't think! He couldn't think!

"Well," Ennius sounded impatient, "have you anything to say, Dr. Shekt? Or you, Dr. Arvardan?"

But Pola's voice suddenly pierced the silence. "Can't you see it's all a lie? Don't you see he's tying us all up with his false tongue? Oh, we're all going to die, and I don't care anymore—but we could stop it; we could stop it— And instead we just sit here and—and—*talk*—" She burst into wild sobs.

The Secretary said, "So we are reduced to the screams of a hysterical girl. —Your Excellency, I have this proposition. My accusers say that all this, the alleged virus and whatever else they have in mind, is scheduled for a definite time, six in the morning, I believe. I offer to remain in your custody for a week. If what they say is true, word of an epidemic in the Galaxy ought to reach Earth within a few days. If such occurs, Imperial forces will still control Earth—"

"Earth is a fine exchange, indeed, for a Galaxy of humans!" mumbled the white-faced Shekt.

"I value my own life, and that of my people. We are hostages for our innocence."

The Secretary folded his arms.

Ennius looked up, his face troubled. "I find no fault in this man—"

And Arvardan could stand it no more. With a quiet and deadly ferocity, he arose and strode quickly toward the Procurator. What he meditated was never known. Afterward, he could not remember himself. At any rate, it made no difference. Ennius had a Neuronic Whip, and used it.

Everything about Arvardan flamed up into pain, spun about, and vanished—

Light—

Blurring light and misty shadows—melting and twisting, and then coming into focus.

A face— Eyes upon his—

"Pola!" Things became sharp and clear to Arvardan in a single leaping bound. "What time is it?" His fingers were hard upon her wrist, so that she winced involuntarily.

"It's past seven," she whispered, "past the deadline."

He looked about wildly, starting from the cot on which he lay, disregarding the burning in his joints. Shekt, his lean figure huddled in a chair, raised his head to nod in brief mournfulness.

"It's all over, Arvardan."

"Then Ennius—"

"Ennius," said Shekt, "would not take the chance. Isn't that strange?" He laughed a queer, cracked, rasping laugh. "The three of us single-handedly discover a vast plot against humanity, single-handedly we capture the ringleader and bring him to justice. It's like a visicast, isn't it, with the great all-conquering heroes zooming to victory in the nick of time. —Except that no one believes us. That doesn't happen in the visicasts, does it? Things end happily there, don't they? It's funny—" The words turned into rough, dry sobs.

Arvardan looked away, sick. Pola's eyes were blue universes, moist, tear-filled. Somehow, for an instant, he was lost in them—they *were* universes—star-filled. And towards those stars little gleaming metallic cases were streaking—devouring the light-years as they penetrated hyper-space in calculated, deadly paths. Soon— perhaps already—they would approach, pierce atmospheres, fall apart into unseen deadly rains of virus—

Well, it was over—

"Where is Schwartz?" he asked weakly.

But Pola only shook her head. "They never brought him back."

Ten o'clock! Three hours past the deadline!

There was an air of activity about the fort. There were the shouts of men—an atmosphere of physical tension that could be felt.

Ennius was at the door, tall, lean, anxious—

The door opened. He beckoned. He said something. To Arvardan, buried in his own, futile thoughts, it meant nothing. But he followed—like an automaton—

And now they were back in the Commandant's office— It might have been last night once again— The Secretary was there also, face dark, eyes pouched—

Ennius had not slept in twenty-four hours. He addressed the Secretary. "Do you know the meaning of what is going on outside? A band of natives is once again besieging the fort. We do not wish to have to open fire against them. Can you control them?"

"If I choose, Your Excellence."

"Well, then—"

"But I do not choose, Your Excellence!" And now the Secretary smiled, and flung out an arm. His voice was a wild taunt, too long withheld, gladly released. "Fool! You waited too long. Die for that! Or live a slave!"

The wild statement produced no shattering effect upon Ennius. It was only that the grayness about him deepened. "Then I lost so much in my caution? The story of the virus—was true?" There was almost an abstract, indifferent wonder in his voice. "But Earth, yourself— You are all my hostages."

"Not at all," came the instant, victorious cry. "It is you and yours that are my hostages. —The virus that now is spreading through the Universe has not left Earth immune. Enough already saturates the atmosphere of every garrison on the planet, including Everest itself. We of Earth are immune, but how do *you* feel, Procurator? Weak? Is your throat dry? Your head feverish? It will not be long, you know. —And it is only from us that you can obtain the antidote."

He turned savagely and suddenly upon Shekt and Arvardan. "Well, have I played my part properly? Have I succeeded?" And he broke into wild laughter.

Slowly, slowly Ennius pressed the button upon his desk. Slowly, slowly a door slid open, and Joseph Schwartz, frowning a bit, swaying a bit with weariness stood upon the threshold. Slowly, slowly he entered.

The Secretary's laughter faded. With a sudden, wary suspicion, he faced the man from the past.

"No," he gritted, "you can't get the secret of the antidote out of me. The men who have it and who can use it are safely beyond your reach."

"Quite safely," agreed Schwartz, "except that we don't need it. There's no virus to stamp out."

The statement did not quite penetrate. Arvardan felt a sudden choking thought enter his mind, but expelled it. He couldn't risk the disappointment.

But Ennius spoke again. "Tell your story, Schwartz, and make it plain. I want the Brother to understand it completely."

"It's not complicated," said Schwartz. "When we were here last night, I knew I could do nothing just sitting and listening. So I worked carefully on the Secretary's mind—for a long time. And then finally he asked that I be ordered out of the room, which was what I wanted, of course. The rest was easy.

"I stunned my guard and left for the airstrip. The fort was on a twenty-four-hour alert. The aircraft were fueled, armed, and ready for flight. The pilots were waiting. I picked one out—and we flew to Senloo."

The Secretary might have wished to say something. His jaws writhed soundlessly.

It was Shekt who spoke. "But you could force no one to fly a plane, Schwartz. It was all you could do to make a man walk."

"Yes, when it's against his will. But from Dr. Arvardan's mind, I knew how Sirians hated Earthmen —so I looked for a pilot who was born in the Sirius sector. I found one. He *hated* Earthmen with a hate that's difficult to understand, even for me, and I was inside his mind. He *wanted* to bomb them. He *wanted* to destroy them. It was only discipline that tied him fast, that kept him from taking out his plane then and there.

"That kind of a mind is different. Just a little suggestion, a little push, and discipline was not enough to hold him. I don't even think he realized that I climbed into the plane with him."

"How did you find Senloo?" whispered Shekt.

"In my time," said Schwartz, "there was a city called St. Louis. It was at the junction of two great rivers. —We found it. It was night, but there was a dark patch in a sea of radioactivity—and Dr. Shekt had said the Temple was an isolated oasis of normal soil. We dropped a flare—at least, it was my mental suggestion—and there was a five-pointed building below us. It jibed with the picture I had received in the Secretary's mind. —Now there's only a hole, a hundred feet deep, where that building was. That happened at 3 A.M. No virus was sent out. The universe is free."

It was an animal-like howl that emerged from the Secretary's lips. —The unearthly screech of a demon. He seemed to gather for a leap, and then—collapsed.

A thin froth of saliva trickled slowly down his lower lip.

"I never touched him," said Schwartz softly. Then, staring thoughtfully at the fallen figure, "When I returned, the Procurator would have blown a fuse if I hadn't argued him into waiting past the deadline. I knew the Secretary couldn't resist crowing; I knew that from his mind. —And now there he lies."

EPILOGUE

Actually, the story ended just above, and an epilogue is quite out of fashion. Still, it has its functions—It's a knot, you see, that ties up the loose ends of the yarn (pun, pun), keeps them from unraveling, and tucks them neatly away. So if you want a sense of completion, just read on—because an epilogue is going to be written here, regardless.

It won't take long—

The only person involved, in fact, is Joseph Schwartz. Thirty days had passed since he had lifted off the airport runway on a night dedicated to Galactic destruction, with alarm bells shrilling madly after him and radioed orders to return burning the ether towards him.

He had returned in his own time—with the Temple at Senloo destroyed and his unwitting pilot first beginning to wonder just exactly what had happened.

The heroism was finally made official now. In his pocket he had the ribbon of the Order of the Spaceship and Sun, First Class. Only two others in all the Galaxy had ever gotten it non-posthumously. That was something for a retired tailor—

No one, of course, outside the most official of officialdom knew exactly what he had done, but that didn't matter. Someday, in the history books—

He was walking through the quiet night now toward Dr. Shekt's house. The city was peaceful—as peaceful as the starry glitter above. In isolated places on Earth, bands of Zealots still made trouble, but their leaders were dead or captive, and the moderate Earthmen themselves could take care of the rest.

—The first huge convoys of normal soil were already on their way. Ennius had again made his original proposal that Earth's population be moved to another planet, but that was out. Charity was not wanted. Let Earthmen have a chance to remake their own planet. Let them build once again the home of their fathers, the native world of man. Let them labor with their hands; let the diseased soil be removed, and healthy replace it.

It was an enormous job; it could take a century—but what of that? Let the Galaxy lend machinery; let the Galaxy ship food; let the Galaxy supply soil. Of their incalculable resources, it would be a trifle—and it would be repaid.

And someday, once again, the Earthmen would be a people among peoples, inhabiting a planet among planets, looking all humanity in the eye in dignity and equality—

Schwartz's heart pounded at the wonder of it all, as he walked up the steps to the front door. —Next week, he left with Arvardan for the great central worlds of the Galaxy. Who else of his generation had ever left Earth?—

He paused, his hand on the point of signaling at the door, as the words from within sounded in his mind. How clearly he heard thoughts now—like tiny bells.

It was Arvardan, of course, with more in his mind than words alone could quite handle. "Think, Pola, you would see things you never saw, live as you've never lived—"

And Pola, with a mind as eager as his and words of

the purest reluctance, "If you think it's a Galactic tour I want—"

"But you'd be with me. —I mean I'd be with you. If you'd rather, we'll come back after this address I've got to make at Trantor."

"Your old Archaeological Society— Hmp."

"But then we can come back. I'll stay here with you. I'll never leave you."

"But I don't know that I wouldn't rather travel."

"Then we'll go anywhere you want."

"But I'm just a poor little Earthg——"

There was a short, muffled exclamation from Arvardan, followed by a tiny, girlish squeal. The conversation stopped.

But of course the Mind Touches did not, and Schwartz, in full satisfaction—and a little embarrassment—backed away. He could wait. Time enough to disturb them when things had settled down further.

He waited in the street, with the cold stars burning down—a whole Galaxy of them, seen and unseen.

—And for himself, and the new Earth, and all those millions of planets far beyond, he repeated softly once more that ancient poem that he alone now, of so many quadrillions, knew:

> *Grow old along with me!*
> *The best is yet to be . . .*

AFTERWORD

I suppose that if I wanted this book to be a kind of teaching exercise on "How to Revise," the best thing to do would be to include the published version of *Pebble in the Sky* immediately after "Grow Old Along with Me." Then the reader can study, in painstaking detail, paragraph by paragraph, what I did.

Of course, that is impossible.

For one thing, that sort of thing would double the length and expense (and price) of the book to very little purpose.

Those readers, after all, who are sufficiently interested in my writing to have bought this book are very likely to have a copy of *Pebble in the Sky* tucked away somewhere. Even if they have never read the book, or have lost it, or have thrown it away, or have been foolish enough to lend it out ("foolish" because from the letters I receive I have come to realize that no one who borrows one of my books ever returns it), they can always buy a copy, since Ballantine books has recently put out a new paperback edition.

Finally, there may even be some who will get a certain pleasure out of "Grow Old Along with Me" and will not care anything at all about reading *Pebble in the*

Sky. In that case, why bother them with a second dose of what is, in essence, the same story?

Nevertheless, I will humor myself by making a few comments on the subject.

Now that I've reread "Grow Old Along with Me" for the first time since I revised it thirty-six years ago, it seems to me to be not so bad. I think *Startling* could have done lots worse than to have accepted and published it.

One thing I am very thankful for, however, is that I cut out the asinine prologue, epilogue, and intermissions. What got into me and caused me to write them, I can't recall. Anyway, during the two-year interval between 1947 and 1949, I obviously gained some common sense and killed them. Then, too, I removed the three-part division and combined the Joseph Schwartz and Bel Arvardan story, commingling the parts in a manner which, in my opinion, is more interestingly complex.

As I went through "Grow Old Along with Me" I noticed, with some horror, pencil marks about various sentences and paragraphs that could only mean I was planning at one time to cut the story—perhaps to make it more suitable for magazine publication. If so, that project was obviously stillborn, and a good thing, too. I actually seem to have wanted to cut the chess game, which is my favorite part of the story.

I had had a vague idea in my head that the chess game had been introduced into "Pebble in the Sky" as one way of elaborating and lengthening the story. I was delighted to see that it already existed in "Grow Old Along with Me." You see, I've always despised fictional descriptions of chess games, in which no real details are given but something that is just silly is included, like, "He opened a slashing attack with his King's Rook"—to which my reaction always is, "Did the King's Rook use a knife or a gun?"

I made up my mind to present a real game, with every move meticulously described, and at least one person who was reading the book late at night was sufficiently astonished and stimulated to get out of bed, get his chessboard, and play it through. He wrote it up for a chess journal under the heading of "Asimov's Game," and pronounced it a pretty good game.

Well, it wasn't my game, and it was better than the reader judged it to be. The real game that I used was played in 1924 in Moscow between Werlinski (white) and Loewenfisch (black), and it won a first prize for brilliance.

One thing about "Grow Old Along with Me" is terribly embarrassing to me. It was written, remember, in 1947, only two years after nuclear fission bombs were dropped on Hiroshima and Nagasaki. I was clearly unaware of the exact degree of danger represented by nuclear wars and by radiation (as was almost everyone else).

I gave the Earth of the future a radioactive crust, at least in spots, yet it had a remnant of life and humanity clinging to it. Clearly, I meant this to be taken by the reader as the result of a nuclear war in our future, and the story's past. Yet surely any nuclear war that is so intense that it turns large tracts of Earth's crust into areas of long-term radioactivity is going to wipe out life on Earth.

At one point in "Grow Old Along with Me" I had Joseph Schwartz guess that the radioactivity of the crust had arisen from a war "with atomic bombs," but fortunately that was not corroborated by any other character, and in terms of the story, it remained just a guess.

Naturally, I kept Earth's radioactive crust in "Pebble in the Sky." I had to, since it is of crucial importance to the plot. In my second novel, The Stars, Like Dust—(Doubleday, 1951), the opening scenes were on Earth, and again I kept the radioactive crust.

As the years passed, however, and grew less naive about nuclear war, especially after hydrogen fusion bombs began to be exploded, I avoided the notion of the radioactive Earth. Nevertheless, when, a generation later, I wrote Foundation's Edge (Doubleday, 1982), I began to weave my various novels into one overview of future history and found myself stuck with Earth's radioactive crust.

I had to fall back on my store of ingenuity. The radioactive crust couldn't be the result of a nuclear war, so what was it? As a result of my thinking on the subject, I wrote *Robots and Empire* (Doubleday, 1985), so that an embarrassment was turned into an asset.

2

THE END OF ETERNITY

FOREWORD

Another novel of mine grew out of a smaller version, and in this second case, matters were more extreme. *Pebble in the Sky* was only 1.4 times as long as "Grow Old Along with Me," but my novel *The End of Eternity* was three times as long as the story out of which it developed.

It happened this way—

The year was 1953, and nearly four years had passed since the publication of my first book, *Pebble in the Sky*. Since then, I had published eight more books (including a biochemistry textbook), for nine altogether. My tenth book, *Lucky Starr and the Pirates of the Asteroids* (Doubleday, 1953), was about to appear, and my eleventh book, *The Caves of Steel* (Doubleday, 1954), was being serialized in *Galaxy*, in preparation for book publication.

I was averaging three books per year in those early days, which, given my rate of writing, was not very much, but I didn't have much time to write then. Half a year before *Pebble in the Sky* appeared, I had begun my teaching duties at Boston University School of Medicine and in 1951 I had become an Assistant Professor of Biochemistry. I was still under the delusion that this was my lifework and that writing was just a sideline—but I kept writing just the same, in odd moments.

Occasionally it was necessary for me to visit the Boston University Library on the main campus (those were its pre-Gotlieb days), and on November 17, 1953, while wandering through the stacks, I came across a file of bound volumes of *Time*.

I began leafing through the early ones and was naturally amused at how much wiser I was than the *Time* writers, with their carefully cultivated style of know-it-all arrogance (because I had the benefit of hindsight, of course). I asked the librarians, without much hope, if it was possible to take out those volumes for home reading. I then discovered that faculty members had some extraordinary privileges. They could take out such volumes, though students couldn't.

I promptly took out the first of the volumes in their collection (which covered the first half of 1928) and moved onward steadily. It took me almost a year to work my way through all the volumes and the librarians called me, with what I hope was affectionate amusement, "the *Time* professor."

The whole procedure was merely a matter of pampering an impulse, except that in one of the early volumes I noticed a line drawing in a small advertisement. Glimpsing it out of the corner of my eye, I got a flash of something that looked like the now-familiar mushroom cloud of a nuclear bomb. That startled me, for the volume of *Time* was some fifteen years before Hiroshima. I took another look. It was only the Old Faithful geyser of Yellowstone National Park, and the advertisement was perfectly ordinary.

But what's the use of being a science fiction writer if you don't take advantage of odd little things like that? ("Where do you get your crazy ideas?" I'm frequently asked. One answer should be, "From old issues of *Time* magazine.")

After all, what if the advertisement were what I thought it was—actually the mushroom cloud? Could the words of the advertisement offer a subtle hint as to the true nature of the drawing? If so, how did it get there? And why?

Clearly, the matter had to involve time-travel, which was at once interesting, for I had never written a major story involving time-travel. —So on December 7, 1953, I began to write a novelette, which I called "The End of Eternity."

It turned out to be 25,000 words long and I was finished with it on February 6, 1954. I was very pleased with it, and I mailed it off to *Galaxy* at once.

On February 9, Horace Gold phoned me. It was a complete rejection. He talked revision, but a *total* one. It would have amounted to my jacking up the title and running a new story under it. I refused point-blank, and that was that.

It seems to me that I should have tried *Astounding* then, but I didn't. I no longer remember why, and I have no indication in my diary as to why I didn't. (I've noticed many times that when something unpleasant happens, I don't say much about it in my diary. My diary may, therefore, give a more carefree, happy-happy impression of my life than is truly warranted by the facts—though my life has been happy enough, to be sure, and I wouldn't dream of complaining.)

It may be (and I'm just guessing now) that from Gold's telephone conversation, I got the idea that too much was happening in the novelette, and that I had a dehydrated novel on my hands. Since Doubleday had now published four of my novels and had two more in press, I felt like an established Doubleday writer who could make use of the perquisites that come with the post. It may, therefore, have seemed reasonable for me to ask Walter Bradbury to read the novelette and tell me if he thought a novel was hiding in it.

On March 17, 1954, when I was in New York, I left the novelette with Bradbury, who good-naturedly agreed to humor me. My judgment, this time, was accurate. Bradbury said that I had a worthwhile novel there, and on April 7 he called me to say that a contract was in the works.

I signed the contract on April 21, and was then faced with the prospect of retelling the story at three times the length. It took me exactly half a year to do so, and I was finished on December 5, 1954. Within a week I submitted it to Doubleday and on August 4, 1955, I received an advance copy of the book.

Here, then, is the original novelette from which the novel was prepared.

The End of Eternity

1.

The section of Eternity given over to the 575th Century is matter-oriented. The energy vortices of the 300's are gone; the field dynamics of the 600's have not yet come. In all the twenty-millennial range from the former to the latter, matter is used for everything from walls to frying pans. Nor have all the recorded changes in Reality affected that. On the whole, in all Eternity, energy-orientation has always been the exception.

That is not to say that Brinsley Sheridan Cooper (28th Century), born in another matter-oriented Time, felt himself at home when he moved into the ante-room that stretched out to a transparent door, and then back and back indefinitely through all of the 575th. After all, there are fashions in matter too. To an "energetic," matter tends to be matter, nothing more. All of it is gross, heavy, and barbarous. To a "matric," however, there is wood, metal (subdivisions, heavy and light), plastic, silicates, concrete, and leather in innumerable varieties and combinations.

To Cooper, whose notion of a world was built about structures of light-metal alloys, the sight of an ocean

of glass and porcelain wherever he looked (the more
impressive because there was no sight, at the moment,
of anything human), had him openmouthed.

He stayed so until a harsh voice, heavy with forty-
millennial accent, said, "Check in, damn you."

Cooper blinked. "Sorry, sir, but I don't think—" In
his confusion, he used his own 28th-Century dialect.

The cragginess of the other's expression softened at
the sound of it and the aquiline nose beneath heavy,
grizzled eyebrows grew somehow less formidable. The
door behind him, through which he had entered, still
swung its heavy glass softly upon one lengthwise field
hinge, a concession to energetics not uncommon in a
matter-oriented Time.

He reached out a large hand to steady the door and
said, "Sorry, son. I thought you were a local out of
Time."

"No, sir," said Cooper, with an attempt at crisp-
ness. "I'm B.S. Cooper, 28th. My credentials." He
had shifted now to the sixty-millennial tongue he had
been practicing for days.

He passed the Personal Capsule to the other, who
did not look at the exposed flimsy but put it to one
side and laughed.

"My apologies," he said. "We're expecting a local
man to take over the reception desk and I jumped at
conclusions. We're having trouble finding a new man,
and we were through with the old one just a little
sooner than we expected. You know how it is."

He said it with a blasé ease that Cooper tried to
imitate in his nod. After all, the local people were
experimental and observational subjects in addition to
whatever jobs they held. He would have to get used to
that.

The other talked on. "You always have to keep an
eye on the locals. They never really understand about
Eternity; never get it through their heads that you
can't treat Time like a football. They loaf around
seconds at a time before checking in. If they have to
check out, they do so, then go to the washroom on *this*

side of the curtain. When they get back into Time, they find themselves on the wrong side of a two-minute hole, and there's hell to pay for it from the Computers. —When are you from?''

"Twenty-eighth." Then, eagerly, "You from anywhen around then?''

"I'm 413th. What's your business here, son?''

Cooper's face lengthened. He might have been able to guess the man's Time by his accent, but where is the Eternal who, on first assignment to a new sector of Eternity, can resist calling out, "Anyone here from the old 123rd?'' or whenever his Hometime is. Or if he is too young and timid, or too old and dignified, to call it aloud, he can at least think it. There is something about sharing a common set of social tropisms and prejudices that not all the washing and training of cub school can quite remove. And the most unpalatable person, if he is dressed in a costume you recognize as the *right* costume, the one that deep in your heart you will cherish all your life as the *only* right costume, becomes a prince and a companion to be cherished.

But 413 was only a number to Cooper. At the moment, he could remember nothing more in connection with it than that it was part of a millennium marked by underpopulation and that it exported seedling trees to the various deforested centuries. It did so in fair quantities, too, since seedlings weren't as sensitive with respect to Reality as were anti-viral serums, human embryos, or vortex relays.

Cooper said, "I'm to see Laban Twissell." He couldn't help raising his voice a bit as he said that.

The other's eyebrows lifted and he picked up the Personal Capsule he had disregarded and now looked at it searchingly. "Senior Computer Twissell?''

"That's right.''

"Well, take a seat, Cooper, and I'll get in touch with him. My name is Nero Attrell, by the way.'' The earlier touch of condescension was gone from his voice.

Cooper sat down and his lips all but quivered with suppressed delight. He was here on Senior Computer

Laban Twissell's request, and Twissell was a member of the Allwhen Council and was considered throughout Eternity as the greatest Computer of them all.

And it was Twissell who had asked that Cooper be assigned to him. He had not given any reasons for it, and yet Cooper was convinced he knew the reason. He had told no one of his conviction, not even Genro Manfield, his instructor and the man whom above all in his short life so far he respected.

After all, it had become obvious to himself for a long time now that he was being groomed for a special mission. He had caught his first glimpse of what that mission must be more than a physioyear ago. (One had to learn, almost at the beginning of one's schooling, the difference between years, which did not exist in Eternity, and physioyears, which were merely the measure of the aging of the human body.)

It had come about in this way. There were five "cubs" in the 28th-Century class, two from the second decade and one each from the fifth, seventh, and ninth decades. He had himself been the ninth-decade student, having been born in 2784 and taken into school in 2798. If he had stayed in Time, he would be 29th Century now by seven years; but they always counted Century from the moment you left Time and entered training. He'd be 28th to the day he died. (In his mind, he changed the phrase to "*till* I die." What was the use of speaking of "days" in Eternity, though, of course, everyone did it. They said "yesterday" and "maybe next year" just as though it meant something.)

But of the five cubs, he alone specialized. He was hastened through computer mathematics as fast as he could be driven, and except for that, all effort else was devoted to Primitive history. He complained once. The others, he pointed out, were receiving well-rounded courses.

Instructor Manfield had rubbed his brown hair into a mat of confusion and had said, "It's direct orders from the Council, son." (People always had a tendency to call Cooper "son," perhaps because his light hair and eyes and his small-chinned face made him look conspicuously younger than his years.) "I don't know why."

There was nothing for it but to go back to their browsing over old periodicals (print on paper from the days before film grew fashionable) until lives and deeds and names long dead were living things to both of them.

A physioyear before he had read one of Computer Twissell's research papers as an exercise in mathematics ("Analyze Twissell's results in terms of temporal tensors"), and that led him through an independent search into other papers by Twissell, and from that he was led into certain byways of speculation concerning which he dared not speak even to Manfield.

But he thought he knew then what was happening to him and why, and he waited, more or less impatiently, for the call from Twissell. It had come.

Just before he left, he had one last talk with Manfield, and he had been unable to forebear hinting. Surely Manfield must know of this, and Cooper wanted corroboration of his thoughts. He wanted it badly.

"What would he be wanting me for, sir?" he asked. "I've been specializing in Primitive history."

"I know. I know." Manfield smiled at him. "I'm afraid that in the years we've spent on it, I've grown over-interested. I'll probably be continuing in the field by myself after you're gone."

Cooper knew what he meant. The newsmagazines of the Primitive centuries, with their chronicles of uncontrolled blood, crime, and passion, stamped indelibly into a Reality that could not be altered, made fascinating reading. He would miss the hours he and Manfield had spent on them together.

Cooper edged a little closer to what he was sure was the truth. "But I want to work on the Primitive centuries. I want to do original research on them. Working in the 500's would not be exactly what I wanted."

Now if Manfield knew, surely he could not resist hinting just a little. But either Manfield did not know,

or he was too wise to fall into traps, or else—and this
Cooper bitterly rejected—Cooper's speculations were
all wrong.

Manfield said, "There'll always be spare time in
which you can engage in a hobby, son."

He smiled again, but even his smiles seemed to have
an edge of sorrow behind them. His students, who
uniformly loved him, knew nothing of his past. He
never spoke of it, even to Cooper, who had spent the
most time with him. Somehow the knowledge that he
was born in the forward millennia ("the upwhens," as
the common phrase had it) had percolated down to
the students, and they accepted that without too keen
a search for evidence. It was said that he had been a
Computer once, an outstanding mathematician, a good
prospect for the Allwhen Council, and that he had
thrown it all over to become an instructor of cubs in
the far downwhen centuries.

"How do you feel?" asked Manfield.

"A little scared. A little excited," said Cooper truthfully. "I've never been anywhen, you know, except for
that field trip to the 40th, and that was only a two-day
report on municipal life under decentralized conditions."

What he did not add was that it was only by dint of
much begging that he had been allowed to go, although it was basic stuff for the rest of the class.

And the next morning Brinsley Sheridan Cooper
had taken a small one-man kettle and passed, alone,
through the corridors of Eternity. The kettle didn't
pass through space in the usual sense of the word, and
of course it didn't pass through Time, since Eternity
short-circuited all of Time from the 28th Century (the
first Century of Eternity, a fact that was the 28th's
greatest and proudest claim to fame) to the unplumbable
entropy-death ahead.

But Father Time! the kettle went through or over or
along *something*. Cooper was still untrained enough,
still young enough, to wonder what that something
was.

His wondering didn't help him. Whatever it was, it

remained unknown to him, but it passed, and then there was a neat little sign that said 575th in the local numeration system as well as in Atemporal Standard. (There was even an Atemporal Standard Tongue that somehow rarely got used outside official reports. Local dialects were more satisfying, it seemed, and Manfield used to explain that by calling it an unconscious expression of the "return-to-Time" drive.)

In a few moments now Cooper would actually meet Twissell. Twissell! The oldest living Senior Computer; the man who had authorized more quantum changes in Reality than any Senior Computer who had ever lived; the man who was the greatest authority on Harvey Mallon, the 24th-Century Primitive who had made Eternity possible.

It was Harvey Mallon who was the key to his own—

The voice of Attrell broke into his reveries. "Senior Computer Twissell will be ready for you soon, son."

"Thank you, sir." Cooper was never offended by the word "son." If he and Attrell existed in Time, he would be some forty thousand years Attrell's senior. He might be Attrell's great-great-great-many-times-great-grandfather. But this wasn't Time; this was Eternity. Here the word "son" meant nothing. Really nothing, since no Eternal might even have a son. All Eternals must be born in Time of Timed parents. Only in that way could it remain certain that Eternals would retain the spiritual connection with mankind that was so necessary for their work. Let Eternals have children of their own, Eternal from birth, and dynasties would be formed, divorced from Earth. From the wise directors and molders of humanity, the Eternals would become its tyrants.

(Cooper was still young enough, still school-fresh enough to feel no pang of self-consciousness at being idealistic.)

Attrell said, "Would you like to look over the Century while you're waiting?"

"Yes!" said Cooper, suddenly grinning. "Can that be arranged?"

"No trouble. They've got a trick viewscope herewhen. They use it clear into the 600's, and then they switch to field-focus. There's one in the next lab that I can hook up for you."

"Well, thanks!"

2.

Nero Attrell cast a cautious glance at the youngster at his side. He had been twenty physioyears an Eternal, and he was not given to pampering cubs who swam in on their first missions through seas of worldsaviorism.

But this one, somehow, must be different. Twissell had sent for him. Now Twissell was a hard man to know, but Nero Attrell had known the old gentleman for a sufficient percentage of his own lifetime to know when the man was excited.

And Twissell was excited.

He had twittered softly into Attrell's ear over the communo only a moment ago, "Yes, I have been expecting the young man. I will be ready soon. I will rush. Itis only a quantum change I must make sure of first."

The excitement was obvious. It lay in the word "rush."

Twissell never rushed for others. He had once made a committee of the Allwhen Council wait five hours, and had never bothered to explain. But now he was going to rush for a thin, pale cub who was overwhelmed at finding himself in an otherwhen so long from home.

The whole thing invested this newcomer, Cooper, with a strange interest, and Attrell found himself nursing the beginnings of friendship for the boy.

It did not take Attrell long to hook up the viewscope. The 575th was neat and logical in its technics. The 'scope seemed just a glass-topped table, but then suddenly the glass was not there and a city was, looking like an excellent photograph in trimensional color. Attrell

smiled slowly when a small exclamation forced itself
out of Cooper. He had expected it. It always came
when an unwary spectator first noticed that there was
motion within the "photograph."

The cub leaned over the 'scope, trying to crowd it all
into his eyes. Then he stepped away, frowning.

"If you want a closer view," said Attrell, "I'll show
you how the controls work. They're quite simple."

The cub shook his head. "It's all right. I— It isn't so
different, is it? Somehow I thought it would be
different."

"Different from when?"

"From—from the 28th. From home, you know."

"Should it be?"

"Well, it's fifty thousand years in the fut—uh—fifty
thousand years upwhen."

Attrell smiled tolerantly. "You know," he said, "I
don't think there's a cub ever invented who hasn't had
the same feeling when he first looked over the Time
he was first assigned to. Things are never any different, somehow."

"You don't really mean that, do you, Mr. Attrell?"

"Well, I'm exaggerating a little, maybe. Look, do
you mind if I explain something to you?"

"I'd appreciate it, Mr. Attrell."

Well, thought Attrell, he's polite. Attrell had been
told often enough (once even by Twissell) that he was
a man from the underpopulated centuries, and that
therefore he was bound to be unhappy in the company
of strangers. That might be, yet he felt himself warming to the kid.

He said gently, "All right, then, this is what I want
to explain. You're going to find out the human pattern
of history isn't a line; it's an irregular sine curve.
Progress doesn't continue in a single curve so that all
times are different from yours. A given era is just as
likely to be similar to your own as different."

"I've been taught that."

"You've been taught that, yes. But a fellow from
the 28th never really believes it till he sees it. Don't

get me wrong; I've got nothing against the 28th, but you've got to admit that the 28th is only the first full century of Eternity. Right?"

"True enough."

"And the 28th is always very conscious of Primitive times; the centuries before Eternity begins."

"Yes. Primitive history is my field of specialization, in fact."

"Then there you are. The last millennium of Primitive times was a kind of straight-line development with a steadily developing technology. Naturally, you get into the habit of thinking that such a straight line will continue. I don't have to tell a major in Primitive history that sometimes the human race doesn't progress, if such a word has meaning; sometimes it retrogresses."

"It's true," said Cooper, with a prim pursing of his lips, "that for a millennium after the first century there was technological decline and no real recovery of the standards of the half millennium before the first century till—"

Attrell, who had been listening to the faintly pompous manner in which Cooper was trotting out his new-painted knowledge, suffered a sudden spasm of suspicion. Was *he* the one being made sport of?

He said, "The half millennium *before* the first century?"

"Yes. Honestly. The first century wasn't the first."

"They just call it the first century for no reason?"

"It's a little complicated. Look, it's like this—"

"Well, never mind." Attrell decided that the boy was serious, and he felt no desire to go into the paradoxes of Time. He said, "It's your specialty, so I'll take your word for it. I majored in lifeplots myself. The point I'm trying to make is this: People go in circles. They may be far upwhen or downwhen, and still be a lot like you. Or they might be just nextwhen, and quite different. Don't let the differentness get you either. What may look like decadence or barbarity to you may be a finding of new and better values to other people. Are you acquainted with the 413th?"

Against his will, Attrell found a defensiveness, almost a belligerence, rising in him at the thought of his homewhen.

Cooper shook his head. "Not in any detail."

"We've only got a hundred million people in it. It's a good Time." Suddenly he was drenched in homesickness. It had been a long time since he had visited the 410's and 20's. He could smell the cold, piney air and see the blue of the glaciers against the horizon. He could almost feel the clear space, the openness of the world.

Gloomily he said, "I guess your 28th is crowded up."

"Quite a bit. Five billion."

"So's this 575th. So's almost everywhen. In my time, there was a small glacial period, you know. The forests took over, the cities broke up into smaller, friendlier aggregations. We like it, you know, but every time there's a quantum change, the underpopulated eras squeeze in. That's what the Allwhen Council calls them, 'the underpopulated eras.' In the other glacial eras they use underground cities, or develop solar energy. Most of them keep the population high.

"Now, I think underpopulation is fine. I don't consider it underpopulation; I consider it sensible population. People from mostwhen are horrified. So there you are."

Attrell was getting emotional, and of course as he felt that, he bit his lips together and there was a sudden silence that lasted uncomfortably.

Finally Cooper said, "When did Computer Twissell say he'd see me?"

"You can't tell about Twissell," said Attrell. Then, unable to resist the urge, he asked, "I suppose you're on the Harvey Mallon project."

It amused Attrell to see the alarm spring into the youngster's eyes. It also confirmed a suspicion.

Cooper said, "What Harvey Mallon project? I know nothing about that."

"If you don't, you will. It's all Twissell is interested in. He holds seminars every once in a while, and Harvey Mallons us to death. Everything he does has something to do with Mallon."

And a gentle voice said, "And why not, Associate Plotter?" with the tiniest of emphasis upon Attrell's title.

Attrell covered his surprise. He had not heard Twissell enter. "No reason at all, Senior Computer."

Cooper stiffened. His fair cheeks flushed, his thin features seemed sharper than ever. He stammered, "Senior Computer Twissell?"

Attrell watched Cooper's reactions, and a corner of his mouth trembled at the edge of a twitch. He had a good notion of Cooper's feelings. He had seen a similar look, half disbelief and half disappointment, in the eyes of a dozen cubs when they caught their first sight of Eternity's great man.

But then, when a man's reputation is colossal and his name magic, it is hard to be faced with the physical reality of a stooped figure, a small, round face, a retreating, bald-smooth forehead, little eyes that screwed up into a thousand wrinkles, an ingratiating smile, and a cigarette. The cigarette above all.

Cooper looked as though it were the first cigarette he had ever seen. He flinched visibly as a puff of smoke reached him.

"Are you my boy? Are you my youngster?" Twissell approached Cooper, looking up into his face, as though trying to peer through the cigarette-manufactured haze, and speaking in a horribly accented three-millennial dialect.

Cooper said, "I am Brinsley Sheridan Cooper, sir, on assignment and awaiting orders." He spoke a painstakingly slow, school-fresh sixty-millennial.

"Oh, formalities!" The Senior Computer waved the hand with the cigarette in it and feathery ash was flicked to the polished floor. "And don't bother with sixty-millennial. I have studied your own language much. I speak it wonderfully good. —So now tell me, what is wrong with being interested in Harvey Mallon, Associate Plotter Attrell?"

Attrell recognized it for the rhetorical question it was, and didn't trust himself in any case to speak three-millennial with fluency, so he maintained a strategic silence.

Twissell said, "Isn't he worth study? He's a Primitive, so that he cannot be reached in person by kettle. Yet he invented the Temporal Field in 2354, and that made the kettles possible four hundred years later. He laid the groundwork for Eternity, and yet we don't even know for certain when he was born or when he died. Let us ask my youngster." (He pronounced it "yunkstarr," with the accent on the second syllable, and even to Attrell's inexpert ears that sounded like a vile perversion of what the word ought to be.)

The Senior Computer turned to the cub. "Do *you* know anything about Harvey Mallon? You are nearer his time. You studied the Primitives."

Cooper said, "His life is poorly documented, sir."

Twissell smiled. "All you can say, my boy?" The cigarette between his fingers had burned itself into a stub and a new one appeared in its place, lighted. The exchange was made with the unobtrusive ease of a lifetime's practice, but to Attrell it seemed, as it always did, like a gratuitous piece of legerdemain.

Twissell said to Cooper, "I would offer you a cigarette, but I know you don't smoke. Hardly nowhen in Eternity is smoking smiled upon. In the 72nd only, they make good cigarettes, and mine are specially imported from there. It is all very sad. Last week I was stuck in the 123rd for two days. No smoking. They don't mind incest in the 123rd, but they would have fainted like old ladies if I had taken out a cigarette. Sometimes I think I should arrange a quantum change and wipe out all the no-smoking taboos in all Eternity, but every time I try to figure one out, I find it makes for wars in the 58th or a slave society in the 1000th. Always something."

Without any transition in emphasis he went on to say, "Would you like to witness a quantum change, boy? I've arranged it for you." He seized the cub's elbow and led him out.

Attrell's eyes followed them gravely. He had never seen Twissell act so queerly, talk so much.

He shrugged. He wasn't going to find out, so why puzzle? He went back to his office and sat down to chart lives in the precise way he had been employing for physioyears. In his time he had plotted the alternate life-paths (including all those with a probability higher than 0.01) of 572 individuals in those centuries that lacked decent cancer treatment of any sort. That included the 27th to the 35th inclusive, which had not managed to develop a workable gene technology, and parts of the rather outré 52nd and 53rd, which had reacted violently to physical medicine (including the use of psychic probes and other physical aids to psychoanalysis) by reverting to a brand of psychiatry that bordered strongly on faith healing.

Of all the 572 whose life-paths he had plotted, exactly 17 had benefited as a result. Or at least, extension of the lifetimes of 17 had been found to involve no quantum changes of negative value, and their premature deaths by cancer had been averted. The treatment was expensive, but still the government officials in those centuries clamored for more; more anti-cancer serums shipped across time at any expense, more lives to be saved.

Attrell knew well that rather than more, fewer would be saved. It was Twissell's favorite thesis; with each quantum change for the benefit of mankind, the next quantum change would grow harder to find. Never impossible; but always harder.

Attrell sighed. Would the day come when no lifetime in all of Time could be altered? When human history would finally follow the ideal path?

The Allwhen Council said no. In an infinite number

of paths, there could be no one ideal. It could only be approached asymptotically. Forever approached. Never reached.

He bent over the lifetime of Lyman Hugh Shapur of the 29th Century, and retraced the queer double fork he had not yet quite succeeded in interpreting. Let's see now—

3.

Anders Horemm, native of the 95th Century (stiffly restrictive of atomic power, faintly rustic, fond of natural wood as a structural material, exporters of certain types of distilled potables to nearly everywhen, and importers of clover seed), took the kettle to the 2456th Century.

His sallow face, with its long cheeks and thin lips, was calm. He showed no nervousness in the face of a delicate job that would not bear botching. It never occurred to him that he could possibly botch a quantum change. So far, his self-confidence had not been misplaced.

Horemm had started his career in Eternity as an Observer. While Computers remained in the rarefied atmosphere of their mathematical labors, and Life-Plotters delved into the wearily endless jungle of infinite possibility, and Socials spun their fragile theories concerning men and things, the Observer went steadily out into Time and brought back the raw data that fed them all.

For this the Observer gets little credit. The literature of Eternity rings with applause for the brilliancies of Computing, the delicacies of Plotting, the intelligence of Socializing, but little is said of the Observer who collects the facts, and less still of the Technician, whose hand pulls the string that changes the lives of billions.

Horemm had been a Technician for five years now. For most of that time he had worked directly with Twissell. Twissell told him what he must do, and for that Twissell was honored. Horemm did as Twissell told him, and for that Horemm was disliked. It was as though the Eternals, unable to avoid the collective guilt involved in playing God with the lives of generations, compromised by placing upon the Technician's shoulders the load of that guilt.

In his observations of those societies that practiced capital punishment, Horemm had noticed the same social distinction between the respected judge who ordered execution done, and the civil servant who carried out the order at the cost of social ostracism.

Horemm felt no bitterness concerning this. He was dourly glad to be a Technician working for Twissell. There was nothing for which he would have changed his position.

Above all else, he was devoutly pleased to be working on what Twissell called the "Mallon mystery." It was Horemm himself who had penetrated eras on errands the results of which had been entered in no public record books. It was he himself who had followed lives that Twissell would not trust to professional Plotters. It was he himself who had first located Brinsley Sheridan Cooper, and his sluggish blood had caught fire when he learned that here at last was he for whom Twissell had been seeking. He, personally, had gone downwhen (as far back in Cooper's life as Twissell had dared reach) to get Cooper first into cub school, then into the proper sort of specialized training. Then, when the minimum of training had passed, it was Horemm who had sent the message in Twissell's name, ordering Cooper to the 575th.

It was all well. If Horemm were a man given to smiling, he would have smiled now. In the hyper-isolation of a kettle passing up the corridors of the endless centuries, he might even have laughed aloud. But he felt only the cold satisfaction of a physiodecade of painstaking work approaching its climax as he watched the centuries vanish through and beyond his kettle.

Then the kettle came to its smooth, automatic halt,

and Reality solidified out of the vague mists that had surrounded it.

Horemm did not even pause to note the novel facets that any century must possess to new eyes, even on the first and most trivial acquaintance. He was too old a hand to waste his time on any observations not immediately useful.

In any case, he was only in that section of Eternity given over to the 2456th, and not in the Time itself. The barrier that separated Eternity from Time was dark with the darkness of primeval chaos, and its velvety non-light was characteristically speckled with the flitting points of light that mirrored sub-microscopic imperfections of the fabric that could not be eradicated while the Uncertainty Principle existed.

Horemm adjusted the position of the barrier quietly, and then stepped through into the exact second of Time indicated by Spatio-temporal Analysis to be optimal for his purpose. The barrier flamed up into unfelt brilliance as mass traveled across it, moving from Eternity into Time.

A million tons of matter disintegrated each second to feed the barriers that dotted Eternity, but energy was no problem. Twenty billions of years upwhen blazed the final Nova that was once Sol, and a million sunpower of energy was there for the taking.

That at least was constant. No conceivable change of Reality, no possible alteration in the petty human affairs of Time, could ever alter the coming of that Nova.

Horemm found himself in an engine room. It was empty, and it would stay empty for two hours and thirty-six minutes under the present Reality; for two minutes longer under the Reality to come. His own presence here, as careful calculation showed, was neutral. While no entrance into Time, however casual, could fail to impose a finite distortion on the fabric of Reality, not all distortions reached the minimum level required to make an actual quantum change.

What Horemm did next was apparently even more

trivial than the mere fact of his presence. He lifted a
small container from its position on a shelf to an
empty spot in the shelf below.

Having done that, he reentered Eternity in a way
that seemed to him as prosaic as passage through any
door might be. To an observer pinned in Time, it
would seem that he had disappeared.

The small container stayed where he put it. It played
no immediate role in world history. A man's hand
reached for it and did not find it. A search revealed it
half an hour later, but in the interim a force-field had
blanked out and a man's temper had been lost. A
decision that would have remained unmade in a previous Reality was now made in anger. A meeting did
not take place; a man who would have died, lived a
year longer; and one who would have lived a day
longer, died a day sooner.

The ripples spread wider.

From the moment that container had been shifted,
through all of Time thereafter, a new Reality existed.
In some centuries the change was extreme, with whole
cultures subtly altered. In some centuries the change
was slight. Nowhere was it zero.

But of course, no human being in Time could ever
possibly be aware of any change having taken place.
And though millions of men did not live who, but for
Horemm's touch, would have, the Eternals understood, and except for irrational instinct, none could
consider Horemm a murderer.

Except, of course, Horemm himself.

4.

Laban Twissell had been a fixture in Eternity for so
long that few living could remember an Eternity without him. It was freely stated that he had been immersed in the problems of mankind for so long that he
had forgotten the exact number of the Century of his
birth. It was also said that at an early age his heart had
atrophied and that a hand computer similar to the

model he carried always in his trouser pocket had taken its place.

Twissell did nothing to deny these rumors. In fact, he rather believed them himself. It would have mortified him if he were told that any of his inner excitement was visible; that his handcomputer heart might be thumping with indecent haste, as though it were only muscle and valves after all.

He was *looking* at Brinsley Sheridan Cooper, actually looking at him. And none knew, outside himself and that odd fish, Horemm, that this undistinguished, nervous youth was—everything.

They were climbing into the kettle. Its sides were perfectly round and it fit snugly inside the vertical shaft. Twissell set the controls with one hand; the other, of course, manipulated his cigarette. There was the little stir, not spin, not motion, that meant the kettle was moving through Eternity.

He smiled at Cooper. "Are you troubled, youngster?"

Cooper's eyes followed the passing of the spinning numbers. "To when are we going, sir?"

Twissell said, "Two-seven-eight-one. Not far. A walk. A little walk."

"The 2781st?"

"You've never been so far?"

"Until today, Computer Twissell, I'd never been further upwhen than the 40th."

"So? Are you afraid?"

Cooper stirred in his seat. "It's over two hundred thousand years from home."

"An Eternal has no home. You should learn that, boy," said Twissell softly.

The numbers came and went, increasing. Cooper said, "How far upwhen have you ever gone, sir?"

"Two hundred thousand centuries, I think. More or less. It's not worthwhile going any further, except for the engineers who tap Nova Sol. About then, the two hundred thousandth, humanity leaves Earth."

The old Computer studied the other's uneasy face. "They didn't teach you that in school, I suppose?"

"I was very specialized in the other direction, sir," Cooper replied, weighing his words.

But Twissell let them lie there. He said, "But Man does leave this old world, eventually."

"Why?"

"It's not known exactly. Entry into Time stops some centuries before the departure. Some say it's evolution; men become something other than men. Some say it's science; men finally learn the secret of the hyper-space drive and can reach the stars."

"There's no reason they should leave Earth, though."

Twissell said, "Some people think they leave to escape us and our eternal fiddling with Reality."

"Can't we make them stay?"

"Why should we? Is there not enough work in our two hundred thousand centuries of Eternity?"

"What happens after they leave?"

"Nothing. Eternity goes on without mankind unfil the Sun blows up, and then it goes on without the Sun until entropy is maximum and all the stars are dead, and then it just goes on. There is no end to Eternity."

The numbers came to a halt and Twissell led the way into an anteroom, mirror-lined.

"Molecular films fashionable here," said Twissell with distaste. "Pseudo-liquids."

He led Cooper past respectful Eternals to whom he paid no attention and marched into a small observation room.

Cooper stared at his own reflection, duplicated with disconcerting frequency. He said, "Is *everything* mirrors?"

"Just about. A posturing generation. They can adjust to less reflection, though." With a sweep of his hand over unobtrusive controls, he toned the mirrors down to a slate-gray diffuseness in which he and Cooper were the barest shadows.

He sat down and said, "We have yet a small wait."

The bare chair frame grew upholstery as his body approached it, a smooth red upholstery shaped to fit Twissell's anatomy.

Cooper sat down cautiously, and upholstery grew beneath him also.

Twissell's withered hand cupped a contact, and the nearer wall melted into glassiness. Figures and objects sharpened.

Cooper gasped. "What is it, sir?"

"A spaceport. Spaceships leave from here and move through the solar system along lines of electro-gravitic force. Quite useless."

"But it's beautiful."

"Nothing is beautiful if it is bought at the price of misery. This is an unhappy century, and the last few quantum changes have tended to make it unhappier. Now, finally, something must be done. The poor creatures go to Mars, but there isn't anything on Mars. There never was. There never will be. On Earth, they turn to drugs. The 2781st has the highest incidence of drug addiction in Eternity."

"They must be awfully advanced technologically."

"You're 28th. Also a technological Century, so you're impressed. Listen, child, do you know how many times space-travel is developed along the Centuries? Twenty-seven times! It never lasts more than a millennium or two. People get tired. They come back home. The colonies die out. Then another four or five millennia, or forty or fifty, and they try again. When I first came to Eternity, there were thirty-four space-travel periods."

"Are the computers quanting space-travel out of Reality?"

"Not at all. Why should we? There was a time when there were only fourteen space-travel periods, and then it moved up again. We of Eternity just improve Reality. Where improvement leads, we follow. One time it may wipe out space-travel here; the next it may restore it there."

Cooper watched the shining green metal of the hangars and the brilliant gleam of the steel ships, lifting silently and smoothly on the mass-free lines of force that bind the planets. Twissell watched Cooper, rather than the scene, and let smoke rise smoothly and undisturbed from his cigarette.

Cooper said tremulously, "Out there, it's so far from homewhen." He added suddenly, "My mother is dead, out there, for over a quarter of a million years."

Twissell glanced at the boy sharply and said, "Your mother exists?"

Cooper shrugged and said in a muffled voice, "I don't know. Quantum changes hardly ever come that near the beginning of Eternity. Maybe she does. After I came to Eternity, though, Manfield told me never to check."

"Manfield was quite right. You're a foolish lad even to think of such things."

"I'm sorry, sir."

"Well, you're forgiven. Watch, now! Three centuries downwhen, Horemm is displacing the mezolite crystals. The moment in physiotime is upon us, eh?"

Cooper cried out sharply, "The spaceport!"

The shininess was gone; the buildings shrank. A spaceship rusted. Motion died.

"Is this what you expected, sir?" asked Cooper.

"Quite. Space-travel decayed a century sooner than otherwise. But no drugs. Happier people. Improvements in other areas you know nothing about."

Unconsciously, Twissell had slipped into his own dialect. He caught that and reverted back to Cooper's tongue, and his irritation at the slip sharpened his words.

"Idiot! Do you cry over metal? Don't you care about people? I warn you, if you place matter over man, you are not fit for Eternity."

Then, with instant contrition, his tone changed radically. "No, no, Cooper, I scold you for something you cannot help. Come with me now. I just wanted you to see this to give you insight, so that you might understand more. But now, come. More important business lies ahead of us; the most important business in all Eternity."

5.

Anders Horemm was returning by kettle from the 2456th.

The anteroom of the 2456th, through which he had passed in going from kettle to Time and from Time to kettle, had been glaringly and obviously empty. The Eternals of that section of Eternity knew that a Technician was at work, and they preferred neither to see him nor to speak to him.

In his own chill way, Horemm understood the reasons. None of the Eternals of that section were natives of the 2456th. Naturally! One of the prime rules of Eternity was that no man might be associated officially with his own homewhen. The possibilities of corruption if that rule didn't exist were too apparent to discuss. Still, the passage of a Technician through a barrier would remind all men sharply that their own homewhen might suffer in the next quantum change. And though all Eternals' minds were educated to know that, if so, it was inevitable and even desirable, hearts (even of Eternals) are not always amenable to education.

Unless, of course, it was the heart of such a man as himself, the Technician thought, and frowned as he thought so. Many a time he had been held up to cubs as an example. Devotion to duty and consciousness of a mission that transcended any personal considerations were all that should go into the makeup of an Eternal, it was said.

Horemm had once lived earnestly by that rule, in the days when he was a simple Observer, slithering out of Eternity to collect data, quietly, unobtrusively, efficiently. Whenever possible he used the homes of Timed employees of Eternity as a base. When it was inexpedient to do so, he stayed at hotels, if the spatiotemporal charts allowed; slept under hedges if they insisted.

Always, at every penetration, the charts were most meticulous as to where he might go and when, what he might and might not do. Always, with an efficiency

that now made him Twissell's prized Technician, he
invaded no forbidden areas of people, space, or time.
At no time in his career had the fabric of Reality
tottered because he had passed the bounds.

What he had just done was an example. His deed
had to be pinpointed in space-time for optimal results.
It was the equivalent of the surgeon's sure cut, the
engineer's deft twist.

It was he who supplied the MNC (no Eternal thought
of the "Minimum Necessary Cause" as anything but
MNC), using his own method after the Computer had
pointed out the general nature of the MNC required.
It was Twissell, three Centuries later in Time, who
observed the MSR (Maximum Significant Result, they
taught you to say in school).

Typical! The Technician instituted the little disgraceful cause. The Computer watched the large honorable
result.

It didn't matter. Nothing mattered but the great
work that lay immediately ahead, now that the cub,
Cooper, had come.

He shuddered very slightly. The thought had come
to him, unwanted, of his first physioyear in the 482nd.

He did not know what the era was like now. He
avoided reading about it. He had avoided assignments
near it. But he remembered so clearly how it had been
when he finished school and received his first assignment in Eternity.

Observer in the 482nd and neighboring Centuries.

Observer! Objective and cold! Incapable of seeing
anything other than it was!

Observer! The man whose job was never done, since
every quantum change more or less voided all observational data on the centuries involved.

He had brought back his first report on the 482nd
and made certain that he remained objective and cold.
He made certain that none of his inner disapproval
showed. It was an era without ethics or principles, as
he was accustomed to think of such. It was hedonistic,
materialistic, more than a little matriarchal. It was the

only era in which ectogenic birth flourished, and at its peak 40 percent of its women gave eventual birth by merely contributing a fertilized ovum to the ovaria. Marriage was made and unmade by mutual consent, and was considered a purely emotional arrangement. Union for the sake of childbearing was, of course, divorced from the merely social functions of marriage, and was decided on by purely eugenic principles.

In a hundred other ways Horemm thought the society sick, and hungered for a quantum change. His jaw tightened with thrilling anticipation as he thought of the millions of pleasure-seeking women (the men were of no account, really) who would find themselves true, pure-hearted mothers in another Reality, with all the memories that belonged with it, unable to tell, dream, or fancy that they had ever been anything else. Millions living would, in a moment, never have lived, and other millions would come into existence convinced as a matter of course that they possessed ancestors and childhoods. And in *their* Reality, that would be true.

But his reports showed none of his feeling, and, he knew, must not. It was not until Noÿs Lambent first entered his sector of Eternity as Computer Hobbe Finge's secretary that his disapproval of the era and all its work first broke surface.

Horemm viewed all Timed employees with suspicion. Ideally, he thought, none but Eternals should ever be found within Eternity. The presence of ordinary Timed individuals made necessary a thousand precautions. But naturally, the Computers always insisted there were a thousand reasons for their use.

Noÿs Lambent, however, was past ten thousand reasons—or so it seemed to Horemm.

After two days, he walked determinedly into the office of Hobbe Finge, Associate Computer. (Finge was dead now; a plump and smiling nearsighted man from an energy-centered Century somewhere in the 600's, who always seemed surprised to find himself sitting on something made of mere flimsy matter and who treaded cautiously on the flooring for fear it would break under his weight.)

Horemm made his point instantly. "Computer Finge, I protest the hiring of Miss Lambent."

"Ah, Horemm." Finge looked up, smiling. "Sit down. Sit down. You find Miss Lambent incompetent, unsuitable—"

"I cannot say whether she is incompetent or not," said Horemm sharply. "I have not made use of her services, nor do I intend to. She is your secretary. But she is certainly unsuitable."

It was not politic to speak so to a superior, but Horemm in his youth had been an idealist about Eternity and he felt it necessary to make his protest at any cost.

Finge stared at him distantly as though his Computer's mind were weighing abstractions beyond the reach of an ordinary Eternal. "In what way is she unsuitable, Horemm?"

"I'm amazed you need ask, Computer. Her costume is most disgraceful."

"Oh, come."

"I cannot help having noticed that she wears very little above the waist." His hands moved vaguely about at chest level. "Besides that, her levity is disgusting."

"I am sure, Horemm, her clothes and attitude are part of the mores of her Time. You as an Observer should be aware of that."

"In its own surroundings, in its own cultural milieu, I would have no fault to find with her character. Here in Eternity, however, a person such as she is out of place."

Finge grinned. He actually grinned, and Horemm would have stiffened if any slack in his body had remained.

Finge said, "I hired her deliberately. She is performing an essential function. It is only temporary. Try to endure her meanwhile."

Horemm's jaw tightened. He had protested and he had been fobbed off. It would do no good to ask what the "essential function" was. A Computer never explained, certainly not to an Observer. One couldn't buck the mental aristocracy that ruled Eternity.

He turned stiffly, walked to the door. Finge's voice stopped him.

Finge said, "Observer, have you ever had a"—he hesitated, seemed to pick among words—"girlfriend?"

With painstaking and insulting accuracy Horemm quoted, "In the interest of avoiding emotional entanglements with Time, an Eternal may not marry. In the interest of avoiding emotional entanglements with family, an Eternal may not have children."

The Computer said gravely, "I didn't ask about marriage or children."

Horemm quoted further, "Temporary liaisons may be made with inhabitants of Time only after application with the Central Charting Board for an appropriate spatiotemporal chart."

"Quite true. Have you ever applied, Observer?"

"No, Computer."

"Well, perhaps you ought to, Horemm. It would give you a greater breath of view. You would become less concerned about the details of a woman's costume."

Horemm left, speechless with rage.

He worked harder than ever thereafter, and hated the era more. He ignored the offending employee, but was always aware of her presence. Somehow, without ever inquiring directly, he learned that her name was Noÿs Lambent and that she was independently wealthy, accountable to no one, an aristocrat in her time.

Why then should she wish to work in Eternity? How could she fulfill a Secretary's duties?

His suspicions of Finge were strong. Finge spoke coarsely of liaisons, even recommended such relations. Eternity had always been aware of the necessity of compromising with human appetite (to Horemm, the phrase carried a quivery repulsion), but the restrictions involved in choosing mistresses made the compromise anything but a generous one.

Among the lower groupings of Eternals there were always the rumors (half-hopeful, half-resentful) of women imported on a more or less permanent basis for the obvious reasons. Always, rumor pointed to the Computers as the benefiting group. They and only they could decide which women could be abstracted from Time without quantum change of Reality.

Such rumors remained rumors. No case had ever been proven against specific offenders, and Horemm had always dismissed such things as the vaporings of idle minds.

But now he suspected Finge. A woman like *that* his secretary? He knew other words for it.

He met the woman in a corridor one day and stood aside, eyes averted, to let her pass.

But she remained standing, looking at him. "You're Observer Horemm, aren't you?"

He nodded briefly, coldly.

"I'm told you're quite an expert on our Time."

"Will you pass or let me pass, please?"

He could not help but look at her, and she smiled at him and moved by with a slow swing of her hips that brought his chill blood tingling to his angry cheeks.

Angry against himself for reddening, at her for speaking to him, and most of all, for some obscure reason, at Finge.

Finge called him in two weeks later. On his desk were the familiar perforated flimsies which the Allwhen Council periodically sent. On appropriate scanning by Horemm's instrument, they would become the spatio-temporal chart that would send him out into Time on another mission.

Finge said, "Would you sit down, Horemm? Scan it right now."

Horemm did as he was told, stopped at midpoint, and tore the flimsies from his scanner as though they were on the point of exploding. He held them between thumb and index finger.

"Computer Finge, there is some mistake."

Finge said, "I think not. Why do you say so?"

"Surely I am not to be expected to use the home of this woman, Lambent, as base."

The Computer pursed his lips. "Such is my understanding. Ordinarily, Observer, I would expect you to carry out your mission without question. In this case, since you have gone to the extent of expressing official displeasure concerning Miss Lambent, I thought I would explain some of the aspects of the present problem."

Finge was speaking carefully, a little stiffly, and Horemm sat motionless, not looking at his superior. Make him come all the way, he thought.

Ordinarily, professional pride would have forced Horemm to disdain explanation. His not to make reply, reason why, and all the rest of it. But here he felt a certain vengefulness that suggested that just a little bending of professional honor might be well.

Horemm had complained, that was it. Finge was fearful that the complaint might go further, that the Allwhen Council might investigate the exact function of Finge's blatant secretary. Finge was forced to give Horemm this new mission, since Horemm was his best man. But if Horemm were placed too near the girl, he might find out too much.

Finge feared that. Finge would try to explain it all away in advance. Horemm, grimly amused at the prospect, was prepared to listen, but not to believe.

Finge said, "Of course, the various Centuries are aware of the existence of Eternity. They know that we supervise inter-Temporal trade, and they consider that to be our chief function, which is good. They have a dim knowledge that we are also here to prevent catastrophe from striking mankind, which is more or less correct. We supply the generations with a mass father image and a certain feeling of security, so we would want them to know about us in any case.

"There are some things, however, they must not know. Prime among them is our function in altering the path of Reality by quantum changes. It was established long ago that the insecurity arising from any knowledge that Reality could be altered at will would work to great disadvantage. So we have always bred such possible knowledge out of Reality and have never been troubled with it.

"However, there are always other undesirable beliefs about Eternity that spring up from time to time in one Century or another. Usually the dangerous beliefs are those that concentrate particularly in the ruling classes of an era, the classes that have most contact with us and that carry the important weight of what is called public opinion. This is always distressing, because in eliminating such dangerous beliefs we must induce Reality changes that often negate hard-won advances in other fields, which must then be re-won by sometimes complicated means."

Finge paused as though he expected Horemm to offer some comment or ask some question. Horemm did neither.

Finge continued. "Ever since the quantum change that last affected the 482nd seriously, the Allwhen Council has been aware of certain undesirable aspects of the new Reality here. It was nothing of a sufficiently gross nature to be apparent on extrapolations even down to the fifth order, which was as far as we could go in this case without increasing the probability error to a prohibitive degree. For that reason, we have been concentrating on new Observation here, and you have been kept busy, Horemm.

"I might say that new computing shows the focus of disturbance rests in a rather unprecedented attitude of Timed people toward Eternity. The Allwhen Council is reluctant to accept the results without direct observational confirmation.

"It was for that reason that I located a member of the aristocracy who thought it would be thrilling or exciting to work in Eternity. I kept her under close observation to see if she was suitable for our purpose—"

Horemm thought: Close observation! Yes!

Again his anger focused itself on Finge rather than upon the woman.

Finge was continuing. "By all standards, she is suitable. We will now return her to Time. Using her dwelling as a base, you will be able to study the social life of her circle, taking due heed of the precautions outlined in the chart. I'll just emphasize the point that you are observing the cultural milieu of a small and specific circle and that Miss Lambent offers an ideal tool for the purpose. Now do you understand her function here?"

To a direct question, Horemm had to answer. "I do, Computer."

"You are willing to accept the mission?"

Horemm could not resist a parting thrust. "I am an Observer with a duty. My manner of performing that duty is independent of explanations."

Horemm left with the comforting thought that while expressing himself with the high idealism to be expected of an Eternal, he had nevertheless made the point that Finge's complicated explanation (how long had it taken him to work it all out?) had left Horemm untouched.

Almost buried in that thought was another: that a new quantum change might be approaching for the 482nd, one that perhaps might wipe out the immorality of the times and install decency in its place.

Noÿs Lambent's house was fairly isolated, yet within easy reach of one of the larger cities of the Century. Horemm had memorized the map of the city, as he had memorized others. He knew its avenues and its buildings; its transport lines; its habits of life. He knew the exact portions he must observe on each of the days of his assignment, when he might make each trip, when he must remain at base.

His first conversation with Noÿs Lambent in her own Time came about as the result of her excitement when she discovered her slight temporal displacement.

She came to him breathlessly. "It's June, Observer Horemm."

He said harshly, "Do not use my title here. What if it is June?"

"But it was February when I joined," she paused archly, "*that* place, and that was only a month ago."

Horemm frowned. "What year is it now?"

"Oh, it's the same year."

"Are you sure?"

"I'm quite positive." She had a disturbing habit of standing quite close to him as they talked, and her slight lisp (a trait of the Century rather than of herself personally) gave her the sound of a young and rather helpless child. Horemm was not fooled by that. He drew away.

"Are you usually in this house during the spring?"

"No. I have a place at the Middle Sea."

(Horemm knew the region under its earlier name of Mediterranean.)

He said, "Then your friends would expect your absence during the interval, wouldn't they?"

"I see," she said thoughtfully. "You mean it would look funny if I were to come back in April."

"Exactly. We are careful about such things in Eternity." He said it proudly, as though he himself were a Senior Computer.

She said, "But then have I lost three months in my life?"

"Your movements through Time have nothing to do with your physiological age."

"Does that mean I have or I haven't?"

"You haven't."

"Why do you act so angry with me?" asked Noÿs Lambent on the second evening. Her arms and shoulders were bare and her long legs shimmered in faintly luminescent foamite.

The spatiotemporal chart confined Horemm to the house during the later hours of the day, and he ate dinner there, picking sparingly at dishes that had been entered in previous reports of his on the dietary of the times but which he had thus far refrained from eating himself. Against his will, he liked them. Against his will, he enjoyed the foaming, light green, peppermint-flavored drink that went with the meal.

He said, "I am not angry. I have no feeling for you at all." At the moment, he felt the statement to be rigidly true.

They were alone together in the house. In this era, with the female of the species economically independent and able to attain motherhood, if she so wished, without the necessity of physical child-bearing, the relationships between the sexes involved no "rules" worthy of the name. It was nothing to be remarked at if a young woman entertained male guests; she was rather an object of pity if she did not.

Horemm knew this thoroughly, and yet he felt compromised.

The meal was over; she poured him another of the tall, lightly foaming drinks. He felt a little warm and somewhat breathless, and stirred about in the soft chair to find a more comfortable position.

The girl was stretched out on her elbow on a sofa opposite. Its patterned covering sank beneath her as though avid to embrace her. She had kicked off the transparent shoes she had been wearing and her toes curled and uncurled as though they were the soft paws of a luxuriant cat.

"It was fun working for Eternity," she said, sighing, "and I waited the longest time for them to let me." She was watching him. Her dark hair had loosened at some point in the evening and fell about her neck and naked shoulders, which stood out creamily in contrast.

He didn't answer.

She murmured, "How old are you?"

That he certainly should not have answered. It was a personal question, and the answer was none of her business. He heard himself saying, "Twenty-five years." He meant physioyears, of course.

She said, "I'm only twenty-two, but you'll live and live and be young, and I'll be gone so many years."

"What are you talking about?" He rubbed his forehead to clear his mind.

She said, "You live forever. You're an Eternal."

Was it a question or a statement?

He said, "You're mad. We grow old and die like anyone else."

She said, "You can tell me." Her voice was low and cajoling. The fifty-millennial language which he had always thought harsh and unpleasant seemed euphonious after all. Or was it merely that a full stomach and the scented air had dulled his ears?

She said, "You can see all Times, visit all places. I'd love to be an Eternal. Why aren't more women Eternals?"

He couldn't trust himself to speak. What could he say? That members of Eternity were chosen with infinite care, since two conditions had to be met. First, they must be equipped for the job; second, their withdrawal from Time must have no deleterious effect upon Reality.

Reality! He must not mention that!

How many excellent prospects had been left untouched because their removal into Eternity meant the non-birth of children, the non-death of men and women, non-marriage, non-happenings, non-circumstances that would have twisted Reality in directions the Allwhen Council could not permit.

Could he tell her that women almost never qualified for Eternity because, for some reason he did not understand (Computers might, but he was merely an Observer), their abstraction from Time was over ten times more likely to distort Reality than was the abstraction of a man?

(All the thoughts jumbled together in his head until he could not tell one from another. They seemed lost and embedded in a vague buzzing that wasn't entirely unpleasant. She was closer to him now, smiling.)

He heard her voice like a drifting wind. "Oh, you Eternals! Make me one!"

He wanted, he longed to tell her: There's no fun in Eternity, lady. We work! We work to plot out all the details of everywhen from the beginning of Eternity to where Earth is empty, and we try to plot out all the infinite possibilities of all the might-have-beens and pick out a might-have-been that is better than what is and decide where in Time we can make a tiny little change to twist the is to the might-be, and we have a new is and look for a new might-be, forever and forever and forever and—

He shook his head, but the whirligig of thought went on. The drink?

The peppermint drink?

She was yet closer, her face not quite clear. He could feel her hair against his cheek, the warm, light pressure of her breath. He ought to draw away, but—strangely, strangely—he found he did not want to.

"If I were made an Eternal—" she breathed, almost in his ear, though the words sounded distantly above the beating of his heart. Her lips were moist and parted. "If I were an Eternal—"

He put out his arms clumsily, gropingly. She did not resist, but melted and coalesced with him.

It all happened dreamily, as though it were happening to someone else.

It wasn't nearly as repulsive as he had always imagined it must be.

And afterward she leaned against him with her eyes glittering and whispering, "Eternity—Eternity—" over and over.

The spatiotemporal chart had not allowed this. Yet for some reason, it was only the thought of Finge that aroused strong emotion in Horemm's breast at that moment. Nor was it guilt, either. Rather— satisfaction; even triumph.

Eventually he returned to Eternity, but before he left Noÿs, he kissed her hands and held her tightly.

He almost smiled at Finge as he presented his report. Finge did not look up, but glanced over the puncture pattern, as though his practiced eye were converting words and phrases into symbols; as though somewhere in his mathematical mind the meshings of equations were already taking place.

He said casually, "This will be checked. And what happened to you, Horemm?"

"To me, Computer?" muttered Horemm, his feeling of assurance suddenly gone.

"Yes. You spent one evening alone in the lady's house. —You did, didn't you? You followed the chart."

"I did, sir."

"Well? Are all pertinent details included in your report?"

Finge's eyes were keenly upon him and the habit of duty tugged at Horemm. An Observer must report everything. Ideally, an Observer was merely a sense-perceptive pseudopod thrown out by Eternity. He had no individuality of his own in the performance of his duty.

Horemm's lower lip trembled momentarily, not with fear, anger, or embarrassment, but with the sudden memory of that evening's exaltation.

He began his narration of the events he had left out of his report.

And then Finge raised his hand and said sharply, "Thank you. It is enough."

Horemm went back to his desk filled with a spiritual wine. Of course Finge would ask about it, and of course the man could not bear to hear it.

Finge was jealous! To Horemm that was obvious, and for the first time in his life he knew an aim that meant more to him than the frigid fulfillment of Eternity. He was going to keep Finge jealous and all the world beside, if he had to, because he was going to keep Noÿs in the face of Finge, the Allwhen Council, and all of Eternity.

Horemm's first request for permission to enter the Century on non-official business was entered two days later. He had meant to wait a discreet five days, but couldn't.

It was refused.

He had more than half-expected that. He entered

Computer Finge's office trembling with all the words he had to say.

He began, "A request for my entry into the Century has been rejected—"

Finge interrupted at once. "You wish to see Miss Lambent."

"Yes." He put all the defiance he could manage into the monosyllable.

"There's been a quantum change. I thought you realized that."

Horemm went white. He had forgotten. "A quantum change?"

"Whatever else did you think we needed information for?"

"A quantum change?"

"A comparatively small one, to be sure."

"Then—"

"But Miss Lambent doesn't exist. Except in the minds of those of us in Eternity who knew her, she never existed. The new Reality excludes her. She was never born." ·

Horemm stumbled backward into a chair.

Finge said, "I explained. I told you of the difficulties we had with Times where inexpedient ideas grow up about Eternity. The 482nd was one of them. From what information we did have, we came, indirectly, to the conclusion that among the upper classes of the era, particularly among the women, the notion grew that Eternals were really Eternal, that they lived forever—"

(Horemm remembered Noÿs's statement, short and straightforward. "You live forever." But he had denied it. —It was with a tremendous effort that he kept from screaming.)

Finge was talking. "Worse than that, the superstition had arisen that intimacy with an Eternal would enable a mortal woman—as they thought of themselves —to live forever."

(Horemm could hear her voice again, so clearly. "If I were an Eternal." —"Make me one." The words he heard drowned in the stronger memory of her kisses.)

Finge went on. "This was hard to believe, Horemm. It was unprecedented. If true, the belief and the causes giving rise to it had to be removed. But before we could act, we needed a direct check. We chose Miss Lambent as a good example of the class. We chose you as the other subject—"

Horemm struggled to his feet. "You chose *me*—as a *subject*."

"It was unusual. Necessity—"

"Damn necessity! You're lying!" He didn't care what he said now.

Finge's eyes widened. His plump lips quivered. "How dare you, Observer?"

"I say you're lying," Horemm shouted. "You're jealous. You had your own plans for Noÿs, but she chose me. *Me!* You're trying to tell me that she—she acted as she did because she wanted to live forever and I tell you, no. It wasn't at all like that, and your lies won't cheapen it for me and won't hide her from me. She exists, and I'll go out there—and—"

The words seemed to fade in Horemm's ears, though he was screaming with all the force his lungs could muster. The red mist before his eyes darkened and swirled. He felt the pressure of the floor against his cheek, yet he was not conscious of pain at first.

Then the pain came. His fingers were crooked against the floor as though trying to grip it. Finge's hated voice was in his ears, but the words were not addressed to him. Finge was talking into a Communo. Horemm could tell that much, even in his helplessness.

Horemm heard what he said without having the capacity to rise from the ground and throttle the man.

Finge was saying, "—slightest idea that it would have such an effect. —Yes, he was the logical choice, almost the only choice. Inhibited; prudish; unprepossessing. The fact that the girl deliberately— She did. It was unmistakably deliberate. His report made it quite clear. I refer you to the addendum. —Yes, hospitalization and rehabilitation, certainly. He's one of our best men in his way. I wouldn't want to lose him."

*   *   *

Hospitalization and rehabilitation! It took months of physiotime, but when it was over, all who had ever known Horemm would have sworn he was himself again.

And so he might have been, except that there now existed something that had not existed before. Noÿs!

What use to say she did not exist? She existed in his mind. And while he lived she would always exist in his mind, and there would be no other woman.

To that resolve he adhered.

He brought, or rather dragged, from the bottom of his soul a still firmer and more impersonal efficiency in his job than even he had ever shown before. He climbed through the various levels of the Observer classification to those of Technician.

He attracted the attention of no less a man than Senior Computer Twissell and was, at Twissell's own request, assigned to him as personal Technician. In the past three years he himself, personally, had misplaced objects, put out lights, adjusted switches, abstracted personal communications, and done a hundred and one unimportant things, each of which had brought to non-existence so many persons and things, and to new-existence so many others.

But he no longer cared what left Reality, and of all things that entered it, not one was Noÿs. In the first year after the catastrophe he had somehow deluded himself into hoping that somewhere in the Times, as quantum changes came and went, Noÿs Lambent would be recreated. But deeper knowledge said No, and as physiotime passed he had to admit that No. Out of the infinite number of possible Realities, the chance that one would be chosen with Noÿs in it was one out of an infinite number, or (bluntly and horribly) zero.

And then, when the weight of futility might have borne down everything, there came a new aim in life. He didn't realize what it was all at once. The thought grew slowly, but for its sake Horemm endured life, work, and Computer Twissell. He bore with the

Senior Computer's pettiness and trivialities. He bore
with all the follies to which genius seemed to entitle
him. Most of all, he bore with the man's burning,
smoking cylinders of paper and weed—a vice he had
never heard of, let alone experienced, in his earlier
years. He breathed the foul smoke, choking and gag-
ging on it, and never by word or glance (scarcely by
thought) did he complain. All for the sake of Twissell's
great project.

Today, on this day, as he returned from his errand
to the 2456th, that project was to come to fruition.

Today it was to happen, with the arrival of the
young Brinsley Sheridan Cooper, whom Horemm himself had painfully tracked down out of how many
quintillion possibilities with an ardor and devotion that
transcended mere duty.

6.

Cooper was quiet on the trip back from the 2781st.
He was a little sick. There had been people bustling
through that spaceport. There had been none doing so
afterward. It didn't mean they were all non-existent,
necessarily. They were elsewhere, with different lives
and different memories; and if some had never been,
others were newly there.

It was all for the better, he told himself, all for the
better.

The kettle spun downwhen and downwhen, slipping
through the centuries.

When the kettle halted and they were back at the
575th, the old Computer wrinkled his forehead into
horizontal furrows and said, "You don't feel well,
youngster?"

"I'm all right, sir," demurred Cooper, unconvincingly.

"Come this way to my office," said Twissell.

They passed groups who stepped aside and made
way. Their greetings made a continuous murmur, but
Twissell returned none. Cooper, embarrassed, kept

his eyes on the ground and hastened at the great man's hurrying heels.

He was grateful when they entered a room and a door closed behind them. Clean porcelain made an antiseptic enclosure. One wall of the office was crowded from floor to ceiling with the little computing units which together made up the largest privately operated Computaplex in Eternity, and indeed one of the largest altogether. The opposite wall was crammed with reference films. Between the two, what was left of the room was almost a corridor, broken by a desk, two chairs, recording and projecting equipment, and a strange object for which Cooper could imagine no use until he saw Twissell flick the malodorant remnants of a cigarette into it.

It flashed noiselessly, and Twissell, in his usual prestidigitous fashion, held another in his hands.

Cooper wondered how it would be if someday his own work would be used as the basis for a quantum change; if someday he would say, "Here and now! Change!" Could he bear it?

His instructor, Manfield, had warned them once. "No man," he said, "can control the lives of all mankind and feel no guilt. It is for that reason that even the greatest Computers are careful to subject even the simplest analogical extrapolations to machine analysis. The machine must take all the blame and all the responsibility. And even then—"

Manfield withdrew into himself at that moment, and did not complete the sentence.

Another time, at one of the informal after-dinner sessions he held regularly with his five boys, Manfield said, "Why must changes in Reality be so radical, eh? Why not ultra-fine alterations that would change a life here and there, and no more? Why must whole centuries be wrenched from their moorings?"

His sad, placid face reddened and became strangely like that of a passionate man, which he was not. He said, "Think about it, gentlemen. Someday you'll be reciting formulas to explain it, but will that be enough?

When ten generations of men have been twisted and remolded at your instance to undo or redo the work of half a dozen individuals, will the pious mutter of an equation suffice?

"You must therefore understand the necessity for it. It is easy to think that every little gesture introduced into Reality will change it, every additional step and glance, every cough, every nod. These so-tiny stimuli should produce so-tiny changes. But they won't.

"Gentlemen, they won't. Reality has a stability of its own. Push it a little, and like a rowboat in a pond, it may rock but it won't capsize. It will restore itself to its original position. To change Reality at all, you must push hard enough to make it jump its tracks, if you will allow me to mix my metaphors. Just as matter and energy exist in discrete particles or quanta, so does Reality.

"And quantum changes are large. They must be. So you will never have a choice, gentlemen. If you are to help mankind at all, you must be prepared to interfere with a billion lives at a stroke. The rowboat must be capsized, not rocked."

Then quite suddenly, without looking at the students, without waiting for questions, he strode from the room. The students buzzed to one another about it, but came to no conclusion. Manfield was a good teacher, and all good teachers, they opined, had their quirks.

Manfield returned after half an hour, composed, a little pale. The discussion continued with cool deliberation, but it confined itself strictly to mathematics.

"Ah," said Twissell suddenly, "here's Horemm."

Cooper emerged from his reverie, stood up hurriedly, and waited respectfully for an introduction.

Twissell said, "My technician, Anders Horemm. This is Brinsley Cooper of the 28th." He added, to Cooper, "Technician Horemm negotiated the quantum change you just witnessed."

Cooper's extended hand withdrew involuntarily. Was

this the man? It gave him a shivery sensation to see
the long, veined hands that had actually done the
deed. Surely the man's face was in actuality dour and
ugly, and did not simply seem so because of his job.

Twissell said, "Come, boy, don't hang back. You're
not superstitious about quantum changes, are you?"

Cooper said, "N—no, sir. Not at all. I'm very pleased
to meet you, sir, very pleased." He extended his hand
once more, anxiously.

The Technician took it for a moment, regarded him
frigidly, and said, "I'm sure you are. Don't overdo it."

Cooper felt rebuffed and thought rebelliously: Well,
I *don't* like him.

Twissell rubbed his hands, letting his cigarette dan-
gle from the corner of his mouth. "Is everything set
up, Horemm?"

"Quite set up, Computer."

Twissell was looking at Cooper. His hands rubbed
one another nervously and his eyes were filled with
gloating as though he were saving the climax of a
lifetime for just a few more moments. He said to
Horemm, "This young man has been studying Primitive Times, Horemm, the strange Time before Eternity. He studied its unchanging Reality; its one,
unalterable course of history; its madness, suffering,
poverty, disease, war, and famine that no one can
change or improve."

Cooper looked at Horemm in surprise. The Technician's lower lip was bitten raw and he was trembling.
"I know that, Computer. There is little time left."

Twissell waved his hand impatiently. "I know the
time. —Well, youngster, have you any idea of what
this is all about?"

Cooper's throat was raw with the smoke from
Twissell's cigarettes and he felt his heart begin to
speed its beat. He found the voice to say, steadily
enough, "I think so."

In the days when he looked forward vaguely to
some such scene as this, Cooper used to imagine

himself making such a remark and Twissell being thunderstruck.

But he wasn't thunderstruck at all, and Cooper felt an edge of disappointment. Twissell simply beamed and said, "Tell me."

Cooper, fighting anticlimax, said, "I specialized in Primitive history, as you say. Instructor Manfield separated me from the others and told me he was acting under orders. My studies were particularly thorough with regard to the 24th Century, and it was in the 24th Century that Harvey Mallon lived."

"Good, good," said Twissell, his face puckering into that of a benevolent gnome.

Cooper went on, gathering courage. "It was astonishing that so little was known about the inventor of time-travel. I came across one of your papers in an assignment. It interested me, and I looked up some of your other papers on my own time. It seemed to me your researches could lead to only one conclusion, even though you never stated it explicitly."

"You hear that, Horemm?" interrupted Twissell with delight.

"I hear," said Horemm.

Cooper said, "It seemed inescapable that Harvey Mallon couldn't possibly have invented the Temporal Field in the 24th Century. Nor could anyone have. The mathematical basis for it didn't exist. The fundamental Lefebvre equations did not exist, nor could they exist until the researches of Jan Verdeer in the 27th Century."

Twissell said, "What if Mallon had stumbled on the Temporal Field without being aware of the mathematical justification? What if it were simply an empirical discovery?"

"But it couldn't be, if your analysis of the original engineering specifications of the first Temporal Field is correct. In a hundred ways the Lefebvre equations were used. Coincidence or luck couldn't possibly have accounted for the way in which Mallon designed the machine with perfect economy and rationale."

"Yes. Yes."

Cooper's confidence swelled. He said triumphantly, "There was only one way Mallon could have learned of the Lefebvre equations. He was told about it by a man from his future, by someone from Eternity. —Am I right, sir?"

"Quite right, my boy. I was confident you would work it out for yourself on the basis of what you experienced. If you were the right man, you would have to. It was a necessary test, eh, Horemm?"

Horemm looked sideways at Twissell with a flicker of his dark, brooding eyes. "You are the Computer, sir. But what other reason would there be never to have warned him during training of his final mission? Surely there could be no other reason."

"Of course there isn't," snapped Twissell angrily. He threw down his cigarette, crushing its life out with the sole of his shoe.

Humbly Horemm bent, picked it up between two fingers, and dropped it into the stub receptacle. Slowly, over the next few minutes he dusted those fingers against one another, over and over and over.

Cooper noted the byplay, but his mind was not concerned with it. Now that he was finally face to face with it, a sickness washed over him. He knew the sickness by name; it was fear. He said, "Then it *is* true; *I* am to be the one to go to the 24th—"

Twissell said, "You have been trained thoroughly in the cultures of these centuries. You will be able to acclimate yourself, perform your task."

"But if I don't?" The sudden realization of an unbearable responsibility took the strength from his legs so that he crumpled into a chair. "If I make a mistake, I'll disturb the creation of the Temporal Field. I'll make Verdeer's researches impossible. I'll invalidate the whole basis of the development of Etern———"

Twissell's voice broke in, soft and gentle. "You can't make a mistake, son. There is only one Reality in Primitive times. You have already been there. You have already done your job. You have already suc-

ceeded. You must keep that fully in mind. You are
going far downwhen to do a job that is already done.
—Now, I have the engineering specifications of the
Temporal Field here—"

Cooper looked up. He stared at the small roll of
film in its translucent container.

He said in shock, "But that's Mallon's own set?"
Surely it could be no other. He had seen the very
object in the Museum of Primitive Art and Science in
his own era. The translucent container, rosy in color,
with its graven map of a portion of North America—

"Mallon's very set."

"But it can't be. It's his. If I take it to him for him
to use, and if he leaves it for us to take and bring to
him for him to use—" Cooper laughed weakly. "It's a
circle. It can't be. Who drew the plans in the first
place? Where does it start? It's impossible."

"There are no paradoxes in Time, son," said Twissell.
"You'll find that out more and more as you grow
older. I, a native of the 1025th Century, have ordered
quantum changes that may have killed my grandfather
as a baby, yet here I am. All apparent paradoxes are
the result of Time-centered thinking, instead of Eternity-
centered thinking. Times exist all at once, just as
Space does. It's only our human limitations, even here
in Eternity, that make us persist in thinking of Time as
happening in consecutive instants. Suppose Mallon's
plans do oscillate in Time from now to then and back.
What of it? A pendulum oscillates in Space. What of
that?"

The Computer's hand was resting on his shoulder
very softly. Cooper looked up, and the wrinkled face
that stared across at him was blurred. The young man
blinked his eyes, but the blurring persisted.

"It's time to go to the 24th, son," said Twissell.

Cooper said, "I'm ready." With a weak smile he
added, "I've got to be ready. I've already been there."

In two hours, Cooper learned a great deal.

He learned something about Eternity's tools. He

learned that in addition to the kettles that moved within Eternity, there was something else that could be hurled out of it. It looked like a kettle, but attached to it was a complex mechanism whose bus-bars looked capable of handling energy transfer at rates Cooper did not attempt to imagine.

Horemm bent low over the bones and vitals of it, checking, adjusting—all without a stir of the facial muscles.

Cooper learned much about his mission. Twissell spoke rapidly and not always coherently. Invariably, though, his words returned to the flimsies he held.

He said, "You will find yourself in a protected and isolated spot in the year calculated as optimal. Food, water, and the means for shelter and defense will be sent with you. The flimsies will be meaningless to anyone but you. They will give you further instructions in detail. When it is time to return—

"How long, sir?" asked Cooper.

Twissell hesitated. "I am not sure. *Two years.* Twenty years. Two days." His tone sharpened. "I tell you, I don't know, youngster. Whenever you're through; whenever you return to the coordinates at which you arrived—you will have a fixed-point Barr locator as part of your equipment—this kettle will be activated."

His old voice went on and on. Horemm straightened, placed his right hand upon one of the porcelain dials, and waited.

Twissell's tone increased in urgency. "We cannot attempt to counterfeit their medium of exchange or any of their negotiable scrip. You will have gold in the form of small nuggets—"

Cooper thought wildly: Why didn't they tell me all this before? I can't do it. I won't—

Cooper learned something about himself. He learned that looking forward to a great romantic feat of danger was not at all the same as finding it in your lap leering at you. He found that he wasn't as old as he thought, not as brave as he thought, not as devotedly idealistic as he thought.

And he also found that despite all that, he was going to manage to go through with it.

Twissell was warning him again about the information he must *not* give and the information he *must* give, then checking himself to exclaim impatiently that Cooper couldn't do anything wrong, since Primitive times were invariant and he had already done it all right.

Cooper scarcely heard him now. He was in the kettle, noting with a slight pricking of interest the economy of space and the manner in which supplies had been introduced nevertheless.

"Are you ready?" Twissell said finally. He stood there, directly in front of Cooper, legs apart, his cigarette for once held motionless between stained fingers, its smoke rising in slow curls.

Cooper thought with a sudden wild surprise: He's more scared than I am.

Oddly, the thought gave him courage. His spirits lifted and he said, "I'm ready."

The last thing he saw, before a strange, giddy grayness closed down momentarily upon his vision, was Horemm's left hand moving a switch down toward contact, while the fingers of his right hand, at which the Technician did not look, gave to the porcelain dial they held a sharp and sudden twist.

7.

Senior Computer Twissell could see that his hand was shaking, and that annoyed him. The boy was gone. The deed was done. The manipulation had been perfect. It was over.

When he put his hand to his forehead, then, why should both be clammy? Was he a Cub Computer, fretting and shaking over his first quantum change, or was he Twissell? It was over and done, damn it.

He said it aloud, angrily. "It's over."

"Yes, Computer Twissell," said Horemm.

Twissell started. "What?"

Somehow he never expected Horemm to speak, except in answer to a direct question. When he did speak, Twissell always had that momentary sensation that an extension of himself, an arm, a leg, had suddenly been endowed (like Balaam's ass in the old myth) with miraculous speech.

But Horemm was doing more than talk. He was smiling.

In all their association, Twissell had never seen Horemm smile. He stared now at the twisted mouth and bared teeth that bore the aspect of a smile while emitting none of its warmth. He stared at the glee that sparkled in the Technician's eyes.

He said roughly (for he was very tired), "What's the matter with you, Horemm?"

Horemm said, "It's over. Everything's over. I'm happy."

"Good. I'm happy, too. Now stop leering at me, please. Take a few days off. You've earned them."

"More than you know, Computer," said Horemm. His grin remained.

Twissell puffed madly at his cigarette, burning it nearly to the skin of his fingers before discarding it. He drew the smoke deep into his lungs and expelled it forcefully through parted lips. "What don't I know, Horemm?" He grew angry, for he felt in no mood for foolish talk.

"Why, that everything *is* over. This. You. I. All Eternity!"

"What in Time are you talking about, man? Do you know?"

"I know!" Horemm drew closer.

Twissell backed hurriedly. With sudden acute discomfort, he remembered something he did not usually bring to mind. The man had a history of mental difficulties. Twissell had known that when he requested Horemm's assignment to himself as personal Technician, but then Horemm's soulless efficiency and his fanatic devotion to the ideals of Eternity *had* to have a neurotic basis. For his own purposes, Twissell needed just such an iron-bound personality. And certainly, in his years with Twissell, Horemm had always behaved himself to the Computer's complete satisfaction. He was queer enough (and who was *not* queer? Twissell demanded of himself), and no one would ever think him a lovable character, yet the fact remained that without his complete loyalty, it was doubtful whether the project could have been carried through.

But now it was no Horemm that Twissell could recognize, moving closer to him and extending a lean hand as though anxious to feel Twissell's flesh, make certain that Twissell was really standing there, that it wasn't all a dream.

It was the only way Twissell could account for Horemm's expression. The man was so happy he could scarcely believe in the reality of his own happiness. Was it the release of an over-taut nature by the final accomplishment of the long-drawn-out project?

"You're over-tired, Horemm," said Twissell.

But Horemm only shook his head. "I want you to understand, Computer. Eternity is over. It's done. Do you think Eternity can have no end? That it is everlasting? Think again. Eternity may not have an end in Time, but it can have one in Reality. You see that, don't you? You're a Computer. You're very intelligent."

Twissell was beginning to guess. His whole body trembled now. He shouted, *"Horemm!"*

Horemm's grin disappeared, but the glitter in his eyes remained ferociously joyous. "Yes, Horemm. Just an Observer and Technician. Someone for Finge to experiment with. A thousand Realities have come and gone since Eternity began. Can you recall all the Realities *you* changed, Computer? I can recall one of them. You changed the 482nd ten physioyears ago. You countersigned Finge's analysis. I learned a great deal about that quantum change afterward, but I wonder if you remember? Finge died. Damn him, he died too soon. But you live. You must remember."

Twissell broke into the breathless stream of the other's words. "How can I—"

What was left of the sentence was swept away. Horemm cried, "How *can* you remember? There were so many changes that a billion lives more or less are too puny to clutter your mind. What are the generations of man to a Computer who can flick them about with a puff of breath! Do this! It is done! Nothing on Earth is left unchanged. —Who gave you the right? *Who gave you the right?*"

The Technician lifted both clenched fists into the air.

Twissell moved toward the door and Horemm brought his arms down, moving quickly to forestall him.

"You will listen to me, Computer. I listened to you for five years, and surely you can spare me as many minutes. Did it ever occur to you that a victim of your tamperings might someday wish to return the compliment?"

Twissell said huskily, "What have you done?"

Horemm said, "I've changed Reality all by myself. And not only for the poor creatures in Time. I've changed it even for us. Think of it. Realize it. Live with it. Soon, tomorrow, next year, maybe next minute, there will be an end of Eternity."

"There can't be," whispered Twissell.

"There can be. There is!" cried Horemm. "You sent that boy back to the 24th to inspire the invention that led to Eternity. What if that invention is not inspired? Will there *ever* be an Eternity? The boy asked where the plans for the Temporal Field came from. You said they oscillated in Time as a pendulum did in space. What if someone cuts the string of the pendulum, eh? What if someone interferes with the temporal oscillations of the precious plans?"

Again Twissell asked, "What have you done?"

"You can guess, I think. Just as I was closing the switch that sent Cooper back in time, I turned the chrono-control. He was *not* sent to the 24th, but to some time earlier than that. Centuries earlier. I do not know the year. I don't even know the century. I didn't

look at the control as I turned it, and I turned it once
again before I released it. And *that* disrupted the
automatic feedback of the kettle to the same spot in
Time if and when Cooper attempts reactivation for a
return trip.

"He's lost, Computer; lost forever in the Primitive
era. Already the fabric of Reality must be stretching
with every moment that Cooper is in a Century in
which he doesn't belong. Sooner or later, the changes
he is introducing will reach the quantum level—you
and I know all about quantum changes, eh, Computer—
and all Reality will leap its moorings. Only this won't
be anything like the quantum changes we've introduced so far. This time everything, even Eternity, will
be included, because the quantum change will involve
the non-invention of the Temporal Field. And then
finally I'll be quits with you and Finge, and all the rest,
and I'll live in the new, unchanging Reality, and find
Noÿs again—"

He flung his arms about wildly, then threw himself
to the floor in an agony of laughter that continued
hoarsely while his shoulders heaved and quivered.

Twissell stared down at him in a moment of frozen
horror. Horemm's laughter cracked and faded. He lay
still.

Twissell burst out of the laboratory, his high old
voice nearly cracking as he shouted, "Someone get me
Instructor Manfield of the 28th on the Communo.
Manfield of the 28th! And an ambulance! *Damn you
all, move!* Manfield! Instructor in the 28th! Get him!"

8.

Genro Manfield had once described himself as a
"pacifist" before no less a group than the Personnel
Committee of the Allwhen Council. He had stood
before them, some nine physioyears earlier, moving
about in a nervous, shuffling bear-gait, his broad shoulders stooped, his brown hair matted, his heavy face
etched with stubborn lines of unhappiness.

"We fight a war here in Eternity," he said in part, while explaining and defending his month-old petition to the Committee. "Against what, I'm not exactly sure. Against Reality, I suppose, or against the machine-polished concepts we have of what constitutes human misery. Our ends I believe to be good, but our means I know to be ruthless.

"As a Computer, I have been an officer in that war; I should judge, from what I've done so far, that my rank is about that of a major." (His slow words rumbled slower still as his mind rested upon the archaic metaphor he had conjured up, and then moved by easy and automatic stages to the beginnings of a consideration of Primitive history, the study of which was his amusement and his escape.)

He shook himself with a visible gesture and passed his hand through his hair once again. "I am temperamentally unsuited to that role. If it is a war we fight, I can participate no more. It is no use to tell me that it is a just war and that it must be fought. I am a pacifist and I cannot fight."

The Chairman of the Committee asked him what he intended to do. Surely he knew that a discharge from Eternity and a return to his original Time was impossible. To pension him off at the age of forty physioyears would set a dangerous precedent. Did he wish to withdraw his petition and ask for hospitalization and rehabilitation?

Manfield was violent in his objections. He knew full well that a Computer of his standing could be subjected to no such program without either 1) his own consent or 2) the clear and present danger of psychosis. The second was always hard to demonstrate, and the first they would never get.

He pointed to his petition and said in part, "I am not asking for complete retirement; merely removal from the front lines. Assignment to the 28th Century would enable me to pursue my researches in peace and would place me in a quiet sector where the assaults on Reality are neither frequent nor serious." He could not drag himself away from his own metaphor.

The Chairman of the Committee inquired whether he fully realized the value of a Computer's training and knowledge; whether he was aware of the loss Eternity would sustain if he voluntarily withdrew from Computer status; whether he had considered the difficulty involved in finding a replacement.

Manfield said, "In my present state I am of no service to you as a Computer in any case. However, I would be willing to be an Instructor. Surely Instructors are as valuable to Eternity as any other classification can be, and one of my qualifications would be hard to find."

It is doubtful if the Committee would have approved even that compromise if Laban Twissell, who was at that time on the Committee and who had until then confined himself to silence and smoking, had not suddenly offered his agreement in forceful terms.

At a meeting with Twissell the next day, Manfield, the official notification of transfer of rating and assignment in his wallet, did his best to thank the man.

Twissell brushed the matter away. The quick, birdlike motions of the hand that held the cigarette, his bald, retreating forehead and his bright, intelligent eyes were familiar to Manfield as they already were to every Computer in Eternity.

Twissell said, "I have the germs of a notion; a great one; maybe a ridiculous one. I won't tell you about it. But I would like to have a good, solid fellow such as yourself back in the far downwhens. An Instructor, too. It may come to nothing, but still—"

Manfield did not try to penetrate these remarks. He was anxious only to leave. His kettle was waiting and he wanted to get as far into the quiet of Eternity's beginnings as possible. In that quiet, perhaps, he would forget his own great crime.

He was in the kettle, with Twissell shaking his hand one last time and saying, "You'll remember, won't you, if I ever need you—"

"I'll remember," he muttered, with just an edge of impatience. "I will always be grateful, Computer."

But he forgot.

Not entirely, of course. As the physioyears passed, he did not forget that he was once a Computer. He did not forget one horrible night, nor the petition he had drawn up the next morning. He did not even forget that Twissell had come to his aid.

He did forget, however, Twissell's vague hintings that his reasons for backing Manfield were prompted not by sympathy but by a highly practical foresight. He forgot—or rather, he never thought about—the fact that he had agreed to consider himself under an obligation to Twissell.

Even when Twissell sent down the request that he accept into his class one Brinsley Sheridan Cooper, with the further request that the cub be specialized in Primitive history, no germ of memory stirred. It did not occur to Manfield that this was part of what Twissell already had in mind when he helped place Manfield as Instructor in the 28th.

Manfield was a known expert in Primitive history, and he did not consider it strange that a student should be sent to him for training in that discipline.

When Cooper left for the 575th and when, not twelve hours later, the call came from Twissell, he went to the Communo calmly.

He even went so far as to protest, in considerable agitation, against Twissell's first demand that he take a kettle immediately for the 575th. He was not a Computer, he explained indignantly. He would prefer not to—

"Great Time, man," Twissell had exclaimed with tight hoarseness, "you'd still be a Computer if it weren't for myself. I need you now."

And then Manfield remembered.

"I'll be there," he said mournfully.

It took more than fifteen minutes for Manfield to

obtain even the most general notion of what was wrong.
At first it seemed to him that Twissell was merely
bemoaning the loss of a mentally unstable Technician
(Manfield had heard of Horemm, the so-called "Prince
of Technicians").

Or perhaps his understanding was slow because he
was ill at ease in these surroundings. In all the years
since he had taken the kettle downwhen to the 28th,
he had not returned further upwhen than the periodic
field trip to the 40th had taken him. Now here he was,
deep in sixty-millennial Eternity, staring at the man
who epitomized the role in life he found most revolt-
ing and loathesome. Not five centuries away—not five—

He dragged his mind out of the all-too-ready pit of
memory and tried to fix it upon what Twissell was
saying.

The old Computer's voice grew steadier, colder, and
the true significance of what he was saying began to
penetrate. Manfield's eyes narrowed and his eagerness
to return to the womb he had built himself in the 28th
lessened as he listened.

Finally he said, "Computer, did the Allwhen Council agree to allow a kettle to be sent past the beginning
of—"

Twissell slapped his hands together in fierce disgust.
"What has that to do with it? We built this kettle,
Horemm and I, to accomplish a purpose. Unfortunately, Horemm's purpose wasn't mine. Unfortunately,
I left too much in his hands.—Will you get that look
off your face, Manfield? The theory of penetrating past
the beginning of Eternity is well known. For obvious
reasons, it is a restricted matter, but I managed it
anyway.—Very well then, I did *not* inform the Allwhen
Council. What meaning has that now?"

Manfield said, "Then I should report you."

"And what will that accomplish now? *Do* you understand what I'm saying? We are facing the end of
Eternity."

Yes, the notion was becoming quite clear to Manfield.
The end of Eternity? An odd notion; almost a pleas-

ant one. Was he, and all the Eternals, to endure the
fate that they had distributed coldly to so many others? Suddenly he wondered: Does a shift in Reality
hurt? Are memories really changed cleanly? Does nothing linger? Would there be no ghost of a vanished
Eternity in anyone's mind?

Faintly, he smiled. It was as though he were being
offered, finally, an expiation for his crime, and he
smiled.

Twissell cried out, "Don't sit there grinning, Manfield.
Don't you understand what I'm saying?"

"I understand you, but—"

"But you're shocked at my having ignored the Council. Is that it? Listen, Manfield," he said violently, "I
had to work without them. It was my idea, entirely
mine. I couldn't wait for their confabulations and de-
lays. As it is, it took me over ten physioyears. I'm
sixty-five now. It may take ten years, even fifteen, for
Cooper to complete his mission. I want to be alive
when he comes back. I want to be able to say that *I*
made Harvey Mallon possible. I, and only I, was the
true originator of Eternity. I want to say it; I want the
Eternals to know it. Then I can die."

For all his burning energy, Twissell's body was not
to be denied. His hands shook and his pale lips quivered dryly. Manfield thought with shock: He's old;
old.

He found pity somehow and said, expecting no reasonable answer, "What do you want of me?"

"You know Cooper and you know Primitive times.
Find him for me."

Manfield shook his head. "How can I? Where shall
I look? How shall I look?—See here, Computer, why
don't you settle the matter by sending someone else
back to the 24th? Surely there are copies of Mallon's
plan for a Temporal Field. Meanwhile, when Cooper
realizes he's in the wrong century and can't get back,
he will be enough of a Computer and enough of an
Eternal to realize the dangers of a quantum change
and to avoid—"

Twissell raged. "You are a fool, an idiot. The boy could bring about a quantum change involuntarily, without being aware of it. Besides, it is impossible to send anyone else."

"Why?"

Twissell looked at Manfield with tortured eyes. "Because Cooper is no messenger to Mallon. He *is* Mallon."

"What!"

"Brinsley Sheridan Cooper is Harvey Mallon, the inventor of the Temporal Field and the father of Eternity."

"But that's impossible."

"You think so? *You* think so. Your field of specialization is Primitive history, and you think so. Why was Mallon's birthdate never established? Couldn't that be because he wasn't born in the 24th? Why does no one know the exact date of his death; why are there no records? Couldn't it be that, having completed his work, he returned to Eternity? And don't tell me about paradoxes."

Manfield shook his head. "I'm not a child. I don't talk about paradoxes. Did you tell this to Cooper?"

"I had to tell him something, yes. But I told him as little as possible to the very end. For optimum results it was necessary to keep his thoughts on the matter as fluid as possible. History in Primitive times is fixed; there is only one Reality, so he had to follow it freely. If I told him, if he arrived in the 24th with set notions, he might not be able to adapt quickly enough.

"The plan was to have him search for Mallon and not find him. He would grow panicky, and in desperation establish himself as Mallon, reveal the plans for the Field himself, close the circle. It must take place that way. We can almost deduce it from history. You know the records—Mallon exhibited his machine only with great reluctance and published his papers only after a delay of two years. We used to call it the humility of true genius, but it isn't. It's Cooper wondering what to do."

Manfield said, "If Primitive Reality is fixed, this

must be part of it. Maybe it isn't Cooper that's Mallon, but Cooper's great-grandchild. Cooper might hand down the plans—"

"No. No. *No!* The plan went wrong inside Eternity. Horemm wasn't in Primitive times when he twisted the controls. He was here, in Eternity, and here Reality can be fluid. Cooper is where he ought not to be. That is definite. And at any time, at any physiotime at all, the quantum change may come and all will be ended."

Manfield responded slowly, thoughtfully, "And if so, I wonder if it might not be a good thing, a desirable thing?"

Twissell said, "You can't be serious!"

"No? The whole notion of Eternity is based on the assumption that men, ordinary men, can be trusted with the lives and Reality of all mankind."

"Not men. We only service the computing machines," said Twissell with difficulty.

"Is that right? Was it a computing machine that followed a project for over ten years without the permission, knowledge, or cooperation of the Allwhen Council? Was it a computing machine that twisted the controls of a kettle with the knowledge it would destroy Eternity? If men like you and Horemm cannot be trusted, Computer, what Eternal can be? And if no Eternal can be trusted, what good is Eternity?"

"Manfield, Manfield, we have no time for cheap philosophy. There are thousands of Eternals who have devoted their lives to Eternity without deviation from its ideals. You, for instance. You yourself."

Manfield shook his head and said, "Not I. I am as criminal as anyone in Eternity can be."

Twissell's eyes transfixed him brightly. "In what way? Tell me! But quickly."

And because Manfield could look another Eternal in the face and feel a kinship in wrongdoing, he found he could finally confess his crime.

The crime began with a woman, as Horemm's had. That was not coincidence. It was almost inevitable. The Eternal who sold the normal satisfactions of fam-

ily life for a handful of perforations on paper was ripe
for infection. Or, like Twissell, he would fall prey to a
basic insecurity and respond with small vanities such
as the incessantly ostentatious twirling of a cigarette in
a smokeless society, or the larger vanity of seeking
personal renown at the risk of all Eternity.

Manfield remembered the woman with pain and
love. She was intelligent and kind. If he were a Timed
man, he would have been proud to have her as his
wife. Not all Eternals (who must take their women
only as Computing permits) were as fortunate as he in
that respect.

Yet his relations with her were clouded by something he knew and she, by the very nature of things,
did not. In the Reality of that physiotime, she was to
die young. She was to die, in fact, within a year of the
beginning of their relationship.

He knew that from the start. When first he felt
attracted to her (first as an individual in an Observer's
report of the 570th, and then, driven by curiosity, as
the result of seeing and speaking to her in the course
of an irregular, but perfectly legal, tour of personal
Observation), he had life-plotted her.

He had not left it to the Life-Plotting department.
He had done it himself, out of a certain shyness. He
learned of her coming death and at first, as he now
remembered with shame, that pleased him. It meant
that the chances for a quantum change resulting from
their relationship could be but slim. He checked, and
that was so.

He visited her as often as spatiotemporal charting
allowed. Her amiability passed the heights of his ex-
pectation, and with her he found contentment. The
Allwhen Council, having duly passed upon his calculations, was indifferent.

So far, he had committed no crime.

But what began as the satisfaction of an emotional
need became something more. Her imminent death
stopped being a convenience and became a calamity.
Three separate times, a point in physiotime came and

passed, during which some simple action of his own would have altered her personal Reality. But he knew that no such personally motivated change could possibly be authorized. Her death became his personal responsibility, and he learned the meaning of guilt.

That was no crime, either, though it was dangerously weak.

(Twissell said so, letting his cigarette burn, lured slightly from his preoccupation with the overwhelming danger that surrounded him. Manfield shook his head and said softly, "You cannot understand.")

He took no action when she became pregnant. Her life-plot, modified to include her relationship with Manfield, indicated pregnancy to be a high-probability consequence. Generally such an eventuality was avoided, but sometimes Timed women were made pregnant by Eternals. It was not unheard of. But because no Eternal might have a child, the pregnancies were ended painlessly and efficiently. There were many methods.

Manfield did nothing. She was happy in her pregnancy and he wanted her to remain so. He knew that she would be dead before the fullness of her term, so he only watched with veiled eyes and smiled painfully when she told him, in triumph, that she could feel life stirring within her.

This still was not a willful crime on Manfield's part, but it was ignorance; and ignorance can be almost a crime.

For she gave birth prematurely. It was something Manfield had not anticipated. It was an aspect of life of which he had little experience, and the possibility of premature birth had not occurred to him.

Yet how had it come about that the life-plot he had made did not indicate it? He went back to his life-plot and found the living child—in an alternate solution to a low-probability forklet he had overlooked. A professional would not have overlooked it.

What could Manfield do now?

He could not kill the child. The mother had two

weeks to live. Let it live till then, he thought. Two weeks of happiness is not an exorbitant gift to ask.

The mother died—as foreseen, and in the manner foreseen. Manfield (for the time permitted by the spatiotemporal chart) sat in her room, aching with a sorrow all the keener for his having waited for it, in full knowledge, for over a year. In his arms he held her son and his.

(Twissell said, with horror in his voice, *"You let it live?"*

"You can't understand," said Manfield.

"But it was a crime.")

It *was* a crime, but it was not *the* crime.

He let it live. He put it in the charge of an appropriate organization and returned when he could (in strict temporal sequence, held even with physiotime) to make necessary payments and to watch the boy grow.

Two years passed. Periodically he checked, making sure the boy's life-plot in no way induced quantum changes. It was a good life-plot, and Manfield was pleased. The child learned to walk and mispronounce a few words. He was not taught to call Manfield "daddy." Whatever speculations the Timed people of the childcare institution might make concerning the large man who paid so regularly remained speculations, nothing more.

Then, when the two years had passed, the necessities of a quantum change that included the 570th at one wing was brought up before the Allwhen Council and Manfield, lately promoted to Associate Computer, was placed in charge.

The pride of the moment was alloyed with apprehension.

("It would have to be," said Twissell. "Children are hostages to Time."

Manfield shook his head in annoyance at the aphorism.)

He worked at the quantum change and did a flawless job. But his apprehension grew. He succumbed to a temptation he had known in his heart he would never be able to resist. He held back his solution while he worked out a new life-plot for his son.

That was a second crime, as great as the first, and still it was not *the* crime.

For twenty-four hours, without eating or sleeping, he sat in his office, striving with the completed life-plot, tearing at it in a despairing attempt to find an error.

There was no error.

The next day, still holding back his solution to the quantum change, he worked out a spatiotemporal chart and entered Time at a point more than thirty years upwhen from the birth of his child.

That was a third crime, greater than the first two, and still not *the* crime.

His son was thirty-four years old; as old as Manfield himself was now. He had no knowledge of his father, no memory of a large man who had visited him in his infancy.

He was an aeronautical engineer. The 570th was expert in half a dozen varieties of air travel, and Manfield's son was a happy and successful member of his society. He was married to an ardently enamored girl, but would have no children, Manfield knew.

("At least there was that," said Twissell, and placed his cigarette stub in a disposal unit.

"I told you I charted his original life-plot for quantum change. I am not completely abandoned.")

Manfield spent the day with his son. He introduced himself in a business connection and spoke to him formally, smiled politely, took his leave coolly. But secretly he watched and absorbed every action, filling himself, living fiercely that one day out of a Reality that tomorrow (by physiotime) would no longer have existed.

He returned to Eternity and spent one last, horrible night wrestling futilely against what must be. The next morning he handed in his computations and prepared a petition to the Allwhen Council for transfer of classification.

"And you helped me, Computer," Manfield concluded.

Twissell said, "Your son, I suppose, did not live in the new Reality."

"Oh, he lived," said Manfield slowly. "He existed—as a paraplegic, from the age of four. Forty-two years in bed, under circumstances that barred me even from arranging to have the nerve-regenerating techniques of the 900's applied to his case.

"*I* did that to my son. It was my mind and my computing machines that computed that new life for him, and my word that ordered the change. I committed a number of crimes, but that was *the* crime that finished me as a Computer."

9.

Twissell blamed himself for his initial panic in proportion as that panic subsided. He had acted quickly enough in sending for Manfield, but then had been thrown off base, first by Manfield's slowness in understanding and then by the man's neurotic reluctance to help.

It was only when Twissell recognized, in Manfield's sullenness, the turmoil of a private grief and a private guilt that he could seize the initiative once more. This he did by allowing Manfield to talk. He felt the ground go solid beneath him, and he steadied.

He did not try to hurry Manfield. He let the minutes pass. By the time Manfield had finished, Twissell was tasting his cigarettes again.

He did not rush into speech. Rather, he allowed more minutes to pass while the catharsis of confession emptied Manfield of his congested guilt.

As a Computer, Twissell had, of course, a working knowledge of Psycho-Engineering. Intellectually, if not emotionally, he could follow in the track of Manfield's mind. What had happened was equivalent to the lancing of a boil. Someday, Twissell thought, Psycho-

Engineering ought to be raised to the status of a separate specialty classification in Eternity.

Finally he said quietly, "If Eternity ends, the equivalent of your tragedy will happen to uncounted men and women. You can prevent that."

He waited, then went on. "You know Primitive history. You know what it was like. It was a Reality that blindly flowed along the line of maximum probability. In the centuries of physiotime that Eternity has existed, we've lifted our Reality to a level of well-being far beyond anything Primitive times knew, but also to a level which, but for our interference, would be very low probability indeed."

Twissell watched the silent Manfield narrowly, then said, "With Eternity gone, a million years of human history will revert to an unchangeable Reality of ignorance, slaughter, and misery. Your own experience should give you a better insight into the meaning of that and the necessity of its prevention than I myself can possibly have."

Manfield raised his head. "But what can I do?"

It was surrender, and Twissell knew it. He acted at once to bar reconsideration on the other's part, and moved quickly to the controls of the kettle through which Cooper had disappeared past the beginning of Eternity.

"Come here, Manfield." Twissell had lost an hour all told, but with that hour he had bought a chance. He did not let himself think how slim the chance was.

He felt excited. At least he was *doing* something. He said, "This is the chrono-control, the rheostat that controls the temporal length of the kettle thrust. If I had added a lock to make certain its setting could not be disturbed once set—but of course, I left details like that to Horemm." He smiled twistedly.

"Now Horemm stood so," he went on. "He turned the control just as he closed the switch. He told me so. And if I can follow the workings of his emotions now, he used his one hand on the chrono-control for one spasmodic twist in hate and anger."

And as Twissell said that, his own face seemed to mirror those emotions and his hand, gripping the porcelain knob, turned it savagely.

"What does it read?" he asked breathlessly.

Manfield bent close. "Somewhere in the 20th. Let's see, nineteen—"

"It's no use reading it too closely," said Twissell. "It can only be an approximation." He put his cigarette to his mouth, peered through the smoke.

"What do you know about the 20th, Manfield?"

The Instructor shrugged.

"You studied it, of course," said Twissell.

"Oh yes."

"All right. Let's imagine ourselves in Cooper's place. He's a bright lad; intelligent, imaginative, wouldn't you say?"

"A very capable youngster."

"And an Eternal. That's the important thing." Twissell shook his finger. "That's the important thing. He's used to the notion of communication across time. He is not likely to surrender to the thought of being marooned in time. He'll know that we're looking for him."

"Yes, but what can he do about it, Computer?"

Twissell's shrewd old face stared up at Manfield, its lines crinkling. "Is there any particular source you used in studying the 20th? Any documents, archives, films, artifacts, reference works? I mean primary sources, dating from the time itself."

"Naturally."

"And he studied them with you?"

"Yes."

"Then doesn't it follow that he might try to insert into one of those objects—an object he'd *know* you were accustomed to looking at and studying—some reference to himself?"

"That's far-fetched."

"Maybe," agreed Twissell quickly, "but what else can he do? If he does nothing, we're done, we're through, it's over. The one chance we have is that he's done something and that we can penetrate his thinking. That's why I need you. First, you know him best. For five years you've had him under your continual care. Second, it is you he would automatically try to reach. If he knows and loves anyone in Eternity, it would be you. Third, you and only you would know where to look; you and only you would recognize his message."

Manfield said with an anxious shake of his head, "But I *don't* know where to look."

"Ask yourself: Was there any one source which more than any other you consulted with respect to the 20th? Is there some particular form of record that Cooper would associate automatically with the 20th? Think, man. It's our only chance."

He waited, his lips pressed thinly together.

Manfield said, "There were the newsmagazines. They were a phenomenon of the early second millennium. One in particular was very useful. Its first issue dates from 1923.—Of course, he might have been sent back earlier than that."

"And he might not. We've got to start somewhere, Manfield."

"It continued well into the 22nd."

"Very well. Is there any way, do you suppose, in which he could make use of that newsmagazine to carry a message? Remember, he'd know you'd be reading it; that you'd be acquainted with it; that you'd know your way about in it."

"I don't know." Again Manfield shook his head. "It affected an artificial style. It was selective rather than inclusive. It would be difficult or even impossible to rely on its printing something you would plan to have it print. Even if Cooper, let us say, managed to get a position on its staff, which is very unlikely, he couldn't be certain that his exact wording would pass the various editors. I don't see it, Computer."

Twissell said, "For Time's sake, think! Concentrate on that newsmagazine. You're in the 20th and you're Cooper with his education and background. You taught the boy, Manfield. And you've been a Computer with Psycho-Engineering training. What would he do? How would he go about placing something in the magazine, something with the exact wording he wants?"

Manfield's eyes widened. "An advertisement!"

"What?"

"An advertisement. A paid notice which they would be compelled to print exactly as requested."

"Ah, yes. They have that sort of thing in the 182nd."

"I imagine they have it in a number of eras, but the 20th is absolutely peak in that way. In fact," said Manfield, suddenly warming to his subject, "the 20th is in many ways the peak of Primitive time. The cultural milieu—"

"Not now, Manfield. Back to the advertisement. What kind would it be?"

"I haven't the slightest idea, Computer."

Twissell stared at the lighted end of his cigarette as though seeking inspiration. "He can't say anything directly. He can't say: Cooper of the 28th calling Eternity—"

"He might."

"He'd be a fool if he did, and I don't think he's a fool. He would be asking for a quantum change."

"More likely arrest for mental observation. In Primitive times, any serious implication of time-travel was pure insanity."

"All right. Indirection. That's what it would have to be. It must seem perfectly normal to the men of the time. Perfectly normal. And yet obvious to us. Very obvious. Obvious at a glance, because it would have to be found among uncounted individual items. How big do you suppose it would have to be, Manfield? Are those advertisements expensive?"

"In the newsmagazine, I should say, moderately so."

Twissell said, "And ideally, to avoid the wrong kind of attention, it would have to be small anyway. Guess, Manfield. How large?"

Manfield spread his hands. "Half a column?"

"All right. Now we have the first approximation. Look for a half-column advertisement which will, practically at a glance, give evidence that the man who put it in came from another time, and yet which is so normal an advertisement that no man of that time would see anything queer in it."

The Instructor said, "What if I don't find it?"

"Then we'll think up some alternative for you to investigate. And if that fails, we'll try something else, and then something else, as long as we live and Eternity exists."

Twissell remembered his panic now only as a bad and unworthy dream. He was *doing* now; he was *acting*. His keen mind was thoroughly occupied with the thrill of the chase and not at all with the consequences of failure.

Twissell stared curiously at the books in Manfield's library. Occasionally, because he could not bear to do nothing, he would take one down from its shelf, peer through its crinkling pages, and silently mouth the archaic words. His knowledge of the three-millennial dialect, while not as extensive as he would like to have men believe, was sufficient to enable him to catch phrases and sometimes whole sentences.

"This is the English the linguists are always talking about, isn't it?" he asked, tapping a page.

"English," muttered Manfield.

Twissell had never quite been this far downwhen before. All of Eternity here seemed to have a musty look, as though it were not really Eternity but merely a somewhat advanced Primitive era.

It might have been the library itself that gave rise to that sensation. Twissell was acquainted with several book eras. His own Century, to be sure, was a film era, as most eras were. Others were molecular-recording eras. Still, books as such, while pleasantly outlandish, were not at all repulsively outmoded.

But when they were lined up in such numbers—

Even in those sections of Eternity given over to the

book eras, books in the libraries of Eternity were converted to film or to molecular patterns, if only out of consideration for space economy.

Twissell glanced across at Manfield. The Instructor's large shoulders were hunched over the spotlighted desk. Brown hair, in complete disarray, was all that showed of his head.

He cultivates archaism, thought Twissell. He *prefers* books. He hides in a universe of fixed Reality. It's his security.

But he was too restless for any one line of thought to linger long. He took another book down from the shelf, opening it at random. What if he just turned a page, and there—there—

He blushed inwardly and put the book back.

Manfield turned the pages regularly, only one hand moving, the rest of the body fixed at rigid attention.

At what seemed eonic intervals Manfield would rise, grunting, for a new volume. On those occasions there would be the coffee break or the sandwich break or the other breaks.

Manfield said heavily, "It's useless *your* staying."

"Do I bother you?"

"Of course not."

"Then I'll stay," and Twissell, feeling cold and alone, resumed his soft, sporadic, and useless assault on the bookshelves, the sparks of his furious cigarette burning his finger ends, disregarded.

And a physioday ended.

Twissell said helplessly, "There's so much. There must be some faster way."

Manfield said, "Name it. I can't let a single page go by."

"How much have you done?"

"Nine volumes. Four and a half years."

Twissell said, "He'll have landed on the edge of the North American Southwestern Desert. That was deliberate, since it's very sparsely populated, even in the 20th, I believe."

Manfield nodded absently and turned another page.

"We intended him to have some time unmolested, in which to adjust himself. He had a good supply of food and water. He would be bound to be cautious. It would be days before he really contacted a settled area and ran much risk of quantum change. We might have weeks." He wasn't quite sure that he believed himself, but he said it again. "We might have weeks."

Methodically Manfield turned another page, and another.

"Eventually," he said, "the print starts blurring and that means it's time for sleep."

A second physioday ended.

And at 10:22 A.M. on the third physioday Manfield said, in quiet wonder, "This is it."

Twissell didn't absorb the statement. He said, "What?"

Manfield looked up, his face twisted with astonishment. "You know, I didn't believe it. By Time, I never really believed it, even while we were working out all that rigmarole about newsmagazines and advertisements."

Twissell had absorbed it now. *"You've found the ad."* He leaped at the volume Manfield was holding, clutching at it with shaking fingers.

But Manfield maintained his hold. He put the volume down with a slap and pointed to a small advertisement at the upper lefthand corner.

It was simple enough. It read:

ALL THE

TALK

OF THE

MARKET

Underneath, in smaller letters, it said: "Investments NewsLetter, P.O. Box 14, Denver, Colorado."

Twissell said confusedly, "Market?"

"The stock market," said Manfield impatiently. "A system by which private capital was invested in busi-

ness. That's not the point. Don't you see the line
drawing against which the advertisement is set?"

"Of course," said Twissell, frowning. To whom should
a drawing of a mushroom cloud be familiar, if not to a
Computer? Three-quarters of the quantum changes in
Eternity were made necessary by the desire to wipe
out the development of fission and fusion bombs without wholly crippling nuclear science.

The Computer said, "It's an A-bomb. Is that all? It
has nothing to do with the subject of the advertisement, but surely that incongruity is not what caught
your eye." He was bitterly disappointed. "It's only an
attention-getter—"

"Attention-getter? Great Time, Computer, look at
the date of the magazine issue."

He pointed to the top heading. It said March 28,
1932. It was page 30.

"Nineteen thirty-two!" said Manfield. "And the first
A-bomb explosion took place in July of 1945."

"Are you sure?"

"I *know* this era. I'm positive! Until July, 1945, no
human being who had ever lived had ever seen a full
nuclear mushroom cloud. No one could possibly re-
produce it so accurately, except—"

"It's just a pattern," said Twissell, trying to retain
his equilibrium. "It might resemble the mushroom
cloud coincidentally."

"Might it? Will you look at the wording again?"
Manfield's fingers punched out the short lines: "All
the—Talk—Of the—Market. The initials spell out
ATOM. Coincidence? Not a chance. Don't you see
how it fits your own conditions? It's something that
caught my eye instantly. It would have caught any
Computer's eye, but mine particularly, because I would
see at a glance that it was an impossible advertisement
for anyone but Cooper to have put in. And at the
same time it would have no meaning except for its face
value, absolutely none at all, to any man of that time.
It's Cooper, Computer Twissell. He is calling us, and
I'm going after him. We have the date. We have the

mailing address. And I'm sufficiently well acquainted
with the period to handle myself safely in it."

Twissell felt very weak. He leaned gratefully on
Manfield's arm as it was extended suddenly toward
him.

"Careful, Computer."

"It's all right," said Twissell. "Let's go."

10.

The next day's events were most unusual in several
respects. No one but Twissell (and Twissell at his most
arbitrary) could have so short-circuited "channels," so
bulled major lines of calculations through computing
machines, so ignored the horrified complaints of oper-
ators who found their work disrupted.

No one but Twissell could have done all this, and no
one but Twissell could have had his kettle ready, at
new adjustments, within twenty-four hours.

To top that, Twissell ignored completely Eternity's
convention of always allowing for physiotime.

He said breathlessly to Manfield, already dressed in
an appropriate costume for the era he was to visit,
"I'm allowing for no physiotime lapse. I'm disconnect-
ing the radiochron."

"All right," said Manfield calmly. He adjusted the
clumsy trousers of his 225th-Century outfit, one which
he had decided was a close enough approach to the
20th-Century version; close enough, at any rate, to
make unnecessary any time-consuming tailoring job.

Twissell went on, "I don't care if it takes you a day
or a month or ten years to get him. I don't care how
long *he's* been there. You'll return to the instant you've
left, once you activate the Temporal Field at the far
end. I can't wait through physiotime. You understand?"

Manfield nodded. It meant that if the chase took
him the unlikely length of ten years, he would return
to Eternity aged ten years with respect to the other
Eternals. Psychologically, that would be unpleasant.
But he nodded.

He buttoned a last button and said, "I'm ready."

So it was that when Twissell, his heart drumming a red tattoo and his clammy hands almost unable to do what was required, finally managed to plunge the lever home, the kettle never moved.

Or at least it left, then returned to the same instant, so that there was no apparent gap in its existence.

In fact, the only change that took place was that in the kettle, immediately next to a suddenly tired-looking Manfield, was a somewhat gaunt, but not visibly aged, Brinsley Sheridan Cooper.

And then Twissell performed in the most unusual fashion. It was quite out of character. Before the amazed eyes of the other two, he burst into sudden and unexpected tears of sheer relief.

Cooper remained a little over one physioday in Eternity. Through all those hours he remained a little hilarious, never quite himself, it seemed, never quite getting used to the fact that he was actually back in Eternity.

"If you knew," he kept saying, "how I felt when I first got hold of a newspaper. I wanted the exact day, you know. Only it turned out to be 1931! I thought I was going mad."

"But what made you think of the advertisement, boy?" asked Twissell. "It was magnificent."

"I didn't think of it for months. If you'd known the things I tried to do first. I tried to leave stones with carvings, only I didn't know how to carve stone without a McIlvain pierce-tube. Then I tried to think up a way of getting into archives. For two months, I tried to get a job at one of the government printing offices, but there was something called Civil Service and I didn't have a birth certificate. Besides, there was an economic depression under way. My supply of bullion was sinking—"

"If you had landed two years later," said Manfield dryly, "your gold would have done you no good. There was a period where the possession of gold was illegal," he went on to explain to Twissell.

"In any case," said Cooper, "*finally* I thought of the newsmagazine we spent so much time over, Instructor Manfield. At first I thought I'd put in something in sixty-millennial dialect for Computer Twissell, you know. But they wouldn't take an ad they couldn't understand, so I tried again in plain Primitive English. I knew Instructor Manfield would understand. Then, the very day it appeared, there was Instructor Manfield's telegram at the post office. Wow!"

Twissell said, "You'll have to leave Eternity again tomorrow. You understand that, don't you, youngster? There's still a job to do."

"That's all right," said Cooper jubilantly. "It's nothing now, after what I've been through. When I found out there wasn't any Temporal Field to reactivate for the return, I knew there'd been an accident. I felt so *lost*. In the 24th, at least, I'll know I'm coming back. Great Time, I feel so sure of myself now that if I don't find Harvey Mallon right off, I have half a mind to just assume his name and give Earth the Temporal Field myself. So *help* me, I will."

And over his head, Twissell's eyes met those of Manfield.

11.

They sat together, the two of them. Alone again.

Twissell said wonderingly, "Maybe it was all meant to be, after all."

Manfield said, "How's that?"

"You heard his remark about taking Mallon's place. And you know he will. Now would he have been willing to do so, would he have had the ability to do so, if he hadn't gone to the 20th first? Would the cycle have been completed?"

Manfield thought grimly: He's going to cancel his mistake. He's going to convince himself it wasn't a mistake at all; that it was all just another stroke of Twissell genius.

Aloud he said, "How can we ever tell?"

"I *feel* it. Even a Computer can be intuitive once in a while, I suppose. I am convinced that Cooper belonged in the 20th just as he belonged in the 24th. Primitive Reality is immutable."

"You didn't think so a week ago. You said the change had taken place within Eternity, not within the Primitive Era."

Twissell waved that away with an angry flip of his hands.

Manfield insisted. "And how can we tell, anyway? Suppose Cooper *had* changed Reality. We would change, our memories would change."

Twissell snorted. "Nothing has changed, I tell you."

"But why not? There was Cooper's first attempt to place an ad in sixty-millennial. Wouldn't that strain the fabric of Reality? Then there was the ad he did put in. How many other people might have blundered upon it between the 20th and the 24th and wondered what a mushroom cloud was doing in a 1932 newsmagazine? Suppose they wondered at the initial letters, spelling the English word for atom. Cooper was there for nearly six months. I was there for nearly two days. In that time—"

"The fact is," said Twissell shrilly, "that no change has taken place. Why do you insist the opposite?"

Manfield's shoulders drooped. He could make no denial to himself. If Twissell's ego was chained to the fact of non-change, his own was as intimately concerned with an insistence on the fact of change. He said, "I was hoping—" and stopped.

"Well?"

"I thought there might be some little change. A micro-change, so to speak, that would expand its ripples all along the Timestream."

"Quantum changes are big changes," said Twissell.

"Ordinary quantum changes, yes. But who knows the mathematics of Reality in the Primitive Centuries? Without the presence of Eternity, it's a different case. Why couldn't there be the possibility of micro-changes?"

Twissell said, "What are you driving at?"

"Why might there not be a new Reality in which my son is healthy, or one in which he does not exist? Anything but what is."

Twissell said quickly, "There is no way you can check on that. You must not play with Time any longer. Nor will I. Nor will I. We've done enough, both of us." And for a moment there was a return of horror to his eyes as though once again he found himself staring into the abyss of the end of all Eternity.

Manfield whispered, "I'll never look. I don't have the courage for it."

Preoccupied, he placed a cigarette in his mouth and lit it, then looked up in surprise at Twissell's sharp cry.

Twissell said, "Get rid of that poisonous trash, for Time's sake. I can't stand it."

Manfield stubbed out the cigarette hurriedly and raised a pair of mental eyebrows at himself. He was far gone indeed to have lit a cigarette in the company of Eternity's most notorious anti-tobacco fanatic.

Twissell's nose twitched at the lingering acrid vapor in the air and he said, "Just make up your mind to it, Manfield. There's been no change in Eternity. None at all. Take my word for it."

And he stared with detestation at what remained of the cigarette.

AFTERWORD

I've presented only the novelette because, as before, it is impractical to try to present the novel itself as well. If you are interested in a direct comparison and do not have a copy of the novel, Ballantine has recently put out a new paperback edition of *The End of Eternity*. Meanwhile, I will say a few words of my own.

In the case of "Grow Old Along with Me," I had to add comparatively little to turn it into "Pebble in the Sky." This meant I could use the plot as was and simply rearrange it and go into a few things in greater detail.

Not so in the case of "The End of Eternity" (novelette), where I had to triple the length. There I had a much freer hand in actually revising the plot.

I made some small changes, of course. First, I changed the name of my character Anders Horemm to Andrew Harlan. Why? I'm not certain.

Some people, after reading the novel, have suggested that I made use of the name Harlan as a reference to Harlan Ellison. That's not impossible. I had met Harlan Ellison in September, 1953, and of course he made a deep impression on me, as he does on everyone.

I would not have been surprised, then, if I had named the character Andrew Harlan in the original novelette, which I began within two months of the meeting. I did not, however; I called him Anders Horemm. Why, then, should I have made the change in the novel?

Here's what seems reasonable to me. Horcmm had been a rather minor character in the novelette, but I made him into the actual hero in the novel, and Horemm strikes me as a particularly ugly name. It was suitable for an unpleasant minor character, but not for the hero. When I do make name changes, I tend to make them as small as I can (I don't know why), so I changed Anders to Andrew and Horemm to Harlan.

Then too, Manfield, an important character in the novelette, disappeared in the novel, or rather, his role was combined with that of Twissell. As for Noÿs, her role was greatly expanded and the love story was made even more central to the development of the story than had been true in the novelette.

But what really astonished me, as I read both versions in preparing for this book, was that I didn't simply dilute the novelette. After all, if the novelette was really a dehydrated novel, I might have merely added water, so to speak—lengthened the descriptions, carried on the dialogue at greater length, and stuck to the plot.

I didn't. Having Bradbury's praise in my ears and suddenly finding myself with 50,000 more words to play with, I added incidents and complications, and made the novel every bit as dense as the novelette had been.

In particular, there was the matter of the ending. In rereading the novelette for this book, I was amazed that I had made the ending as weak as I had. At least, it seemed weak to me now in comparison with what I had done for the ending of the novel. After all, I called the story "The End of Eternity," and yet I had not had the courage (or the heart, perhaps) actually to end Eternity in the novelette.

In the novel, I determined to make a better job of it, perhaps because (it being a novel now) I wanted to tie it in somehow with earlier books of mine dealing with the rise and fall of the Galactic Empire. (It's a weakness of mine to try to make my science fiction novels consistent with each other, and it influences my writing to this very day.)

In any case, the end of the novel is far more complex and dramatic than is the end of the novelette. In the novel, I tried (as I often do in my novels) to uncover several surprises, one after the other, until it seems to me that the reader feels he has come to the end—and then I produce one last surprise that I have held in reserve. It's fun to do—but not easy.

In the case of *The End of Eternity* as a novel, the density did not work entirely in its favor. I showed the novel to Horace Gold, in case he felt I had improved the story and was therefore willing to serialize it prior to publication. (Such serialization, in those days, meant an additional $1500 or so for the ever-impoverished author.) Gold, however, rejected it as swiftly and as uncompromisingly as he had rejected the novelette. Nor would Campbell accept it for *Astounding*. Doubleday tried to peddle it for serialization to some of the general magazines and got nowhere at all (not surprising in 1955, when science fiction was virtually an aberration outside the few speciality magazines devoted to it).

The result was that "The End of Eternity" never saw magazine publication of any kind. "Pebble in the Sky" also appeared in book form without any magazine publication, but after its book appearance, it appeared twice in slightly condensed form. It appeared in the first issue of *Two Complete Science-Adventure Books* and in *Galaxy Science Fiction Novels*. "The End of Eternity" never experienced such "second serialization."

Nor were some of the critics particularly kind to it. Their objections usually rested on its density. Damon Knight referred to the confusing nature of the opening chapters in a rather caustic fashion, for instance.

Even Anthony Boucher, then editor of *Fantasy and Science Fiction*, who was an unusually gentle fellow and a good friend of mine, thought it was too complicated.

I remember that we were both at the World Science Fiction Convention in Cleveland in 1955 (at which I was the guest of honor and he the toastmaster). We were both being interviewed by someone who asked me what my most recent book was.

I said, "A science fiction novel named *The End of Eternity*."

He shoved the microphone under my nose and said, "Can you give us an idea of the plot in a few sentences?"

I stammered and made a false start, and Tony Boucher chuckled and said, "Even you can't do it for *that* book, Isaac."

I said, "Yes, I can, Tony. I was just caught by surprise. Ask me the question again, sir."

The interviewer obliged, and I rattled off several clear sentences outlining the plot.

Its sales were comparable to those of my other novels of the 1950s. It has appeared in paperback form a number of different times and has been translated into fourteen foreign languages that I know of (including Russian and Hebrew), so I don't consider it a failure.

I do consider it underappreciated, however, and feel it is unfairly drowned out by my Foundation novels and my Robot novels. Someday, after I'm dead perhaps, it may come into its own.

Before I leave the world of my novels, I want to mention briefly the case of another novelette, even shorter than the novelette version of "The End of Eternity," which I expanded to a novel somewhat longer than the novel version of *The End of Eternity*.

At a local science fiction convention, on January 15, 1971, someone on the stage, seeking under pressure for an example of an obscure isotope, referred to "plutonium-186." I was amused because there is no such thing as plutonium-186, and there can't be.

I decided, therefore, to write a short story on the subject of plutonium-186 and to submit it for inclusion in an anthology of originals that was going to be edited by the person who made the remark, and published by Doubleday.

Unfortunately, the story ran away with me and, at 20,000 words, proved to be a novelette. I was afraid it was now too long for the anthology, and so I consulted Lawrence P. Ashmead on that point. He was my editor at Doubleday at that time and he it was who would also be handling the anthology. Larry read my story and said he didn't want it in the anthology; he wanted me to make a novel out of it.

So I did, but I didn't touch the novelette at all—not one word. I kept it as a beginning, and added two more long novelettes that continued the story. All together, the three made up a 90,000-word novel, *The Gods Themselves* (Doubleday, 1972).

In that case there is no "alternative Asimov," however, for the novelette out of which it grew is right there in the book as the first of three parts.

3

BELIEF
(First Version)

FOREWORD

What about those stories of mine that began as short stories or novelettes, and were published in the magazines as short stories or novelettes, but only after such extensive revisions that my original story would qualify as an "alternate Asimov"?

There are not very many of those, at best, but let's poke around and see.

In my first few years as a science fiction writer, I wrote nine stories that never sold to anyone, and were so beyond help that no one as much as whispered a word concerning revision. They were simply still-born. These stories are, in chronological order:

> Cosmic Corkscrew (1938)
> This Irrational Planet (1938)
> Paths of Destiny (1938)
> Knossos in Its Glory (1938)
> The Decline and Fall (1939)
> Life Before Birth (1939)
> The Brothers (1939)
> Oak (1940)
> Masks (1941)

I might be tempted to include these stories as "alternatives" to my published work, and as historical curiosities and teen-age miscalculations at which my readers could laugh indulgently. Fortunately, it is easy for me to resist that temptation. The manuscripts no longer exist.

"Masks" was the twenty-ninth story I had written, so if nine of the stories written up to that time were total flops, the other twenty, which were sold, make me only a 30 percent flop, even in my teen-age years. Sometimes it was only after considerable effort that those early stories were sold, but most of them appeared (for better or worse) as I had written them, so there is no "alternate" there.

There was, however, one exception. In March, 1939, I wrote a story called "Pilgrimage." Campbell didn't like it, but was willing to have me try my hand at revision in order that I might eliminate the things he disapproved of. Actually, I revised it three times, giving each new version to Campbell, and each time he rejected it. The fourth rejection was final.

I continued revising it with a determination worthy of a far better cause, and the story was finally published in the Spring, 1942, *Planet Stories,* after a total of seven (!) revisions. *Planet Stories* published it under the dreadful title of "Black Friar of the Flame" and by then, I simply hated the story. I decided I would never again revise a story more than once—and I never have. However, none of the early versions of "Pilgrimage" exist, so I can't include them here—thank goodness.

"Masks," the ninth and last story I wrote and was unable to sell, was written at the beginning of February, 1941. I wrote two other stories that month, both of which were published in minor magazines. Then, in March, 1941, I wrote "Nightfall" as my thirty-second story.

How it was possible for me to write "Nightfall" after having written thirty-one stories of quality varying from fair to downright horrible, I don't know. Of course, I don't rate "Nightfall" as highly as most science fiction readers seem to, but there's no denying that it settled down almost at once into the status of "classic." On a number of occasions it has even been voted the best science fiction short story or novelette ever written. (I disapprove of that estimate strongly. I believe that I myself have written a number of stories that are better than "Nightfall." It is even possible that others have done so.)

In any case, after "Nightfall" I never wrote another science fiction story I couldn't sell, usually at the first try. With growing confidence in myself, I became less and less amenable to drastic revision. I could always be talked into making trivial changes that involved the introduction or excision of sentences, or even paragraphs, but was rarely willing to do more than that.

Of course, "rarely" is not "never," and there were always exceptions. Usually those exceptions involved either Horace Gold or John Campbell. Both were top-ranking science fiction writers in their own right, and both were overbearing individuals who were never satisfied with a story that was not exactly as they would have written it themselves. The difference between the two of them was that Campbell was genial and pleasant, while Gold was cantankerous and sometimes abrasive.

Usually my brushes with Gold were traumatic. In 1950, when I was writing *The Stars, Like Dust*—my second novel, he insisted that I introduce a small plot line involving the Constitution of the United States. I objected strenuously on the ground that in a novel with Galactic sweep, something associated with a small part of one planet was simply inappropriate. Gold continued to insist, and inserted it in the form of scattered paragraphs that could easily be excised without damaging the novel in any way. When I handed the manuscript to Bradbury, I apologized for the offensive paragraphs and said I would excise them, but when Bradbury read the novel he wanted them to stay. You have no idea how frustrated I was—but the inappropriate paragraphs have remained ever since, and *The Stars, Like Dust*—is my least favorite novel, in consequence.

Then, when Gold serialized *The Stars, Like Dust*—in the January, February, and March, 1951, issues of *Galaxy*, he made things worse by titling it *Tyrann*. He had the *worst* taste in titles, in my opinion.

In June, 1952, I sold "The Martian Way" to Gold. He wanted lots of revisions and I balked. He finally reduced his demands to one: I had only male characters in the story, and would I please introduce one female, any female.

I couldn't see a reason for it, since the plot didn't demand a female and I wasn't at ease with them. (I mean, as characters in a story; in real life, I was very much at ease with them, thank you.) But I agreed, because I didn't want to seem totally unreasonable. I therefore revised a section or two of the story and inserted the shrewish wife of one of the males.

This was *not* what Gold wanted, and I knew very well it was not what he wanted, but I had done what he said. I had introduced a female. Gold was forced to run the story as revised. It appeared in the November, 1952, issue of *Galaxy*, and on the cover my name was misspelled. I don't suppose that was Gold's way of getting back at me, but at the time the thought *did* cross my mind.

I don't have the original version of "The Martian Way." Those were the days before Gotlieb and "Isaac's Vault," and I daresay it was burned in the barbecue pit. It doesn't matter, however; the difference between the first version and the published version was not great enough to warrant the inclusion of the former here.

Another peculiar incident took place with my story "Hostess," which I had sold to Gold in December, 1950. Apparently Theodore Sturgeon had earlier sold him a story that had the same central point as mine, though the stories were miles apart otherwise. Gold insisted that I make some minor changes in the final part of the story in order to lessen the completely coincidental resemblance. I did so under vehement protest because the changes would greatly weaken my story, but Gold was not to be withstood in this matter.

"Hostess" appeared in the May, 1951, *Galaxy*, but when I included it in my collection *Nightfall and Other Stories* (Doubleday, 1969), I made sure that it appeared in my original version. The original has therefore seen print, so it is not suitable for inclusion here.

My heroine in "Hostess," by the way, was originally named Vera Smollett. This Gold resolutely refused to permit because the editor in chief of the magazine (a purely nominal position, as far as I know) was, at the time, Vera Cerutti. I was puzzled as to what difference that made, since my Vera was a totally sympathetic character, but I suppose Gold had his reasons, so I changed Vera to Rose. In all later appearances of the story, I kept the name Rose. (Something like that happened to me only one other time—when one of the two characters in a short-short mystery of mine happened, unknown to me, to bear the name of the editor's deceased wife. The editor asked that the name be changed, and I obliged.)

Once, and once only, was this rocky relationship between Gold and myself over revisions resolved entirely in his favor.

In the fall of 1957, I wrote a story called "The Ugly Little Boy." I sent it to Larry Shaw of *Infinity Science Fiction* because he had asked me for a story. He took it at once, but the magazine was on its last legs (unknown to me), and on February 5, 1958, he admitted he had no money to pay for it and sent the story back.

This was a very disconcerting event, for I intended to make "The Ugly Little Boy" the concluding story in a new collection of mine to be called *Nine Tomorrows*. I had shown the story to Bradbury, and he was doubtful. I had to talk him into accepting the story as it was—the first time I ever had to use my eloquence on him for such a purpose. If now I couldn't find a magazine to take the story, and quickly, Bradbury might reconsider his willingness to include it.

I submitted the story to *Astounding* and Campbell sent it back on March 11, quite firmly. There was no request for revision. So, very reluctantly, I tried Horace Gold, bracing myself for the usual harsh rejection.

It wasn't like that at all. On March 20, we talked on the phone and he said he would take the story if I would make some revisions. He was quite apologetic about it because by that time he knew very well that requests for revision would be met by me with the sternest possible resistance and that he might have to wait a long time before I was willing to try him again. He outlined three points he wanted to make and said he would be satisfied if I would adjust the story to meet just one of them—any one of the three.

But even as he spoke I realized I had the story all wrong. No wonder Bradbury had been reluctant and Campbell totally negative. Gold's critique had explained that to me.

"Never mind, Horace," I shouted into the phone, "I'll rewrite the whole damned story."

And I did. Between March 24 and April 1, 1958, I wrote an entirely new version of the story, and both Gold and Bradbury accepted the new version gladly. It appeared in the September, 1958, *Galaxy* under the senseless title of "Lastborn." However, it was included in *Nine Tomorrows* (Doubleday, 1959) under its original and sensible title of "The Ugly Little Boy."

I don't have the original version of "The Ugly Little Boy," and this I regret bitterly. If I had it, I would have included it here, *with* the published version, and you would have seen with your own eyes how an experienced writer can miss the boat and *need* a little bit of correction from outside. But there you are—. Once I finished the second, infinitely superior, version, without a Howard Gotlieb to tell me I must save *everything*, I probably simply tore the first version into confetti.

I do have one story to present, however, and it is not a Gold story at all, but a Campbell story. In December, 1952, Campbell suggested I write a story about a man who found that he could levitate but could not get anyone to take it seriously. He wanted to call it "Upsy-Daisy." In those days, you see, Campbell was becoming increasingly interested in the fringe areas of science, and he never lost a chance to get authors to write stories about telepathy, telekinesis, clairvoyance, and other "wild talents."

I was careful not to make it a story about the fringe, however, but dealt with levitation strictly from the viewpoint of physics, in the full realization that this might make Campbell refuse the story. But that wasn't it. Campbell objected to the downbeat ending and talked me into agreeing to something upbeat.

I therefore rewrote the final third of the story, whereupon he took it and published it in the October, 1953, issue of *Astounding*. Because of the revised ending, I was never entirely happy with "Belief." However, I allowed the published version to be anthologized several times and included it in two of my collections: *Through a Glass, Clearly* (New English Library, 1967) and *The Winds of Change and Other Stories* (Doubleday, 1983).

I still have the original version, however, and, for the first time, it will see publication here.

Belief

"Did you ever dream you were flying?" asked Dr. Roger Toomey of his wife.

June Toomey looked up. "Certainly!"

Her quick fingers didn't stop their nimble manipulations of the yarn out of which an intricate and quite useless doily was being created. The television set made a muted murmur in the room and the posturings on its screen were, out of long custom, disregarded.

Roger said, "Everyone dreams of flying at some time or other. It's universal. I've done it many times. That's what worries me."

June said, "I don't know what you're getting at, dear. I hate to say so." She counted stitches in an undertone.

"When you think about it, it makes you wonder. It's not really flying that you dream of. You have no wings; at least I never had any. There's no effort involved. You're just floating. That's it. Floating."

"When I fly," said June, "I don't remember any of the details. Except once I landed on top of City Hall and hadn't any clothes on. Somehow no one ever seems to pay any attention to you when you're dream-nude. Ever notice that? You're dying of embarrassment, but people just pass by."

She pulled at the yarn and the ball tumbled out the bag and halfway across the floor. She paid no attention.

Roger shook his head slowly. At the moment, his face was pale and absorbed in doubt. It seemed all angles, with its high cheekbones, its long, straight nose, and the widow's-peak hairline that was growing more pronounced with the years. He was thirty-five.

He said, "Have you ever wondered what makes you dream you're floating?"

"No, I haven't."

June Toomey was blonde and small. Her prettiness was the fragile kind that does not impose itself upon you, but rather creeps on you unaware. She had the bright blue eyes and pink cheeks of a porcelain doll. She was thirty.

Roger said, "Many dreams are only the mind's interpretation of a stimulus imperfectly understood. The stimuli are forced into a reasonable context in a split second."

June said, "What are you talking about, darling?"

Roger said, "Look, I once dreamed I was in a hotel, attending a physics convention. I was with old friends. Everything seemed quite normal. Suddenly there was a confusion of shouting, and for no reason at all I grew panicky. I ran to the door, but it wouldn't open. One by one, my friends disappeared. They had no trouble leaving the room, but I couldn't see how they managed it. I shouted at them and they ignored me.

"It was borne in upon me that the hotel was on fire. I didn't smell smoke. I just knew there was a fire. I ran to the window, and I could see a fire escape on the outside of the building. I ran to each window in turn, but none led to the fire escape. I was quite alone in the room now. I leaned out the window, calling desperately. No one heard me.

"Then the fire engines were coming, little red smears darting along the streets. I remember that clearly. The alarm bells clanged sharply to clear traffic. I could hear them, louder and louder, till the sound was split-

ting my skull. I awoke, and of course, the alarm clock
was ringing.

"Now I can't have dreamed a long dream designed to
arrive at the moment of the alarm-clock ring in a way
that builds the alarm neatly into the fabric of the
dream. It's much more reasonable to suppose that the
dream began at the moment the alarm began and
crammed all its sensation of duration into one split
second. It was just a hurry-up device of my brain to
explain this sudden noise that penetrated the silence."

June was frowning now. She put down her crochet-
ing. "Roger! You've been behaving queerly since you
got back from the College. You didn't eat much, and
now this ridiculous conversation. I've never heard you
so morbid. What you need is a dose of bicarbonate."

"I need a little more than that," said Roger in a low
voice. "Now what starts a floating dream?"

"If you don't mind, let's change the subject."

She rose, and with firm fingers turned up the sound
on the television set. A young gentleman with hollow
cheeks and a soulful tenor suddenly raised his voice
and assured her, dulcetly, of his never-ending love.

Roger turned it down again and stood with his back
to the instrument.

"Levitation!" he said. "That's it, by Heaven. There
is some way in which human beings can make themselves float. They have the capacity for it. It's just that
they don't know how to use that capacity—except
when they sleep. Then, sometimes, they lift up just a
little bit, a tenth of an inch maybe. It wouldn't be
enough for anyone to notice even if they were watching, but it would be enough to deliver the proper
sensation for the start of a floating dream."

"Roger, you're delirious. I wish you'd stop. Honestly."

He drove on. "Sometimes we sink down slowly, and
the sensation is gone. Then again, sometimes the float-
control ends suddenly, and we drop.—June, did you
ever dream you were falling?"

"Yes, of c——"

"You're hanging on the side of a building, or you're

sitting at the edge of a seat, and suddenly you're tumbling. There's the awful shock of falling and you snap awake, your breath gasping, your heart palpitating. You *did* fall. There's no other explanation."

June's expression, having passed slowly from bewilderment to concern, dissolved suddenly into sheepish amusement.

"Roger, you *devil*. And you fooled me! Oh, you rat!"

"What?"

"Oh no. You can't play it out anymore. I know exactly what you're doing. You're making up a plot to a story and you're trying it out on me. I should know better than to listen to you."

Roger looked startled, even a little confused. He strode to her chair and looked down at her. "No, June."

"I don't see why not. You've been talking about writing fiction as long as I've known you. If you've got a plot, you might as well write it down. No use just frightening me with it." Her fingers flew as her spirits rose.

"June, for Heaven's sake, this is no story."

"But what else—"

"When I woke up this morning, *I dropped to the mattress!*"

He stared at her without blinking. "I dreamed I was flying," he said. "It was clear and distinct. I remember every minute of it. I was lying on my back when I woke up. I was feeling comfortable and quite happy. I just wondered a little why the ceiling looked so queer. I yawned and stretched and *touched* the ceiling. For a minute, I just stared at my arm reaching upward and ending hard against the ceiling.

"Then I turned over. I didn't move a muscle, June. I just turned all in one piece because I wanted to. There I was, five feet above the bed. There you were on the bed, sleeping. I was frightened. Lord, I was frightened to death. I didn't know how to get down, but the minute I thought of getting down, I dropped. I dropped slowly. The whole process was under perfect control.

"I stayed in bed fifteen minutes before I dared move. Then I got up, washed, dressed, and went to work."

June forced a laugh. "Darling, you had *better* write it up. But that's all right. You've just been working too hard."

"Please! Don't be banal."

"People do work too hard, even though to say so is banal. After all, you were just dreaming fifteen minutes longer than you thought you were."

"It wasn't a dream."

"Of course it was. I can't even count the times I've dreamed I awoke and dressed and made breakfast, then really woke up and found it was all to do over again. I've even dreamed I was dreaming, if you see what I mean. It can be awfully confusing."

"Look, June. I've come to you with a problem because you're the only one I feel I can come to. Please take me seriously."

June's blue eyes opened wide. "Darling! I'm taking you as seriously as I can. You're the physics professor, not I. Gravitation is what you know about, not I. Would *you* take it seriously if I told you *I* had found myself floating?"

"No. *No!* That's the hell of it. I don't want to believe it, only I've got to. It was no dream, June. I tried to tell myself it was. You have no idea how I talked myself into that. By the time I got to class, I was sure it was a dream. You didn't notice anything queer about me at breakfast, did you?"

"Yes, I did, now that I think about it."

"Well, it wasn't very queer or you would have mentioned it. Anyway, I gave my nine o'clock lecture perfectly. By eleven, I had forgotten the whole incident. Then, just after lunch, I needed a book. I needed Page and— Well, the book doesn't matter; I just needed it. It was on an upper shelf, but I could reach it. June—"

He stopped.

"Well, go on, Roger."

"Look, did you ever try to pick up something that's just a step away? You bend and automatically take a step toward it as you reach. It's completely involuntary. It's just your body's overall coordination."

"All right. What of it?"

"I reached for the book, and automatically took a step upward. On air, June! On empty air!"

"I'm going to call Jim Sarle, Roger."

"I'm not sick, damn it."

"I think he ought to talk to you. He's a friend. It won't be a doctor's visit. He'll just talk to you."

"And what good will that do?" Roger's face turned red with sudden anger.

"We'll see. Now sit down, Roger. Please." She walked to the phone.

He cut her off, seizing her wrist. "You don't believe me."

"Oh, Roger."

"You don't."

"I believe you. Of course I believe you. I just want—"

"Yes. You just want Jim Sarle to talk to me. That's how much you believe me. I'm telling the truth, but you want me to talk to a psychiatrist. Look, you don't have to take my word for anything. I can prove this. I can prove I can float."

"I *believe* you."

"Don't be a fool. I know when I'm being humored. Stand still! Now watch me."

He backed away to the middle of the room and without preliminary lifted off the floor. He *dangled,* with the toes of his shoes six empty inches from the carpet.

June's eyes and mouth were three round O's. She whispered, "Come down, Roger. Oh dear heaven, come down."

He drifted down, his feet touching the floor without a sound. "You see?"

"Oh my. Oh my."

She stared at him, half-frightened, half-sick.

On the television set, a chesty female sang mutedly that flying high with some guy in the sky was her idea of nothing at all.

Roger Toomey stared into the bedroom's darkness. He whispered, "June."

"What?"

"You're not sleeping?"

"No."

"I can't sleep either. I keep holding the headboard to make sure I'm—you know."

His hand moved restlessly and touched her face. She flinched, jerking away as though he carried an electric charge.

She said, "I'm sorry. I'm a little nervous."

"That's all right. I'm getting out of bed anyway."

"What are you going to do? You've got to sleep."

"Well, I can't, so there's no sense keeping you awake too."

"Maybe nothing will happen. It doesn't have to happen every night. It didn't happen before last night."

"How do I know? Maybe I just never went up so high. Maybe I just never woke up and caught myself. Anyway, now it's different."

He was sitting up in bed, his legs bent, his arms clasping his knees, his forehead resting on them. He pushed the sheet to one side and rubbed his cheek against the soft flannel of his pajamas.

He said, "It's bound to be different now. My mind's full of it. Once I'm asleep, once I'm not holding myself down consciously, why, up I'll go."

"I don't see why. It must be such an effort."

"That's the point. It isn't."

"But you're fighting gravity, aren't you?"

"I know, but there's still no effort. Look, June, if I only *could* understand it, I wouldn't mind so much."

He dangled his feet out of bed and stood up. "I don't want to talk about it."

His wife muttered, "Oh, for Heaven's sake, I don't

want to either." She started crying, fighting back the sobs and turning them into strangled moans, which sounded much worse.

Roger said, "I'm sorry, June. I'm getting you all wrought up."

"No, don't touch me. Just—just leave me alone."

He took a few uncertain steps away from the bed.

She said, "Where are you going?"

"To the studio couch. Will you help me?"

"How?"

"I want you to tie me down."

"Tie you down?"

"With a couple of ropes. Just loosely, so I can turn if I want to. Do you mind?"

Her bare feet were already seeking her mules on the floor at her side of the bed. "All right," she sighed.

Roger Toomey sat in the small cubbyhole that passed for his office and stared at the pile of examination papers before him. At the moment, he didn't see how he was going to mark them.

He had given five lectures on electricity and magnetism since the first night he had floated. He had gotten through them somehow, though not swimmingly. The students had asked ridiculous questions, so probably he wasn't making himself as clear as he once did.

Today he had saved himself a lecture by giving a surprise examination. He didn't bother making one up; just handed out copies of one given several years earlier.

Now he had the answer papers and would have to mark them. Why? Did it matter what they said? Or anyone? Was it so important to know the laws of physics? If it came to that, what were the laws? Were there any, really?

Or was it all just a mass of confusion out of which nothing orderly could ever be extracted? Was the universe, for all its appearance, merely the original chaos, still waiting for the Spirit to move upon the face of its deep?

Insomnia wasn't helping him either. Even strapped in upon the couch, he slept only fitfully, and then always with dreams.

There was a knock at the door.

Roger cried angrily, "Who's there?"

A pause, and then the uncertain answer. "It's Miss Harroway, Dr. Toomey. I have the letters you dictated."

"Well, come in, come in. Don't just stand there."

The Department Secretary opened the door a minimum distance and squeezed her lean and unprepossessing body into his office. She had a sheaf of papers in her hand. To each was clipped a yellow carbon and a stamped, addressed envelope.

Roger was anxious to get rid of her. That was his mistake. He stretched forward to reach the letters as she approached and felt himself leave the chair.

He moved two feet forward, still in sitting position, before he could bring himself down hard, losing his balance and tumbling in the process. It was too late.

It was entirely too late. Miss Harroway dropped the letters in a fluttering handful. She screamed and turned, hitting the door with her shoulder, caroming out into the hall and dashing down the corridor in a clatter of high heels.

Roger rose, rubbing an aching hip. "Damn," he said forcefully. "Damn that ninny."

But he couldn't help seeing her point. He pictured the sight as she must have seen it—a full-grown man lifting smoothly out of his chair and gliding toward her in a maintained squat.

He picked up the letters and closed his office door. It was quite late in the day; the corridors would be empty; she would probably be quite incoherent. Still— He waited anxiously for the crowd to gather.

Nothing happened. Perhaps she was lying somewhere in a dead faint. Roger felt it a point of honor to seek her out and do what he could for her, but he told his conscience to go to the devil. Until he found out exactly what was wrong with him, exactly what this wild nightmare of his was all about, he must do nothing to reveal it.

Nothing, that is, more than he had done already.

He leafed through the letters, one to every major theoretical physicist in the country. Home talent was insufficient for this sort of thing.

He wondered if Miss Harroway grasped the contents of the letter. He hoped not. He had deliberately couched them in technical language; more so, perhaps, than was quite necessary. Partly, that was to be discreet; partly, to impress the addressees with the fact that he, Toomey, was a legitimate and capable scientist.

One by one, he put the letters in the appropriate envelopes. The best brains in the country, he thought. Could they help?

He didn't know.

The library was quiet. Roger Toomey closed the *Journal of Theoretical Physics,* placed it on end, and stared at its back strip somberly. The *Journal of Theoretical Physics!* What did any of the contributors to that learned bit of balderdash understand anyway? The thought tore at him. Until so recently they had been the greatest men in the world to him.

And still he was doing his best to live up to their code and philosophy. With June's increasingly reluctant help, he had made measurements. He had tried to weigh the phenomenon in the balance, extract its relationships, evaluate its quantities. He had tried, in short, to defeat it in the only way he knew how—by making of it just another expression of the eternal modes of behavior that all the Universe must follow.

(*Must* follow. The best minds said so.)

Only there was nothing to measure. There was absolutely no sensation of effort to his levitation. Indoors (he dared not test himself outdoors, of course) he could reach the ceiling as easily as he could rise an inch, except that it took more time. Given enough time, he felt, he could continue rising indefinitely; go to the Moon, if necessary.

He could carry weights while levitating. The process became slower, but there was no increase in effort.

The day before he had come on June without warning, a stopwatch in one hand.

"How much do you weigh?" he asked.

"One hundred ten," she replied. She gazed at him uncertainly.

He seized her waist with one arm. She tried to push him away, but he paid no attention. Together, they moved upward at a creeping pace. She clung to him, white and rigid with terror.

"Twenty-two minutes, thirteen seconds," he said, when his head nudged the ceiling.

When they came down again, June tore away and hurried out of the room.

Some days before, he had passed a drugstore scale standing shabbily on a street corner. The street was empty, so he stepped on and put in his penny. Even though he had suspected something of the sort, it was a shock to find himself weighing thirty pounds.

He began carrying handfuls of pennies and weighing himself under all conditions. He was heavier on days on which there was a brisk wind, as though he required weight to keep from blowing away.

Adjustment was automatic. Whatever it was that levitated him maintained a balance between comfort and safety. But he could enforce conscious control upon his levitation just as he could upon his respiration. He could stand on a scale and force the pointer up to almost his full weight—and down, of course, to nothing.

He had bought a scale two days before and tried to measure the rate at which he could change weight. That didn't help. The rate, whatever it was, was faster than the pointer could swing. All he did was collect data on moduli of compressibility and moments of inertia.

Well— What did it all amount to, anyway?

He stood up and trudged out of the library, shoulders drooping. He touched tables and chairs as he

walked to the side of the room and then kept his hand
unobtrusively on the wall. He had to do that, he felt.
Contact with matter kept him continuously informed
as to his status with respect to the ground. If his hand
lost touch with a table or slid upward against the
wall—that was it.

The corridor had the usual sprinkling of students.
He ignored them. In these last days, they had gradually learned to stop greeting him. Roger imagined
that some had come to think of him as queer, and
most were probably growing to dislike him.

He passed by the elevator. He never took it anymore
—going down, particularly. When the elevator made
its initial drop, he found it impossible not to lift into
air for just a moment. No matter how he lay in wait
for the moment, he hopped, and people would turn to
look at him.

He reached for the railing at the head of the stairs
and just before his hand touched it, one of his feet
kicked the other. It was the most ungainly stumble
that could be imagined. Three weeks earlier, Roger
would have sprawled down the stairs.

This time his autonomic system took over, and leaning forward, spread-eagled, fingers wide, legs half-
buckled, he sailed down the flight glider-like. He might
have been on wires.

He was too dazed to right himself, too paralyzed
with horror to do anything. Within two feet of the
window at the bottom of the flight, he came to an
automatic halt and hovered.

There were two students on the flight he had come
down, both now pressed against the wall, three more
at the head of the stairs, two on the flight below, and
one on the landing with him, so close they could
almost touch one another.

It was very silent. They all looked at him.

Roger straightened himself, dropped to the ground,
and ran down the stairs, pushing one student roughly
out of his way.

Conversation swirled up into exclamation behind him.

* * *

"Dr. Morton wants to see me?" Roger turned in his chair, holding one of its arms firmly.

The new Department Secretary nodded. "Yes, Dr. Toomey."

She left quickly. In the short time since Miss Harroway had resigned, she had learned that Dr. Toomey had something "wrong" with him. The students avoided him. In his lecture room today, the back seats had been full of whispering students. The front seats had been empty.

Roger looked into the small wall mirror near the door. He adjusted his jacket and brushed some lint off, but that operation did little to improve his appearance. His complexion had grown sallow. He had lost at least ten pounds since all this had started, though, of course, he had no way of really knowing his exact weight loss. He was generally unhealthy-looking, as though his digestion perpetually disagreed with him and won every argument.

He had no apprehensions about this interview with the Chairman of the Department. He had reached a pronounced cynicism concerning the levitation incidents. Apparently witnesses didn't talk. Miss Harroway hadn't. There was no sign that the students on the staircase had.

With a last touch at his tie, he left his office.

Dr. Philip Morton's office was not too far down the hall, which was gratifying to Roger. More and more, he was cultivating the habit of walking with systematic slowness. He picked up one foot and put it before him, watching. Then he picked up the other and put it before him, still watching. He moved along in a confirmed stoop, gazing at his feet.

Dr. Morton frowned as Roger walked in. He had little eyes, and wore a poorly trimmed grizzled mustache and an untidy suit. He had a moderate reputation in the scientific world and a decided penchant for leaving teaching duties to the members of his staff.

He said, "Say, Toomey, I got the damndest letter

from Linus Derring. Did you write to him on—" (he consulted a paper on his desk) "—the twenty-second of last month? Is this your signature?"

Roger looked and nodded. Anxiously, he tried to read Deering's letter upside down. This was unexpected. Of the letters he had sent out the day of the Miss Harroway incident, only four had so far been answered.

Three of them had consisted of cold one-paragraph replies that read, more or less: "This is to acknowledge receipt of your letter of the 22nd. I do not believe I can help you in the matter you discuss." A fourth, from Ballantine of Northwestern Tech, had bumblingly suggested an institute for psychic research. Roger couldn't tell whether he was trying to be helpful or insulting.

Deering of Princeton made five. He had had high hopes of Deering.

Dr. Morton cleared his throat loudly and adjusted a pair of glasses. "I want to read you what he says.—Sit down, Toomey, sit down. He says: 'Dear Phil—' "

Dr. Morton looked up briefly with a slightly fatuous smile. "Linus and I met at Federation meetings last year. We had a few drinks together. Very nice fellow."

He adjusted his glasses again and returned to the letter: " 'Dear Phil: Is there a Dr. Roger Toomey in your department? I received a very queer letter from him the other day. I didn't quite know what to make of it. At first, I thought I'd just let it go as another crank letter. Then I thought that since the letter carried your department heading, you ought to know of it. It's just possible someone may be using your staff as part of a confidence game. I'm enclosing Dr. Toomey's letter for your inspection. I hope to be visiting your part of the country—'

"Well, the rest of it is personal." Dr. Morton folded the letter, took off his glasses, put them in a leather container, and put that in his breast pocket. He twined his fingers together and leaned forward.

"Now," he said, "I don't have to read you your own letter. Was it a joke? A hoax?"

"Dr. Morton," said Roger heavily, "I was serious. I don't see anything wrong with my letter. I sent it to quite a few physicists. It speaks for itself. I've made observations on a case of—of levitation and I wanted information about possible theoretical explanations for such a phenomenon."

"Levitation! Really!"

"It's a legitimate case, Dr. Morton."

"You've observed it yourself?"

"Of course."

"No hidden wires? No mirrors? Look here, Toomey, you're no expert on these frauds."

"Good God—" With an effort, Roger broke off. He resumed coldly. "This was a thoroughly scientific series of observations. There is no possibility of fraud."

"You might have consulted me, Toomey, before sending out these letters."

"Perhaps I should have, Dr. Morton, but frankly, I thought you might be—unsympathetic."

"Well, thank you. I should hope so. And on department stationery. I'm really surprised, Toomey. Look here, Toomey, your life is your own. If you wish to believe in levitation, go ahead, but strictly on your own time. For the sake of the department and the College, it should be obvious that this sort of thing should not be injected into your scholastic affairs.

"In point of fact, you've lost some weight recently, haven't you, Toomey? Yes, you don't look well at all. I'd see a doctor, if I were you. A nerve specialist, perhaps."

Roger said bitterly, "A psychiatrist might be better, you think?"

"Well, that's entirely your business. In any case, a little rest—"

The telephone had rung and the secretary had taken the call. She caught Dr. Morton's eye and he picked up his extension.

He said, "Hello.—Oh, Dr. Smithers, yes.—Umm. —Yes.—Concerning whom?—Well, in point of fact, he's with me right now.—Yes.—Yes, immediately."

He cradled the phone and looked at Roger thoughtfully. "The Dean wants to see both of us."

"What about, sir?"

"He didn't say." He got up and stepped to the door. "Are you coming, Toomey?"

"Yes, sir." Roger rose slowly to his feet, cramming the toe of one foot carefully under Dr. Morton's desk as he did so.

Dean Smithers was a lean man with a long, ascetic face. He had a mouthful of false teeth that fitted just badly enough to give his sibilants a peculiar half-whistle.

"Close the door, Miss Bryce," he said, "and I'll take no phone calls for a while.—Sit down, gentlemen."

He stared at them portentously and added, "I think I had better get right to the point. I don't know exactly what Dr. Toomey is doing, but he must stop."

Dr. Morton turned upon Roger in amazement. "What have you been doing?"

Roger shrugged dispiritedly. "Nothing that I can help." He had underestimated student tongue-wagging after all.

"Oh, come, come." The Dean registered impatience. "I'm sure I don't know how much of the story to discount, but it seems you must have been engaging in parlor tricks; silly parlor tricks, quite unsuited to the spirit and dignity of this institution."

Dr. Morton said, "This is all beyond me."

The Dean frowned. "It seems you haven't heard, then. It is amazing to me how the faculty can remain in complete ignorance of matters that fairly saturate the student body. I had never realized it before. I myself heard of it by accident—by a very fortunate accident, in fact, since I was able to intercept a newspaper reporter who arrived this morning looking for someone he called 'Dr. Toomey, the flying professor.'"

"What?" cried Dr. Morton.

Roger listened haggardly.

"That's what the reporter said. I quote him. It seems

one of our students had called the paper. I ordered the
newspaperman out and had the student sent to my office.
According to him, Dr. Toomey flew—I use the word
'flew,' because that's what the student insisted on calling it—*flew* down a flight of stairs and then back up
again. He claimed there were a dozen witnesses."

"I went down the stairs only," muttered Roger.

Dean Smithers was tramping up and down along his
carpet now. He had worked himself up into a feverish
eloquence. "Now mind you, Toomey, I have nothing
against amateur theatricals. In my stay in office I have
consistently fought against stuffiness and false dignity.
I have encouraged friendliness between ranks in the
faculty and have not even objected to reasonable frat-
ernization with students. So I have no objection to
your putting on a show for the students *in your own
home.*

"Surely you see what could happen to the College
once an irresponsible press is done with us. Shall we
have a flying professor craze succeed the flying saucer
craze? If the reporters get in touch with you, Dr.
Toomey, I will expect you to deny all such reports
categorically."

"I understand, Dean Smithers."

"I trust that we shall escape this incident without
lasting damage. I must ask you, with all the firmness
at my command, never to repeat your—uh—performance. If you ever do, your resignation will be requested. Do you understand, Dr. Toomey?"

"Yes," said Roger.

"In that case, good day, gentlemen."

Dr. Morton steered Roger back into his office. This
time he shooed his secretary out and closed the door
behind her carefully.

"Good heavens, Toomey," he whispered, "has this
madness any connection with your letter on levitation?"

Roger's nerves were beginning to twang. "Isn't it
obvious? I was referring to myself in those letters."

"You can fly? I mean, levitate?"

"Either word you choose."

"I never heard of such— Damn it, Toomey, did Miss Harroway ever see you levitate?"

"Once. It was an accid——"

"Of course. It's obvious now. She was so hysterical it was hard to make out. She said you had jumped at her. It sounded as though she were accusing you of—of—" Dr. Morton looked embarrassed. "Well, I didn't believe that. She was a good secretary, you understand, but obviously not one designed to attract the attention of a young man. I was actually relieved when she left. I thought she would be carrying a small revolver next, or accusing *me*— You—you levitated, eh?"

"Yes."

"How do you do it?"

Roger shook his head. "That's my problem. I don't know."

Dr. Morton allowed himself a smile. "Surely you don't repeal the law of gravity?"

"You know, I think I do. There must be anti-gravity involved somehow."

Dr. Morton's indignation at having a joke taken seriously was marked. He said, "Look here, Toomey, this is nothing to laugh at."

"*Laugh* at! Great Scott, Dr. Morton, do I look as though I were laughing?"

"Well— You need a rest. No question about it. A little rest, and this nonsense of yours will pass. I'm sure of it."

"It's not nonsense." Roger bowed his head a moment, then said, in a quieter tone, "I tell you what, Dr. Morton, would you like to go into this with me? In some way this will open new horizons in physical science. I don't know how it works; I just can't conceive of any solution. The two of us together—"

Dr. Morton's look of horror had penetrated by that time.

Roger said, "I know it all sounds queer. But I'll

demonstrate for you. It's perfectly legitimate. I wish to Heaven it weren't."

"Now, now," Dr. Morton sprang from his seat. "Don't exert yourself. You need a rest badly. I don't think you should wait till June. You go home right now. I'll see that your salary comes through, and I'll look after your course. I used to give it myself once, you know."

"Dr. Morton. This is important."

"I know. I know." Dr. Morton clapped Roger on the shoulder. "Still, my boy, you look under the weather. Speaking frankly, you look like hell. You need a long rest."

"I *can* levitate." Roger's voice was climbing again. "You're just trying to get rid of me because you don't believe me. Do you think I'm lying? What would be my motive?"

"You're exciting yourself needlessly, my boy. You let me make a phone call. I'll have someone take you home."

"I tell you, I *can* levitate," shouted Roger.

Dr. Morton turned red. "Look, Toomey, let's not discuss it. I don't care if you fly up in the air right this minute."

"You mean seeing isn't believing as far as you're concerned?"

"Levitation? Of course not." The Department Chairman was bellowing. "If I saw you fly, I'd see an optometrist or a psychiatrist. I'd sooner believe myself insane than that the laws of physics—"

He caught himself, harumphed loudly. "Well, as I said, let's not discuss it. I'll just make this phone call."

"No need, sir. No need," said Roger. "I'll go. I'll take my rest. Good-bye."

He walked out rapidly, moving more quickly than at any time in days. Dr. Morton, on his feet, hands flat on his desk, looked at his departing back with relief.

James Sarle, M.D., was in the living room when Roger arrived home. He was lighting his pipe as Roger stepped through the door, one large-knuckled hand enclosing the bowl. He shook out the match and his ruddy face crinkled into a smile.

"Hello, Roger. Resigning from the human race? Haven't heard from you in over a month."

His black eyebrows met above the bridge of his nose, giving him a rather forbidding appearance that somehow helped him establish the proper atmosphere with his patients.

Roger turned to June, who sat buried in an armchair. As usual lately, she had a look of wan exhaustion on her face.

Roger said to her, "Why did you bring him here?"

"Hold it! Hold it, man," said Sarle. "Nobody brought me. I met June downtown this morning and invited myself here. I'm bigger than she is. She couldn't keep me out."

"Met her by coincidence, I suppose? Do you make appointments for all your coincidences?"

Sarle laughed. "Let's put it this way. She told me a little about what's been going on."

June said wearily, "I'm sorry if you disapprove, Roger, but it was the first chance I had to talk to someone who would understand."

"What makes you think he understands? Tell me, Jim, do you believe her story?"

Sarle said, "It's not an easy thing to believe. You'll admit that. But I'm trying."

"All right, suppose I flew. Suppose I levitated right now. What would you do?"

"Faint, maybe. Maybe I'd say, 'Holy Pete.' Maybe I'd bust out laughing. Why don't you try, and then we'll see."

Roger stared at him. "You really want to see it?"

"Why shouldn't I?"

"The ones that have seen it screamed or ran or froze with horror. Can you take it, Jim?"

"I think so."

"Okay." Roger slipped two feet upward and executed a slow ten-fold *entrechat*. He remained in the

air, toes pointed downward, legs together, arms grace-
fully outstretched in bitter parody.

"Better than Nijinsky, eh, Jim?"

Sarle did none of the things he had suggested he
might do. Except for catching his pipe as it dropped,
he did nothing at all.

June had closed her eyes. Tears squeezed quietly
through the lids.

Sarle said, "Come down, Roger."

Roger did so. He took a seat and said, "I wrote to
physicists, men of reputation. I explained the situation
in an impersonal way. I said I thought it ought to be
investigated. Most of them ignored me. One of them
wrote to old man Morton to ask if I were crooked or
crazy."

"Oh Roger," whispered June.

"You think that's bad? The Dean called me into his
office today. I'm to stop my parlor tricks, he says. It
seems I had stumbled down the stairs and automatically levitated myself to safety. Morton says he wouldn't
believe I could fly if he saw me in action. Seeing isn't
believing in this case, he says, and orders me to take a
rest.—The hell with all of them. I'm not going back."

"Roger," said June, her eyes opening wide. "Are
you serious?"

"I can't go back. I'm sick of them. Scientists!"

"But what will you do?"

"I don't know." Roger buried his head in his hands.
He said in a muffled voice, "You tell me, Jim. You're
the psychiatrist. Why won't they believe me?"

"Perhaps it's a matter of self-protection, Roger,"
said Sarle slowly. "People aren't happy with anything
they can't understand. Even some centuries ago when
many people *did* believe in the existence of extra-
natural abilities, like flying on broomsticks, for instance, it was almost always assumed that these powers
originated with the forces of evil.

"People still think so. They may not believe literally
in the devil, but they do think that what is strange is
evil. They'll fight against believing in levitation—or be
scared to death if the fact is forced down their throat."

Roger shook his head. "You're talking about people, and I'm talking about scientists."

"Scientists are people."

"You know what I mean. I have here a phenomenon. It isn't witchcraft. I haven't dealt with the devil. For Heaven's sake, Jim, there must be a natural explanation. We don't know all there is to know about gravitation. We know hardly anything, really. Don't you suppose it's just barely conceivable that there is some biological method of nullifying gravity? Perhaps I am a mutation of some sort. I have a—well, call it a muscle—which can abolish gravity. At least it can abolish the effect of gravity on myself. Well, damn it, let's investigate it. Why sit on our hands? If we have antigravity, imagine what it will mean to the human race."

"Hold it, Rog," said Sarle. "Think about the matter awhile. Why are *you* so unhappy about it? According to June, you were almost mad with fear the first day it happened, *before* you had any way of knowing that science was going to ignore you and that your superiors would be unsympathetic."

"That's right," murmured June.

Sarle said, "Now why should that be? Here you had a great, new, wonderful power; a sudden freedom from the deadly pull of gravity."

Roger said, "Oh, don't be a fool. It was—horrible. I couldn't understand it. I still can't."

"Exactly, my boy. It was something you couldn't understand, and *therefore* something horrible. You're a physical scientist. You *know* what makes the universe run. Or if you don't know, you know someone else knows. Even if no one understands a certain point, you know that someday someone will know. The key word is *know*. It's part of your life. Now you come face to face with a phenomenon which you consider to violate one of the basic laws of the universe. Scientists say: Two masses will attract one another according to a fixed mathematical rule. It is an inalienable property of matter and space. There are no exceptions. And now you're an exception."

Roger said glumly, "And how."

"You see, Roger," Sarle went on, "for the first time in history, mankind really has what he considers unbreakable rules. I mean, unbreakable. In primitive cultures, a medicine man might use a spell to produce rain. If it didn't work, it didn't upset the validity of magic. It just meant that the shaman had neglected some part of his spell, or had broken a taboo, or offended a god. In modern theocratic cultures, the commandments of the Deity are unbreakable. Still, if a man were to break the commandments and yet prosper, it would be no sign that that particular religion was invalid. The ways of providence are admittedly mysterious, and some invisible punishment awaits.

"Today, however, we have rules that *really* can't be broken, and one of them is the existence of gravity. It works even though the man who invokes it has forgotten to mutter, 'em-em-over-ahr-square.' "

Roger managed a twisted smile. "You're all wrong, Jim. The unbreakable rules have been broken over and over again. Radioactivity was impossible when it was discovered. Energy came out of nowhere; incredible quantities of it. It was as ridiculous as levitation."

"Radioactivity was an objective phenomenon that could be communicated and duplicated. Uranium would fog photographic film for anyone. A Crookes tube could be built by anyone and would deliver an electron stream in identical fashion for all. You—"

"I've tried communicating—"

"I know. But can you tell me, for instance, how I might levitate?"

"Of course not."

"That limits others to observation only, without experimental duplication. It puts your levitation on the same plane with stellar evolution, something to theorize about but never experiment with."

"Yet scientists are willing to devote their lives to astrophysics."

"Scientists are people. They can't reach the stars, so they make the best of it. But they can reach you, and to be unable to touch your levitation would be infuriating."

"Jim, they haven't even tried. You talk as though I've been studied. Jim, they won't even consider the problem."

"They don't have to. Your levitation is part of a whole class of phenomena that won't be considered. Telepathy, clairvoyance, prescience, and a thousand other extra-natural powers are practically never seriously investigated, even though reported with every appearance of reliability. Rhine's experiments on ESP have annoyed far more scientists than they have intrigued. So you see, they don't have to study you to know they don't want to study you. They know that in advance."

"Is this funny to you, Jim? Scientists refuse to investigate facts; they turn their back on the truth. And you just sit there and grin and make droll statements."

"No, Roger, I know it's serious. And I have no glib explanations for mankind, really. I'm giving you my thoughts. It's what I think. But don't you see? What I'm doing, really, is to try to look at things as they are. It's what you must do. Forget your ideals, your theories, your notions as to what people *ought* to do. Consider what they *are* doing.* And try to accept it as a condition of life you must live with. I don't say it's easy."

"How do you propose that I live with it?"

James Sarle knocked the dottle out of his pipe and put it away. "You want my advice?"

"I'm ready to listen."

"In your present mood, you can't remain in science. You must live in such a way that your levitation will be accepted by others as some sort of fact. Don't you think so?"

"It would be a comfort."

"Then I can suggest something. I know a man called

*From this point on, I began to revise. The revised ending, from this point on, begins on page 298.

William Magoun. I think I can persuade him to help you. He's a sort of theatrical producer. He owns the Black Mask, which is a nightclub. Or at least that's the closest description."

"What the devil are you suggesting?"

"Isn't it obvious? Why not go on the stage? Call yourself a magician."

Sarle gathered up his topcoat and stood up.

Roger said, "A magician!"

"I have Magoun's card. I brought it with me just in case. Take it, will you? And Roger, you look awful. When did you last have a good night's sleep?"

Roger mumbled something vague.

"Do you want a prescription for some sleeping pills?"

Roger roused himself. "No, that's all right. I got some a while back from one of the men at the Medical School.—A magician!"

"It's a respectable living." Sarle stepped to the door.

June took Sarle's hand. She said softly, "Thanks, Jim. Thanks for talking to him."

Sarle squeezed her fingers. "It's all right, June."

Roger called, "Jim?"

"Yes?"

"Why is it that my flying didn't disturb you?"

Sarle smiled. "I'm not a physical scientist, Roger. In my line of work, I'm afraid, we have no rules at all. Or at least, every little school of psychiatry has its own rules, which are all mutually exclusive, and that amounts to the same thing. So what's a broken rule? Just the same—"

"Well?"

"I don't think I'll attend any of your performances at the Black Mask if Magoun takes you on. You won't mind?"

"No," said Roger dully, "I won't mind."

Sarle was gone, and Roger and June were left alone together.

Roger said, "What do you think, June?"

June did not stir out of her apathy. "I don't know."

"A magician!"

"What's the difference?" she said and walked out of the room.

Roger looked after her but did not follow. Slowly he looked down at the pasteboard square Sarle had given him.

Bill Magoun patted his desk with thick fingers. His head was bare and shiny, his cheeks broad and jowly. His voice was hoarse and he exuded an aura of coarse but good-natured prosperity.

He said, "Yeah. Dr. Sarle told me about you. Great guy, the doctor."

"Yes," said Roger dispiritedly. There was a cold morning-after smell about Magoun's cluttered office and the Black Mask, through which he had just passed at the off-hour of 11 A.M., was dankly miserable.

"The best!" said Magoun with feeling. "If he goes to bat for you, you got an in with me that's a good one, know what I mean? What's your pitch?"

Roger stumbled over the words. "I'm a magician."

Magoun looked dashed. "That so? Frankly, that's not so hot. Magicians don't go nowadays unless they got some novelty angle. You got to be a comic too these days, know what I mean? You got a specialty?"

"I can levitate."

"Levi-who?"

"I can float—float in the air."

"Yeah? You mean you, or an assistant?"

"I myself."

"Well, that's funny. I been in show business a long time, know what I mean? I get to know most of the name artists in the country. It seems to me I'd of hoid of a magician with a floating act name of Toomey. Where'd you work last?"

"I've never worked before at this, Mr. Magoun."

"You *haven't?* How'd you get your act, then? A floating illusion isn't penny-ante stuff, know what I mean?"

"I developed it myself at home."

Magoun looked unimpressed. He said, "I'd like to

help you out as a favor to the doc, so I tell you
what— Suppose you give me a little demonstration.
Just self-protection, know what I mean? You come
back some time with your props and we'll run through
it, and maybe I can place you. Maybe not here, but
somewheres."

He was rising and smiling broadly. Interview over,
the smile seemed to say.

Roger said, "I can show you right now if you'd
like."

Magoun looked startled. "Now!"

"Now!"

"Like you are. In those clothes."

"Surely."

"Well, that beats me. You *must* be an amateur. The
magicians I know wouldn't cut a pack of cards in a
business suit. They'd feel naked, know what I mean?"

Roger said, "I wasn't planning any special costume."

"No? Well, maybe you got something at that. People are getting tired of this Mandrake the Magician
getup. There might be a real kick in looking at a guy
in blue soige or something making with the tricks. A
novelty, sort of, know what I mean? Okay, let's get
you on to the stage and I'll take a seat in among the
tables. Where're your props?"

"I'll take care of them," muttered Roger.

They passed out into the tawdry hollowness of the
empty nightclub. It was gray with the dullness of thickly
curtained window light. Magoun found a switch that
poured light on the stage when he clicked it.

"Go ahead," he said, retreating into the table section. "You don't have to bother with the come-on acts
or the patter. Just let's see you float, know what I
mean? Make out like there's a roll on the drums."

At one end of the room, a waiter leaned interest-
edly on his broom.

Roger looked about him in confusion. He had one
horrible but momentary sensation of inability. Now
that, for the first time, he wanted to float, he would
forget how. There was Magoun, nodding at him, purs-

ing his lips over a fat cigar he was lighting. There was
one waiter watching. And there was a huge emptiness
where some night a hundred eyes might be on him.

He thought to himself grimly: Upsy-daisy.

And up he went.

He floated halfway to the ceiling. He heard Magoun's
hoarse shout, and saw the waiter dash precipitously
through the nearest door.

He turned a somersault, then dropped to the stage.

Magoun was on top of him when he landed. "Sensa-
tional, Toomey, terrific. Marvellous illusion. How do
you do it?"

"Well— Professional secret, you know."

"Oh, sure. I apologize. Should've known better than
to ask, but it sort of knocked me for a loop, know
what I mean? Listen, you're on. With what I seen, you
don't have to do nothing else. You'll fracture them."

"How much?" said Roger.

"Well—" Magoun cocked an eye at the ceiling.
"Fifty a week."

"A hundred and fifty," said Roger.

"What? For a new act?"

"You never saw anything like it, did you?"

Magoun said, "All right. I'll let you get away with
it, on account of the doc. Two shows a night except
Sunday. And the engagement's only for one week, till
we see how you go with the cash customers. Tell you
what— You start Monday, and I'll get in some advance
publicity. I'll bill you as the Great Flotino. How's
that?"

"All right," said Roger.

James Sarle stepped through the front door, unbut-
toned his coat, and said in a low voice, "You're looking better, June. How's Roger?"

Roger's voice sounded before June could answer.
"I'm right here, Jim. No point in whispering."

"Was I whispering?" asked Sarle cheerfully. He
fetched his pipe out of his coat pocket before delivering the garment to June. "What's new?"

Roger remained deep in the armchair. He said, "I sent in my resignation to the College today."

"Oh?" Sarle stepped to the couch and sat down facing the other. "I called Magoun. He says you're a thundering hit."

"Yes," said Roger sourly. "I've only put on a few shows, but I'm apparently well on the way to stardom."

"He says you're worth the money."

"That's nice of him. He's paying me more than the College did."

"Seriously. How is it?"

Roger stirred restlessly. "How would you suppose? I float up into the air for a bunch of idiots, listen to them yell, come down, bow, and collect my pay. Today I passed over the table of one party and hovered there a while. One of the women squealed, 'Oh, I see the wires. I see them.' Her escort climbed on the table and flailed with a newspaper through the space over my head. Another fellow jumped to grab my legs. I moved upward a bit.— Damn fools."

"It shows they're interested.—Here, June, sit down."

June smiled and did so. She had brought drinks. Roger accepted his moodily and tossed it down.

He said, "Lots of the boys from the College show up. They seem to enjoy it as long as they think it's an act. Isn't that funny?"

"No," said Sarle, "not really. It may be a good thing, all this. Once you establish your reputation as a magic man, you may be able to get back into academic life."

"And float off every once in a while, eh? Go upsy-daisy at a faculty meeting or while I'm delivering a paper."

"Perhaps not. Once the burden of this levitation business is off your mind, it may plague you less. It may be under better control."

Roger gazed at the other searchingly. "Do you really think so?"

"I consider it a strong possibility."

"If I thought there were a chance of that— You

know, if I could be sure I wouldn't go up in the air at inconvenient times, it would help a lot. I could work on the problem myself. I wouldn't need anyone's help."

"Uh-huh," said Sarle encouragingly.

"If they would only leave me alone."

"Well, why wouldn't they?"

"Yes. Keep this up a year or so. Play other cities when the Black Mask is sucked dry. Then get back to the real thing. I'll even have saved up a little money, probably. And who knows?" He laughed a little. "I may even get to like show business."

He played with his empty cocktail glass and sat there, buried in thought.

Sarle turned to June and smiled at her. Holding his left hand close to his body, he put thumb and forefinger together in a circle and held the other fingers outstretched. June didn't see him. Instead, she was staring at Roger, her expression strained and unhappy.

"Roger," she said.

"What?"

"Please. You're doing it again."

Roger, startled, looked down. His body was six inches off the upholstered seat of the armchair.

"I'm sorry," he said, as he lowered himself. "I get abstracted and it just happens."

"I know," said June dully. "I know."

Roger received his first pay envelope in Magoun's office. Magoun tried to look hearty and succeeded in looking uncomfortable.

"It was a good week, Mr. Toomey," he said, "and I'm putting a little bonus in the envelope for you. You'll find two and a half G's when you look."

"Thank you," said Roger.

"It's okay." Magoun slapped his shoulder. "You can use me as a reference, and I'll give you the name of a reliable agent if you want one."

Roger looked startled. "What does that mean? I'm through here?"

Magoun took a cigar out of the box and stared at it.

"The engagement was only for a week. You remember that."

"Well, damn it, you said one week, meaning you'd see how I went with the crowd."

"Yeah, yeah. That's it. The act's a good one, but there ain't enough to it, know what I mean? You float, but that's all. You got no patter, no variety. You ain't even got one of those assistants in tights. A pretty goil lends class to an act. If the men get tired of magic, they watch legs, know what I mean?"

"But you're making money. The cashier told me this was the best week you ever had."

Magoun put his cigar down unlighted. "Look, Mr. Toomey, you want the truth? I'll give it to you. I ain't the type to give anyone no fake pitch, know what I mean? Look, I've been watching your act. I ain't no fool; I got experience. I've seen more magicians than you could count. I know their tricks. Only you don't use them. You got no hocus-pocus. You don't get their eyes off you while you quick substitute one gizmo for another. You ain't got wires strung to the ceiling. You ain't got mirrors.

"I thought maybe it was hypnotism, even though I ain't never seen hypnotism used on a whole crowd. Anyway, I sat out in the audience and closed my eyes when you came on. I waited till the shouting started and then opened them. There you were, standing on your head ten feet over the stage. It couldn't be hypnotism. I had my eyes closed."

"Let me understand this," said Roger. "Do you mean that you're firing me because you think I'm legitimate; that I really *can* fly?"

Magoun spread his hands. "I don't like to say that, know what I mean? I ain't going on record that I believe in fairies. I'd just like to say good-bye in a nice way with no hard feelings."

"Wait. Just suppose my floating *is* legitimate. What's that to you?"

"Well, it's like this. The customers are liable to get the idea that it's all too legit. They won't like that.

You know how people are. Superstitious, know what I mean? Lots of them ain't got too good an education. First thing you know, someone's hollering, 'Evil eye' or 'He's the devil' or something crazy. Say listen, you don't know show business like I do; you don't know the things that can go on. I can't afford a riot, Mr. Toomey. I got my reputation to think of."

"But you're all wrong, Mr. Magoun. The public likes to be fooled."

"Maybe. But only as long as they know it's only fooling. A guy gets out of handcuffs, okay. They know he's palmed a key even if they ain't seen it. He makes an assistant disappear? They know there's a mirror on stage or a false bottom to something. Somebody reads minds? They know a confederate's in the audience.

"But *you*, Mr. Toomey, you're *too* good. I've seen a goil float over a couch for ten seconds or so. It's rigged up, naturally. She can't move; she can't change position. But you float all over the place. You do handstands on air. You move right over the tables. There just ain't any way out. It's the real thing. That's the way they got to figure.—Tell you what, Mr. Toomey, let me know how you do it, and we'll do business. How's that?"

Roger was silent.

"So there you are," said Magoun.

Roger said, "You're not worried about riots. No producer in his right mind would turn down a money-making act like mine because it was too good. You're afraid of me. You're personally afraid of me."

"Not afraid," said Magoun. "I just don't like it myself. It makes me uncomfortable, know what I mean?"

"Why?"

"Because it ain't right, Mr. Toomey. It's against nature. It *just ain't right.*—Look, Mr. Toomey, ain't you ever hoid of gravity?"

Roger got to his feet. "Good-bye."

Magoun held out a broad palm. "No hard feelings?"

Roger walked out without answering.

*   *   *

He ignored the subway and walked home. It was all
a jumble, all a mess. No one would face the truth. No
one would look a fact in the face. Even a magician had
to be able to prove himself a fake. Illusion was fine.
Quackery was fine.

Only truth had to be hidden.

The two-hour walk in the small hours of the morning found him no solution. He walked up the flight of
stairs to his second-floor apartment in a state of circu-
lar exhaustion. He closed the door gingerly behind
him. The latch didn't quite catch, but he didn't notice
that.

He undressed without putting on the lights so as not
to disturb June. The couch was made for him and the
straps were neatly in place.

He found everything suddenly unbearable. He had
to tell June. He had to wake her up and tell her right
now. He had to, or damn it, he'd choke.

He walked softly into the bedroom and reached out
for the place on the pillow where her blonde head
would be. Nothing was resting there.

"June," he called softly. He thought confusedly:
She must be in the bathroom.

He fumbled for the bed lamp and blinked at the
empty room. He called again, questioningly, then saw
the sheet of paper pinned to the pillow. He tore it
loose.

It began: "Roger." No endearments; simply, "Roger."
The handwriting was hasty, disrupted, almost incoherent.

> Roger: I can't stand it and I've got to get away. I
> know it's not your fault, but I can't help that. I
> didn't want to leave while things were going so
> badly. It would have been too mean. But now
> you've got a new career and you'll be doing well
> without me. Please don't try to find me, and don't
> worry about me. I've only taken my personal
> things and half the money in the joint account.
> Good-bye. June.

Roger read the note, and slowly its contents seeped through his stunned mind. He let it drop. He thought: My new career. He said it aloud, half hysterically, "My new career!"

Half-dazed, he moved to the chest of drawers. From the top drawer, he took out the box in which he kept his private minutiae: tie clips, cuff links, an old fountain pen, the Phi Beta Kappa key he no longer wore. From it, he took out the vial of sleeping pills he had accumulated from the prescriptions his friend at the Medical School had given him. Some presentiment of possible necessity had always lurked in his mind.

He picked up June's note and scribbled a few words on the other side with his fountain pen. He got a glass of water, put it on the night table, sat on the edge of the bed, and tumbled half a dozen tablets out of the vial and into the palm of his hand. Then the rest. Slowly, thoughtfully, he swallowed them down with water, two at a time.

He lay down flat on his back and covered himself neatly with the sheet. He closed his eyes.

The turmoil in his brain dimmed and slowly peace descended. Levitation didn't matter. Nothing mattered. Except sleep. Only sleep.

His last, slow, dreaming sensation was that he was flying.

He lay there, cooling.

The onset of *rigor mortis*, when occurring unevenly, will sometimes imbue an arm or leg with ghastly pseudo-life and cause it to bend.

Whatever it was in Roger's body that controlled levitation, the first pangs of death tightened and activated it.

Near noon, a neighbor noticed the two milk bottles just outside the Toomey's apartment door. Good-naturedly, she knuckled the door. "Mrs. Toomey. Mrs. Toomey."

The door, its latch uncaught, moved inward under the pressure of her rapping.

She stepped inside and was oppressed by the silence. "Mrs. Toomey?—Why, I wonder what's wrong."

Half in fright, she tiptoed through the empty living room and peered into the bedroom.

Her composure shattered into a wild scream. Roger's rigid body was obviously dead, and she did not wait long enough or observe closely enough to detect what else was wrong.

The two plainclothesmen looked over the apartment dispassionately and gave the corpse the briefest of bored glances.

Plainclothesman Dooley picked up the note on the night table.

"It's from a dame," he said, holding it gingerly by one corner.

Plainclothesman Herlihan read it over Dooley's shoulder. "Wouldn't you know? Poor stiff!"

Dooley said, "I'll call Doc Curley. Straight suicide. No problem."

Herlihan picked up the empty vial between two fingernails. "Sleeping pills, I suppose?" He put it back in position.

"Sure." Dooley stepped into the hall.

Herlihan stared speculatively at what was left of Roger Toomey. He looked closer.

"That's funny," he muttered.

With a twitch, he removed the queerly hanging sheet, and nearly. fell over backward. "Holy Mother," he breathed.

Six inches of space separated the body and the mattress.

Herlihan put his hand beneath the body, but there was nothing supporting it. Only space. He snatched his hand out again, shaking it and staring at it.

Wildly, his flesh crawling, he put his hands on the dead chest and abdomen and pressed downward.

Something snapped. There was a clean, thin crack, tiny but distinct, and the body dropped—a dead weight. The mattress creaked to prove it.

The snap had come from inside the body, as though a muscle had been stretched just a little too tight and fine.

Herlihan backed away.

Dooley's voice, speaking into the phone, ceased. He came into the room.

Dooley said, "Doc Curley will be over in half an hour. And hey, Mike, this guy wrote something on the other side of his wife's note. Listen: 'You can lead a man to data, but you can't make him believe.' What do you make of that?"

Herlihan was still staring at the corpse.

Dooley frowned. "Anything wrong?"

Herlihan shook his head numbly. "Nothing! Nothing at all!"

4

BELIEF
(Published Version)

In this case, since the story was written as a novelette and appeared as a novelette, there is room for both versions. Nor is it necessary to produce each in full, since the first two-thirds is identical in both.

The difference comes in the scene, just past the middle of the story, between Roger Toomey, the levitator, and James Sarle, the psychiatrist. In my original version Sarle recommends that Toomey consider doing a magic act as a way of regaining control of his life.

At the asterisk I have inserted in that speech, I began my revision, changing completely everything that followed. Here, then, beginning at the asterisk, is the version of the ending that was published:

Once a person is oriented to face facts rather than delusions, problems tend to disappear. At the very least, they fall into their true perspective and become soluble."

Roger stirred restlessly. "Psychiatric gobbledygook! It's like putting your fingers on a man's temple and saying, 'Have faith and you will be cured!' If the poor sap isn't cured, it's because he didn't drum up enough faith. The witch doctor can't lose."

"Maybe you're right, but let's see. What *is* your problem?"

"No catechism, please. You know my problem, so let's not horse around."

"You levitate. Is that it?"

"Let's say it is. It'll do as a first approximation."

"You're not being serious, Roger, but actually you're probably right. It's only a first approximation. After all, you're tackling that problem. June tells me you've been experimenting."

"Experimenting! Ye Gods, Jim, I'm not experimenting. I'm drifting. I need high-powered brains and equipment. I need a research team, and I don't have it."

"Then what's your problem? Second approximation."

Roger said, "I see what you mean. My problem is to get a research team. But I've tried! Man, I've tried till I'm tired of trying."

"How have you tried?"

"I've sent out letters. I've asked— Oh stop it, Jim. I haven't the heart to go through the patient-on-the-couch routine. You know what I've been doing."

"I know that you've said to people, 'I have a problem. Help me.' Have you tried anything else?"

"Look, Jim. I'm dealing with mature scientists."

"I know. So you reason that the straightforward request is sufficient. Again it's theory against fact. I've told you the difficulties involved in your request. When you thumb a ride on a highway you're making a straightforward request, but most cars pass you by just the same. The point is that the straightforward request has failed. Now what's your problem? Third approximation!"

"To find another approach which won't fail? Is that what you want me to say?"

"It's what you have said, isn't it?"

"So I know it without your telling me."

"Do you? You're ready to quit school, quit your job, quit science. Where's your consistency, Rog? Do you abandon a problem when your first experiment fails? Do you give up when one theory is shown to be inadequate? The same philosophy of experimental science that holds for inanimate objects should hold for people as well."

"All right. What do you suggest I try? Bribery? Threats? Tears?"

James Sarle stood up. "Do you really want a suggestion?"

"Go ahead."

"Do as Dr. Morton said. Take a vacation, and to hell with levitation. It's a problem for the future. Sleep in bed and float or don't float; what's the difference? Ignore levitation, laugh at it, or even enjoy it. Do anything but worry about it, because it isn't your problem. That's the whole point. It's not your immediate problem. Spend your time considering how to make scientists study something they don't want to study. That is the immediate problem, and that is exactly what you've spent no thinking time on as yet."

Sarle walked to the hall closet and got his coat. Roger went with him. Minutes passed in silence.

Then Roger said, without looking up, "Maybe you're right, Jim."

"Maybe I am. Try it and then tell me. Good-bye, Roger."

Roger Toomey opened his eyes and blinked at the morning brightness of the bedroom. He called out, "Hey, June, where are you?"

June's voice answered, "In the kitchen. Where do you think?"

"Come in here, will you?"

She came in. "The bacon won't fry itself, you know."

"Listen, did I float last night?"

"I don't know. I slept."

"You're a help." He got out of bed and slipped his feet into his mules. "Still, I don't think I did."

"Do you think you've forgotten how?" There was sudden hope in her voice.

"I haven't forgotten. See!" He slid into the dining room on a cushion of air. "I just have a feeling I haven't floated. I think it's three nights now."

"Well, that's good," said June. She was back at the stove. "It's just that a month's rest has done you good. If I had called Jim in the beginning—"

"Oh please, don't go through that. A month's rest, my eye. It's just that last Sunday I made up my mind what to do. Since then I've relaxed. That's all there is to it."

"What are you going to do?"

"Every spring Northwestern Tech gives a series of seminars on physical topics. I'll attend."

"You mean, go way out to Seattle?"

"Of course."

"What will they be discussing?"

"What's the difference? I just want to see Linus Deering."

"But he's the one who called you crazy, isn't he?"

"He did." Roger scooped up a forkful of scrambled eggs. "But he's also the best man of the lot."

He reached for the salt and lifted a few inches out of his chair as he did so. He paid no attention.

He said, "I think maybe I can handle him."

The spring seminars at Northwestern Tech had become a nationally known institution since Linus Deering had joined the faculty. He was the perennial chairman and lent the proceedings their distinctive tone. He introduced the speakers, led the question periods, summed up at the close of each morning and afternoon session, and was the soul of conviviality at the concluding dinner at the end of the week's work.

All this Roger Toomey knew by report. He could now observe the actual workings of the man. Professor Deering was rather under middle height, was dark of complexion, and had a luxuriant and quite distinctive mop of wavy brown hair. His wide, thin-lipped mouth, when not engaged in active conversation, looked perpetually on the point of a sly smile. He spoke quickly and fluently, without notes, and seemed always to deliver his comments from a level of superiority that his listeners automatically accepted.

At least, so he had been on the first morning of the seminar. It was only during the afternoon session that the listeners began to notice a certain hesitation in his remarks. Even more, there was an uneasiness about him as he sat on the stage during the delivery of the scheduled papers. Occasionally, he glanced furtively toward the rear of the auditorium.

Roger Toomey, seated in the very last row, observed all this tensely. His temporary glide toward normality that had begun when he first thought there might be a way out was beginning to recede.

On the Pullman to Seattle, he had not slept. He had had visions of himself lifting upward in time to the wheel-clacking, of moving out quietly past the curtains and into the corridor, of being awakened into endless embarrassment by the hoarse shouting of a porter. So he had fastened the curtains with safety pins—and had achieved nothing by that; no feeling of security; no sleep outside a few exhausting snatches.

He had napped in his seat during the day, while the mountains slipped past outside, and arrived in Seattle in the evening with a stiff neck, aching bones, and a general sensation of despair.

He had made his decision to attend the seminar far too late to have been able to obtain a room to himself at the Institute's dormitories. Sharing a room was, of course, quite out of the question. He registered at a downtown hotel, locked the door, closed and locked all the windows, and shoved his bed hard against the wall and the bureau against the open side of the bed; then slept.

He remembered no dreams, and when he awoke in the morning he was still lying within the manufactured enclosure. He felt relieved.

When he arrived, in good time, at Physics Hall on the Institute's campus, he found, as he expected, a large room and a small gathering. The seminar sessions were held, traditionally, over the Easter vacation and students were not in attendance. Some fifty physicists sat in an auditorium designed to hold four hundred, clustering on either side of the central aisle up near the podium.

Roger took his seat in the last row, where he would not be seen by casual passers-by looking through the high, small windows of the auditorium door, and where the others in the audience would have had to twist through nearly a hundred eighty degrees to see him.

Except, of course, for the speaker on the platform— and for Professor Deering.

Roger did not hear much of the actual proceedings. He concentrated entirely on waiting for those moments when Deering was alone on the platform; when only Deering could see him.

As Deering grew obviously more disturbed, Roger grew bolder. During the final summing up of the afternoon, he did his best.

Professor Deering stopped altogether in the middle of a poorly constructed and entirely meaningless sentence. His audience, which had been shifting in their seats for some time, stopped also and looked wonderingly at him.

Deering raised his hand and said, gaspingly, "You! You there!"

Roger Toomey had been sitting with an air of complete relaxation—in the very center of the aisle. The only chair beneath him was composed of two and a half feet of empty air. His legs were stretched out before him on the armrest of an equally airy chair.

When Deering pointed, Roger slid rapidly sidewise. By the time fifty heads turned, he was sitting quietly in a very prosaic wooden seat.

Roger looked this way and that, then stared at Deering's pointing finger and rose.

"Are you speaking to me, Professor Deering?" he asked, with only the slightest tremble in his voice to indicate the savage battle he was fighting within himself to keep that voice cool and wondering.

"What are you doing?" demanded Deering, his morning's tension exploding.

Some of the audience were standing in order to see better. An unexpected commotion is as dearly loved by a gathering of research physicists as by a crowd at a baseball game.

"I'm not doing anything," said Roger. "I don't understand you."

"Get out! Leave this hall!"

Deering was beside himself with a mixture of emotions, or perhaps he would not have said that. At any rate, Roger sighed and took his opportunity prayerfully.

He said, loudly and distinctly, forcing himself to be heard over the gathering clamor, "I am Professor Roger Toomey of Carson College. I am a member of the American Physical Association. I have applied for permission to attend these sessions, have been accepted, and have paid my registration fee. I am sitting here as is my right, and will continue to do so."

Deering could only say blindly, "Get out!"

"I will not," said Roger. He was actually trembling with a synthetic and self-imposed anger. "For what reason must I get out? What have I done?"

Deering put a shaking hand through his hair. He was quite unable to answer.

Roger followed up his advantage. "If you attempt to evict me from these sessions without just cause, I shall certainly sue the Institute."

Deering said hurriedly, "I call the first day's session of the Spring Seminars of Recent Advances in the Physical Sciences to a close. Our next session will be in this hall tomorrow at nine in—"

Roger left as he was speaking and hurried away.

There was a knock at Roger's hotel-room door that night. It startled him, froze him in his chair.

"Who is it?" he cried.

The answering voice was soft and hurried. "May I see you?"

It was Deering's voice. Roger's hotel as well as his room number were, of course, recorded with the seminar secretary. Roger had hoped, but scarcely expected, that the day's events would have so speedy a consequence.

He opened the door and said stiffly, "Good evening, Professor Deering."

Deering stepped in and looked about. He wore a very light topcoat that he made no gesture to remove. He held his hat in his hand and did not offer to put it down.

He said, "Professor Roger Toomey of Carson College. Right?" He said it with a certain emphasis, as though the name had significance.

"Yes. Sit down, Professor."

Deering remained standing. "Now what is it? What are you after?"

"I don't understand."

"I'm sure you do. You aren't arranging this ridiculous foolery for nothing. Are you trying to make me seem foolish, or is it that you expect to hoodwink me into some crooked scheme? I want you to know it won't work. And don't try to use force now. I have friends who know exactly where I am at this moment. I'll advise you to tell the truth and then get out of town."

"Professor Deering! This is my room. If you are here to bully me, I'll ask you to leave. If you don't go, I'll have you put out."

"Do you intend to continue this . . . this persecution?"

"I have not been persecuting you. I don't know you, sir."

"Aren't you the Roger Toomey who wrote me a letter concerning a case of levitation he wanted me to investigate?"

Roger stared at the man. "What letter is this?"

"Do you deny it?"

"Of course I do. What are you talking about? Have you got the letter?"

Professor Deering's lips compressed. "Never mind that. Do you deny you were suspending yourself on wires at this afternoon's sessions?"

"On wires? I don't follow you at all."

"You were levitating!"

"Would you please leave, Professor Deering? I don't think you're well."

The physicist raised his voice. "Do you deny you were levitating?"

"I think you're mad. Do you mean to say I made magician's arrangements in your auditorium? I was never in it before today, and when I arrived you were already present. Did you find wires or anything of the sort after I left?"

"I don't know how you did it, and I don't care. *Do* you deny you were levitating?"

"Why, of course I do."

"I saw you. Why are you lying?"

"You saw me levitate? Professor Deering, will you tell me how that's possible? I suppose your knowledge of gravitational forces is enough to tell you that true levitation is a meaningless concept except in outer space. Are you playing some sort of joke on me?"

"Good Heavens," said Deering in a shrill voice, "why won't you tell the truth?"

"I am. Do you suppose that by stretching out my hand and making a mystic pass . . . so . . . I can go sailing off into air?" And Roger did so, his head brushing the ceiling.

Deering's head jerked upward. "Ah! There . . . there—"

Roger returned to earth, smiling. "You *can't* be serious."

"You did it again. You just did it."

"Did what, sir?"

"You levitated. You just levitated. You can't deny it."

Roger's eyes grew serious. "I think you're sick, sir."

"I know what I saw."

"Perhaps you need a rest. Overwork—"

"It was *not* a hallucination."

"Would you care for a drink?" Roger walked to his suitcase while Deering followed his footsteps with bulging eyes. The toes of his shoes touched air two inches from the ground and went no lower.

Deering sank into the chair Roger had vacated.

"Yes, please," he said weakly.

Roger gave him the whiskey bottle and watched the other drink, then gag a bit. "How do you feel now?"

"Look here," said Deering, "have you discovered a way of neutralizing gravity?"

Roger stared. "Get hold of yourself, Professor. If I had antigravity, I wouldn't use it to play games on you. I'd be in Washington. I'd be a military secret. I'd be— Well, I wouldn't be here! Surely all this is obvious to you."

Deering jumped to his feet. "Do you intend sitting in on the remaining sessions?"

"Of course."

Deering nodded, jerked his hat down upon his head, and hurried out.

For the next three days, Professor Deering did not preside over the seminar sessions. No reason for his absence was given. Roger Toomey, caught between hope and apprehension, sat in the body of the audience and tried to remain inconspicuous. In this, he was not entirely successful. Deering's public attack had made him notorious, while his own strong defense had given him a kind of David versus Goliath popularity.

Roger returned to his hotel room Thursday night after an unsatisfactory dinner and remained standing in the doorway, one foot over the threshold. Professor Deering was gazing at him from within. And another man, a gray fedora shoved well back on his forehead, was seated on Roger's bed.

It was the stranger who spoke. "Come inside, Toomey."

Roger did so. "What's going on?"

The stranger opened his wallet and presented a cellophane window to Roger. He said, "I'm Cannon of the FBI."

Roger said, "You have influence with the government, I take it, Professor Deering."

"A little," said Deering.

Roger said, "Well, am I under arrest? What's my crime?"

"Take it easy," said Cannon. "We've been collecting some data on you, Toomey. Is this your signature?"

He held a letter out far enough for Roger to see, but not to snatch. It was the letter Roger had written to Deering which the latter had sent on to Morton.

"Yes," said Roger.

"How about this one?" The federal agent had a sheaf of letters.

Roger realized that he must have collected every one he had sent out, minus those that had been torn up. "They're all mine," he said wearily.

Deering snorted.

Cannon said, "Professor Deering tells us that you can float."

"Float? What the devil do you mean, float?"

"Float in the air," said Cannon, stolidly.

"Do you believe anything as crazy as that?"

"I'm not here to believe or not to believe, Dr. Toomey," said Cannon. "I'm an agent of the Government of the United States and I've got an assignment to carry out. I'd cooperate if I were you."

"How can I cooperate in something like this? If I came to you and told you that Professor Deering could float in air, you'd have me flat on a psychiatrist's couch in no time."

Cannon said, "Professor Deering has been examined by a psychiatrist at his own request. However, the government has been in the habit of listening very seriously to Professor Deering for a number of years now. Besides, I might as well tell you that we have independent evidence."

"Such as?"

"A group of students at your college have seen you float. Also, a woman who was once secretary to the head of your department. We have statements from all of them."

Roger said, "What kind of statements? Sensible ones that you would be willing to put into the record and show to my congressman?"

Professor Deering interrupted anxiously, "Dr. Toomey, what do you gain by denying the fact that you can levitate? Your own Dean admits that you've done something of the sort. He has told me that he will inform you officially that your appointment will be terminated at the end of the academic year. He wouldn't do that for nothing."

"That doesn't matter," said Roger.

"But why won't you admit I saw you levitate?"

"Why should I?"

Cannon said, "I'd like to point out, Dr. Toomey, that if you have any device for counteracting gravity, it would be of great importance to your government."

"Really? I suppose you have investigated my background for possible disloyalty."

"The investigation," said the agent, "is proceeding."

"All right," said Roger, "let's take a hypothetical case. Suppose I admitted I could levitate. Suppose I didn't know how I did it. Suppose I had nothing to give the government but my body and an insoluble problem."

"How can you know it's insoluble?" asked Deering eagerly.

"I once asked you to study such a phenomenon," pointed out Roger mildly. "You refused."

"Forget that. Look." Deering spoke rapidly, urgently. "You don't have a position at the moment. I can offer you one in my department as Associate Professor of Physics. Your teaching duties will be nominal. Full-time research on levitation. What about it?"

"It sounds attractive," said Roger.

"I think it's safe to say that unlimited government funds will be available."

"What do I have to do? Just admit I can levitate?"

"I know you can. I saw you. I want you to do it now for Mr. Cannon."

Roger's legs moved upward and his body stretched out horizontally at the level of Cannon's head. He turned to one side and seemed to rest on his right elbow.

Cannon's hat fell backward onto the bed.

He yelled, "He floats."

Deering was almost incoherent with excitement. "Do you see it, man?"

"I sure see something."

"Then report it. Put it right down in your report, do you hear me? Make a complete record of it. They won't say there's anything wrong with me. I didn't doubt for a minute that I had seen it."

But he couldn't have been so happy if that were entirely true.

"I don't even know what the climate is like in Seattle," wailed June, "and there are a million things I have to do."

"Need any help?" asked Jim Sarle from his comfortable position in the depths of the armchair.

"There's nothing you can do. Oh, dear." And she flew from the room, but unlike her husband, she did so figuratively only.

Roger Toomey came in. "June, do we have the crates for the books yet? Hello, Jim. When did you come in? And where's June?"

"I came in a minute ago, and June's in the next room. I had to get past a policeman to get in. Man, they've got you surrounded."

"Um-m-m," said Roger absently. "I told them about you."

"I know you did. I've been sworn to secrecy. I told them it was a matter of professional confidence in any case. Why don't you let the movers do the packing? The government is paying, isn't it?"

"Movers wouldn't do it right," said June, suddenly hurrying in again and flouncing down on the sofa. "I'm going to have a cigarette."

"Break down, Roger," said Sarle, "and tell me what happened."

Roger smiled sheepishly. "As you said, Jim, I took my mind off the wrong problem and applied it to the right one. It just seemed to me that I was forever being faced with two alternatives. I was either crooked or crazy. Deering said that flatly in his letter to Morton. The Dean assumed I was crooked and Morton suspected that I was crazy.

"But supposing I could show them that I could really levitate. Well, Morton told me what would happen in that case. Either I would be crooked, or the *witness* would be insane. Morton said that . . . he said that if he saw me fly, he'd prefer to believe himself insane than accept the evidence. Of course, he was only being rhetorical. No man would believe in his own insanity while even the faintest alternative existed. I counted on that.

"So I changed my tactics. I went to Deering's seminar. I didn't *tell* him I could float; I showed him, *and then denied I had done it.* The alternative was clear. I was either lying or he . . . not I, mind you, but *he . . .* was mad. It was obvious that he would sooner believe in levitation than doubt his own sanity, once he was really put to the test. All his actions thereafter—his bullying, his trip to Washington, his offer of a job— were intended only to vindicate his own sanity, not to help me."

Sarle said, "In other words, you had made your levitation his problem and not your own."

Roger said, "Did you have anything like this in mind when we had our talk, Jim?"

Sarle shook his head. "I had vague notions, but a man must solve his own problems if they're to be solved effectively. Do you think they'll work out the principle of levitation now?"

"I don't know, Jim. I still can't communicate the subjective aspects of the phenomenon. But that doesn't matter. We'll be investigating them, and that's what counts." He struck his balled right fist into the palm of his left hand. "As far as I'm concerned, the important point is that I made them help me."

"Is it?" asked Sarle softly. "I should say that the important point is that you let them make *you* help *them*, which is a different thing altogether."

AFTERWORD

I would like to leave it to the readers to decide which version they themselves like better—but if you promise not to let yourself be influenced by them, here are some of my own thoughts on the matter.

In these past thirty years, I have thought of the two endings as "my ending" and "Campbell's ending" and have, in my thoroughly prejudiced way, strongly preferred "my ending"; that is, the one in the first, unpublished version. However, now that, for the first time in thirty-two years, I have read both versions of the story, one immediately after the other, I have come to the realization that *both* of them are my endings and are very well written—but I still like the first one better.

Oddly enough, the second ending, the one that was published and was considered by me to be "Campbell's ending," is the one of the two that is the far more typical of me. In story after story after story, I have had my hero win by superior cleverness, superior rationality, superior brains. In short, Roger Toomey does *exactly* what a typical Asimov hero *ought* to do. Why, then, am I dissatisfied?

Because Roger Toomey is *not* a typical Asimov hero.

The story as I conceived it after Campbell expressed his desire that I write a story about a person who levitated, but couldn't get anyone to believe it, required a non-Asimovian hero. My thesis (not directly expressed in so many words, but implied over and over) was: "For belief to exist, truth alone is insufficient."

My usual cheery, upbeat view of life is such that I don't accept that thesis. I continue to write books on science and history—and science fiction too—in which I try to explain the world in a natural, rationalist way, with the confident certainty that one has but to do that to cause people to abandon their foolish superstitions.

And yet I occasionally have my darker, cynical moments, when I am aware of millions of people—even educated and presumably intelligent people—who accept a wide spectrum of nonsense from astrology all the way down to creationism, in the face of all the evidence patiently and painfully gathered by rational human beings through the course of the history of civilization.—And then I feel like Roger Toomey.

To demonstrate this cynical view, levitation is ideal, for it is something that every rational person who is aware of modern scientific thought agrees is impossible and goes against natural law. Even people who are ill-educated and superstitious would not believe levitation was possible except by divine (or demonic) intervention.

Those who are faced with the *fact* of levitation must therefore seek some explanation involving hoaxes of some sort, or recoil in terror at what must seem to them to involve the presence of the divine or demonic.

If you came to me, for instance, and demonstrated that you could levitate, and if I failed to find wires holding you up, I would probably proceed to disbelieve my eyes. Sorry.

So when Roger Toomey cannot find belief (note that that is the title of the story), his life must follow a steady downward course in order to demonstrate the central thesis of the story as powerfully as possible.

In the second version of the ending, however, "Campbell's ending," I have Toomey make a right-about-face between one line and the next, so that although he is clearly *not* an Asimovian hero, he becomes one.

I don't think I should have agreed to do it.

FINAL WORD

The various items of editorial insistence on change which I have described in this book have dated from 1939 ("Pilgrimage") to 1958 ("The Ugly Little Boy").

Since 1958—over a quarter of a century now—there have been no such incidents. Either something I write is rejected (very rarely, to be sure), or it is accepted and is then printed substantially as I have written it, with only the kind of routine change that is the result of line-by-line editing for typos and infelicities.

This is not necessarily a Good Thing, as far as some critics are concerned. I have seen reviews of my recent novels, for instance, that seem to imply that I suffer from the lack of editorial control. The impression they seek to convey is that I have become an arrogant superstar of the science fiction world and that editors cower in corners, fearing my frown; that I get away with all sorts of self-indulgent shenanigans while those same editors shrug their shoulders at each other (when I am not looking) and bemoan their inability to control me.

I wish reviewers who think that would consult my editors on the matter (in my absence, if that will make them feel better), for I am quite certain they will be assured it is not so.

What *is* so is that I am an aging, experienced science fiction writer who has learned my craft in the hard school of such powerful, idiosyncratic editors as John W. Campbell, Jr., and Horace L. Gold, so that there is now no longer any great need to rewrite me.

The time may well come when advancing age and mental decay (if I live long enough) may deprive me of the fine edge of my power; and in that case, I dare say my editors will draw straws to find out which one of them gets to tell me that I don't have it any more.

Their reluctance to be the one to do so won't be out of fear of me, I know, but (I hope) out of a reluctance to make me feel bad, for I have made friends with every editor I have ever had, and my relations with them—all of them, from John Campbell, forty-seven years ago, to Sam Vaughan right now—have been marked by friendliness and warmth, and even arguments over revision have ruffled the surface of our friendships only slightly, and only temporarily.

Isaac Asimov has written over three hundred books on subjects ranging from the Bible and Shakespeare to math and alien encounters. He is perhaps the best known, and certainly the best loved, of all science fiction authors, with his award-winning Foundation Series an international phenomenon. He lives in New York City.